Moonshine Darling

Jacqueline Parchment

AuthorHouse™ UK Ltd.
500 Avebury Boulevard
Central Milton Keynes, MK9 2BE
www.authorhouse.co.uk
Phone: 08001974150

First published by AuthorHouse 4/5/2010

ISBN: 978-1-4490-1674-6 (sc)

This book is printed on acid-free paper.

To my mother Mercedes Wallace and my brother Dudley.
Mama you have been an inspiration to us all. And Dudley,
you have taught me so much about me, and life.

Chapter One

England 1966

....

Six little bodies lying in a row, head to toe - the double mattress - a field of hills and valleys, which yielded up a rich harvest of razor-sharp springs to poke fun at us during the night. Come daylight, we would have to move on again; vacate the one room shared by a family of eight. Home had always been just one room after the other and over time, I had learnt to despise the familiarity of change. A rush of warm, moist air drifted in through half opened windows, lifting the net curtains to cast moving shadows on the walls of this dimly lit room. It was a peculiar night; hot, tense, almost silent except for the industry of respiration happening around and the far off rumbles of thunder creeping ever closer. A storm was coming to put a pause to the hot sultry weather we had been having lately.

In the darkest corner of the room lay my father on his back snoring, deep in slumber. His lower jaw moved in unison to the rises and falls of his large chest as he sucked in, then released air. Occasionally he whistled, snorted or twitched which caused a chain reaction around the room.

For some reason I was unable to drift into the unconscious world where sleeping souls live a timeless, parallel life. Instead, I lay awake listening to the composition of sleep, trying to find a pattern, a tune or melody to the song of rhythmic breathing. In another corner of the room, surrounded by the fuzzy glow of a table lamp, sat my mother, sewing. For a brief moment, she looked up from her sewing, over to the bed where all her children lay huddled together. It hadn't always been like that. Poverty had caused six long years of separation that spanned the distance of the Atlantic Ocean - a sacrifice for a better future in England. It was a hard sacrifice, for during that time of pining for her loss, she had been hospitalised, twice, for severe post-natal depression following the birth of three more children, of which I was one. Now, as luck would have it, the hands of fate had mended a family fragmented by circumstance, allowing a little peace and contentment to grace Mama's life again, after being absent for so very long. It was after all, her hopes; her ambitions, which had brought us here to Hackney, London; to congregate in this one room, a landing bay.

Without warning, a flash of lightning illuminated the room in brilliant blue-white. A fearful cry escaped my lips as I dashed across the room. Mama caught hold of me. 'Shh! Don't wake your father. He'll be mad if you wake him.'

Nevertheless, all I could think about was the crash of thunder that would follow. I could hear it coming.

Like a huge ball of dark grey rock gathering mass, it rolled towards us. Mama listened too, her eyes gauged towards the ceiling. When eventually it crashed into us, she quickly stifled my cry to a muffled moan by putting her hand over my mouth.

'Shh! There's nothing to be scared of Melanie,' she whispered anxiously. 'It's just God moving his furniture around.'

Suddenly, Dada grunted and both Mama and I stood deadly still for a few seconds, then, when he had settled, Mama carefully pulled the sheets about him, pausing for a while to admire his face as it fell back into the peaceful countenance of a sweet little boy at rest. She was still obviously crazy about her husband; and even though he had told me often enough that I was an unwanted child, I loved him too - we all did, unconditionally. With the next rumble of thunder, Mama pulled me onto her lap and held me close. Soothing odours of nutmeg, butter and Palmolive soap distracted my fears, comforted my senses as she sang that same song, over and over again until my tensed body began to relax and eyelids grew heavy:

'Hush little darling don't say a word

Mama's goin buy you a mocking bird

If that mocking bird don't sing

Mama's goin buy you a diamond ring.'

The birth of a new day brought a new beginning for this family. Outside in the street, the engine of a transit van was revving and ready to go. Sitting in between Pauline and Douglas, I was squashed but that didn't matter. The air was thick with optimistic excitement and I wallowed shamelessly, as children do, in the centre of that euphoria. Eventually I took one last look out of the back window, then realised that I had to get off.

'Melanie where you going? Melanie Get back in the van,'

'Wait Mama! There's something I've forgotten to do.'

I had to say goodbye to Dolly, the little old lady who had lived downstairs in the basement flat since losing her husband in the First World War. She was all right really. By night, she'd use the handle of a broom to bang up against the ceiling shouting: 'Shut that noise up, you black bastards,' and by day, she produced handfuls of boiled fruit sweets from her apron pocket and tickled us affectionately under the chin. Our relationship was strange to say the least but for some bizarre wisdom, we inadvertently sought each other's company daily. There were times when Dolly and I talked for hours on end about everything and anything and times when just being in each other's company was enough. I was going to miss her and all the stories she told about what life was like during the wars. Somehow, she made these times seem like better days - days for which we should all be thankful. We looked each other up and down for a while and I could see that visibly, she was more upset than I was.

'Ahh, come here,' I said, 'Gi me a hug.' That's what she always said to me when I was upset. So now, I hugged her, as though it was for the last time because maybe, somewhere inside my seven-year-old mind, I knew I was never going to see her again; knew our paths had met and were now parting.

'Goodbye Dolly. I'll be thinking of you.'

I remember Dolly's big, wrinkled, white hand in the air, waving at us as we drove off; then I imagined her climbing slowly down the stairs to her dark basement flat, before shutting the door on the world outside.

Number 27 Grayling Road was a mansion compared to the space we had just left, but in actual fact was a three bedroom terraced house, slap-bang in the centre of the street. It was the eyes of the street, staring straight ahead up Yoakley Road, as far as the churchyard. At last a place we could call home, a stepping-stone - an interlude in a journey that would take us full circle, back across the Atlantic, from whence we had come. But for now, the whole family, as though hypnotized, had gathered outside to stare up in silent wonderment, at what was now ours. We just stood there, and stood there, in the hot, hazy, September sunshine, mouths agape, as our dreams materialised in front of our eyes. This house meant so much, to so many people. It was a symbol of hope and prosperity; a sign of better things to come, and with the opening of a new door came the assurance that all things would now naturally fall into their given place. Mama's eyes glistened with renewed hope of a fresh beginning, and after a while, I too became absorbed in the beauty of what this house signified for us. Everything was going to be all right from here-on. I was sure of that.

'Well don't all just stand there with your mouth wide open catching flies; mek we unpack before it get dark noh.'

Mama came to her senses first. Her voice signalled everyone to work and for the first time, that house was filled with the freedom of our uninhibited noises - the sounds of the grown-ups shouting to each other as they shifted large pieces of furniture.

'Lift up your end! To me! To me! Go back! Turn it to me now,' and us children running under and over, squeezing past just in time to avoid being squashed to a pulp between the sharp corners of a piece of furniture and that of a wall.

Shortly after arriving, we discovered that quite a few black families on our street had bought their own houses prior to us and that akin to any other neighbourhood, it also had its fair share of busy-bodies who took it upon themselves to talk about everyone else's business but their own. Like a 'News' bug, they drifted from person to person whispering revelations that would carry in the air; quickly spreading like bushfire. Keen witnesses when mishaps occurred, they were always in the right place at the right time, just waiting and waiting. Always the first ones at the front of a gathering; the first to say; "I tell you what happened; I see everything; I know that would happen, didn't I say it would?"

Mrs Green and her twin sister Mrs Andrews, two middle-aged women without husbands, lived in adjacent houses, four doors down. There was no holding them back. They had introduced themselves to the family as soon as the first pieces of furniture were being lifted off the van.

'So it was you who bought the house. I told my sister you'd be back. Who's this your daughter?' said Mrs

Green, grabbing hold of my cheek and giving it a good hard squeeze.

'She cute ain't she?'

I pulled away from her, took two paces back and stuck out my tongue at them.

'Melanie behave yourself,' gasped Mama.

'Oh she's alright. So you got six kids,' piped up the other sister.

'We counted them as you arrived, I'm Mrs Green and this is my sister Mrs Andrews. What do they call you?'

'Girlie,' said Mama.

'Well now Girlie, tell me, which one of those handsome men is your husband?'

Mama pointed to my father.

'That one! gasped Mrs Green, then proceeded to suck in her breath. 'He's the most handsome in the bunch. I hope you know what you doing.'

'Huh! Look like trouble to me,' scoffed Mrs Andrews, folding her arms indignantly as though somewhat offended. 'Give me a ugly man any day. You always know where you are with a ugly man and what's more,' she said wagging her finger at Mama, 'he knows his place. I tell you something, that man going bring you trouble.'

'Hush you mouth. That's no way to welcome our new neighbour.'

'It's true. You always hear me say a handsome man is a dangerous man, don't you, well I speak from experience.'

'Which handsome man you ever had?' enquired Mrs Green giving her sister a surprised look. 'You could not be speaking about that ex husband of yours. Come on, talk the truth, he was as bald as they come.'

'He was not bald. He was a little bit thin on top that's all. And he did have a nice smile'

Sandwiched between two women who squabbled at astronomical speed, Mama shifted impatiently trying to get away from their endless bickering, but each time she tried, Mrs Green would grip her wrist in an attempt to draw her into the conversation.

'Sister,' gasped Mrs Green, 'you must be having one of your dizzy spells again. The man hardly had any teeth in him head, and well, I'm sorry, I don't know how anybody can be handsome with half their teeth missing,' she said, looking Mama square in the eyes.

Mrs Andrews muttered something under her breath, and then resigned herself to kissing her teeth and cutting her eyes, both at the same time. There was no doubt of her sister having the upper hand, or plain and simple, she knew not to cross certain boundaries.

'Girlie,' said Mrs Green, taking Mama's wrist again and turning her back towards Mrs Andrews, 'you take no notice of my sister you hear. I can't bear when she get like this. Anyway, we been here for five years come March and I can tell you all you need to know about the area and the people.'

Mrs Andrews composed herself quickly, shuffling over to her sister's side.

There was obviously some tension between these two women but when it came to passing on information about other people, they were united. They called everyone who lived on the street by name, pointing out all the Jamaican families and then proceeded to give personal background information about what was going on in their lives.

'Now I'm not one to talk,' said Mrs Andrews before looking over both shoulders in turn. 'But that woman at number fifty-eight I told you about, Mrs Jones, I'd like to find out what she does with all the money they earn, I mean this week alone she's had at least half a dozen eggs, a loaf of bread, practically two pounds of sugar and God only knows what else.'

Mama looked uncomfortable not wanting to be an accomplice or to appear to be colluding with this two-some.

'Well she has got eight children to feed now sister,' replied Mrs Green sympathetically to her slightly confused sister.

'I thought you said two of them didn't belong to her.'

'That's right,' replied Mrs Green, recalling the knowledge of that event as though it were fresh in her mind. 'Her husband had those kids with two other women - *her sisters,* if I remember right.'

'She's got three children, the same age, under one roof, and I tell you something,' said Mrs Andrews swinging her gaze towards Mama's direction, 'they not triplets.'

'That's because he was doing it with those two sisters the same time as he was doing his wife. Nasty!' said Mrs Green.

Mama couldn't hold it any more. 'Anyway, thanks for calling by,' she interrupted with some conviction, 'but as you can see I got a lot to get on with.'

Mrs Green took hold of one of Mama's hands, patted it affectionately and said: 'Now if you need anything, and I mean anything, just call round. We be only too glad to help.'

Getting the house ready for habitation on that first day was a mammoth task. In between shouting warnings, Mama worked like a Trojan because now that all the furniture was safely inside the house, Dada had left with his friends for a celebratory drink in The Three Crowns pub. So to keep us out of the way, Mama threw open the two doors to the backyard, revealing sixty foot of what seemed like fields upon fields of lush green outdoor space. A huge pear tree, heavy with ripe fruit, stood majestically to the right centre smiling down the most beautiful smile imaginable. There was a quaint brick shed, about nine foot tall, with a flat roof to one side, and at the very end of the yard was a hill leading up to the back wall and on the other side of that wall was a huge, thriving, bustling factory. We jumped and tipped on our toes to follow the sound; to see over the wall. The tallest children lifted the smallest ones so that we could all peer over the fence into the dusty white faces of workmen in their hardhats and masks, as they packed and unpacked scaffolding poles and planks of wood. Over that backyard wall, men shouted to be heard over the grinding sound of machinery as it cut wood, filling the air with jewelled sawdust particles, which sparkled in the sunlight. Occasionally a flash of a smile would evoke excited giggles from us and we would duck down behind the wall or run around the yard, getting breathless before taking another peek.

With the evening drawing in, Mama rounded up her reluctant brood for dinner with a sharp slap to the back of the legs, if you were not quick enough to avoid it. Converging in one of the back rooms upstairs, we waited for dinner to be put in front of us. To while the time away, we searched for interesting things in opened boxes, whereas Pauline - who was all but one year older than me, as though hypnotized, was immediately drawn to the sink in the corner of the room. Hoisting herself up, she swung her legs to and fro, to and fro, until eventually she ended up on the floor with the sink - broken in two pieces. Mama came rushing in to check that Pauline was not seriously injured in any way. When Pauline stood up meekly, smoothing her crumpled dress over her thighs, only then did Mama deliver a few sharp slaps to the backs of her legs, which reverberated around the room.

'I can't believe it. Look what you do to the sink.'

We all stared silently down at the sink as though it were a living person who had been killed - murdered - cut down in its prime.

'We don't even get to use it yet and you brok it arf,' said Mama.

'Yeah,' chipped in Clovis, 'You pop it arf.'

'Hush up you mouth and talk proper Henglish. You ina Hengland now - brok it arf, not pop it arf,' corrected Mama.

Determined to better herself and her family, Mama decided that what we desperately needed, more than anything, was a good education and some spiritual guidance. The four youngest children - my younger brother Douglas, myself, my sisters Pauline and Julia, were enrolled at a local primary school. The two eldest boys, Clovis and Glen, were placed in a special school - their Jamaican accents deemed too strong and incomprehensible to the English ear, although I understood them well enough. I suppose Glen having a stutter didn't help much either. Dada always said ignorant people suffered the affliction of a stutter; by 'ignorant' he meant quick-tempered.

Over the coming weeks and months, new pieces of furniture arrived for each of the rooms - huge mahogany wardrobes, beds, tables, chairs. It kept on arriving and our home at last began to look and feel like how a home should - comfortable and luxurious in parts. A strange yet positive force was in motion. Everyone and everything became a part of it; pulling in the same direction, or so it appeared.

In the background to this, Mama was the first to notice how restless Dada had become; pacing the living room floor, peering out the bay window every few minutes, then sitting back down to shuffle the pack of cards he kept in his trouser pocket. She brought him a semi-circular bar with cream padded edge and filled it with all the different types of drinks and liqueurs you might expect see in a pub. How she laboured to make him see that he was not missing anything. But without doubt, the most beautiful thing to come through the door of our house was a dark oak gramophone, which resembled a long oak coffin on four legs. The sliding door on the top, opened to reveal a radio and a record player with stacking system for up to ten records at a time. As well as being mad about her husband, Mama was mad about Sam Cooke, so she tested the gramophone out with 'You Send Me.' Hugging herself, she gently swayed to the music as we all watched bemused, Dada included. Heavenly music filled the air, intoxicating everyone within earshot. When the record finished playing, Dada, who had been waiting impatiently for his turn, tested it out with Percy Sledge's 'When a Man Loves a Woman,' instructing everyone to stand back. It was Dada's turn to show off, and boy could he show off. This was one of those beautiful yet rare moments . It was not often he let his guard down and was in this kind of mood but when he did, he was full of style and endless charm. We idolised the playful Dada, we adored him. He gave us permission to laugh aloud, to be ourselves and to embrace our own individuality. Bitter-sweet was the knowledge that he was always there beneath the stern Dada we were all so anxious at being around.

As the record launched into play, Dada began to dance a slow step to the tune and then, after a James Brown type spin, he turned to Mama, and extended a hand for a dance.

'What a way your husband can *move*, eh Girlie!'

'Pa Daidee,' that's what she called him when they were on good terms, 'why you have to be so boas'y?' she asked, taking his hand.

'Is a gift from God. I can't help it Him bless me with so much style.'

As they swayed to the music entwined in each other's arms, they cast a lovely silhouette on the wall - two giants very much in love. We giggled lots before leaving the room to run joyfully around the backyard, happy because Mama and Dada were happy. They put on a whole stack of records before leaving the gramophone for us to enjoy. It was our turn to show off, so we danced around the gram as though it were our dancing partner. We danced until we were tired, and before Mama put us to bed that night, we knelt down on our knees beside the bed to say our nightly prayers in unison.

'Now I lay me down to sleep

I pray the Lord my soul to keep

If I should die before I wake

I pray the Lord my soul to take.'

At the end of prayers, we thanked God for the things that were most important in our lives, as Mama had taught us.

'Thank God for Mama and thank God for Dada, and thank God for each other, and thank you so much God for the backyard and oh for the Gram...'

'Come on get in the bed. God can read your mind and He already knows what is in your heart.'

'Is that true Mama?' I asked as Mama tucked us in.

'Of course it's true. God knows what you are thinking. He know you better than anybody know you.'

'Even you Mama? Does God know me better than you do?'

'Yes, of course! He knows everything about everybody. I don't.'

'What am I thinking now Mama?' I asked.

'God he knows, but *I'm* thinking it's bedtime, so hush up and go to sleep now.'

Sundays was church day at number 27 Grayling Road. Normally we were not allowed to raise our voices full stop, but on Sundays, our voices would automatically reduce to a whisper. It was the Lord's Day, a quiet day, a day of rest, a day for reflection. Playing in the backyard was discouraged on a Sunday morning because playing children have a tendency to shout and squeal and with Dada asleep in the back room that just was not on - on a Sunday. Boys had to behave like young men on a Sunday and as for the girls, well, we became respectable young ladies. No charging up and down the stairs, or straddling the banister to slide down: this was a serious offence, punishable by being torn from the banister by Mama and given a good, hard shaking.

'Girl, you tek leave of you senses? Don't let me blood you up this fine Sunday morning...'

Then she would catch herself and realise that blood should not be spilled on a Sunday. It was not very Godly. Neither was whistling. It was unladylike at all times but on a Sunday, it was a sin. It was a sound made only by grown working men as it helped them to keep a cheerful head. It was for the likes of the milkman, the postman and men on building sites and besides, according to Mama, it was bad luck. Whistling around the house on a Sunday through sheer forgetfulness was not only stupid but also irresponsible and if you unknowingly took the chance and it was loud enough to be heard, an unexpected hand would shoot out from nowhere to make contact with your mouth - hard enough for you to remember what day it was. Speaking from experience, whistling with swollen lips isn't easy. However, if Dada heard you, then God help you. Towering above us, he spoke in a menacing tone, with words that filled us with more pain than anything Mama could deliver, so we respected and obeyed without question. Therefore, there were no arguments or fights of any sort or bickering with each other on this day, for this day was a sacred day, a holy day, where children were transformed into little angels.

The transformation process, began early on the Sunday morning. After a bath for Julia, Pauline and me, we queued to have our hair pressed with the hot iron comb. Having your hair straightened was serious grown up business, not for cowards. The comb was heated up on the paraffin heater until deemed hot enough, by which time it would be dragged smoking through your hair, from the scalp to the tip, leaving the hair dead straight. One false move though, and your scalp or ears might be accidentally fried. Then we'd put on our Sunday best. White socks, white shoes, white dress with either pink or yellow ribbons mixed in. Ladies powdered their noses and faces and Mama powdered ours with the darkest shade for white skin, seeing as there wasn't any make up for black skin; a hideous combination which left all three girls looking like ghosts, to the stifled amusement of the boys. To top it all, a huge wide brimmed white hat, woven with more generous amounts of, yes you've guessed it, lace and ribbon, was placed on top of each of our heads and coins for the collection box placed carefully into our palms.

Outside the boys laughed out loud, laughed and pointed at our ghostly faces, calling us girls "The Three Dupees," attracting even more attention to our plight whilst we tried hard to pay them no mind, by holding our backs straight and our heads high, bold enough to look into the faces of people going by. We walked quickly down to the end of Grayling Road, stopping only to look down into the basement window of a large Victorian house used as a Pentecostal church. Through the misted window, we could see well-rounded ladies, old enough to be someone's maiden aunt, clapping wildly and beating their tambourines to:

'Have you been to Jesus for the cleansing power?

Are you washed in the blood of the lamb?

Are you truly trusting in his grace this hour?

Are you washed in the blood of the lamb?

Are you washed, in the blood?

In the soul cleansing blood of the lamb

Are your garments spotless are they white as snow?

Are you washed in the blood of the lamb?'

We held our bellies to laugh, a sweet, sweet laugh, pointing at women who were in the spirit, shaking violently and blabbering in tongues. Members of the congregation had to catch hold of their limp bodies as the spirit tossed them about, causing hats and even wigs to slip from their graceful places. We laughed till we were weak, watching the parishioners struggle to scrape their comrades off the floor, trying to salvage what little was left of their dignity. Eventually, an elderly man caught sight of us enjoying the spectacle just a little bit too much. He held onto his trilby, taking the basement stairs leading up to the street, two steps at a time to chase us away.

'Get away from there, and go bout you business. Go on! Get out a here! Rude! Outta order!'

We scrambled to get away, still holding our aching bellies, coming to a halt at the corner, to catch our breaths and begin yet another transformation of our own. For it was on this corner on a Sunday morning that we would try to undo some of Mama's horrors. First, we girls would all deposit a very large amount of spit into our cupped palms, to wash away the ghostly powder from our faces. We each knew this had to be done, for we had looked into each other's faces when Mama finally stood back to admire her handiwork. Next we tore the huge white hats from our heads, so the breeze could tease our pressed heads and then rolled three pairs of long white socks down to ankle level before running wildly through Clissold Park. At the sight of the Baptist church on the corner of Albion Road, we pulled our socks up and reluctantly placed our hats on our heads in case anyone connected to the church reported back to Mama.

'How much have you got?' asked Clovis, the eldest of the clan. 'Give it to me and I'll count how much money we got between us.'

'Don't listen to him,' insisted Julia, the eldest of the girls. 'Mama said to make sure we put all the money in the collection box.'

'With my idea, we could buy loads of sweets and still put money in the collection box; now don't that sound like a good idea?.'

It did not take us long to agree, causing us to make a quick detour to the shops. We bought 'Toffoes,' 'Spangles,' and 'Treats' and chewed relentlessly throughout the service, taking care not be caught putting sweets into our mouths. The Sunday school service was bland as usual. Sitting around with a bunch of other kids who had been forced out of the house, as we were, so the grown ups could have "Nookie" time in peace, was no fun. Singing songs like 'This little Light of Mine' was the highlight, and of course going home at the end, but before that, we had to join the adults in the grown up service. As the door leading to the hall was flung open, the minister's words reached our ears and echoed with such great velocity that it followed us all the way home.

'For the Lord knows everything. E-V-E-R-Y-T-H-I-N-G. I tell you he knows what is in each of our hearts. He sees E-V-E-R-Y-T-H-I-N-G. With Him there is no secret.'

We gulped, staring at each other in amazement, all thinking the same thing. God had found out about the collection money. The guilt gnawed away at our guts as we walked home in reflective silence, trying to decide on ways of recompense.

'You lot are fools,' announced Clovis after a while. 'God loves little children. He's a kind God. He doesn't mind.'

A light came on for us all then. There was truth in what Clovis said. They told us that at Sunday school, and they had told us that God is forgiving, so we reasoned with God, telling Him how we had listened carefully to His teachings about sharing and how it benefited everyone. He must have heard because somehow it seemed all right after that and God was kind enough to share the collection money with us every Sunday. However, Mama soon became suspicious when we started asking for more money to give to the Lord.

Life was wonderful, dreamy, a flawless mastery of art that had captured the full light of the sun in all its glory. If only things could have remained on that course. But something happened to change all of that forever.

Clovis brought home a nest of three sparrows one day and placed it in my hands.

'I think the mother bird must have abandoned them or maybe a cat's got it. We'll care for them until they can fly. Find something to put them in,' he said, then dashed out again, slingshot hanging precariously from his back pocket.

The distressed high-pitched cry of the birds bounced off the walls and ceiling of the small room as I looked down at them with an ambivalence of tenderness and pity. I must not let them die. Life is sacred; to be preserved at all costs. Their survival depended on me. The nearest thing to hand was Mama's old grip - the one she came to England with, the one she would most certainly use again when we all returned to the Caribbean. I slid it out from under the bed and carefully placed the birds inside, along with some bread and water, which they refused to touch. To stop them from escaping, the last thing I did that night before climbing into bed, was to shut the lid of the grip.

The discovery of three limp bodies in the morning was a knife of shame, guilt and devastation, thrust deep into my guts. I had brought death into the house by starving the birds of air. I had killed them; committed mortal sin for which I would have to pay. That was the law of the land. It was a painful lesson, but that morning I learnt that if you truly love something, you have to give it air; space to grow and room to breathe. The birds would still be alive had I known that, but instead I had stifled the air out of them and with it, all our hopes of a happy future. From thereon, I carried that guilt around with me for most of my life, along with the fear of what was to come for nothing was ever going to be the same again.

Chapter Two

Love Thy Neighbour

....

There is nothing greater than love. To give love is a joy, a tribute to one's own heart and to receive it in abundance is truly a blessing. Living according to the first of the new commandments was easy, and so we loved with all our hearts, with all our souls, and with all our minds. Unfortunately, for us, the second commandment was not as effortless. In fact, it was a real struggle. Try as we did, to love the likes of Mrs Green and Mrs Andrews, it was evident after a while that pointless energy was being poured out on those who did not hold love in equal esteem.

Extravagant spending in the early months had finally caught up with us. It meant that belts had to be tightened, sacrifices had to be made, and so the dividing doors in the middle of the lounge were shut to make an extra room where Mama and Dada would have to sleep.

Worst of all, it meant that everyone had to shift around to make space for our two new tenants.

Massah Stanley, the first to arrive, was allocated the biggest room, the master bedroom, which looked out onto the front of the house. He was blown into our lives one evening, during winter of the following year, on a gust of superiority. After shaking raindrops from his overcoat for what seemed an eternity, he stepped in on the mat, straightened up, and began to assess his surroundings. From behind a ravine in the hallway, I inspected him closely with inquisitive eyes. I had never seen anything like it before in my life. There was an air about this tall, slender, quaint looking man, almost as though he was of noble birth but through some cruel twist of fate, his birthright had been denied him. The feeling of being watched directed his gaze down to where I stood. There was no warmth in his eyes or even a flicker of hello, instead his nostrils flare impatiently for a brief moment, and then quickly, he averted his eyes to continue his observation.

'Your room is nice and warm. I put a paraffin heater in there for you.'

Massah Stanley opened his mouth to respond to Mama, and out of it poured the Queen's English in a voice far too high-pitched for a man.

'That is very kind of you but I'm afraid the paraffin does not agree with my chest.'

He spoke through his nostrils as though he had suffered from sinusitis, or adenoids or a blockage of some other kind, for a significant period of his life. Hidden beneath the layers of floral Queen's English and his sinusitis, if indeed that is what is was, one could still detect the slightest murmur of a Jamaican accent.

He paid the princely sum of three pounds a week from his government job as a civil servant for the rent, wore a bowler hat and carried a long black umbrella to work every morning, come rain or shine. He appeared stuffy and somewhat effeminate to us kids. Maybe it was the way he carried his silver tray of fine bone china down to the kitchen to be washed every morning. If anyone happened to be half-way up the stairs and he was at the top, ready to descend, they would automatically retreat backwards to give way to him. Always displaying airs and graces, he walked sideways down the stairs, like a sidewinder in the desert; his bony kneecaps protruding through his trousers with each step he took, his long nailed little fingers, cocked high in the air at either end of the tray. Occasionally, he would miss a step or two, and when he did, what came out of his mouth was by no means floral. On the contrary, when taken unaware, these exclamations of surprise de-robed him of being anything but an English gentleman, for they were always exclamations with a definitive Jamaican edge.

'Raas Claat!'

We sniffed and coughed away the hysteria ready to burst from our mouths. There would be trouble to pay if we laughed in his face. So we tried our best to hold it in, whilst he looked down on us with scorn, as though we were nothing more than pickaninnies. For some reason unknown to us, he had a natural aversion to children.

His white woman Daphne, who I might add was a married woman, came to stay every Friday night; at the same time - nine o'clock on the dot. They walked down the road, at least twenty metres apart from each other, him, way up ahead and she, trailing five minutes or so behind. It was not safe or fashionable for a white woman to be seen walking the streets, in certain areas, with a coloured man in 1960s England. He left the front door slightly ajar so that she could enter without drawing any attention to herself. Her strawberry blonde hair was piled high on her head - a monument to fashion. Wearing a short psychedelic dress, she mounted the stairs to his room, leaving a trail of potent, heady perfume that filled the whole house. We knew they were in there having wild jungle sex. We heard the loud rhythmic creaking of the bedsprings, the long groaning and moaning, followed by gasps of 'Oh Stanley! Oh Stanley! Oh yes! Oh yes!' coming through the door. She would leave early next morning after he had made her tea in one of those fine china cups of his. I wondered about her husband; whether he was aware that he was not enough for her.

Massah Keith, a level headed man who wore a clenched black fist around his neck on a suede string, resided in a bedroom facing the backyard. His African woman, Yemi was always asking Mama to take one of the younger children to the shops, where she would buy hoards of sweets. When we got back from the shops, Clovis and Glen, being pubescent boys, would be waiting in the usual spot at the bottom of the stairs for their reward. A prime position to study Yemi's huge posterior vibrating in her tight pants as she mounted the stairs one at a time.

Four of us children slept in the other back bedroom, therefore the only other room left for Clovis and Glen to sleep in, besides the bathroom, was in the kitchen, on an old battered grey settee, which folded down into a bed.

With a strict upbringing based on keeping a tidy home and keeping the family happy, Mama was as house proud as they came. A martyr to the routines of family life, she scrubbed and cleaned all day long. It kept her mind occupied; stopped the disquieting voices of doubt and fear, which threatened to consume her when she was still. Her day began whilst everyone slept. Waking my father in the mornings was never the easiest of tasks. It took numerous attempts, in between stirring the corn-meal porridge to keep it lump-free, running a bath and preparing something for his lunch. On good days, he lifted hopes of them being the perfect couple with a loving peck on the cheek at the front door, but on bad days, he would follow it with a startling warning.

'Make sure you remember to take your tablets, Girlie.'

That statement had the power to change her whole persona in a way that could only be compared to throwing a wet blanket over someone.

'Go to work, I won't forget.'

'Make sure you don't. You know what the doctor said will happen.'

If only he knew how tired and groggy those tablets made her feel; how difficult it was to get through the daily workload and if the house was not up to its usual standard, he'd have something to say about it. Conveniently forgetting to take her tablets until the work was done was a necessary evil. She had no choice. What else could she do?

Surrounded by mountains of clothes in the washroom, Mama got down on her knees. She washed piles of white sheets, colours, towels and everyone's Sunday best, of which she took great care, especially with Dada's clothes. She liked the fact that he liked to look good. For hours on end the squirting sound of her washing drifted out into the backyard, through the backroom window.

On one side of our fence stood an old, empty, desolate house; overrun with weeds: it cried out to be lived in, desperate for the warmth and love of a family. On the other side of us lived our Jewish next-door neighbours, the Albergs. The parents were now grandparents as four of their five children had grown up, and two were married with babies. The youngest of their children, Rachel was about five years old. We tried to make friends with her one day after her voice floated over the backyard wall. Curious, we beat the dust from our clothes before climbing up, to sit on the wall to look over into what was a completely new world on the other side of our fence. Rachel was plump, healthy and clean. She was wearing the most beautiful, fluffy yellow dress with little blue bows. We gasped at the sight of her. Mama would never let us play in the yard wearing our Sunday best. Rachel's shiny brown pigtails were tied up with two shiny blue ribbons and what's more, when we looked down at her feet, she was wearing her "Good" shoes, and in the backyard as well. We only ever wore our "Good" shoes to church or if Mama decided to venture round to Cousin Enid's on a fine Sunday afternoon.

'Who are you talking to?' I asked her.

'I'm talking to my toys silly. We're having a tea party.'

'But they can't hear you.'

'Of course they can hear me, haven't you got any toys?'

We looked at each other. We knew we did not have any, not one between us, but we were not about to reveal that to her.

'Hey, we got loads and loads of toys in our house. We just don't want to play with them right now.'

Rachel picked up, then introduced us to each of her toys. She spoke with enthusiasm, giving information about their origin and how they came to be here. She was in the middle of answering another question when her mother, on seeing her conversing with us through the kitchen window, shouted to her.

'Rachel! Rachel! Time to come in!'

When Rachel's movement was not fast enough, her mother called again, only this time there was a penetrating urgency in her voice. .

'Quickly Rachel! Quickly!'

We wondered what could be so important. Rachel continued to talk as she packed her toys into a box, still holding the attention of a keen audience. With quick steps, her mother bolted into the garden, took hold of Rachel's hand and whisked her away, towards the house.

'Rachel has to go in now,' she said with a fixed smile.

'Oh, but why?' we called after her in, a pleading tone, but it was too late. The door had already been shut tight.

Still sitting on the wall, somewhat stunned and deflated, the silence that followed brought us an eerie truth. Like the dawning of a new day, it was obvious now that there had not been any great emergency or need for Rachel to be inside the house at that precise moment. The truth was that her mother did not want her milk-white daughter playing with dusty, little coloured children. The realisation of this dampened our young spirits, alienated and pushed us away, causing us to question internally what it was about coloureds that so many people hated. The great crime we had supposedly committed baffled me as one of life's mysteries. Yet the hurt we felt only drew us closer together, made us stronger, together, for amongst ourselves, we knew our own worth, and no one was going to take *that* away from us.

A safe comforting sound, an elixir of life, poured out to us into the backyard and we were drawn to it. To while the time away, Mama sang; she sang her heart out to get through all that washing. Songs that could make you stop whatever foolish childish games you might have been playing, songs of love and heartbreak that would hypnotize and like a magnet draw you in the direction of the washroom. Kneeling over the bath, as though in prayer, with her back to the door, she wouldn't even know you were there; so lost was she in the melodic cleansing of her spirit. When all the clothes had been wrung, we pegged them onto the line, and helped Mama to hoist it high in the air to catch the cool breeze.

Whilst dinner cooked, I laid snuggled up in the soft doughy arch of my mother's arms, on the battered old settee, listening to stories about what life was like for her as a child, back in Jamaica. Again, she told me that one day we would all go back to Jamaica to live; that she had made a solemn oath to return in time to take care of Aunt Mary, Mammee Jule and Pinto in their old age; the three people who had made her journey to England possible. Whenever she spoke of Jamaica, Mama's eyes, although distant, shone brighter than ever. Wearing a fixed smile, her face was an embellishment of sheer joy and divinity. Clear as day was the fact that what she wanted, needed, more than anything in the world was to once again, bless her eyes on her homeland; to ingest the piquancy of the hot Jamaican sun, safe in the knowledge that she had achieved her ambitions and that all the struggles and the sacrifices she had made for a better life had been worth it. A house on a plot of land with a sea-view, that's what she dreamed of. I felt an enormous sense of responsibility towards her, and the seeds of a profound desire to see Mama's hopes fulfilled had at last sprouted in my heart. Yet still, I knew that I could be fighting a losing battle.

Just a little over one year, since the death of those birds, was all it took for the ice-cold hands of change to touch our lives, one by one. I didn't quite know when exactly it had touched Dada, but touched him it had and there was something different about Mama too. At first, it was subtle in its manner, for she did a good job pretending everything was OK. But I could see that a cloud of sadness was descending on her. I could hear it in the gentle undertones of her melancholy voice; the silent calling of a spirit, so longing to be rescued. Something quite sinister was stirring. Deep down in the core of my bones I could feel it; a feeling of immense sadness, despair and loss. Suddenly, I wanted for her to get away from this house because I knew it meant her no good. But like the birds in the grip, she too was trapped, and so was I. That realisation came to me as she spoke harmoniously about sunshine, blue seas and palm trees. In an effort to discount my fears, I closed my eyes, allowing myself to bathe with Mama, in the warm glow of paradise. Delicious.

'Dada's coming! Dada's coming!' Someone shouted after catching a glimpse of my father, bouncing down Yoakley Road towards home. The sight of him evoked a gut-wrenching feeling in the pit of my stomach. Everyone was on red alert. Panicking bodies bumped into, and tripped over each other so that everything would be just right for when he came through the door; the way he expected it to be. We took up our places in readiness; and Mama began to look about his dinner. In this house, he was king, all mighty and powerful, and we were all his subjects, praying that he would come home in a good mood. First, someone would take his coat, and then he went and sat in his favourite armchair, still dusty from the building site, slamming his feet down on top of the coffee table.

'Come take off my shoes and socks,' he commanded Douglas and me. 'And you,' he said to Pauline, 'get me a pan of water to wash my feet, and bring the towel.'

'Yes Dada,' we said obediently.

'Girlie! Girlie! Where's my dinner?'

'It's coming, its coming Winston,' Mama called back hurriedly from the kitchen.

Getting his shoes off was hard work; a perilous job we tried hard to avoid. He shouted at us if we were too rough but we couldn't help it sometimes. It was as though his shoes had been welded onto his feet because when eventually they were released, it would send us sailing triumphantly, backwards onto the floor. Stifling was the strong odour of cheese that wafted up from his feet after we had pulled his socks off, worse still on a hot day. After his feet had been dried on a fluffy towel, Mama would give one of us kids a heavy tray of food to carry in for him. We carried it slowly, taking great care to lift our feet high so as not to trip and drop his dinner because if by some misfortune that happened, we knew all hell would break loose. Of course Mama would produce another plate of food, although to him it was not the same. We sat there staring blankly into the television, making sure not to speak or look at him as he ate, trying to ignore the clapping sound his mouth made as he chewed on a boiled cornmeal dumpling. Then, when he had finished eating, we all sat on the floor so that he could sleep on the settee. Listening to the television was difficult because he snored so loudly. Occasionally we turned it up a notch or two, but he always knew; raising his head from the armrest he'd look directly at the perpetrator with bloodshot eyes.

'Turn it down before I beat you!'

For reasons unknown to us, we all looked up to him in admiration, eager for his approval, eager to please.

His favourite out of all us kids was Julia. The pretty one; brown skinned with a head of black curly hair. He'd play her off against Mama by buying her little presents, telling her how beautiful she was in front of Mama and showing her off to his friends whenever they came round. It put a big strain on Mama's relationship with her eldest daughter. Over time, she grew to resent Julia, most of all, for seeming to be the object of Dada's love and attention. He played precarious games with our lives, by way of finding out where our loyalties lay. On days like that, he called us together in the sitting room, in full earshot of Mama.

'Out of me and your Mama, who do you love the most?' he asked us in turn. Dear God, what kind of a question was that to be asking a child? We loved them both but forcing us to choose had reduced us all to tears then. If we said we loved him, it was only through fear, and out of our desperate need to put a halt to his shenanigans. However, those who chose him above Mama were always shown preferential treatment for their compliance.

'Come on,' he goaded, a mischievous smile etched on his face, 'Your Mama or me?'

'I don't want to choose. Please don't make me choose Dada,' I cried pleadingly. 'I love you and Mama.'

'You can't choose both of us; you can only choose one. Who do you love the most?'

What made it worse was that I knew Mama could hear every word; knew how it must be tearing her apart and all I wanted to do was to comfort her; hug all her pain away.

'Then I choose Mama,' I said boldly through my tears.

'Go to your Mama then!' he said, slapping my legs, pushing me in the direction of the kitchen. I threw my arms about Mama's waist as she washed dishes.

'Never mind darling,' she would say, hugging me with wet hands. 'He's only playing.'

But just like his gambling, his games were devious and underhand. The four loves of his life were: his clothes, jewellery, gambling and women.

Us kids, we couldn't wait for him for go out. The relief we felt after he had left, made us able to breathe again, and so willingly, we helped that process along.

Preparation for a night out more than often, started early in the day. He would send us out to the shops to get a packet of Gillette razor blades, ten Benson and Hedges, and to pick up his suit from the drycleane'rs.

'And if the suit's not ready, then wait for it.'

Everyone knew of us. The Greek men who worked in the drycleaner's on Church Street knew him well. They were all terrified of what he stood for. If by chance, Marios, the owner, lost one of Dada's suits, he recruited the whole family to help look for it.

Once when we had gone to pick up a suit, they told us it was not ready yet and unfortunately, I had drawn the short straw to convey the message to Dada back at home whilst he ate his dinner.

'Oh shit! Almighty God! He shouted, throwing his fork down onto the plate, and his arms high into the air. 'You go back to the laundry and tell him, tell him, I said, if I have to leave my dinner, to come and get my suit, I'm going to come down there to kick his arse. Go on! Tell him! Tell him there's going to be trouble if I don't get my suit right away! Tell him I want it *now!*'

We ran all the way back to the shop, fearful and anxious because we knew what Dada was capable of. He was a man of his word. If he said he was going to do something then he usually did.

Mario's face dropped when he saw us entering his shop a second time. He could see we too were scared.

'Big Winston said he wants his brown pinstripe suit now, or he's ...'

'It's OK. It'll be ready in five minutes.'

The name 'Big Winston' struck fear in people. Everyone in Stoke Newington knew of him as a fighting man - fearless of everything and everybody but God. On that occasion, we left with Dada's suit about ten minutes later. After that, he would send us to get his clothes from the drycleaner's, even when it was shut. In the dark, we knocked on the windows repeatedly with urgent knuckles, peered into the dark shop, for signs of life, smearing the cold glass with our warm panting breath and waited until a face appeared from behind the curtains of their second floor living quarters. Marios must have known that it was too perilous for us to return home empty-handed so as always, he would rush downstairs, turn the lights on, and open the shop.

Tricksters can turn their hands to many things. Using a razor, Dada wet shaved first, sticking bits of toilet paper where he had cut himself. He then took a fresh pack of new playing cards from his jacket pocket. As he did this, we sat there, silent witnesses to his cunning action. Ever so carefully, he loosened the clear cellophane wrapping from the pack of cards. Sitting beside a table lamp for extra light, cigarette hanging precariously from the corner of his mouth, deep in concentration, he used the razor to mark the picture cards in the top right hand corner so he could tell them apart by touch. Then, when he had finished, he did something quite out of character. He set up the ironing board in the living room. The first time we saw him do this, our jaws dropped open with shock. We thought a miracle was taking place right before our eyes. Had his nurturing skills finally kicked in at last? God knows it was well overdue. However, he did not intend to make sure we all had a weeks' worth of freshly ironed clothes. Using his handkerchief and the hot iron, he re-sealed the cellophane wrapper carefully over the box again, good as new.

'Set the bath for me.'

A royal command had been given, and there were echoes of 'set the bath, set the bath,' until we could all hear the water running, fast and furious. We took it in turn to do the different tasks to the best of our ability for him. Mama ironed his shirt, sewing a button on if need be; Clovis knotted his tie, someone would be looking for a particular pair of cufflinks, whilst someone else searched for a pair of black socks. I polished his shoes, as if they were my pride and joy.

'Are they shiny enough now Dada? I've been shining them for a long time.'

'They're so shiny, I can see my face in them,' he beamed on inspection, showing them to everyone else who pretended to look.

'Looks like I'm going to have to get you to shine them all the time,' he said ruffling my hair affectionately.

It was not as if I was going to grow up to be a shoeshine girl or anything, but his approval boosted my self-esteem.

He was handsome all right; standing there all dolled up admiring himself in the mirror. Immaculate in his suit and felt hat, he was sharper than the razor he used to mark his cards. His gold teeth gleamed as he smiled one last glittering smile in admiration of how good he looked. He preferred to travel on foot as opposed to driving his car' that way he got the attention he so craved. Finally he left, bouncing up the road with that distinctive walk which got him noticed. He left us with the sweet odour of his aftershave, clothes to collect from the floor and a scummy bath to clean. The relief was great for us children, although not so great for Mama. She pined for him. Mama withdrew to her bedroom, alone to muse with her sadness. I sang to her, told her jokes, and did just about anything I could to bring a smile to her face.

Dada returned at a ridiculous hour, hungry for food, so he woke his girls to get up at after three o'clock in the morning to make him fried dumpling, eggs and beans. It was a hurried affair, for by the time we brought it to him; he was always deep in a drunken sleep, out for the count.

Although our faith was strong, I kept hoping and praying that our lives would improve; that what we were going through was just a temporary setback; that my debt of recompense with the powers that be would end. However, I was sorely disappointed with what happened next. Far from being exonerated, more trouble came, in many different guises.

It came in the shape of Mrs Adams, our new next-door neighbour. She had two children, a teenage boy named Jeffrey and a little girl, Sandra - about five or six years in age. A flirtatious, over-friendly woman, she paraded around the place wearing colourful low cut V-neck dresses, showing off her wobbling, ample bosoms, bending over unnecessarily at every opportunity. To start with, she called round frequently for cups of sugar in the early days. Then after a while, Mama told her not to come back; that she would have to get her own sugar from the shops, just like everyone else.

Mrs Adam's husband, Henry, was a serious looking, well built, bald headed man with a beautiful chocolate complexion. With his thick moustache and beard, he resembled a strong man, the kind you see at the circus. He acted as her bodyguard, tentative, always loitering in the background, but being a working man, he could not be there all of the time.

When Dada had first clapped eyes on Mrs Adams, they nearly popped out of his head. Soon afterwards, she started speaking to him over the fence at the front of the house first. Then after a while, I noticed something else - Dada in the backyard. He never went into the backyard. He never had any business being out there before. But now she spoke to him over the backyard fence, slowly running her middle finger over the exposed flesh of her huge breasts as she did, occasionally looking down on her chest, as though checking they were still there. He'd come back into the house all hot and flustered, dabbing his head and neck with a kerchief, clearing his throat as if something was stuck in it.

Then, one day, it happened. When he thought no one was looking, he crept to the end of the yard, to the lowest part of the neighbouring wall, quickly climbed over and disappeared into her house. I saw it with my own two eyes, and it mystified me. I could not understand why he used the back door and not the front. Then one day, not long afterwards, Mama helped my innocent mind to understand. We were in the washroom, which looked out onto the backyard. Mama was soaking some clothes in huge tin basins. I kept her company, helping her with the washing. As Mama bent down to immerse the garments in warm soapy water; something suddenly caught my eye from where I was standing.

'You listening to me?' Mama said.

But I couldn't hear her. My mind was occupied; trying to make out the suspicious looking figure of Dada making his way back through Mrs Adams' backyard and over the fence. With eyes bulging on the lookout, he Jim Screeched around behaving like an undercover agent.

'Melanie! Melanie! Mama called, and still I couldn't hear her. Then she stood up and followed my eyes to what it was that had momentarily struck me dumb. There he was, my father, with one leg either side of the fence, trying to clamber back over. I managed to tear my gaze away to look up into Mama's shocked face.

'Winston, What you doing over that woman's house?'

'What you talking about now?'

'I saw you step over from that woman's fence,' said Mama following him into the bedroom. 'Oh God! Don't tell me you went over there and fucked that bitch. How could you do that to me? How?' Mama was distraught now.

'Girlie, I think you getting sick again. If you must know, I went over there to use her phone.'

'I don't believe you. Something's not right; I know it,' sobbed Mama.

'It's all in your mind.' he said tapping her temple with his forefinger. 'You know what? I think I'm going to call the doctor for you?'

'No,' said Mama, sobering up quickly, now willing to question whether in fact she had overreacted. 'I don't want to go back to that place, and I don't want you to have an excuse to go back into that woman's house.'

Fleeting looks and suggestive grins hung in the air whenever Dada and Mrs Adams spotted each other.

'Good morning Mrs Adams,' Dada said after charging outside on hearing her milk bottles rattle - a clear signal that required attention.

'Winston.' Mrs Adams' response made his name sound like good morning itself.

'Why do you still have to talk to that woman, and in front of me,' Mama asked tormented by the threat Mrs Adams posed.

'Girlie, she is my neighbour,' Dada said, grinning away. 'What you want me to do, ignore her? It says in the Bible to love thy neighbour.'

'Yes, but nowhere does it say to fuck them.'

A look of utter repulsion affixed itself to my father's face.

'That's why I can't take you sometimes you know.'

'You mean you can't face the truth.'

'I'm going out.'

'Yes, run away like you always do. Maybe that's what I should do as well. Take my children and run.'

'Run where? Look at you. You don't even make an effort to look good for me any more, and besides,' he laughed cynically, 'who's going to have you with six kids strapped to your waist?'

'Winston I can't live like this anymore. It's killing me. I used to love this house, but now I hate it,' cried mama.

'I keep telling you it's all in your head, and you know you're head's not right.'

'Maybe if you helped me out with the children a little, spent more time with us, I wouldn't be so tired and miserable all the time.'

He made no response to her pleas. Instead, he took a step towards the door.

'And what about the housekeeping?'

Dada took out a wad of notes from his pocket and peeled off five pounds, throwing it onto the demi table in the hallway. 'I'm gone.'

'Five pounds! What am I supposed to do with five pounds?'

He didn't even answer her - just marched out of the house and up the street as though he did not have a care in the world.

Emotionally exhausted, Mama plodded along like a tired out pit pony, pulling everyone along behind her; trying to give the impression that she was coping, even though it was apparent to all who cared to see, that her state of mind had become frayed around the edges. Her life did not belong to her anymore. She had no control to change that. No control over her husband's infidelity or how used and dirty it made her feel. Pouring more antiseptic than was needed into the bath, she scrubbed her body inside out, sometimes until it bled, in the bid to wash away the sins of the man she loved. Occasionally she'd go as far as to take a swig from the antiseptic bottle just to feel cleansed on the inside as well. However, not even soap and water or antiseptic for that matter, could do the trick and that's when all the burning started.

They say fire is cleansing, so she used it to purge her life of the things that carried bad memories. At first, she burnt things - small things - old clothes, progressing onto photographs she found in Dada's pockets. We were all so busy waiting and watching all the time for what would happen next that no one noticed that Douglas, the runt of the family, was going through his own inner turmoil. Poor Douglas. Because we were all too afraid to take our eyes off Mama, and what she was going through, his silent calls for help went unnoticed. In a short space of time, Douglas endured not one, but two, serious, life-threatening accidents. On one occasion, he had gotten in the way as Mama moved a burning plastic dustbin to another area of the backyard. I will never forget the screams for as long as I live. Douglas' leg was on fire. The plastic from the bin melted the skin on his knee almost down to the bone. Mama frantically wrapped his leg in soaking wet towels then Dada placed Douglas' shaking body into the back of the car and they sped off towards the hospital. Thankfully, Douglas recovered, though he was scarred for life. The authorities turned a blind eye to our plight: to them we were invisible, so no one from social services came round to assess the situation or to give support to a family in need.

A few months after that, another accident occurred. We knew that playing in the house was not permitted - something might get broken. Yet Douglas and I chased each other from room to room. In pursuit of me, Douglas pushed open the glass door to the sitting room and his hand went straight through the full pane of glass, severing a main artery in his wrist, pumping out blood that spurted everywhere. Again, the family car screeched off in the direction of the hospital. By the grace of God, they get there just in time and Douglas received thirty stitches to the wound and had his bandaged arm in a cast for weeks.

The phase of madness continued in our lives, for in addition to everything else that was happening Clovis, grossly unhappy, ran away from the misery of home life at every opportunity, which added to Mama's grief. A few hours after we had reported him missing, a visit from the police brought welcome news for Mama; news that Clovis was safe and ready to be picked up from the station. However, when they returned home, Dada dealt with him the only way he knew how - by drawing his belt, or a piece of curtain rod to punish Clovis for absconding but even though Mama took a few blows in coming to his defence, that did not deter Clovis from trying to escape again. In the end Dada washed his hands of Clovis, refusing to go and collect him again, leaving Mama to trudge down to the station in the cold, time after time. It was on one such occasion that Clovis, on seeing Mama racked with pain, decided that he would give up the desire to escape because he could not afford to entrust Mama to the mercy of his father.

Chapter Three

Hidden Treasure

....

In the autumn of 1969, when a spray of seasonal colours began to fall as silently as snow, Dada secured himself a job as a lorry driver and for a while things seemed as though they were slowly coming back to normality. Quite unexpectedly, he was more interested in the four youngest of his children, leaving the engine of that huge monstrosity running whilst he waited for us to get ready at short notice. No taller than one of the wheels, we were lifted up to a great height to sit in the cab beside him. It felt like being on top of the world looking down at all those people. He took us way out of London to counties we could not even pronounce. Having breakfast or lunch in a motorway café was a novel experience, but when he started taking us to the pictures on a Saturday, giving Mama a welcome break, we concluded that he had reformed.

I did not really notice them the first week we went to the pictures, helped by the fact that they had probably left early, but I became aware of their presence for the two consecutive weeks that followed. Two mysterious figures sat with us in the dark at the end of our row of seats at the picture house; mother and baby daughter from what I could make out from their silhouettes. Every time we went to the pictures, they were always there and each time the audience roared with laughter, I craned my head towards them, straining my eyes to get a look, hoping the lights would come up but as usual, they left before the end of the show. Dada must have twigged that I seemed more interested in him and his companion than in the film. When we got outside onto the street, he made it perfectly clear that there were some things you talked about and some things you did not.

'Anyhow you tell your mama bout that woman and the little girl, I'm going to have to beat you. Do you hear me?'

'Yes Dada,' I said, grasping the full seriousness of his threat.

'Bev is just a friend and if Girlie find out, she going to take it the wrong way.'

So this faceless woman had a name after all. Bev, he had called her. If she was just a friend then why couldn't I tell Mama? Why had I been placed in the firing line to protect her? Some friend. She must have known he was married.

'What film did you see at the pictures?' Mama asked, after Dada had dropped us off.

I avoided eye contact when answering because I was sure that Mama could read my mind through my eyes.

Truly I wanted to tell her but two things stopped me. The knowing that she would be hurt and upset and the prospect of being beaten.

'I... I can't remember, what it was called. But it was good though.'

Luckily, for me, Pauline stepped in at the right moment and started to tell Mama all about the film. My eyes fell to my feet. A feeling of disgust and self-loathing washed over me. I should have been protecting Mama, and instead here I was, sheltering two people intent on keeping her in the dark. If by chance she found out from someone else then she would most certainly believe that I too had deceived her and that alone would break my heart.

That same evening Mama decided a change of scenery was what was needed so we took a stroll out to Cousin Enid's house.

Cousin Enid was all the family Mama had in England since her brother Richard had immigrated to America. A powerfully built, no nonsense woman, Cousin Enid was a serious character not to be trifled with. Us kids had to remember not to speak to her unless she spoke to us first and always to attach the prefix 'Cousin' to her name when addressing her. Forgetting to do so would at best get you scolded and at worst result in having your legs slapped for insolence. On occasions, we had skipped to Cousin Enid's house too carefree to remember our manners. A slip of the tongue was all it took for us to cry all the way home. Cousin Enid had been in England since 1955. You could not accuse her of being a retiring character for she had established good connections, bought her own house a year later and not long after that, had had a win on the pools. Some people are just born lucky. We had the highest respect for her because every so often, she took us out in turns to kit us out with clothes and we would remember our manners and say: 'Thank you Cousin Enid.' In a way, one could say she had been cut from the same cloth as Dada, although the two did not see eye to eye; they detested each other with vehemence.

We heard her vexation before she opened the door. On her head she wore a translucent headscarf; a tea towel tucked around her waist. We followed her through the long hallway and into the kitchen. She moved rapidly around the house, stomping and cussing as she went and I stayed close to Mama for protection.

'I am the ruler in this house,' she said, slamming her clenched fist down onto a floured table, sending flour dust into the air. 'And so help me God, while there is still breath in my body, no one is going to rule me, in my own home, least of all a child.'

Yvette, her eldest daughter, sat crying hysterically at the table.

'Enid, what's wrong with the child? Why she crying so?' asked Mama.

Enid marched over to the fridge, opened the door and took out a plate that was covered with a dish. She uncovered it to reveal a plate of solid cold white rice - nothing else, just so-so rice, on its own. She placed it down roughly in front of Yvette.

'Eat it!' she ordered.

'Oh God Enid, don't do her so,' said Mama picking up the plate from the table. 'At least let me warm it up for her.'

'Three days I been waiting and still she won't eat it. Think she too good to eat the food I put on my table. But I tell you this, she not going to beat me in my own house.'

She went on and on like that for ages, so busy cussing she had not even noticed that Mama had fried an egg and thrown it on top of the rice to make it more appealing.

'Eat some of it for you Cousin Girlie, come on,' Mama whispered to Yvette and she polished off the lot.

'Now get out of my sight,' said Cousin Enid triumphantly to Yvette. 'You just showing off youself.'

Yvette looked back at Mama and the two smiled before she left the kitchen.

'So how you do Girlie?' asked Enid whilst washing the plate.

'I'm all right, nothing to complain about.'

'Yet! You don't sound all right to me. Winston done something?'

'No - well yes. You know he got a job as a lorry driver?'

'Rodney tell me last week.'

'Well he started helping me out, a lot.'

'Helping you out? How?'

'By taking the children off my hands, every week.'

'Huh. Every week. Mark my words, he's definitely up to something.'

'Not necessarily. I think now that he's got this job he's more settled in himself.'

'Girlie,' said Enid trying to enlighten Mama, 'I know you worship the ground he walks on and God knows he doesn't deserve it but he's a leopard and I say he's up to something. Men like Winston never change.'

If cousin Enid found out about Bev and her little girl before I had a chance to break it to Mama, I would be in line for yet another beating. Therefore I had to choose my moment wisely.

As the following Saturday approached I began to think up excuses for not going to the pictures with Dada.

'Melanie's not going today. She say she don't feel well.'

Dada looks down at me, causing my eyes to fall on my feet and a cough to escape my mouth.

'She look fine to me.'

'That's what I tell her,' said Mama.

'Get your coat on,' sneered Dada, giving me a knowing look, 'you're coming.'

And even though I didn't want to, I had to go.

The same husky voice we heard last week was now talking to Dada. Bev had put her daughter to sit next to us children, so she could sit directly next to Dada. I didn't enjoy the film, thinking about Mama all the way through. When at the end of the show the lights came up, I saw Bev and her daughter Maxine clearly for the first time. I took a good long scrutinizing look at Bev and decided almost instantly I didn't like her and her smug knowing smile. She was taking me for a fool because I was a child. Yet I was my mother's daughter and so I despised her.

'Goodbye Melanie,' she said, expecting an innocent response.

I looked her up and down and then cut my eyes at mother and daughter in a way I thought was discreet.

'Say goodbye to Bev,' said Dada through clenched teeth, poking me in the back whilst still trying to sound friendly and non-threatening.

As soon as he had waved them off, he turned abruptly to me.

'I'm warning you, if you ever tell your Mama about Bev, I'm going to beat you so bad, all of you. Do you hear me?'

'Yes Dada,' we muttered, more riddled with guilt that we were being made to keep a nasty secret from Mama, than terrified.

A week later, we sat next to that little girl as usual while the adults got cosy with their arms around each other. We had no idea we had been sitting next to our little sister all that time. It made my blood boil to see him slobbering all over that woman. But the guilt was killing me and all I could think about was freeing myself of it. By not telling the truth, I was a liar, we all were. Mama always said that every liar is a thief. I didn't want to be a liar nor a thief, so together, Julia, Pauline, Douglas and I, we made up our minds and told Mama about Bev one Saturday afternoon, after Dada had dropped us off to go visit a friend.

When Mama confronted him with it the next day, he told her we were wicked for telling such lies, upsetting her like that; and then would you believe it, he drew his belt and beat us and although Mama tried to defend us as usual, she was thrown to the ground a few times. Then, with the dirty deed done, he took his leave from this whimpering, chaotic household.

After the crying had died down and faded away into a solemn atmosphere of helpless despair, Mama took us off to her Cousin's house for a break that evening. A listening ear, a shoulder to cry on was what was needed so Mama sought solace in Cousin Enid's strength.

'Leave him!' was Cousin Enid's answer to all Mama's troubles. The way Dada treated her cousin infuriated her.

'How can I leave with six children? I don't have anywhere else to run. And how will I feed and clothe the children on my own?'

'Girlie if you stay with him he's going to drive you as mad as can be. You going to start walking the streets with you drawers on you head. Make up your mind fast, and leave him. Come to me when you ready and I will send you to my friend Barbara in Brixton. She only have room for you and three children, so for now you would have to take the youngest ones with you and when you settled, in six months or so, go get the other kids. The Assistance Board will help you till you find work. Get that little shithouse out of your life once and for all.'

Into her cupped palms, Mama cried for a while, before catching her breath.

'I didn't come to England to accept charity from anyone. Enid I tell you I'd rather die than take money from the Assistance Board.'

'Girlie what choice you got? You have to run.'

'But you saw what happened last time. He made me go back. Said if I ran away again he was going to put me in the mental hospital for a long time.'

'That nasty bastard trying to control your life,' Cousin Enid was enraged. 'I bet you don't go through his pockets. There's a lot you can learn by going through a man's pockets - see who you dealing with. Nasty bastard,' she cursed again. 'It should have been me. I'd have fixed him good and proper; raising his hand to a woman an' all. Rodney made that mistake one time and lift his hand to me. I tell you Girlie, I give him one punch, and to this day he has never raised his hand to me again.'

Suddenly Mama's tears became tears of laughter and she and Enid laughed at the idea of Rodney being stunned by Enid's fist.

'Even if he talk to me in a certain way,' Cousin Enid now relished, 'I will bring him right back to his senses.

We were not supposed to be staring into Enid's face or listening with ears propped like Alsatians, nor were we permitted to join in with the laughter of grown ups, which we were now doing.

'Damned children.' Cousin Enid's tone wiped the smiles from our faces. 'Always listening in on big people's business; go outside and play.'

Our heels clicked against the floors of St Ann's Home, as we walked the length of the long draughty corridor. Nuns ran this hospice for the terminally ill, nuns who glided silently across the floor as though on wheels, disappearing into dark corners of the building. In this sobering place, life hung precariously on a fraying piece of string. Voices, stricken with pain, cried out for mercy. Mama brought me along with her for company two evenings a week. She had three part-time jobs in total, all cleaning, and because Dada knows this, he was not forthcoming with the housekeeping. Money was tighter than ever and slowly the bills began to pile up. Though Mama was resourceful to say the least - she had stretched what little housekeeping she got to capacity in an effort to put food on the table, keep the creditors at bay and still hold on to her ambitions, lest they should fade away to nothing. The prospect of letting go of her passions was not an option. When she was not cleaning the hospice or St Leonard's Hospital or the Metropolitan Hospital, she was cleaning her home.

Outside in the backyard, the cruel grip of winter had fastened itself to bare, skeleton trees, which bent and menaced in the wind; to anything that had life in it.

Inside, Mama temporarily restrained its grip with the warmth, which emanated from her discourse on Jamaica and by steam from pots on the stove, which caused the windows in the kitchen to mist over. Her passionate dreams were like beautiful wild horses, to which she held on tight, as though her life depended on it. Now when she spoke her tone was pleading - almost willing something that has decided to depart, to stay. We felt her sadness because we needed her so much and because her hopes were all we had. Nevertheless, we were all still too young, too terrified to do anything. All we could do was watch helpless and defenceless.

Moments later, she was in the washroom sobbing over one of Dada's shirts. Perhaps it was a whiff of perfume that taunted her senses or an illuminated, unrecognisable, shade of lipstick that blurred her vision. Taking Cousin Enid's advice, she turned detective, going through Dada's pockets for clues about his life. Her hand encountered a flat, glossy object, which she pulled out - a photograph of him. Sitting either side of him, were two blonde women and next to one of these women, sat a 'half-caste' boy, smiling, unknowing and happy. She did not wash his shirt then. It was evidence with which to confront him later. I looked at the glossy photograph whilst Mama cooked. He was smiling, with both arms about their shoulders. Outside of our home, we knew only Cousin Enid, but Dada obviously had another life away from his family. Anger pricked. I felt sick. If it made me feel this way, I could only begin to imagine what it must be doing to Mama.

We scattered out of the way on seeing him bounce towards us, down Yoakley Road. Swinging his arms in boastful fashion he sauntered as if he hadn't a care in the world, smiling and waving at folk as he did. He was so free and we were so very captive. Back here things were getting so bad.

'Winston, we need to talk,' she said to him as we were taking off his shoes and socks. Defensive he got up, almost knocking us over, to march into the bedroom.

'What you going to nag me about now woman?'

'These,' said Mama throwing the picture and the shirt onto the bed.

'You been going through my pockets! I told you never to go through my pockets,' he said shoving her out of the way.

'I was about to take your clothes to the drycleaner, for you. Who are those women in the picture?'

'I think I'm going to have to call the doctor to you. Have you been taking your tablets?'

'I want to know who those women are. What am I supposed to think if you won't even talk to me? For God's sake, just tell me the truth.'

'Alright, you want the truth. Here it is. These two women are my friends; I know them from the pub. This one,' he said pointing to the one on the left 'is the landlord's wife. She's a married woman; all right!'

'So what about the lipstick?'

'For God sake Girlie, people love me out there. She hugged me! Her husband was right there with us. That's how I got lipstick on my shirt.'

It's true he was a very popular man but Mama's tears didn't help the situation. It made him worse.

'I can't take this. I'm going out. If you keep this up, I can see that I'm going to have to put you right back in the hospital,' and with that, he was gone, leaving a stale trail of Benson and Hedges.

From then on whenever Mama found photographs, she said nothing; just took them out from their hiding place; usually his jacket or from under a carpet and left them lying around for all to see. She was exposing him for what he was.

'What!' she'd say when he noticed them lying around, 'I got to clean my house.'

He'd just stand there looking down on her with contempt.

I continued to pray for deliverance from my sins but I don't think God heard me because I remained a helpless child with no control over what happened to me, or those I loved.

Living the high life is an expensive business and someone somewhere will have to pay for it. Eating greasy Spam, mash and baked beans, we paid for it when Dada came through the front door one Friday night crying real tears. Looking from one to the other we chewed and swallowed in silence, ears tuned and eyes wide open.

'Winston what is it?' panicked Mama. 'Oh God tell me what's wrong.'

'I lost my wage packet. I lost my wage packet. One minute I had it right here,' he wept, beating one side of his trouser pocket, and the next minute it's gone. It must have fallen out.'

'Check your jacket pocket, maybe you put it in there.'

'It's not in my jacket Girlie, I said it's gone.'

I could see the horror etching itself on Mama's face.

'But there's nothing in the house to feed the children and we have to pay the rates or they will take the furniture away again.'

'I'm sorry Girlie. I'm so sorry,' he wailed miserably.

'Oh God Winston, what are we going to do? What, are we going to do,' said Mama cradling Dada's sobbing head in her lap to hush his loud cries.

'Put on your coat and shoes and run round to Cousin Enid's house,' she instructed Julia, Pauline and me. 'Tell her what's happened. Tell her I haven't got no money to feed the children and that I am asking her for ten pounds to borrow until next week. Make sure you tell her I'm going to be paying her back next week.'

In the dark, we ran all the way to Cousin Enid's house. She seemed shocked to see us at that time of the evening. Nervous, we followed her through to the kitchen not knowing which order to start this pitiful story, so we just blurted it out how it came.

'Cousin Enid, Mama's asking for your help,' said Julia.

'Ten pounds to be exact,' I chipped in.

'Dada's lost his wage packet and there's no food in the house to eat,' Pauline added.

'And Mama said she'll pay you back next week,' I finalized.

Would you believe it, after all that, she just kissed her teeth and went back to what she was doing before we arrived, kneading flour.

'I know he's your father,' she said, now beating the air out of the dough with her fist, 'but I'm tired of telling Girlie to leave that no-good bastard; bout him lose the wage packet - nothing more than he gamble it and lose.' We stared at her with pleading eyes.

'Tell her I can't just give her ten pounds like that. I'm going to have to ask Rodney first and I don't know if he's going to say yes.'

Mama was vexed to high heaven when we told her what Cousin Enid had said. When we got hungry later that night, after Dada had done one for his disappearing acts again, we offered to go back round to Enid's to find out whether a decision had been made. But Mama said 'No! I will never ask Enid for anything again.'

As if things were not bad enough, notices for possession from the bailiffs, threatening to seize what little furniture we had left had been piling up. We ate cornmeal porridge, fried dumplings and beans for three days before a sudden stroke of luck came our way, quite unexpectedly. Cousin Enid did not come to our rescue. In fact, it was Dada, except he didn't know it. As usual, Mama took her stress out on the house - cleanliness being next to Godliness and all that. With her belly empty of sustenance, she scrubbed and cleaned the house from top to bottom. The settee in the sitting room was old and battered now but it refused to lie down and die. It was our life support machine because on many occasions it had rewarded us with enough loose change to at the very least buy bread and milk. Therefore, as Mama cleaned, Douglas and I stuck our hands down the sides of the settee, checking for coins that might have fallen haphazardly, out of the full pockets of visitors. However, there were no coins now, not even one, only what felt like heaps of paper. Grabbing a handful, I pulled it out, and came up with a wad of mixed notes. I scratched my head in disbelief, looked at Douglas, and then back at the wad of money in my hand. So stunned, we were rendered speechless for a while. Paper money! Real paper money!

'Look Mama,' I said eventually.

'Lord have mercy, where you get that from?'

'It was down the side of the chair at the bottom, cross my heart and hope to die and there's more too.' This was like something out of those fairytale books we read every night for comfort.

'Maybe little fairies hid it there because they felt sorry for us.'

But Mama did not buy that for one minute. She knew exactly who had hidden it there.

'We got to put it back,' she said anxiously, taking two five-pound notes, tucking it carefully into her apron pocket. 'Don't say a word about this to anyone, you hear me? Not a word.'

'We'll help you tidy up some more Mama.'

We did not do it half-heartedly like before. Good fortune fuelled our enthusiasm. We found more money under the carpet in the bedroom. You would think Mama would have been happy, finding all that money but strangely enough, it made her sad, angry and even more tormented. She paid T Stephenson five pounds towards the debts for the rates when he came to the door with his van that very same day, enough to keep him at bay for a while. Enid came round with offers of help the day after. Mama told her she did not need her help, but at least they were still on talking terms.

That most certainly was not the case with Mrs Adams next door. She and Mama couldn't bear the sight of each other because they both wanted Dada. They fought a war of words over the backyard fence and whenever they passed each other in the street. Mrs Adams was just living too close for comfort. The irony of it all was, they were not the only ones fighting over Dada, so were many other women. Complaining to Dada about Mrs Adams got Mama nowhere.

'It's you who started the trouble, accusing the woman of all kinds of things,' he said putting on a fresh pair of socks.

'By the way,' said Mama, taking all the money we had found from the drawer and changing the subject, 'where did all this come from? The kids found it in the settee and under the carpet.'

'Give me that. It's not mine. I'm holding it for someone I know,' said Dada, guilty as sin and grabbing the money out of Mama's hand.

'Winston how could you have that sort of money in the house knowing that me and the kids don't have nothing? We in so much debt and you got more than enough money there to pay them all off.'

'I told you it's not my money,' he spat. 'It belongs to someone else. I hope you didn't take any or there'll be trouble,' he said, tying his laces.

'It's all there. Count it if you like,' Mama bluffed.

But he didn't. Instead he gave her a curious look for he was not even sure himself how much was there. He took all the money with him, heading off to his favourite haunt, The Three Crowns Pub at the corner of Church Street where it met the high road. That was his real home.

That night I slept in Mama's bed and when she thought I was fast asleep I heard her call for help.

'Dear God, shine a light in my darkness; show me the way to go; leave a door open for me somewhere Lord,' prayed Mama aloud and every time the old house creaked, she braced herself for Dada's sudden appearance, thinking her prayers had been answered.

Chapter Four

Every Dog Has Its Day

....

The next morning I woke up in Mama's bed. Dada had not come home last night and now it was daylight. As usual, Mama carried on with her housework, stopping only to take me for a visit to the butcher, we knew only as F28. F28 was the number on his door - the dentist who pulled teeth for fun and money, telling you to 'shut up,' if you so much as winced or cried out in pain. My reward was a mouth full of blood but at least I got the day off school.

Smart enough to see that school was not meeting his needs, Clovis refused to go back so Mama gave him jobs to do instead. That afternoon, she sent him to the corner shop to buy bread and milk. He returned, bag in hand, sniffing wildly at the air as he walked through the passageway to the kitchen.

'Is Dada upstairs then? he asked.'

'What makes you say that?' said Mama looking up at him suspiciously.

'I can smell his cigarette in the passage.'

'Can't be your father, he never come home last night.'

'He must be here,' insisted Clovis, 'the passage stinks of cigarette smoke. Go smell it yourself if you don't believe me.'

Mama followed Clovis into the passageway. She smelt it too and froze. Her eyes shifted from side to side. It was a sign.

'Dear God, something's wrong,' she said gripping Clovis' arm. 'Run down to The Three Crowns pub. Try to find out what's happened to him. Hurry! Make haste!' she called after him as he took off in the direction of the pub.

As he got closer to The Three Crowns, Clovis saw the flashing light of an ambulance, parked awkwardly on the corner of the high road. He ran the rest of the way until he was standing outside the pub. Transfixed, he stared at the wide open doors of the ambulance, waiting to receive the poor unfortunate person who was going to grace the inside with his presence. Now he focused his eyes on to the saloon-style pub doors. However, just as he lifted his hands, the doors were flung open, almost knocking him to the ground.

An injured man was being carried out. Grown men carried him, as if about to give him the bumps. Four men supported his upper body. Some had their arms under the back of his knees, either side of him and some held his lower legs. In total eight men struggled under his weight. What caught Clovis' eye were the drops of blood that spattered on the concrete pavement, leaving a trail. Suddenly, someone shifted to one side and to Clovis' horror; he saw that it was Dada. Groaning loudly, Dada looked as if he was losing consciousness, his eyes rolling around in his head like a couple of marbles. He came round for a moment though, opening his eyes to see Clovis standing there.

'Tell Girlie - Tell Girlie I …' that's all he managed to get out before drifting back into unconsciousness.

The eight men who bore his weight bundled him into the waiting ambulance, only then allowing the astonished crew to take over. Before accompanying Dada to the hospital, Honey and Steadman, relayed to Clovis what had happened. Apparently, they had all been gambling. As you can probably guess, Dada had won. Scraping up the wad of notes, he had made his way over to the bar, boasting about his luck. Then someone had tapped him on the shoulder, and cracked a bottle over his forehead as he turned to see who it was. The king had been crowned.

Mama waited by the front room window, looking out. Seeing Clovis tearing towards home with the wind under him, she tore open the front door.

'Mama,' said Clovis breathlessly, when he had reached the house, 'Dada's hurt real bad. They took him in the ambulance to the hospital.

'Lord have mercy, what happened to him?'

'He's bleeding bad; you got to go to him now Mama.'

Without a word, she bolted out of the front door, throwing on her coat as she went.

Hours later, they arrived home in a black taxi. He came through the door weak and sheepish, sporting a bandage on his head. Mama made him up a bed in the sitting room so he could watch television from where he lay and there he stayed for three long days. We fetched and carried for him, taking extra care to keep the noise down low to help his recuperation and even though my jaw was still swollen from my earlier extraction, Mama took me back to school. I knew there was something on her mind when she stopped and bit her lip.

'Do you want to know a secret?'

'Yes Mama, I love secrets.'

'You got to promise me not to tell anyone though. Do you promise?'

'Cross my heart and hope to die.'

'Don't say that you bring crosses on yourself. Just say you promise.'

'I promise I won't tell anyone Mama.'

'You like babies don't you?'

'I love babies.'

'Well Mama's going to have another baby.'

I was so overjoyed; a new baby. She must have kept that secret for a while now. For it was only after she told me that I noticed her midriff was bigger than normal. Waiting for a baby was like waiting for a precious gift from God and I couldn't wait to get my hands on it. But three days later, on the Friday evening I heard crying coming through the door of Mama's room. On quick inspection of the sitting room, I noticed the settee was empty. Dada was up and about again.

'For Gods sake, why can't you take the pill like other women?'

'You know how I feel about that. I don't have the right to take a human life.'

'I told you when you was pregnant with Pauline, that I didn't want no more kids, and then when you had Melanie and then Douglas I still stuck by you and now you telling me you going to have another baby. It's not going to happen.'

'Winston please, this is our child we talking about.'

'Girlie I don't care. As there is a God, I'm telling you, if you have this baby I'm leaving you!

'This will be the last time Pa Daidee, I promise,' said Mama, trying to appeal to his better side.

'You had your last time. I mean it. Get rid of it, I don't care how, or me and you, we're done.'

Mama hoped that he would calm down after he had had a chance to get used to the idea. But he didn't calm down. He showed his anger and disapproval by staying away, sometimes for up to two or three days.

It was one of his periods of absence that T. Stephenson's van and Mercedes car pulled up outside. He wanted the rates money now and he wasn't going to leave empty handed. Mama opened the door, her spirit blighted by the sight of this cold, calculating, loathsome man.

'What do you want? We haven't got nothing for you to take.'

'So we meet again,' said, T Stephenson, pushing past Mama with three hefty accomplices. 'You've had more than enough time to pay off your debt for the rates. Either you give me fifteen pounds right now and we'll go away or, I'll have to take what I can to that value.'

'You know I don't have that kind of money, I got six kids to feed.'

'Alright! Take it away lads,' he said, and one by one, all the pieces of furniture we had were shuttled outside into the waiting van. Helpless, all we could do was watch.

'Please Mr Stephenson; I'm begging you don't do this. Just give me a little more time,' pleaded Mama.

'I don't have time for people like you,' he sneered, turning to leave, now that the dirty deed had been done.

'You know what Mr Stephenson,' called Mama after him with tears streaming down her face.

'What? He asked, turning to face her with a cynical grin.

'As long as I live,' she wiped the tears from her face with the back of her hand. 'As long as I live, I will never understand why God ever blow breath into a dog-hearted man like you.'

He didn't say anything to that; just looked us all over, then got into his big Mercedes and drove off without a second glance.

They hadn't taken the beds and mercifully the battered old settee in the sitting room was worthless to them; a potential gold mine to us. There was no TV to watch, just plenty of spaces where furniture had been. When Dada eventually got home, he pretended it hadn't happened, fobbing Mama off with 'I'll buy it back like I did last time.'

A week later, Mama called us together to tell us she was going away for a while.

'Where you going Mama? Can we come?'

She had tears in her eyes and we had tears in ours. We didn't know where she was going then. Didn't understand why she needed to go away. She left quickly with the little suitcase the birds had died in and we cried because we knew something had gone amiss.

That first night without Mama was torture, especially for Douglas, the youngest of the family. He needed Mama more than anyone did. Dada's resentment towards Douglas was obvious. It had been present for as long as I could remember, probably as long as Douglas could remember.

On the second night of Mama's absence, something peculiar happened. It was after ten o'clock and we had just gone to bed. We heard Dada's key in the lock. He was home. I wondered how he was bearing up, not having Mama around to do everything but then we hear voices - two to be precise - one male, one female.

'He's got a woman with him,' whispered Pauline.

Her words echoed around my head. Silently we scrambled out of bed and opened our bedroom door only an inch so that we could get a good look at her. I couldn't tell you what she was wearing. All we saw was her milk-white profile and piles of blonde hair. What was she doing giggling in the passageway of our house while Mama was in hospital?

'Ssh! Don't make so much noise, you'll wake the kids,' whispered Dada, before disappearing with her into Mama's bedroom.

On edge, we paced around in the dark, upset, tormented, and angry. The intense desire to do something, anything, was overwhelming. But terror held us back. If we disturbed him now he would surely beat us badly for depriving him of this woman's sinful flesh. We concluded that maybe our eyes and hearts had indeed deceived us; that as bad as he was, he would never bring another woman into Mama's bed. That would be sacrilege and he was not that low. Nevertheless, we took a risk, creeping quietly down the stairs for confirmation. We did so avoiding the steps, which creaked, testing the ones we were unsure of with the tips of our toes before applying our full weight. Hardly daring to breathe, we listened. He had a woman in there with him and it was not Mama. Disgusted by my own powerlessness I sat up wide awake for most of the night contemplating wicked, vengeful thoughts.

In the morning, we heard him show this woman to the door. After we had run him a hot bath, he vanished into the bathroom. What we did next was an attempt to save Mama from herself; to help her find the strength she needed to cut my father loose. We put Pauline on lookout. She was good at that. She stood outside ready to give a clear warning signal, the moment Dada appeared.

Mama's bedroom was in a terrible mess, clothes strewn over the floor, half-eaten Chinese take-away, the shoe-polish box in the middle of the room, pillows and ruffled covers thrown off the bed. Dazed, all we could do was to stare around in disbelief. Never before had Mama's room been in such a state. Suddenly something at the top of the bed caught my eye.

'What's this?' I said picking up an object from the bed.

'It's a hairpin,' said Julia, and here's another, and look, - hairs, her hairs are all over the bed. Quick collect it up.'

Working against time, we gathered all the hairpins and strands of hair we could find. But then, what was wrong with Pauline? Why was she coughing and clearing her throat so? To our horror, we realised that Dada was out of the bathroom and on his way down to the room. We froze on hearing his size twelve feet booming down the stairs towards us - nearer and nearer. Clasping a handful of pins and hairs, I stood there, trembling with fear. Panicking now, our eyes zoomed around the untidy room, looking for a place to conceal our findings. He was nearing the bottom of the stairs now. He was going to catch us. I prepared myself for a beating but in a split second, Julia's quick thinking saved us. She grabbed the hairs and pins from my hand and stuffed them into the shoe polish box.

'What you all doing in here?'

'I ... We... We, we're looking for the polish,' Julia said.

'We thought we'd polish all our shoes Dada,' I added, trying to sound convincing.

'Take it and go then,' he said, eyeing us suspiciously, 'and give my shoes a polish while you at it.'

'Yes Dada.'

Mama came home that same day. She looked so drained and defeated, as though ready to burst into tears at the drop of a hat, but she put a brave face on things, hugging us and telling us how much she had missed us all. We did not have the heart to tell her about Dada's sordid secret that day. It was not our intention to disturb what little peace she had left on that day. But then she must have sensed the tension. Something was not right, so she gathered us around her and started pressing to find out what had gone on in her absence. We told her then. Told her the awful truth, in the hope that it would give her the boost she needed to leave him and we would all escape from this madness. We got the shoebox and pulled out all the hairs and pins to show her we were not lying, and when Dada's keys rattled in the front door, we vacated the room.

'How could you do that to me Winston? How?' Mama cried hysterically.

'Do What? What you talking about now?'

'You had no right bringing another woman into my bed. No right!'

'You talking foolishness again Girlie.'

'After all I've done for you and that's how you repay me.'

'Those kids been telling you lies again?'

'This is not lies,' said Mama opening the palm of her hand, revealing strands of hair and the pins used to hold it in place.

'Where did you get that?' said Dada startled at being made to face the evidence.

'It don't matter where I got it. You brought that woman into my bed with my children in the house. You bastard. How could you?'

'Those damn kids been telling you lies again, and you listening to it. Where are they?'

'How can I stay with you now? It's finished. I'm leaving you.'

'Leaving who? You not going nowhere.'

Then, in front of Mama, he drew his belt and beat us all. That day we all felt pain of one kind or another. We screamed in pain when the belt made contact with our skin and Mama wailed hysterically from the pain of the revelation and chaotic madness going on around her.

'How could you do it to me, after what I did for you? How could you do it to me?'

That is all she kept saying, over and over again, rocking herself to and fro on the edge of the bed.

'You having a breakdown again,' he said looking down at Mama with disgust. 'You need to be in the hospital. I'm calling Doctor Glassman to get the ambulance out to you.'

He then marched next door to Mrs Adams' house and called for an ambulance, leaving our front door wide open for everyone to witness our grief. There was no hesitation on the part of Dr Glassman to send an ambulance speeding round to our address. Like everyone else, he too was terrified of Dada. Slowly people gathered on hearing the eruption and hung about like a theatre audience waiting for a performance to begin. The ambulance pulled up outside about twenty minutes later. Mrs Adams came out of her house to stand at the end of her gateway so she could see straight into our house. Stood there with arms folded; a satisfied smirk on her face. Even her new tenants came out to watch the spectacle. Without thought, us children put on a good show for those spectators. Two burly ambulance men came into the hallway to drag Mama out kicking and screaming. First, she begged Dada for mercy.

'Please, Winston, don't let them take me. I'm sorry, I'll behave.'

But Dada, flatly refused to listen to her pleas, 'Girlie, it's for your own good.'

Then she turned to us her children. 'Oh God don't let them take me, please don‘t let them take me!'

Screaming, we clung to all parts of Mama in an effort to retrieve her from the ambulance crew. She was pulled and tossed, this way and that, by everyone present; everyone except Dada who stood back to watch. A few times, we all fell onto the floor in a big humungous heap, ambulance crew included, before the tug of war for Mama continued again. However, we were still too young, weak, and defenceless against Dada to be of any real help. The ambulance sped off with Mama still screaming in the back and Dada walked off into the sitting room. Onlookers gasped, held their mouths. Massah Stanley came downstairs carrying his silver tray of fine china. He stopped for moment to look upon us with scorn as we cried hysterically for Mama; the front door still wide open.

'Uncivilized,' he muttered and carried on, as if we were tarnishing his good name.

'Are you all alright?' Mrs Green and Mrs Andrews drew closer to ask, but we were in no mood for small talk.

'Leave us alone. Just leave us alone,' we shouted, slamming the door. It was Mama we all needed right now, not someone who was going to sensationalize our grief into the latest gossip.

That day Dada ordered us to the shop to buy ingredients for a day's dinner, which he cooked, and for the first time in our young lives, we showed him defiance. He placed plates of pork, cabbage and boiled dumplings in front of us to eat. We sat there watching as he tucked into his dinner with a hearty appetite, droplets of gravy dripping from his fork, back onto the plate. I felt sick to my stomach. When he noticed that no one else was eating, he stopped abruptly.

'What's wrong? Why you not eating?'

'I'm not hungry and you can't force me to eat,' I said.

'Eat it!' he shouted, but I just sat there giving him the most hateful stare possible.

'I said to eat it. If you don't eat it, I... I'll never cook for you lot again.'

By rights, I expected him to get mad and beat me again for even daring to speak to him in such a way.But right there and then, I couldn't have cared any less if he had beaten me to death. It would have been sweet release from the curse of my guilt and that dreadful life. He didn't though. Maybe he didn't have the energy or perhaps he actually felt remorse, who knows? Left alone with him for weeks, after a while, we had no choice but to live, to settle down as best we could. He brought new furniture, delegated extra tasks for each person so that we all shared the work Mama used to do. Once or twice a week we visited the old Hackney Hospital, a terrifying place where even partially naked male lunatics roamed, screaming blood-curdling cries of distress. Clovis and Glen being the oldest, visited every day.

In a way, Julia took on the role of mother and Glen, the second eldest, took on the role of a loving father. Clovis just became angry at the world and everyone in it. A lost, lonely stillness, enveloped the lives of Pauline, Douglas and me.

Five weeks is a lifetime to a child. A lifetime of getting ourselves up in the morning, doing our chores, going to school and putting ourselves to bed at night.

Five weeks of blurred emptiness, wondering if Mama was ever coming home again.

Then suddenly the ambulance men delivered Mama back into the bosom of her family, except we did not recognise the woman standing in the doorway wearing Mama's quilted dressing gown. They had held her down and given her electric shock treatments which had aged her by about twenty years, and the side effects, coupled with the medication she was ordered to take, had left her face heavily twisted to one side. Eyes that were totally crushed, stared straight ahead. No, she was not the same person who had left us on that fateful day. We were happy to see her but now we stared at her with jaws hanging open. Mama looked a sorrowful sight standing there. Behind her against the backdrop of a cloudy day, rain poured furiously. The realisation of that sent us to the doorway to pull her into the house.

'Mama what you doing standing there? We missed you so much,' we said hugging her, taking her little suitcase. For days, she could not speak; she just mumbled to communicate with us. Her mouth did not work properly. At least we had her home, where we could take care of her ourselves. Julia cooked for the family, with Dada's occasional help; Pauline cleaned, and being the lazy one, I entertained Mama, talking to her about all sorts of things that required a response, singing and dancing for her, telling jokes and mimicking well-known characters from the TV but nothing worked. She sat there, staring into space day after day. I was beginning to lose all hope that she would ever be herself again, and then I remembered that I had overlooked her favourite TV comic. My speciality was putting on her wig and doing my Dick Emery impression for her. And at last, after many efforts to make her laugh, a smile that so gently lifted the corners of her lips enriched her face. She laughed then, laughed so much, she cried. I threw my arms around her and hugged her tight. Now she was back with us.

Within days Massah Keith and his woman Yemi, had packed up and left. Maybe they were just as sick and tired of all the chaos as the rest of us. At least they had freed up a bedroom for Clovis and Glen to share. We were grateful for that alone. Mama had been against having tenants in her house from day one; it was Dada who had persuaded her otherwise, telling her it would only be for a while.

There is something magical about Christmas, a time of the year when dreams supposedly came true. Like Mama, our visions had shifted drastically. No longer did we hold on tight to aspirations of returning to the sunshine island of Jamaica. That notion was an obscurity that lingered in the background of our desires. What we dreamt about now was keeping Mama out of hospital, having enough food on the table, and survival until we were strong enough, old enough to stand up to Dada. For some strange reason, at Christmas Dada made every effort to impress, by slamming a huge turkey onto the kitchen table, purchasing a real Christmas tree and crates of long life beer, Babycham, Cherry B, Snowball and Pepsi. For that one day out of a year, he *was* Father Christmas. Presents and gifts were things that did not feature in our yuletide celebrations. We never had any, so we never missed it. We did not get any pocket money so from the month of September onwards we became petty criminals. God forgive us, Douglas, Pauline and me, we stole coppers out of Mama's purse, or whenever we went on errands. In a well-coordinated effort, we amassed enough money to purchase the item we had all agreed upon. The item in the shop window we had fallen in love with; going back time after time just to take another look, to check it was still there. On Christmas Eve, Mama laid out our best clothes to wear the next day. We awoke to the aroma of turkey and stuffing wafting up the stairs to our nostrils, down into our ever-hungry stomachs. Excited, we wrapped Mama's present and gave it to her to open.

'What you buying me presents for? And where did you get the money?'

'We've been saving coppers for months Mama.'

'I don't want no presents, you wasting good money.'

'Go on, open it,' we chanted.

And Mama pretended to look vexed but we could tell she was glad for the presents.

'Open it,' we chanted again, holding our breath for her reaction.

In a flash, she removed the wrapping paper, holding a huge crystal punch bowl up to the light.

'It's beautiful, beautiful,' she gasped and her delight was our present, our joy, and the gift of love.

Next we bathed, put on our best clothes and made a proud entrance downstairs. Visitors came on Christmas Day, mostly Dada's family. He picked up waifs and strays he knew, crusty looking scratchy-back men who were down on their luck, to share Christmas dinner with us. For them alone, he would run the bath, and then when they were all shaven and fresh, he'd give them a pair of his old pants to wear. We did not mind them dining with us, now that they looked and smelled clean. They were welcome to share our turkey with us, as long as they didn't ask for a second helping.

After dinner we watched television together, the whole family, with the lights off. The fairy lights on the Christmas tree twinkled, illuminating the room in a sequence of pretty colours and the coal fire crackled in the background. Just for today, we were a normal, loving family.

Later in the evening more visitors arrived. Sometimes there'd be so many, it would turn into a real party.

Cousin Enid and Brother Rodney called round in the evening with their four children.

'Merry Christmas, children,' she called to us, cutting her eyes at Dada, before going off to chat with Mama in the kitchen. She came with boxes of sweets and presents for everyone.

Uncle Fitzbert knew how to make an entrance; a walking party, women, music and merriment followed him wherever he went. He was a replica of Dada, six years older, tall, good-looking, well dressed and boastful like his brother. They were the same, cut from the same cloth. The kind of men women dreamed of capturing and taming, but the kind who were too slippery to hold on to for long. A generous man, he would cross all our palms with silver, a shilling maybe or a half a crown. In fact, we made quite a lot of money from visiting guests. Johnson and his wife Aunt Mabel breezed in as usual, all high and mighty like royalty. They had made it big in England in the mid sixties; two cars, two homes, two businesses. A tight-fisted couple, they simply could not bear to stretch their hands and give anything away. The one time he gave anything away was the previous year, when Uncle Fitzbert had shamed him into doing so.

'Big big Christmas and you broke? Come on man, a rich man like you must have plenty of money. Man you too mean.'

Johnson reluctantly dug way down deep into the pockets of his well-cut pants.Eventually, after much rummaging around, he produced a miserly thru'penny bit for all six kids to share. The pain in his eyes as he handed it over was evident. Uncle Fitzbert just shook his head laughing and told everyone at the top of his voice how stingy Johnson was, shaming him even further.

Christmas was a brief reprieve from the entanglement of mental torture, which riddled our day-to-day lives. Dada did all he could to make sure it was a happy time. It was the one day he could redeem all his sins, to do his bit for mankind.

With Christmas over, Dada went straight back to marking his cards by the window, a clear signal that once again, he had resumed where he had left off. A mysterious relationship existed between him and the betting shop. On quiet, calm, serene mornings, he would startle everyone by jumping up from his sound sleep; like Lazarus, having risen from the dead. Having dreamt the horses the night before, he would send us running to the shop to buy a newspaper.

'Run! Run!' He shouted from the front door, wearing only his vest and underpants. If by chance, he happened to see a passer-by with a newspaper, he would accost them until we came home with his.

'Oi! Oi!' he shouted.

The sound of his voice cause us to freeze in our tracks half way up the road, thinking it was us he was calling and not a complete stranger.

'Let me have a look at your paper a minute! Come on! Give me you paper!'

These people were too frightened, too unsettled at the sight of him in his under garments to say, no, wholly because he looked desperate enough to give chase, so they handed it over readily; telling him to keep it.

It was bizarre because we all knew he could not read nor write, yet despite this hindrance, he was able to read the names of horses. In deep concentration, he matched elements of his dreams - names, symbols, feelings or colours, to names of jockeys or horses, printed at the back of the newspaper. Soon afterwards, he sent us charging off up the road to the betting shop where a multitude of broken promises littered the floor.

'Tell them Big Winston sent you.'

I was sure we did not need to open our mouths. People knew us on sight.

As we entered, thick, choking smoke made it impossible to breathe let alone spot a familiar face, so we waited outside, sussing out whom to ask. It was a frenzied race against time because woe betides us if the race started before we found someone to place the bet. Dada had won plenty of money on his dreams and premonitions. Occasionally, some of it came our way but mostly we did not see a penny.

'Winston where you going?' asked Mama. 'Why can't you spend more time at home with me and the kids? The only time I see you is when you're sleeping, eating or ready to go out. Why can't we sit and talk like when we used to or go out for a drink? What happened to us?

'I'll tell you what happened - you went ahead and had all them kids without even thinking about me and how I feel.'

'You know it wasn't like that. I had our children out of love for you. Not to bind you with.'

'Woman don't chat fart in my ears. You forced me to marry you when you got pregnant with Pauline; you tried to chain me down with them kids.'

'That's not true Winston. I love you,' Mama interrupted desperately.

There was a callousness in his tone as bitter as the cud he regurgitated for Mama.

'But I broke those chains. I'm a free man. No one tells me what to do, you hear me? I do what I like. I am my own master.'

'I'm still your wife for God's sake. Don't that mean anything to you?'

'My wife,' said Dada, cynically, laughing at the same time as knotting his tie. 'In name only. Everything we had is lost because of you. You ruined it by having all those kids. We could have been back home in Jamaica already, rich and successful but you destroyed that like you destroy everything; like you trying to destroy me now. Well I don't need that and I don't need you. '

His words were below the belt; a punch in the groin that caused Mama to cry out in pain.

'How could you stand there and lay all the blame at my feet? You know how I feel about contraception. I love my children, even the one I killed for you but if you felt so strong about it, then why didn't you take precautions?'

'Who me? laughed Dada. That's your responsibility, not mine.'

'I needed your support and you wasn't there for me,' cried Mama. 'Instead you were out there with those loose women who don't have no respect for the sanctity of marriage.'

'There you go again, always accusing me of something. I keep telling you it's all in your mind but you don't believe me because you're a raving lunatic and you expect me to take you out for a drink, looking like that.'

Mama's hand made an involuntary movement to her head in an effort to smooth her hair into place.

'We both know, you wasn't exactly blessed with good looks but you don't even make an effort to look good for me any more. All you do is interrogate me, from morning till night, accusing me of all kinds of things. Well you made your bed.'

Insulted and rejected, Mama wiped away the stream of tears that flowed freely down her cheeks.

'You're a cold hearted no-shame dog, you know that. You can't go through life treating people like dirt and expect to get away with it. You watch; something bad going to happen to you. Something really bad.'

'You mean happen to you, if you don't stop nagging me,' he threatened, putting on his jacket. After admiring himself in the mirror, he walked out to his new burgundy Ford Capri, parked outside the house. It was supposed to be the family car, but rarely did the family get a chance to ride in it. Mama hated that car. To her it was just another extension of his infidelity. Under the stairs we kept empty bottles, which we exchanged for a small fee at the shops. Something must have gotten into Mama that afternoon, for within seconds she picked up a one and a half litre Guinness bottle, wielding it behind Dada. We watched with open mouths as she sailed it spinning high into the air. It missed him by inches, smashing into the side of the car where it shattered into many pieces.

On hearing what sounded like a commotion, Mrs Adams rushed out of her house to take up her place for a good viewing.

At lightening speed Dada came thundering back into the house for Mama, his eyes like his temper, blazing wildly. Mama turned to run, but he lunged at her, hitting her about the head repeatedly. Too scared of what his hands might do to us, we stood back, screaming for him to stop. Struggling in the passageway they bounced off walls and the banisters of the stairs, whilst neighbours stood outside moving their heads from side to side, to wherever the action was, trying to get a look into the house.

Massah Stanley, who was on his way down to the kitchen wearing his morning jacket, did an about turn, heading straight back up to his room, muttering the word 'disgraceful!' At the same time, Glen tore out of his upstairs bedroom on hearing the uproar, sending Massah Stanley and his tray flying. Holding on to the banister and the wall, Glen descended the stairs to Mama's rescue in two swift movements. Bless him because he was our saviour, the peacemaker; always jumping in the middle of their disputes to save Mama; to regain possession of what frangible calm existed before. If anyone could bring a halt to this fight then it was him.

'Take your hand off my Mama,' he spat hatefully, pushing Dada with his full weight. I suppose he had had just about enough of being referee but in the next dreadful second, Dada turned on him, and then Glen was lying on the floor, panting for breath.

'Next time keep out of my business.' Then Dada stepped over Glen, made his way to the car and sped off.

Crying, still trembling, we knelt down to where Glen lay. Mercifully, he shook himself awake then stood up on shaky legs. He didn't say a word to Mama who was now frantically trying to console him, or to anyone else. He did not even cry. He just marched up to his room in silence, slamming the door behind him.

We took it in turns to knock at his bedroom door, concerned that he might be in pain, suffering alone. However, he ignored our pleas for him to come out and talk. Eventually he opened the door for Clovis. The fact that they shared a room is probably what influenced his judgement. It took a further thirty minutes or so before Clovis was able to persuade Glen to join the rest of us in the sitting room.

Despite the background noise exuding from the TV, an atmosphere of explosive silence sat among us.

'What are we going to do?' asked Julia. We can't go on like this any more. He's dangerous. He's going to kill someone - Mama or even one of us.'

'I'm sick and tired of him using my mother - my mother,' cried Clovis, 'as a punch-bag.' We patted him on the back and shoulders to comfort him. 'Look at the size of her to him,' he cried. 'I don't care what any of you think, I hate him so much. I wish he was dead.'

'I'm so tired of being scared,' sobbed Pauline. Scared of being awake, scared of going to sleep, scared of what's going to happen next. I don't want to live no more - I'm too frightened.'

Julia held Pauline. 'Don't talk like that. You got to be strong.' Then with tears in her eyes she whispered; 'you must never say such a thing again Pauline.'

But Pauline's dejected sobbing only heightened our anger to fever pitch. When and where was it ever going to end?

'He's got to be stopped,' said Clovis.

Glen looked at him directly. 'How you going to stop him?'

'The way I see it, there's only one way to stop him.' Clovis was deadly serious now. 'Murder. We're going to have to kill him.'

A cold frost marched across all our hearts then, a sign of even darker things to come.

'Murder! gasped Julia, nervously. 'Look, I feel the same as all of you but we can't kill him. Mama loves him.'

'But what if he kills Mama or even one of us? What you going to say then - oh Mama loves him. Julia, that's not love. I might be only a child but even I know that's not love. It's too ugly to be love.'

'I just want it all to stop,' cried Pauline.

'Well I say we kill him and get it over and done with.'

'How you going to kill him?' asked Glen, waiting patiently for a plausible plan to surface.

We thought for a moment and then Clovis came up with a novel idea, which broke the grave seriousness behind our scheming.

'We crack a bottle over his head when he's sleeping. That ought to do it.'

That idea makes us burst into laughter. It was ridiculous because a bottle over the head, never killed anyone in the Westerns on TV, or in real life. Dada was living proof of that. Yet sweet was the parody of Dada staggering around half dazed and disorientated, with outstretched arms, ready to kill the first person who made contact with his fingertips.

'Seriously though,' said Glen, bringing us back to a state of sobriety, 'if we don't do it properly, he'll kill us all.'

'What about if we poison him,' I said feeling suddenly inventive. 'I heard that rhubarb leaves are poisonous. We could dry some, in the oven, grind it up and put it in his food.'

'Don't be so stupid,' said Clovis, 'It's going to take more than a few leaves to kill a man that size. You'd need something strong like arsenic or cyanide and we ain't got none of that have we?'

'Well at least it's better than cracking a bottle over his head.'

'Shh! Listen!' said Julia suddenly transfixed to the television.

She was listening to the news with precision focus, flapping one hand for us to be quiet and slowly we too gave it our full attention.

A teenager who had killed his abusive father was shown coming out of court after being acquitted on the grounds of provocation. Well dressed, he looked totally done in, fazed by all the attention. People were sympathetic to his plight - his family, who stood beside him, the camera crew and even the way in which it was reported. It was proof to us that if we killed Dada, the law would be on our side.

After the report had ended, we sat there obsessing Dada's downfall. We knew we had to kill him, but what we hadn't quite grasped was how. Nevertheless, we needn't have worried about how, who, where or when. Someone else was going to do it for us.

That same evening, dark threatening clouds coaxed Mama and me into the backyard. We were half way into collecting clothes from the line when the sound of Mrs Adams, unlocking her back door unnerved us both. At every opportunity, she played on Mama's insecurities with great gusto, fuelling the sick pleasure she got out of goading her rival to distress. Difficult though it was, Mama had devised a way of dealing with her - a vow of silence to which I also had to adhere. Indifferent to my presence, Mrs Adams began her assault.

'You can't handle him can you? Winston is a whole lot a man; too much of a man for you, that's why I've been helping you out, by giving him what he needs. You should be grateful to me.'

Astounded at her audacity and Mama's persistent silence, my blood began to boil whilst Mama's pace quickened.

'He tells me everything you know; everybody knows you're a mad woman.' Mama pulled the last item of clothing from the line.

'When you see him next,' Mrs Adams called after her, 'tell him I said hello. Tell him I got something for him.'

My whole being was possessed with the compulsion to do something; say something, anything. I could not let her get away with it this time. Mama hurried inside but I stood my ground still holding an armful of clothes. Looking Mrs Adams square in the eyes, I pulled a face, made a rude gesture with the fingers of my free hand and then for the *piece de resistance*, the cherry on the cake: bold as ever, I put my thumb nail behind my front teeth and flicked it at her, like the Italians - my way of saying fuck-off without a an expletive having actually passed my lips.

'Oh you nasty little girl. You wait, I'm going to tell your father,' she said.

'Go ahead,' I whispered, breaking my vow of silence for Mama, 'and I'll have to tell Mr Adams who you been sleeping with.'

'Bitch!' she gasped, and then I gave her one of my deadliest cut-eyes before going inside and slamming the back door.

We did not see Dada for three whole days. Three days of calm, that could be broken at any minute.

'I wonder if he's all right or if he's lying dead somewhere?' panicked Mama.

We looked at each other and then back at her in disbelief when she said that. Still simmering with anger, we couldn't care less. This house was a better place without him. We could not understand why she loved him so despite all the things he had said and done to her.

With resources running low, Mama sent three of us out there to find him. She told us all the places to look. Our love for Mama and the pinch of hunger was the only thing that fuelled our efforts. We tried The Three Crowns, all the betting shops and pubs along Church Street and the high road, asking people whose faces were vaguely familiar along the way but to no avail. On the third day, Mama went looking herself. She did not let the rain put her off either. In her absence, we tidied the house. She returned hours later, dripping wet, empty handed and visibly upset.

The afternoon had worn into early evening. A fragile calm filled the house, the only kind we knew. Relaxed, we all settled back for the night, to watch TV

Suddenly, from outside came the loud screech of burning tyres; followed by the slamming of car doors and loud voices, then moments later, fists were beating down the front door.

Mama opened it wide and almost fainted at the sight of Dada propped up by five friends and bleeding profusely. Burgundy-red blood gushed from an open stomach wound, soaking his clothes, dripping onto the carpet. Someone had stabbed him in a fight.

'Girlie, get him into the house, quick!' shouted Honey, his voice rich with fear.

'Oh God he's going to die, I know he's going to die on me,' Mama cried repeatedly, as they all carried him into the bedroom. They tore off his clothes, shouting for hot water and bandages. We never kept bandages in the house so Mama used old sheets and towels.

'Why didn't you take him to the hospital?' she screamed frantically, whilst applying pressure to the wound. 'He's going to bleed to death.'

Dada raised his head now, gripping Mama to him by the front of her dress.

'You mustn't take me to the hospital,' he said with eyes rolling around his head.Take care of it yourself.'

'But Pa Daidee you need to go to the hospital, you bleeding to death.'

'No hospital - no police,' he panted. 'Do it for me Girlie,' and then he drifted into unconsciousness.

We brought basins of hot water to the doorway of the room, which were swiftly taken from our hands, and then we were shoved outside again. His friends helped to get him bandaged before leaving him in Mama's hands.

For days, he laid there unconscious. Not allowed into the bedroom, I loitered around outside, trying to catch a glimpse of him whenever Mama entered or left the room. She sent us to the chemist to buy gauze and bandages and once a day she rolled him ever so gently onto his side so that she could change the blood soaked bandages from around his stomach. She sponged cold sweat from his forehead, constantly checked that he was still breathing, and prayed night and day for his recovery. And whilst she prayed for his life, we prayed for his death, that it would be swift.

He must have been born under a lucky star or something because five days later, he regained consciousness. Relieved, Mama smiled as she fed him chicken soup.

'I saved your life. Bout you don't need me,' she says confidently with a new air of self-worth and significance.

He didn't say a word, just looked at her as he swallowed spoonful after spoonful of hot liquid. He was confined to that bed for over two weeks before deemed well enough to have a bed made up for him in the sitting room during the day. At least now Mama had a chance to change the bed sheets without disturbing him too much.

We knew he was getting better when he started holding his stomach and laughing at the comedians on telly. Mama made us change the channel to something more serious. Said his stomach would bust open if he laughed too much. Then when she went back into the kitchen, he would get us to change the channel back again and we all laughed together - him laughing at the jokes on TV, and us laughing at him, laughing at the jokes on TV. The one thing we craved desperately, the only thing that could make us throw immature notions of murder to the wind, was our longing to be a family again. And at that precise moment in time we had it in our grasp once more. The strange thing was, Dada seemed to enjoy being at home with us. It had taken a stabbing to bring him closer to his family.

Mrs Adams sauntered about in her backyard, hips swaying from side to side. In truth, she had long since lost interest in Dada, seeing as she was getting more than enough under her own roof, but now as always, she could not resist taunting Mama about her conquests with Dada from across the fence.

'You know what?' said Mama tearfully, as she pegged the last vest onto the line. 'Every dog has its day, and I'm waiting for yours.'

That day Mama talked about had been a long time coming. Turns out it was just around the corner.

It was one of those boring days when we were stuck in the house with nothing to do, apart from fetch and carry for Dada, who was still laid up in the sitting room, so Mama told us to wash the windows at the front of the house.

'I bet that old ice-cream van is going to come and tempt us like how he knows we ain't got no money,' I said.

Most of our purchases from the ice-cream van were limited to a block of raspberry ripple or vanilla ice-cream as a special treat after Sunday dinner. There is no sound sweeter than the ice-cream van chiming down the road. On the odd occasion, when we had pestered Mama for a cornet, she would give in at the last minute but by the time we got outside, the van was usually disappearing up the road, but that did not deter us. Pulling on our pumps, we gave chase, like cheetahs; eyes focused on the 'Mind the children,' sign. We'd chase him to the ends of the earth if need be. When eventually we caught up with him, which was sometimes two streets away, we were so sweaty and out of breath, we could hardly speak.

'Well, we'll just have to try our best to ignore him; that's all we can do,' said Julia, full of inner strength.

There we were in our raggedy house clothes all wet from the soapsuds, putting our backs into the work, and having fun at the same time before we realised we had an audience of one. A pair of old blue eyes had been observing us from over the wall. An elderly woman wearing a dreamy smile, watched intently.

'Oh you look like such good children. You,' she said pointing to me, 'come over here a minute. Come on, I won't bite you.'

I walked over to her coyly. She reached into her handbag and pulled out her purse; out of which she produced a half a crown.

'Here, buy yourselves an ice-cream when the van comes round again.'

'Thank you, but we're not allowed to accept money from strangers.'

'Come on, take it,' she said, stretching her hand towards me, but I backed away. 'Please tell them it's alright to take it,' she said looking at Mama.

We looked at Mama, and she paused for a moment, then with a nod of her head, we gratefully accepted, each thanking the old lady in turn; glad that there was still some goodness in the world.

Not long after we had completed the task, the ice-cream van tinkled down the road attracting wide-eyed children from out of their homes.

We took our ice creams inside, and I sat on the stairs eating mine, lost in the deluxe, creamy world of Mr Whippy. We were licking those ice creams passionately, when suddenly; from within our house it sounded as though the walls were being smashed in. Curious I opened the front door.

Outside neighbours too had gathered after hearing the noise. They probably thought another drama was unfolding from number 27, but thank God, this time it had nothing to do with us. It was coming from Mrs

Adams' house. Now it sounded like two people had fallen down the stairs. We wondered if someone was in there murdering her. For a few fleeting moments we even pondered on running to her aid, but then came the words; 'You fucking whore!' and their front door was thrown wide open to the world. There in the doorway stood Mrs Adams' husband, Henry, gripping her by the throat. Her head was bleeding and so was her lip. Would you believe it, he was going to throw her out of the house in front of all these people. First, he spun her round to face her public, pushing her a little way forward from the door and then, my God, he swung his foot back and gave her one almighty kick, right up the arse, launching her into the air.

Loud gasps escaped from the spectators.

Not wanting to land on her face, Mrs Adams managed to twist her body in mid air before she fell. She landed on her back in the gateway of her house, but the force of that kick made her roll back, almost onto her shoulders, causing her skirt to rest on her stomach; showing all the world her under-garments.

Gasps of 'Lord have mercy!' 'But see here my God!' and 'Kiss my neck!' echoed from female spectators. Mama had to cover her opened mouth with one hand. And us kids just stood there, ice creams dripping down our hands, clothes and onto our feet. I'll never forget the look of satisfaction that came over Mama's face. It was subtle, but it was there all right.

Henry was now outside, like a man possessed, puffing, panting, and smarting at the mouth, looking around him, as though he had lost something. Then he saw it in Clovis' hand - a wooden spindle that had come loose from our stair banister. Grabbing the chunk of wood from Clovis, he raced back into the house, slamming the door behind him. He had caught them in the act and now he was going to kill the male tenant whom his wife had been vigorously riding when he arrived home early that day. The house thundered under the force of two grown men battering each other, tumbling down the stairs from behind closed doors. Mrs Adams raced round into our front yard. Now she wanted to go through our house so she could get into her own, through the back door. Trembling and bleeding she looked up at Mama who was calmly leaning against the wall with her arms folded. She needed Mama's permission. Smugly Mama nodded her head and Mrs Adams tore through, running from the front of our house to the back, leaving droplets of blood spattered every metre or so along the way. She got back into her house and after a few minutes, everything went dead quiet again. We wondered if the three adults were all dead in there, until the tenant, a male single parent, emerged suitcase in one hand and his little daughter in the other.

Her husband Henry left empty-handed minutes afterwards, so we figured he would be back at some stage after he had had time to cool down. From thereon, filthy looks from across the fence was all Mama got from Mrs Adams - the hounding had stopped.

Chapter Five

Under the Influence of Love

....

Delivered into the world in Post Colonial Jamaica, February 1938; on an island where places with beautiful sounding names like, Old Harbour Bay, Portland Cottage and Treasure Beach, conjure idyllic images of harmony, good fortune and candy cotton comfort. However, for many, born into an unfair world, the harsh reality differs somewhat from the sublime. Poverty, the greatest crime against humanity, is a dire misfortune, which places one firmly at the mercy of those in a position to help.

From the moment Girlie had pegged her first tooth, her Great Aunt Hilda had been there, waiting in the wings to whisk her away and make somebody of her. For many years thereafter, Girlie's whole life was governed by her Aunt Hilda who was determined to mould this spirited child, by any means necessary, into a replica of herself. Girlie did not know her own mother, or so she thought. That tightly guarded secret was kept in the matriarchal circle of aunts that existed. Children had no business asking whose womb had conceived and pushed them out into the world. All they needed to know was that they had a roof over their heads and that they would get something to eat at night - and for that, they should be eternally grateful, showing the adults respect by not asking such intrusive and impertinent questions. For Girlie, the absence of a mother in her life and the lack of knowledge surrounding how she came to be with her aunt, created a gaping dark void where love should have been. It inflicted upon her an indelible sense of loss that she had been forbidden to express or enquire about in any way. But Girlie was such an inquisitive child, which, let's say, was not greeted with fondness.

'Aunt Hilda, where did I come from?'

A wet plate almost slipped from Aunt Hilda's hand as she washed up, so taken aback was she by this child's audacity.

'And what kind a question is dat, you asking me inside here today,' she said, hands akimbo.

The effect of her aunt's aggressive stance and sudden intent gaze on Girlie was to strike her with the imminent need to moisten her now dry throat and to replace hastily, the air that had so suddenly left her lungs.

'I mean, where did you get me?'

'Where did I get you? I get you from Aunt Mary.'

'And who did Aunt Mary get me from?'

'Tell me something, you milk de goat or feed the chicken yet?' asked Aunt Hilda with that all too familiar glint in her eyes.

'Aunt Hilda, I - I was just going ...' stammered Girlie.

There was no time to complete the sentence. Girlie took off out into the yard when Aunt Hilda made for the wet rag, hoping that this woman would be far too preoccupied with other things on her mind to pursue, catch and beat an impertinent child.

A staunch believer that children naturally needed correction meant that Aunt Hilda obliged frequently in what she considered her Christian duty. Once she had started to release her pent up energy, she did not know when to stop. Sometimes, in the middle of a beating she would stop to catch her breath, which often tricked Girlie into thinking the assault had at last, ceased - then, without warning she would say: 'And you know what? I don't finish wid you yet,' and continue to beat until she had exhausted herself. All the time she was beating, her mouth attacked with words of insult, so sharp they cut deeper than the lacerations on Girlie's flesh and hurt twice as much.

In Aunt Hilda's eyes, the worst disadvantages that could be afflicted upon a human being was to be born poor, black (dark-skinned) and female. To her it was a drawback, a handicap, a cross to bear, which she carried for the child in her care, sure that one day, her martyrdom would be rewarded in heaven. But right now, it presented a challenge that could only be rectified with force and Aunt Hilda had no qualms about sharing that knowledge with friends or regular customers.

'But Miss Hilda, you look very tired today; what you been doing?' asked Beulah, her life long friend and sewing companion.

Is *she*!' Miss Hilda scolded, pointing to a solemn Girlie. 'I nearly beat her; kill her in this very house today.'

Miss Beulah and a few other visitors glanced over at Girlie, not sympathetically - nor to offer nurturing words of wisdom from an elder, but to sneer, or tut or kiss their teeth; to show their disapproval because Miss Hilda was a saint and had been very good in taking her in. They were not interested in the marks on her body or which weapon her aunt had used to bring them about. Aunt Hilda had a stash of assorted instruments with which to carry out her assaults. Most popular was the wet rag because it was always quick to hand. Like the bamboo stick, it was great for lower torso and leg beating. Then there was the thick leather strap, which left its mark with every lash and if her aunt was real mad, it would be the buckle of the belt. Blood flowed when it made impact with the body - yet later on, Aunt Hilda would patch up her victim; tending to those very same wounds which she herself had inflicted.

'There, as good as new. Now don't let me have to beat you like dat again,' was all she would say - no sorry or anything.

Aunt Hilda was older and a little better off than the other aunts in the circle. Therefore, she took in girls from her extended family and ran her home in Old Harbour Bay Jamaica, like a finishing school for young ladies. A seamstress by trade, she encouraged the girls in her care to aspire to marriage; to being devoted wives, as opposed to having more than one man father their offspring. She taught her girls to sew, cook and to clean a house from top to bottom, until it sparkled. Each and every

Sunday, Aunt Hilda dressed her girls from head to toe in white frilly garments she had cut and stitched herself. She looked ever so proud on a Sunday morning, her respectable head held high with her girls in tow behind.

'Good morning, Miss Hilda,' people called as she breezed past them.

If they were considered worthy enough, Aunt Hilda acknowledged them with a slight nod of the head or a quiet 'morning,' as she continued on her way, giving the girls a warning after-glance as if to say, 'And you will not bring shame on me.'

Although many considered Aunt Hilda to be a pillar of the community, Girlie had not been afforded the luxury of seeing her aunt in quite the same light. Instead, she was averse to the remote idea that she would ever be anything like her aunt - an unfeeling woman, incapable of love. Life with Aunt Hilda was a living hell - an unusual prison sentence from which, mercifully, Girlie was able to escape, three times a year.

The summer vacation, granted Girlie a temporary reprieve to stay with Aunt Mary in Portland Cottage for near on eight long glorious weeks of freedom. Siblings lucky enough to have a benefactor in the form of a distant relative threw all their cares away as one by one they gathered excited and free for this annual homecoming. Girlie loved Portland Cottage with a passion. It brought a contented smile to her face just thinking about it as she travelled by bus to get there. The tantalizing aroma of freedom in the country air captivated her senses.

Waiting in the distance to greet her was her Aunt Mary. She had been born dirt poor at the turn of the twentieth century, had nothing of value, but for the breath in her lungs and the beating of her heart, and, like ancestors who had come and gone before her, was destined by fate, to live and to die in the same privation with which she first greeted the world. She had come from a long line of strong matriarchs who took pride in making the best out of what life had thrown at them. She had not been placed here, on the face of the earth to aspire to earthly riches; her purpose was only to fulfil the book of life, and to learn from the bittersweet era she had been born into. It was not true that she did not have anything to offer the world, for she was a woman of substance, abundantly rich in qualities of the wise. A good hearted, strong willed woman, Aunt Mary had had twelve children of her own, two of whom had been stillborn at birth and were buried in a corner of the backyard where no one played. There was hardly money for food let alone fancy funerals, so, heartbroken after carrying these babies for nine long months, she buried them herself, saying a prayer of her own, and asking the Lord each time, to take her child into His tender loving care until the appointed time when He would call upon her to join them. Grief was a luxury she could not afford.

'Girlie is that really you?'

Girlie dropped her bags, leaving them for a disgruntled Aunt Hilda to carry.

'Come let me look at you. Turn around for me. Turn around again,' and before Girlie had completed her turn, Aunt Mary's arms gathered her into a warm embrace.

'Look at you; you're practically a young lady now. Oh my, I'm so proud of you.'

Aunt Hilda's distaste at such a spectacle was clear and she excused herself promptly.

'I can't stay. I'll come and see you in a week or so.'

Girlie quickly unpacked; and so began her long awaited summer vacation.

A corrugated zinc roof adorned the top of the small wooden house in which Aunt Mary lived. It was situated in the community of Portland Cottage, on the Portland Ridge peninsula, on the south coast of Jamaica. It backed onto miles of dry limestone forests and to the south, mangrove swamps stretched their bony arms along the ridge of the shoreline, as far as the eye can see. Girlie was eager to reacquaint herself with the rugged terrains, to explore the Portland Bight Lighthouse - an unattractive structure in itself that stood at the highest part of Portland Point. Then there was Barmouth Beach, the gun-club where tourists shot beautiful birds out of trees or sky; Jackson Bay Cave, which had passageways extending some twelve thousand feet or so, with underground lakes and chambers; the nearby sugar estate and the cane fields. Every day was a new adventure. With only one driveable road from Lionel Town to Mitchell Town, Portland Cottage, back then, remained relatively undiscovered, an oasis of unspoilt natural beauty. Girlie saw that same beauty in her Aunt Mary; the woman whom she had come to believe was her mother. To Girlie, *she was* Portland Cottage.

On a hot, bright morning, towards the winter of her holiday, Girlie awoke to face the awful reality that was to come - resuming her life with Aunt Hilda.

Out in the yard, she could see Aunt Mary, on her knees, tidying the area around the grave of her babies with heart-rending pride. The lullaby she sang to lift her dejected spirit, was a sweet whisper, carried on a warm breeze. Sensing her pain, Girlie approached; she knelt beside the older woman, placing an arm around her waist. A sudden wave of sadness engulfed them both, causing a long thought-filled silence to dominate as Aunt Mary contemplated the loss of her two children and Girlie, the loss of growing up without her mother. She would much rather be with Aunt Mary, poor and hungry as she was, than go back to living with her Aunt Hilda. It was being apart from her mother that had made her realise that she was poor in the first place. If a child has love, they don't even know that they are poor and Aunt Mary was full of love.

'Aunt Mary, can I stay with you? I'll do anything you want, and I don't eat much either.'

Girlie clung to the hope that by some miracle, Aunt Mary would agree to her staying on in Portland Cottage.

'Come on,' said Aunt Mary after a long while, 'lets go back up to the house.'

After rubbing the soil from their knees, they put their arms around each other to walk the short distance. Patiently Girlie waited for her aunt's response.

'You know,' said Aunt Mary after a while, 'we very lucky to have Aunt Hilda. She can give you the things I can't.'

'But I don't want to go back to Bay. I hate living with her,' said an impassioned Girlie, 'I want to stay with you.'

'We can't always have what we want,' Aunt Mary said gently, 'and sometimes things happen for the best, except we can't always see that straight away. Aunt Hilda is paying for your schooling. Where else will you get a good education? Remember, I'm expecting great things from you.'

When Aunt Hilda turned up at the end of August to take Girlie back to Bay that was not a very good sign. It brought to a close the end of the summer vacation and all its freedom. It meant waving Aunt Mary a sorrowful goodbye until the next time and travelling all the way back to Old Harbour by bus, with Aunt Hilda for company.

As she always did on her return from Portland, Girlie would dart over at the earliest opportunity to see her old friend Mammee Jule, who baked bread and buns for a living. Originally from St Elizabeth, Mammee Jule greeted Girlie with open arms and fondness. She always had time for the child whom she believed had been dealt an unfair card in life, one of the only people who made this place bearable in the least. As ever, Old Harbour remained predictable. Nothing ever changed there, except for Aunt Hilda. She became more bitter and cantankerous as the years rolled by, vexed with puberty for changing her little girls into sinful women. Her beady eyes watched resentfully as Girlie grew from a child into a young woman, knowing that soon; hot-blooded young males on heat would come buzzing around. They would sniff the air and detect her scent. They'd follow the trail all the way back to the house. Aunt Hilda timed Girlie's every movement away from the house; kept a written log of her menstrual cycles and constantly reminded her that she was still a child, even though her well developed, yet slender body said otherwise.

Admiring looks from males in the area, who had suddenly shown interest in her womanly form, had not gone unnoticed; she simply paid no attention to it, not because her aunt did not approve but because she was not the least bit interested in any of them. They said she was too uptight: hard work, because she in no way pandered to their advances, but there was good reason for that. She had eyes only for one person.

It all started as she walked to school one day with her cousins Enid and Mavis. She noticed him then, watching her intently and not breaking from her gaze until she was out of sight. That's how it began and continued for well over a year; him contemplating her like a piece of candy; just wanton. She enjoyed playing along with the game, putting on a very sultry yet subtle display, enough to feed his interest. Then after a long time, he took it a step further and started calling to her from behind bushes or sheds, stealing every opportunity he could to see or speak with her without her aunt's knowledge but that was made all the more difficult by the fact that she always had company.

'Don't look at him Girlie,' Enid said, pulling her cousin along in an attempt to escape the hungry young buck who pursued. 'Keep your head straight and walk fast - run if you have to.'

'Is he coming?' enquired Girlie eagerly, pleased that at last he had plucked up the courage to declare his interest in her.

'You know Aunt Hilda would beat you just for looking at him.'

'There's no harm in looking. God gave us eyes to see.'

Determined to speak to her now, this dashing young man ran to keep up with their fast walking pace.

'Girlie, cool you foot, I just want to talk to you, wait a minute noh.' Winston had at last finally caught up with her and playfully took one of her hand in his. She could see that he was not going to let this opportunity slip away from him.

'Take you hand off my cousin, she don't want nothing to do with you. Isn't that right Girlie,' said Enid, slapping their hands apart and placing herself between her cousin and this handsome young man. Girlie looked at her with pleading eyes.

'Enid just one minute, that's all I am asking you for.'

'You got one minute and then I'm going home to tell Aunt Hilda.'

Winston took her aside for a moment.

'You know I been watching you don't you?'

'I see you all the time. Why you spying on me?'

They both ignored Enid's obvious impatience.

'Well that's because I like you. I want to take you out to the beach or even the picture house or something. You want to come?' he drawled.

'No. I mean - I want to, but my Aunt Hilda don't like me talking to boys, much less going out with them.'

'She don't have to know,' he whispered secretively, taking hold of her hand again. 'Who's going to tell her? I won't,' he said looking deep into Girlie's eyes.

'I'm going home to tell Aunt Hilda!' shouts Enid, heading off down the path.

'I have to go. I'll be in big trouble if I don't.' Girlie hurried after her cousin.

'I will be waiting for you tomorrow,' he called after her.

True to his words, he was there the next morning, then in the afternoon again. After that, they met up whenever the coast was clear, having followed their plans to first distract Cousin Enid in order to snatch brief moments alone together. There was something about him she could not name, for it was as yet unknown to her. Something so powerful it kept her awake at nights and made her dream during the day. Every word uttered from the mouth of this beautiful young man was poetic perfection to her ears. He was the one to discard the nasty labels her aunt had left imprinted on her mind, words like: black, ugly, sinful, worthless; and replaced them with expressions of love, beauty and strength, to create a new self image for her which, she wore with pride. Little did she know that she did the same for him; they were soul mates, kindred spirits exchanging gifts of the heart. If only her cousin could see him in the same way.

'Somebody tell me they see you talking to Winston again. You crazy?'

'Crazy with love Enid. Please don't tell Aunt Hilda. He's taking me to the beach next week. I can't wait.'

'Oh Lawd! I can't hear you, and I don't want to know,' said Enid covering her ears for a moment. 'Aunt Hilda's going to peel the two of us like banana when she finds out and all you can think about is *love.* Anyway, how will you see him when you got to be in school all day?'

The fixed dreamy smile on Girlie's face was frighteningly indicative of her intentions.

'You can't cut school! What will I tell Miss Sweeney? I won't lie for you; you going to put me in so much trouble.'

'Enid I don't care about Aunt Hilda and Miss Sweeney. You will have to think of something because I'm going. Just do it this one time. I won't ask you to lie for me ever again.'

'Girlie you know it's a sin to tell lies. If Aunt Hilda ask me to swear on the Bible, I will have to tell the truth, cause I don't want to go to hell.'

'It won't come to that Enid, just trust me. I know what I'm doing.'

The fact that Girlie could not get Winston out of her mind, was not only attributed to her feeble efforts to do so, but also to the fact that everywhere she turned, he was there. Love had indeed evaded her for most of her life but now, athirst for her uniqueness alone; it sought her, pined for her, hankered for the opportunity to be close to her, to be a part of her.

Aunt Hilda flapped her chubby arms in excitement when she saw the new material that had just come into the store. Early that morning Girlie had accompanied her aunt to town. Her aunt was in good spirits for she was to purchase material to make a dress for Girlie's passing out ceremony in three months time.

'This one is lovely. Oh my! Come and look at it Girlie.' But Girlie did not come straight away. She was far too busy looking at something else.

'Cut me three yards,' Aunt Hilda told the assistant, excitedly.

The chemistry of fevered ardour, coupled with bewilderment had suddenly gripped Girlie, for in the distance he stood, tall and gallant, a vision of loveliness.

'Beautiful,' she heard herself say aloud. Luckily, Aunt Hilda's love of purchasing new materials had rendered her oblivious to Girlie's distraction.

Outside, a while later, weighted down with packages in hand, Girlie could not tear her eyes away from his six foot two physique. Toned muscles peeked out from an opened white shirt, bulging under the short sleeves: streaks of sweat glistened on his smooth brown skin, and as Girlie and Aunt Hilda drew closer, his gaze sought, and locked on tightly to the object of his affection. He cracked a beautiful movie star smile then, a thousand times more handsome than anything she had ever seen - how she longed to kiss and caress his lips, his face; the deep cleft in his chin. Aunt Mary always said that people with dimples had been touched by God and that He had left his imprint. Well God had definitely touched this man, for he was too heavenly for words. What was he doing here? Had he followed her and Aunt Hilda all the way to town or was this just wild coincidence? Her aunt must not see her looking at him.

'Come on Girlie, keep up,' Aunt Hilda commanded, as though able to sense impending danger.

Oh please God, don't let him say anything to me, she thought, please, please.

'Howdy do Miss Hilda,' Winston teased, putting on his best Yankee accent.

Miss Hilda kissed her teeth loudly and immediately started cussing under her breath.

'Hello Girlie. What a way you look good enough to eat.'

Aunt Hilda did not like his tone one little bit. Being able to spot trouble when she saw it, she quickened her pace so that Girlie would follow suit, shooting Winston a poisoned glance at the same time.

'Ooh, look at those hips. Hey Miss Hilda! You still got it girl!'

Not being able to help herself, Girlie burst out laughing, and then quickly styled it into a few loud coughs when her aunt shot her a glance. By now her aunt who was spitting mad, marched over to Winston with such speed that Girlie was sure she was going to attack him.

Winston stood up swiftly, using his muscular frame to stop Aunt Hilda in her tracks, forcing her to reconsider quickly any rash movement she might be about to make.

'You know what your problem is?'

'Tell me noh Miss Hilda. Tell me.'

'You don't have a drop of manners! Not one drop! And I'm warning you,' she spat, pointing a finger towards his face. 'I don't want no broke-pocket fisher boy talking to Girlie. I never send her to school for all these years so she could turn out to be a fishwife to *you*.'

'Nothing wrong with being a fisherman. I'm earning good money from it. Look,' he said, pulling wads of notes from his pockets - fruits of a good day at sea.

'I got plenty of money.'

'And where is it all going to go eh? I tell you where - gambling, liquor and women. I hear all about you; so you listen to me, and you listen good: my girls don't want nothing to do with you. They have more class in they little fingernail than what you have in the whole of your body. Why would they be interested with a stinking fisher boy like you?'

'You eat fish don't you?'

'What! What's that got to do with anything?'

'Well someone has to catch the fish don't they Miss Hilda, because somehow, I just can't picture you with that big fat behind of yours on a boat, say you catching fish.'

This time he had gone too far. Both Girlie and Aunt Hilda's mouths swung wide open. Sensing danger, Aunt Hilda grabbed Girlie's arm so tight it went numb. Dragging her off, out of earshot: 'You know what will happen to you if anyone tell me they see you talking to that nasty naegger don't you? Don't you?'

'Yes Aunt Hilda, I know. You're hurting me.'

'Good; as long as you know.'

But despite the impending danger her aunt posed, Girlie was determined to keep her rendezvous with Winston. She would go to school as normal and then at recess, sneak away to where Winston would be waiting a little way off from the school. It was all planned and soon enough, that day was the here and now.

She had spent ages the previous night curling her hair with newspaper to give her that film star look and had stuffed one of her Sunday dresses into her satchel for later.

'What am I going to tell Miss Sweeney?' panicked Enid.

'I'll deal with Miss Sweeney. Wait for me at the back of the schoolhouse. Don't let nobody see you though. We have to go home together.'

At last, it was recess. Excited children poured out into the dusty schoolyard. Taking her satchel, Girlie sneaked round to the back of the school where hardly anyone went. After changing into her white Sunday dress and stuffing her uniform into her bag, she ran across the field, looking back frequently to make sure she had not been seen or followed. A sickly feeling of fear in the pit of her stomach battled in vain against her desire for love. Her aunt must never find out. She would murder her for sure if she ever did. Then, in the distance, Girlie saw the man of her dreams up ahead. Winston's pearly white teeth shone in the sunlight when he saw her coming; melting away all her fears, and nothing else seemed to matter after that.

'You look beautiful. Are you ready?'

Beautiful. No one in the world had ever told her she was beautiful before, except this man, her first and last love.

'Where you taking me?'

'It's a surprise. You have to wait and see.'

'I have to be back by two o'clock or my Aunt will kill me.'

'Don't worry; I will get you back in plenty of time. I hear she beats you. If she touch you again, she will have to deal with me.'

'And what you going do, fight my aunt Hilda for me? Girlie laughed aloud. What a sight to behold, you and my Aunt, fighting.'

He took her down to the bay harbour. They watched as the fishermen returned from a day's work, laying out their nets and hauling their boats close to shore. Raised voices of hagglers, hustling for the right price, laughing women stooped to clean fish in the sea, the smell of fish roasting on fires and the sound of children; crying, laughing and playing, echoed around. A boat with an engine bobbed gently up and down on the water's edge.

'You like it? It's mine,' said Winston, pushing out his already big chest at least a further three inches. This is your first surprise. Get in.'

'I don't think I should, I've never been on a boat before, plus I can't even swim.'

'Girlie if you drown, then we drown together. I'm a strong swimmer, come on, get in.'

'Turn around then,' said Girlie, coyly. 'I need to take off my stockings.'

After removing them, Girlie hoisted the hem of her dress and waded through the cool shallow, crystal-clear water to climb into the boat. When she was seated comfortably, Winston clambered aboard, started the engine, and steered the boat in a straight line, away from the shore. Girlie glanced back at the colourful splash of people on the beach, and thought how beautiful a picture they etched along an otherwise ugly shoreline. Their voices grew fainter the further the boat moved away until it was hard to distinguish between the voice of man and the voice of the sea.

When they were far away from land, Winston switched off the engine and took up his place - about a foot or so away from Girlie. Both pretended to be looking out to sea, but every so often Girlie, now nervous about not being able to run if she needed to, glanced at him suspiciously from out of the corner of her eye, trying to convince herself that she was in no immediate danger. Slowly, Winston began moving himself closer and closer to her, and then, when he was sat right beside her, she felt his arm creep up around her shoulder, to droop, ever so subtly, at the top of her left breast.

'What you think you doing?' Girlie asked alarmed at how swiftly he was moving.

'I'm just putting my arm around you. What's the matter with that?'

By this time, girlie had somehow sprung to the other side of the boat, ready to fight him off if necessary, knowing that she would most probably drown in the process.

'If you lay one finger on me, I…I…I'm going to scream.'

First, there was a hushed silence, and then he released a huge mocking laugh into the air, before catching his breath.

'So tell me something Girlie, who you think is going to hear you? There's nobody out here - Just you and me, and the cranes. He pointed to big white birds, squawking above their heads.

'You touch me and Aunt Hilda will kill you.'

'Kill *me*!' He laughed aloud again. 'You mean kill *you*. Remember your aunt must never know about this. He moved slowly down the boat towards her, staring straight into her eyes, and then, without warning began rocking the boat, gently to start with and then with such force Girlie thought they would both keel over into the water. Her screams for him to stop, reduced her to a pathetic, weeping wreck and she fastened herself to the seat for balance. In the next crazy moment, he had pulled her close to him. His big hands wiped the tears from her face, as he apologised profusely.

'Girlie I'm sorry, I didn't mean to frighten you or make you cry. I just wanted to be near you that's all.'

On hearing this, Girlie clung to him and that's when it happened - the kiss. It was like lightning striking, as though a flight of angels had descended to ordain their union. He kissed her - a long lingering kiss that made her go all light-headed and giddy. Her heart pounded so loud in her chest she thought it would burst. When eventually he pulled away, she stood there, her eyes shut tight; lips still puckered up. The sound of Winston laughing again made her open her eyes.

'Why you always laughing at me?'

'I don't mean to laugh at you Girlie. I just need you to trust me. I wouldn't dream of taking liberties with you; I'm a gentleman: look no hands,' he said holding his hands in the air. Then, gently, he pulled her to him again.

'I know that like me, you've had a hard life but that's going to change for the both of us. From this moment onwards, I will always be there for you. I now vow to be a part of the rest of your life. One day I'm going to take you away from Miss Hilda, so you better be ready, because I'm serious. And I mean what I say, if Miss Hilda beats you again, she will have me to deal with.'

They talked and laughed until the scorching hot sun forced them to make their way back inland.

Girlie found out what his next surprise was after they had hitched a lift in a dusty American truck, all the way to busy Kingston. The town centre teemed with people going about their business. The latest sounds of Fats Domino, carried on signals from far away places like Miami and New Orleans, blared out from radios, putting rhythm to everyone's steps. Together they explored exciting places, ending up hours later at a recording studio to watch the queues of waiting talent perform, in turn, to an outside audience. These musicians came with all sorts of instruments. Some came with banjos, guitars or even tin pots to accompany them as they sang - their hearts filled with the hope of making it big. Rejection or humiliation by the producer provided extra entertainment for eager onlookers. Occasionally someone would get a lucky break - a chance to cut a record.

Realising that time had passed, Girlie and Winston hurriedly hitched a lift back to Bay, to carry out the last part of Girlie's plan so that her aunt would be none the wiser as to her diversion that day.

Safely back in Old Harbour Bay, Winston kissed her once more. He looked deep into her eyes.

'Remember what I said. Be ready, I might come and get you at any time.'

Eventually she managed to pull herself away and thanked him for giving her the time of her life.

'I'll see you tomorrow,' he promised.

She watched him disappear out of sight round a corner before hastily running as fast as she could to meet up with her cousin. She decided then that she would confide in Enid. She would tell her everything on the way home. However, when she arrived at the spot where her cousin had promised to wait for her, there was no sign of anyone. The yard where children played stood empty and desolate. Where was Enid and what time was it? Alarmed by this, she sneaked up to the schoolroom window, to try to get a look at the clock hanging on the wall inside. With the windows placed so high in a structure supported by stilts, she had to jump a few times to read what the clock said. She made three jumps in total, catching sight of the clock on the second jump, and made the third jump in total disbelief before stumbling backwards onto the dusty ground.

Half past four! She was more than late. Only God could save her now. Without thinking, she picked up her feet and ran; ran like a woman possessed, as though she herself was being pursued by duppies. Her chest hurt and her sides pained with a stitch. She could hardly breathe, but Girlie could not afford to stop running until she was home. She could feel her body overheating. Sweat poured down her head then onto her neck, rolling down onto her back and chest. So fast were her movements that when she had taken the corner for the last leg home, she did not see Miss Beulah and the two collided together, sending all the provisions Beulah carried catapulting through the air. Miss Beulah stood there in shock; mouth wide open, trying to take in Girlie's dishevelled state. Girlie stood there too, legs trembling nervously all by themselves, like an engine revved up and ready to hit the open road.

'Lawd have mercy, is that you Girlie? Girl, you know how long Miss Hilda's been waiting on you? Look at you hair. And what you doing in your Sunday dress?' she asked in a bewildered tone.'

Her dress! Such was her haste to get home; she had forgotten to change back into her school uniform. It was too late now that Miss Beulah had seen her. Without the utterance of a word, she tore off down the road towards home. Miss Beulah shouted something after her; but Girlie just kept on running. There was no time for elaborate explanations of how her hair and dress had come to be in such a state of disarray. She must get into the house and get changed as quickly as possible before her aunt saw her. With any luck, her aunt would be in the back room and would not hear her enter through the side entrance. True she would have some explaining to do but at least if she looked half decent, then maybe her life would be spared.

The house was quiet and still, but for the ticking of the large pendulum clock on the wall in the sitting room. There was no sign of anyone. The whole place appeared deserted, but nevertheless she tiptoed through the house, eyes bulging, taking two steps at a time before stopping: looking around, and holding her breath to listen for signs of life. Her imagination ran wild. For a brief moment, she thought she could hear a faint sound coming from one of the rooms but then it would go quiet. There it was again. Girlie knew she was getting closer to the source of the sound, which had started out as a low humming, but now sounded like someone sobbing quietly. Awareness of what must have gone on in the house before her own arrival horrified her. Instead of entering the room straight away, Girlie stood outside for a moment: forehead pressed against the door, heartbroken that her cousin had had to face Aunt Hilda on her own. With tears in her eyes, she pushed open the door and saw Enid, sat on the bed crying her heart out.

'Oh Enid, I'm home now, please forgive me,' Girlie whispered.

'I told you not to go,' cried Enid. 'Told you Aunt Hilda would find out but you wouldn't listen.'

'I'm so sorry. Enid you're my first and best cousin, I didn't mean for none of this to happen.'

'Girlie you have to leave this house right now cause Miss Hilda is setting for you and I won't be able to help when she starts beating you.' Enid whispered this with great urgency in her eyes, as though it were a matter of life or death.

'I can't leave, Enid. You know I don't have nowhere else to go. I have no choice but to face her. It will be all right. I'll take the beating, but not for much longer.'

'What about your Aunt Mary? You could go and stay with her. She loves you. She will take care of you.'

'Aunt Mary got enough mouths to feed without me adding to her woes. She can't afford to send me to school and that's the only way I'm ever going to turn out to be somebody.'

'Well then you have to be like the rest of us and do what Aunt Hilda tells you to.'

'For you, I'm going to try really hard; harder than before. I don't ever want you to get hurt because of me again.'

Sensing a presence other than their own, both Girlie and Enid's eyes were drawn to the large ominous figure standing in the doorway.

'Get up!'

'Aunt Hilda!' blurted Girlie in stunned surprise.

Her aunt stood there, hands on hips, puffing and blowing like a mad bull in a pen - except someone had left the gates open. A thick leather strap dangled menacingly around her neck. She could hardly wait to get started for within three swift steps she had grabbed Girlie by the scruff of her white dress with one hand, pulling her from the bedroom and into the sitting room, whilst beating her about the head with the other hand. Still holding onto her dress, her aunt shook her vigorously a few times, then pushed her back at the same time as releasing her grip, causing Girlie to fall backwards, hitting her head on a piece of furniture.

'Don't move,' her aunt commanded, before going over to the dresser. Stretching high on tip-toes, Aunt Hilda took the Bible out from the top shelf of a bookcase in which it was kept. In what seemed like slow motion, Girlie watched her every move, more petrified of swearing on the Bible than she was of her aunt. Her aunt walked over to where Girlie now stood trembling and placed the Bible carefully on the table. She took the leather strap from around her neck and it slithered off her shoulders like a long black snake. Then carefully, she wound the tail end twice around her hand, leaving the heavy, shiny buckle to dangle, swinging side to side like the pendulum in the clock.

'Where did you and Winston go today when you should have been at school?'

'We didn't go anywhere Aunt Hilda; we just went for walk.

Girlie saw the buckle of the belt coming towards her. She turned away to avoid being hit in the face but was not quick enough. The buckle smashed into the back of her head. Sharp pain reverberated through her skull, making her scream out. She held her head tight for a few seconds to ease the pain.

'I'm going to ask you one more time. I said where did you go with Winston?'

Breathless now with fear, warm blood trickled down her nose and into her mouth. She wiped it with the back of her hand, then unconsciously down the side of her white dress.

'We only went to the beach. We sailed on his boat. We didn't go far.'

'Did he touch you?'

'No Aunt Hilda. He's not like that, he's a…'

'How do you know what he's like?' Again, this question was asked with the belt.

'I'm sorry Aunt Hilda. It will never happen again, I promise you. Please don't beat me, please.'

'You damn right it's never going to happen again. I'm going to make sure of that.'

The older woman moved swiftly towards her, her face contorted with unbridled rage and disgust. Girlie cowered backwards with both hands raised in the air ready to protect her head again. Aunt Hilda lunged at her, gripping her right hand to drag her back over to the table. She placed Girlie's right hand on top of the Bible and held it there.

'I want you to swear on the Holy Bible, he didn't touch you.'

'Oh God no, Aunt Hilda - don't make me swear on the Bible, please.'

'I said to swear on the Bible he didn't touch you or so help me God I'm going to strip you naked and beat you.'

God, I can't lie to you, thought Girlie. Winston had touched her when they had kissed, but not in the same way Aunt Hilda was thinking. If she did not swear on the Bible, here and now, her aunt would show no mercy. And if she told such a big lie, then surely God would punish her for telling untruths, some ill-begotten woe would befall the rest of her life. Aunt Hilda always said to fear God more than anybody else, and so Girlie did.

'I said to swear. Go on! Do it!.'

'I can't do it Aunt Hilda! I can't!'

'Her aunt raised the belt, high into the air. Blows rained down on Girlie from all angles. She struggled to protect herself as best she could, falling over the furniture, crawling around on hands and knees, then quickly scrambling to her feet each time as soon as she got the chance. She could hear the piercing shrills of her own screams, or was it coming from her cousin Enid, still paying the price for being an accomplice?. Girlie felt her body wet with sweat, or blood. She could not tell.

'You dirty bitch. I'm going to murder you in here. I warned you to keep away from him - warned you. A man like that only want one thing. Why don't you listen to me? Why do you want to bring shame on me? Who's going to want you when you spoil? You nasty whore.'

Panting for breath, and weak with pain, Girlie begged her aunt to stop but her pleas fell on deaf ears. The buckle flashed towards her again. Girlie put her hands in front of her face for defence. A loud cracking sound followed. Looking down at her bloody hand for a moment, she could see the bone protruding out of her thumb. Then as if in slow motion, the buckle cracked into her forehead, catching her off guard. It sent her reeling to the ground in agony. Her body was too weak to get up this time; too limp and disconnected from her brain to obey orders to survive. Now she must take her punishment lying down.

'Jesus Christ; help me,' she heard herself say, as she drifted in and out of a darkness that promised eternal rest.

'Oh, so now you taking the Lord's name in vain,' her aunt said with sudden rejuvenation.

From where she lay on the floor, Girlie tried to shake her head in protest, to tell her Aunt Hilda that was not so, but it had no effect - nothing could stop her now. She just kept on beating and cussing, ranting and raging - until mercifully, it came to a sudden halt.

'Lawd God Miss Hilda, stop, you going to kill her!'

Miss Beulah had prised the belt from Hilda's hand, thrown it aside, and now struggled to calm this frenzied woman.

'Let me go Beulah! Let me go!' Miss Hilda panted, 'I don't finish wid her yet.'

'Can't you see she's near death already? What's the matter with you?'

'After all I done for her: all the money I spend to send her to school.'

'But Miss Hilda,' said Beulah shaking her back to reality, 'she's somebody else's child. That don't give you the right to take her life.'

The silence that followed was deafening. At that precise moment, everything became motionless. All that energy Miss Hilda had to beat Girlie with, suddenly drained from her body, like blood from a corpse.

'Enid! Take Girlie to her room. Get her cleaned up and put her to bed.'

Enid obediently did as Miss Beulah told her; struggling to help her cousin clamber to her feet, tightening her grasp every so often whenever Girlie stumbled, whilst the two older women looked on.

'And I want that dress washed and back in the wardrobe by tomorrow, or it's you and me again,' spat Aunt Hilda. She just had to have the last word to show her power over the younger females.

Girlie found it hard to take in Enid's hysterical ramblings as she tended her wounds. Shocked and dazed, Girlie stared into space, in total disbelief that she had just been beaten to within an inch of her life.

'Oh God! She beat you bad Girlie. I think she broke your hand. All I can do is bandage you up but you really need a doctor. Why you not saying nothing? Say something - anything, just talk to me, please Girlie.'

Fumbling nervously, Enid bandaged Girlie's hand to the best of her ability and then bandaged her head before bathing the welts on her back and legs that had split open. Enid was more calm now as she helped Girlie into her nightdress and then into bed.

'I will soak your dress for you later and wash it out in the morning. You try and get some rest now.'

The evening gave birth to night, and still not a sound had escaped Girlie since the moment when she had called out to the Christ: not a word, nor cry or cough or sigh, only silent tears that formed small pools of sorrow in her ears. Staring piteously up at the ceiling, her thoughts rested on how unbearable her whole life was. Being poor was a curse; a damnation inflicted on her, against her will. Poor as she was, that night, she vowed to break the chain of poverty, which had followed generations of her family. It was poverty, which had separated her from the love of a mother and placed her in the care of her seemingly unfeeling aunt whom she detested with such vehemence. As soon as she could, she would pack her belongings into a bag, ready to depart her aunt's company, and all the bad memories, for good. Her life here was done. Light from the full silvery moon filtered in through the half drawn curtains, capturing Girlie in its mystical glow. Still wracked with pain, she mused on the kiss shared with Winston, not so long ago - the kiss that had changed her life. He was her knight in shining armour and only he, and he alone, would save her from whatever she needed to be saved from. He had promised as much. With love and salvation on her mind and hope in her heart, a near peaceful sleep came to claim her, for a time.

Her white Sunday dress flapped on the line in the sunlight of the early morning breeze the following day - every trace of blood removed. Gone were all the telltale signs of what horrors had occurred the previous night. Aunt Hilda was stood in the centre of the yard staring up at the dress as though puzzled by how it came to be there.

At least Girlie was certain of one thing; Aunt Hilda's days of terrorizing were over.

Suddenly, out of the corner of her eye, a moving figure attracted Girlie's attention. Bobsy, Miss Beulah's son walked by the house; eyes and mouth opened wide; mystified by the sight of Miss Hilda standing motionless in the middle of the yard and a heavily bandaged Girlie a few paces behind.

'Good Morning Miss Hilda,' he called, but he might just as well have been invisible for she didn't hear him nor see him for that fact. All she could see was the dress. With every stride he took, Bobsy observed first the older woman and then Girlie in turn, looking from one to the other a number of times, until his vision became obscured by trees and bushes, but not before calling to Girlie.

'Good morning Girlie,' he called, then disappeared on his way.

Suddenly aware that she was not alone, Aunt Hilda spun around to face Girlie. Aunt Hilda's immediate reaction was that of total shock at the sight of Girlie, her bandaged hand swollen to twice its normal size and blood still visibly seeping through the fabric.

'Girlie! I…I…Look what you made me do to you.'

'I did not make you do nothing,' said Girlie, as bold as she had ever been. 'You did what you always do.'

'You tell me, what was I supposed to do,' said Hilda, trying to defend her actions.'I send you to school to learn, yet you find yourself in a boat with a man; and not just any man, you have to take up with that nasty naegger Winston who I warned you about so many times.

'I am not a child, I'm almost sixteen years old for God's sake.'

'Sixteen,' laughed Aunt Hilda. 'I don't care if you're sixty, *I* am your guardian and you will do what I tell you to do as long as you're under *my* roof,' and with that she abruptly took her leave.

Just then, Miss Beulah entered the yard to see the back of Aunt Hilda disappear into the house. Pityingly, she looked Girlie over. For a moment her mouth parted as if about to express words of compassion but she must have changed her mind for she too hurried away towards the house just as Enid started out into the yard.

'Girlie, you feeling any better?

'I'm all right, no thanks to Aunt Hilda.'

'You know you're going to have to play Aunt Hilda's game to get back right with her again.

'Enid you don't have to worry any more, I won't be here for much longer: I'm leaving.'

'Leaving!'

'I can't stay here for much longer Enid. I'm going away with Winston, and soon. All my life that woman's been beating me and it has to stop. I can't take it no more; No! I won't take it no more! For God's sake, I *am* somebody, with or without Aunt Hilda's money and damn it, I deserve better.'

'What's he been telling you?'

'He promised to take me away from here. We talk all the time, he understands what I'm going through. Oh Enid yesterday when we kissed ...'

'He kissed you!'

'Yeh,' said Girlie. That same twinkle in her eyes that had got her in this whole mess in the first place, briefly reappeared. He told me he'd always be there for me.'

'And you believed him?'

'Of course I believe him. Nobody in the whole world ever said that to me before, so yes, I know he'll come and take me away from this.'

'Why can't you get it in your head that Winston is full of sweet talk. He's not the kind to settle down with one woman. Him is a pretty boy and you know what Aunt Hilda say about man like that.

'All of a sudden you're beginning to sound just like Aunt Hilda, bad-mouthing him all the time. You never have a good word to say about him. He won't let me down Enid. He'll come, you'll see.'

Troubled by Girlie's high expectations of Winston turning up to save her, Enid took hold of her cousin's hands.

'Girlie I know life has been hard for you with Aunt Hilda, but this is the best place for you. You can't expect to change a man like that.

'Only yesterday you said I had to get away and now all of a sudden, this is the best place for me. I don't understand you sometimes, Enid.'

'Please Girlie, don't set your heart on it,' pleaded Enid discouragingly. 'You're wasting your time. Winston won't come and I don't want to see you get hurt again.'

The ears of the two sleeping dogs in the yard suddenly pricked up like radar dishes turning on a stand. They had detected something. Eager to investigate, they strained against the leashes, which kept them bound. Girlie hushed them. Out of nowhere, Winston's tall handsome figure appeared. Girlie took to her feet and he saw her then.

'I told you he'd come Enid. I knew he wouldn't let me down. I knew it. Oh Enid, do one last thing for me. Pack my bags and bring them to me. Quick Enid, Run! Run!'

After a brief hesitation, Enid suddenly darted into the house through the side entrance and Girlie ran towards Winston.

'I knew you'd come, she panted, as she threw her arms about his neck and hugged him tightly.

'Oh God Girlie, look at you. Was it Miss Hilda? Did she do this to you? I'm going to kill her. Where is she?'

'No! You're here now. Let us go quietly. I don't want no more trouble,' said Girlie.

'But Girlie I need to speak to you.'

Just then, hearing the commotion, Aunt Hilda raced outside to meet him head on.

'You take you hands off that child and get out of my yard before I set the dogs on you.'

The expression on Winston's face terrified Girlie. This was not a face she had seen before. Frantically, she looked around for any sign of her cousin, but there was none.

Like a flash that came from out of nowhere, Winston moved towards Aunt Hilda at speed, and then smote her across the face so severely that she staggered backwards into Beulah's waiting arms.

'You should never have done that,' Aunt Hilda said, after she had recovered from the initial shock - Beulah's arms still around her waist, gently restraining her friend.

Holding on to Winston's shirt, Girlie pulled him to a safe distance, her heart racing at this final conflict. In a blinding rush, Enid at last emerged, bags in hand.

'I got it Girlie! I got it! Go before…'

'Stop right there,' said Aunt Hilda stepping into Enid's view. 'Where you going with those bags?'

'They're mine,' Girlie interjected, neglecting Winston's efforts to still her mouth. The sweet, over-powering tang of everlasting freedom was too strong to hold at bay, so she unleashed it to proclaim to Aunt Hilda, and all those who stood around, her parting speech. 'You will never beat me again as long as you live, Aunt Hilda. Last night was the *last* time. I'm leaving with Winston today, right now.'

A look of bewilderment attached itself to Aunt Hilda's face, but she needn't have worried: her astonishment was short lived, and the shock, which had gripped her briefly, departed from her just as quickly to rest on Girlie's own countenance as all her hopes came tumbling down.

'But Girlie,' blurted Winston, 'I ... I cannot take you with me.'

Those words pierced her heart like a charger that had come through the other side of her: it rendered her weak with confused disbelief. Had she really heard those words or was it just an echo of her inner fears? A rush of heat enveloped her. Her heart, her breathing, competed in a panic-stricken race. She turned to Winston, and sullenly, he repeated those words.

'I can't take you with me Girlie.'

'What do you mean you can't take me with you? You promised! You can't leave me here with her!'

Folding her arms about her bedraggled self, Aunt Hilda stood there triumphant that Girlie's plan to escape had been thwarted.

'I know what I said Girlie,' pleaded Winston, 'but the time is not right. You know I'm looking for somewhere for us to be together but I need more time. You got to give me more time.'

'I don't have any more time Winston. Are you blind? I'm depending on you. You got to help me. Please don't leave me here with her, please. Winston don't do this to me. Take me with you. Look,' she said grabbing the bags from Enid's hands. I'm packed, I'm ready. In a few days, I will find a job. I'll do any...'

'Girlie stop it,' Winston screamed, shaking her back to reality. 'I said I can't take you with me and that's final.'

Girlie's whole world had fallen apart. In the heat of the blazing moment, distraught and overcome with passionate remorse, she made clear to him the poignancy of his intended action - a desperate, last-ditch effort to make him change his mind.

'I was depending on you. I thought I could trust you,' she appealed, but the silent response coupled with the expression on his face, said it all. 'If you let me down like this, I will never forgive you. How could you do this to me? How?'

'I'll come back and get you just as soon as I can Girlie,' said Winston backing away.

'Don't bother,' said Girlie. It's finished.'

'See what you cause,' beamed Aunt Hilda with vigour. 'Now take you nasty naegger-self out of my yard and don't come back!'

'And *you*!' said Winston, taking a step towards Hilda, which startled her, 'if you ever lay a finger on her again and I get to hear about it, I'll come back and murder you, as God is my witness.' And with that, he departed.

Aunt Hilda turned towards Enid, swiping her across the face with the open palm of a hand, raised high.

'Get those bags back in the house right now. I am surprised at you Enid. I will deal with you later.'

Enid scurried away obediently, holding her hot cheek.

'And you,' she said looking directly at Girlie, 'under no circumstances are you to leave this house. Do you understand?'

Everything had gone so horribly wrong. This was not how it was supposed to happen. With no place of refuge to hide her shame, she held her head low, in the cups of her palms to cry tears of dejection. The man she loved, the one to whom she had imparted the gift of her heart for keeps, had humiliated her in front of everyone. How could she ever forgive him?

She never did see a doctor for her broken thumb and so over time, it healed, deformed - a constant reminder that love hurts. During the time of confinement, her finals had come and gone, leaving her behind, therefore, she did not graduate from high school with any qualifications to speak of.

Getting herself ready for church one Sunday morning, Girlie adjusted her hair in the mirror, pleasantly pleased with the result.

'You know, it's high time you were married,' said Aunt Hilda, watching her intently from a chair in Girlie's bedroom, where she waited.

'Me? Married?' said Girlie, with cold indifference. In almost a year, she had grown up with a seriousness of sobriety about her, because life no longer had that splash of rose-tint that had coloured her world for so brief an interlude.

'I know just the type of man you need,' said Aunt Hilda outside the church after a lengthy service.

The fact that marriage was still on Aunt Hilda's mind hours later conveyed to Girlie that her aunt was indeed up to something; not that she cared in the least, for although she detested her aunt with such vehemence, she had learnt to toe the line.

'You need a clean-living, church-going man with a good job - not a womanising gambler who will leave you and your children hungry. You leave it with me. I will take care of everything.'

Girlie had no idea who Aunt Hilda had in mind until Miss Beulah hurried over with her son Bobsy.

'What a lovely service hey Miss Hilda?'

'Wonderful Beulah, wonderful.'

Beulah's son Bobsy just stood there, staring straight at Girlie, grinning like a Cheshire cat.

'You remember my son Bobsy, don't you Girlie.'

Remember him! Of course she knew him. He was a few years older than she was but she could not help remembering him as a snot-nosed boy, running errands for his mother in short pants way into his teens. He was always loitering nearby in the background somewhere, but she had never been interested in him in that way. Now he was a man. Girlie stole a sneaky look to study his face and appearance quickly and concluded that, but for the stupid grin, he had not grown too badly.

'Yes. Hello Bobsy. How you doing?'

'Fine thank you Girlie. And yourself?'

'Good, good, good,' interrupted Aunt Hilda. We got to be going now. Why don't you bring Bobsy over to the house when you call on Friday, then him and Girlie can catch up. They have a lot to talk about.'

'You know that's a very good idea Miss Hilda,' said Beulah obviously in on the conspiracy to pair the two off.

Sure enough, there they both were on Friday afternoon, standing at the gate, calling to Miss Hilda to hold the dogs.

'Do I have to be there as well Aunt Hilda? I have a lot of work to do inside.'

'What work? Of course, you need to be there. Who's going to talk to Bobsy?'

'But I don't have anything to talk to him about.'

'Hush up. You will think of something. Put out the lemonade while I get the dogs round the back.'

Miss Beulah sat next to Girlie on the veranda and Bobsy sat opposite with Aunt Hilda. It was an uncomfortable set up, being forced to take root in such close proximity to a man she had nothing in common with whilst being observed by two meddling, middle-aged women.

Irritating for Girlie was the fact that Bobsy came with a big bag of compliments, which he paid to Aunt Hilda at frequent intervals.

'My, you looking radiant today Miss Hilda,' or 'You have a lovely house Miss Hilda,' or, this is the best lemonade I ever taste Miss Hilda.'

Miss Hilda this and Miss Hilda that. Girlie was sure she would be violently sick on his best Sunday shoes, if he came out with another insipid compliment.

'What a lovely young man you've grown into Bobsy,' said Hilda, and Beulah beamed with pride. However, to Girlie's annoyance, every time her eyes made four with his, he would have that same stupid grin on his face. If she married him, she would have the misfortune to wake up beside that stupid grin every morning for the rest of her life, and if they had children, well, that didn't bear thinking about.

'Why don't you two go for a stroll? Walk out.'

Good God, thought Girlie as she and Bobsy strolled away from the house. Aunt Hilda must really like this man to trust the two of them out alone together and she could see why. Squeaky clean in his best Sunday pants and shirt, he tentatively supported her elbow as they walked over uneven ground; as though he were a safety net; ready to save her from any fall. He had about him an appearance of quiet self-assurance.

'I hope you don't mind,' he said, cutting away the long drawn out silence.

'Mind what?' asked Girlie growing increasingly annoyed at how presumptuous he was being.

'My mama and your aunt throwing us together like this.' He slowed his steps to a halt now, his face taking on a more serious countenance.

'You must know that I have loved you for a longer time, since I was a boy. You're unhappy because right now your life is not your own. You want to get away from Miss Hilda and I thought that by offering to marry you, we'd be helping each other out. We could make a good life together, you and me.'

Girlie open her mouth to interrupt but he quickly put a finger to her lips to hush any protest.

'Hear me out. I know you don't think much of me and I know I am not as handsome as some of the guys in Old Harbour, but I'm a good man and my heart is in the right place. I don't come with any contention or malice. I just want to take care of you Girlie. You probably don't love me now but in time I know you will.'

Looking at him, Girlie could see that he was deadly serious. He meant every word he said. He intended to marry her. For a moment, she was touched in a quirky sort of way by his compassion, coupled with the fact that he fancied himself as a hero of some kind - her hero. Sadly though, she was just not attracted to him; nothing could change that. Right now, he was just a poor deluded pawn in the scheme of things. Ever so subtly, without even looking at him, Girlie slipped her hand into his. He clasped it firmly as though never to let go and must have thought then that he had won his prize. A relaxed and contented smile replaced the earlier strain.

'Do you think your aunt would mind if I took you out again, that is, if you don't mind being seen with me?'

'With all the compliments you give her, she must still be feeling as sweet as honey. Oh how I would love for a swarm of African killer bees to attack and sting her in her raas.' They both laughed aloud at the prospect for some time.

'Did you enjoy your walk?' asked Aunt Hilda, flustered with excitement.

'Oh yes, thank you Miss Hilda,' said Bobsy. 'You know, you did a fine job raising Girlie. She's a lovely woman.' Girlie grinned. 'Truly a credit to you.'

Now it was the turn of Aunt Hilda's big chest to swell with pride, satisfied that her plan had come into fruition.

'I'd like to take Girlie dancing on Saturday. Is that all right with you Miss Hilda?'

'Dancing!' exclaimed Aunt Hilda. She looked Girlie over and then, reassured by Bobsy's responsible composure: 'Well I don't agree with young ladies wining their bodies for the world to see, but make sure you keep your eye on her and have her back here at a decent hour.'

And so began a wonderful taste of freedom for Girlie, not the kind of freedom for which she had yearned all her life, but freedom nevertheless, because restrictions had been lifted. Over the months that ensued, Girlie and Bobsy spent a lot of time in each other's company. Frequently they went to the picture house, open-air dances and for long walks under the shade of the cooling sun. Bobsy was courteous, caring, understanding, and funny even, at times. She could not help but to like him and gradually, this saddened her deeply because she knew in her heart that she probably would never love him the way he wanted her to. The last thing she wanted to do was hurt this loving, gentle man whom she had grown so fond of, but by marrying him, she would be living a lie, and that prospect did not rest easy with her.

'You know, I have a feeling he's going to ask you to marry him soon - maybe even tonight,' declared Aunt Hilda, helping Girlie to look her best for an evening out with Bobsy. Never before had her aunt shown so much concern over Girlie's appearance until now.

'What makes you say that?'

'Well the two of you been courting for a while now. I think the time is right.'

'Right for what?' asked Girlie nervously.

'Marriage of course. Where's your head?'

'It's too soon Aunt Hilda. I'm not ready for marriage yet.'

'Not ready! shouted Aunt Hilda, gripping Girlie's arm. 'Gal, you stupid or something? I can't afford to keep you no more. You costing me money, so if he asks you to marry him, you say yes, you hear me?'

Girlie noted that Bobsy was more nervous than usual when he showed up. Normally he was confident, cool, calm and colleted but now he stumbled over his words, tripped over his own feet, twice, and then spilt half his drink over some other woman, to the anger of her male companion. He was behaving very oddly indeed, which coincided with Aunt Hilda's revelation. It dawned on Girlie that this was the night he would ask her to marry him. Each time he looked as though he was about to say something, Girlie threw him off course with trivialities, until he could wait no longer.

'Stand still for one minute Girlie,' said Bobsy courageously. He spun her round to face him. 'I have a question to ask you and I am not taking no for an answer.'

He took her hand in his and Girlie watched horrified as he got down on one knee. A small group of people headed by Enid and her male companion, Rodney, had slowly crept into the frame.

'Girlie will you do me the honour of being my wife?'

This was the precise moment her world would change for good, regardless of what decision she might make. She was in a quandary about what to do. If she said yes and did what everyone expected she knew she would have to marry a man whom she was very fond of, but did not love. Moreover, if she refused his offer, then it would be like placing him in the jaws of humiliation and she knew only too well the torture he would have to endure. And if that were the case, her aunt would inevitably throw her out in disgrace, which strangely enough, she no longer feared. She looked down at Bobsy again. His wide glistening eyes pleaded longingly with hers for consent. However when she looked up again she was totally taken aback by what she saw. Her heart raced wildly in her chest, her mouth suddenly became parched and her stomach churned over and over again. Her eyes had locked onto the figure of Winston. In the early days following her heartbreak, she had thwarted his efforts to speak by ignoring his mere existence. Last she heard, he had moved away from the district, but now he was back. At first, he was oblivious to her presence, but on catching her gaze, his arms had fallen by his side as he tried to decipher what was taking place. Girlie looked down at Bobsy again, then glanced over to her cousin Enid who quietly mouthed the word, 'Please,' then back again at the man kneeling in front of her. It was tearing her apart. She tried to do her utmost not to embarrass him in front of so many people.

'Bobsy, I… I need more time,' she heard herself say.

But in the next craze-filled minute, Winston, enraged with jealousy, had hauled her by the arm.

'What are you doing? Let me go!' she screamed.

'I want one last dance with you,' he ordered, pulling her along to where everyone could see.

Bobsy moved forward but Winston ordered him: 'Stay back, unless you want to get hurt.'

Defeated, all Bobsy could do was to watch. He was second best and he knew it, but if there was a slim chance that Girlie would choose him of her own accord then surely it would prove that she felt something for him.

Girlie struggled to free herself of Winston's grip but he pulled her closer still, to steady her resistance, trapping her in his arms, staring deep into her eyes whilst music blared in the background. The same sweet smell of his musky aftershave drifted up her nostrils, heightening her emotions all over again.

Still holding her tightly, he lowered his head slightly to whisper in her ear.

'If you think I'm going to let you marry that fool, then think again. There is no way on this God-given earth it's going to happen. I know you don't love him like you love *me*. You belong to me, always have done, always will and you know it to be so. I want you to pack your things and leave all of this behind tonight. If you truly love me, you'll do it. I'll wait for you by the church.'

Then without warning, he kissed her, as though to claim her as his own and her heart in an instant, melted all over again.

She watched him walk briskly away then turned to face the dismayed expressions of her group. There was no way she could stay in Old Harbour after this, even if she wanted to. The fact that she still loved Winston was evident for all to see.

Embarrassment caused her to flee the scene, followed closely behind, not by Bobsy, but by her cousin Enid who eventually caught up with her.

'Girlie don't do this to Bobsy, you owe him more than that.'

'I can't marry Bobsy,' she said tearfully, 'I don't love him.'

'Bobsy is over there, probably worried sick by now. He don't deserve this so you go find him and do whatever it is you have to do. But do it quick.'

Through her tears, Girlie thought of how dreadful poor Bobsy must be feeling as she made her way over to him.

The group she came with had long since dispersed, leaving only Bobsy, sitting alone on a wooden bench with his head hanging low. She walked over to him and placed a hand on his shoulder. Abruptly he stood up.

'I'll walk you home,' he said - all his joy depleted.

Neither spoke a word during the short walk back to Aunt Hilda's home.

'Bobsy, I'm so sorry. I can't marry you.' She blurted it out just like that, knowing that it had to be said and the heartache it would cause.

'Girlie, I'll do anything you want me to do, be anyone you want, just so long as you marry me. I've always loved only you for as long as I can remember.'

This time, Girlie put a finger to his lips as a signal for him to hear her out.

'You probably guessed that I still have feelings for Winston. I wish I didn't, but I can't help how I feel.' Bobsy hung his head low. She raised his drooping chin with her hand and saw the tears in his eyes. 'Bobsy you are a wonderful man but I don't love you the way I should. You deserve someone who is going to love you back the same, if not more. Right now you need the space for that to happen. That's why I'm going away - tonight.'

'Going away! Where will you go?'

'Anywhere far away from this place. You're the only one I've told.' she looked down at her hands. 'I wouldn't blame you if you went inside and told Aunt Hilda this minute.'

'I would never betray you like that Girlie. I want you to know that if ever you change your mind, I'll be right here waiting for you.' Then gently, he kissed her on the cheek - loyal to the end - that was Bobsy.

Sometimes we make mistakes that take us a whole lifetime to forgive ourselves for. For Girlie, this was to be one such mistake. She watched as Bobsy walked back up the path, disappearing into the darkness of night. That was to be the last time she saw him.

Emotions still bubbling over, she rushed into the house. The hissing of what sounded, like a steam engine coming from behind Aunt Hilda's bedroom door told her that she was at least free from immediate interrogation. After throwing a few things into her suitcase, Girlie was ready. In her haste to get out of the dark house, she stumbled but managed to recoup herself before a fall. Reassured by the enduirng silence, she tiptoed nervously towards the door.

'And where in God's name do you think you're going?' Like a ghost, Aunt Hilda's figure materialised in the darkness, her nightdress shimmering white.

Girlie gulped, and then felt freedom racing through her veins. 'I'm leaving, Aunt Hilda.'

'Leaving? What you mean you leaving? You getting married!'

'No - I'm not. I'm leaving you and this house for good.'

'I won't let you do that.'

'I'm leaving and you can't stop me.'

Aunt Hilda lunged forward raising her hand ready to deliver a sobering blow.

Girlie did not move, instead, she tilted her chin in a final show of defiance, stared at her aunt and said, in a hushed but forceful, voice full of newfound strength. 'You will never beat me again Aunt Hilda. As long as I live, you'll never beat me again.'

Something old and primeval passed between the two women then; a recognition that alas, old age must step aside and eventually pass away to make room for youth. Hilda's large hand as though dashed by a great weight, flopped back to her side. As Girlie turned and walked

Chapter Six

Beside the Still Waters

....

Father God, you knew that our trials were not yet over - knew that this family was about to be propelled onto the road of obscurity. Yet true to your word, you stayed with us.

Death followed the family for the next three consecutive years. It sniffed around Dada. It wanted to take someone close to him and it needed his help to snatch a person unknown to us from this world. Earlier in the day, he had spent hours pampering himself for a night out on the town. Since the age of sixteen, he had inherited a clump of grey hair at the front of his head, the size of a half crown. His mission in life though was to stay forever young but his grey hairs had different ideas. They were on the move all over his body and he was determined not to succumb to their age-old power. Taking over the bathroom, he dyed the hair on his head jet black. After he had done that, he turned the old faithful toothbrush he used onto his chest, dying the hairs there black as well. He wandered around the house bare backed for the next thirty minutes with a large black patch on his chest, waiting for the dye to take effect. He sat there now, by the sitting room window polishing his own shoes for once. Whistling, he turned it this way and that, taking care not to miss a spot. I watched him now and thought how carefree and youthful he looked compared to Mama.

That same evening, Uncle Fitzbert paid us an unexpected visit. We jumped up and down, happy to see him, but there was something different about his countenance. He was not in his usual playful mood.

'Where's Winston?'

'In the sitting room,' we said excitedly.

'Go get your Mother. Tell her Winston need her, and you kids stay in the kitchen.'

Were those tears I saw in his eyes as he walked into the sitting room?

'You all right Fiztbert?' Dada called on hearing his uncle's voice?

'Not at all Winston. It's bad news.'

'What bad news, what you talking about?

'Bad news, bad, bad news,' he panted, shaking his head as if trying to get Dada to prepare himself for the worst.

Mama came rushing in. 'Fitzbert, what's wrong, what's happened?'

'I get a phone call from Jamaica today, bad news.'

Mama covered her mouth with her hands and started crying before Fitzbert could even say what was wrong. Dada, sensing that it was bad news for him, sat there chewing on his tongue, staring straight ahead at Fitzbert with red eyes.

'Winston, Your father Pinto; him dead! Winston, Pinto is dead,' cried Uncle Fitzbert in disbelief, awash with the grief.

A loud wailing noise filled the house.

'Woy! Woy!' That was the wailing sound grown ups made when the pain was too hot to bear, when fear of loss was in full control.

So distraught was Dada, he cried at the top of his voice like a baby till Mama caught hold of him and cradled his head in her arms. However, there was no consoling him. It was a shock to witness. In all my life, I had never seen him cry like this before; never knew he had it in him to feel such intense love for somebody other than himself. All evening, nothing else but the loud sorrowful cries of the adults came from the sitting room. One by one we drifted in - first Clovis, then Glen and then Julia. They cried too when they heard Pinto was dead for they also loved him dearly, and the three younger children, well, we all cried because everyone else was crying; it seemed the right thing to do at the time.

Luck had finally deserted Dada. The fact that he did not have the money to be in Jamaica standing at his father's graveside at this crucial time almost killed him. Deeply anguished, he was unable to comprehend that he would never again bless his eyes on his beloved father. All the riches of the world could have landed in his lap right now, but it would be of no use to him whatsoever - it could not bring back that which he loved the most. He could spend his whole life searching every corner of this earth for his father and still he would never find him.

His father, Pinto, was gone forever from this mysterious world in which we live.

With his spirit freefalling at colossal speed, into the pitch darkness of his soul, fear of death and the dark terrified him. Then in the misery of his darkness, came a light from within. That beam of light - the memories of tender moments, carried him, lovingly, all the way back to Jamaica. He remembered his father teaching him to swim in the bay, carrying him on his shoulders and then playfully throwing him into the gleaming waters of the Caribbean Sea. And as he splashed down onto the water, a multitude of bright water droplets, lit by the brilliant light of the hot sun, ascended high above him and then fell back onto the surface of the sea. Memories like waves, flooded back of when he was seven years old and how his father had taught him how to row a small boat. Pinto had taken him far out to sea until the shores were no longer visible in the distance. All he could see around him was horizon, in what seemed to be a world of only sea and sky. His father had stopped rowing the boat now and lay back to relax with his straw hat over his face. If he had been all by himself Winston was sure he would have panicked or drowned even though he was a strong swimmer. But comforted by the knowledge of his beloved father being right by his side, he also laid back to share in the calm silent serenity of the sea as the boat bobbed up and down, to and fro, and occasionally, the sound of a gentle wave would be the only intrusion into their tranquillity. Who would believe that World War 11 was in full swing? It could have been a million miles away. He was not afraid of death back then for he trusted his father with his life. After a long while, his father told him to take the oars.

'Come on boy! Row the boat. I got all the time in the world. We're not going back to shore until I see you rowing like a fisherman.'

This was yet another of his father's life lessons. With concentration, love, guidance and plenty of sweat, he had achieved his father's objectives.

A deep sadness presided over this house like a huge, thunderous cloud threatening to release torrents of angry tears at any moment. His father dead, it was easy to assume now that maybe Dada would love, appreciate and cherish his own family more - and show it. My grandfather's death had changed him all right, but for the worse. He was consumed with anger, guilt and regret. I suppose Mama and us kids reminded him of all the reasons why he was trapped here, and like his guilt, we were a heavy load for him to carry. But somehow, Dada still could not bring himself to walk away from his six children - to the detriment of all of us.

The second death to follow this family came like a curse during the miner's strike of '72 - a time of great industrial unrest. Inspired by world protest against the US war in Vietnam, and the biggest miners' strikes in France's history, miners stopped working to picket vital ports, depots and power stations around the country. They were there on the news with blackened faces, shouting defiance, showing such an admirable display of solidarity - dockers, train and lorry drivers too, all refusing to transport fuel or cross picket lines. The Prime Minister, Edward Heath, imposed a three-day working week. Then began all the power cuts, plunging the whole country into darkness. A state of emergency was declared and power stations up and down the country closed in order to conserve energy. No longer did we hear the peal of the bell as the coal van patrolled the streets, providing fuel to households that needed it. There simply wasn't any. We had to resort to using paraffin to heat the whole house. Taking the five-gallon container with us, we joined long arduous queues to buy paraffin and used it sparingly to preserve it. But the cold winter was so perishing that we had no alternative but to burn it or suffer hypothermia. We watched gladly as the head of the heater burned bright red, warming our feet, hands and dampened spirits. As the fuel reduced to nothing in the five-gallon container, we listened worriedly as the thirsty heater hungrily gulped down the paraffin. To drain the last drops from the bottle, we tilted the heater back onto planks of wood until eventually, the wick was starved of sustenance and the paraffin heater died another death, leaving us with the cold comfort of choking fumes from the burning wick, and the unwelcome cold that was outside invaded our lives once more. All the fuel gone, we roamed the streets, looking for wood to burn. We collected sticks and branches from the park and smashed old peaces of furniture left abandoned on street corners before taking it home. Things were in short supply, not only at home but in shops also.

Mama put us to sit around the table in front of a plate of thinly sliced, greasy Spam with rice and baked beans. It was food and we were hungry, so we tucked in, grateful for small mercies. Whilst eating dinner there was a knock at the door.

'Who could that be at this time of day,' said Mama puzzled because no one ever called at this hour in the afternoon.

On the doorstep stood Dada, shaking from head to toe.

'Winston why didn't you use your key?' Mama asked, annoyed that she had been pulled away from her work. Looking down at him, she noticed the trembling of his hands.

'What's wrong this time?' she dared to ask half cynically, although fear lurked beneath that cynicism. 'Don't tell me you lost your pay packet again?'

On shaky legs, Dada walked towards the bedroom, in a daze. His mouth moved as if he was speaking, but only he knew what he was trying to say. For the moment, audible words could not escape - not a sound, just empty breath. Nervously, Mama followed him into the bedroom, pressing him to tell her what was wrong.

Used to his antics by now, we carred on eating, unperturbed, yet looking curiously into each other's eyes as we chewed. We heard it then. Dada's hysterical cries.

'Girlie, I killed a woman today, I killed her!'

'Killed who? Killed who?' asked Mama trying to shake him back to his senses.

'An old woman. I hit her with the lorry, it was an accident. Oh God, what have I done?'

'Did they take her to hospital? Maybe she's not dead, maybe she's just hurt bad, you have to find out.'

'I tell you she dead! Smashed to pieces! I saw …' he paused for a moment, unable to describe what he had seen. 'I saw when they pulled her out from under the lorry. Oh God, the blood Girlie, the blood. And I killed her,' he sobbed. 'I - I just turned a corner. I, I had the wheel in my hands. I was turning the wheel with both hands. She just stepped out in front of me. I didn't have time to brake. I swear to you Girlie, she just stepped out in front of the lorry.' He repeated it over and over again, whilst Mama, as though being force-fed the grief of it, cried and cried.

'What about your job. Have you still got your job?' Mama asked, eyes tearing out of her head.

'They won't allow me to work until after the court case, and that's if they let me off.'

'But Winston, what we going to live on till then? How will we pay the mortgage, the bills?'

He looked up for a moment at Mama, and then hung his head low again, knowing that what he was about to say would destroy her pride - that it would tear her apart.

'We got to get help from the Assistance Board. We got no choice.'

'Oh God! Not Assistance Board money!' she said holding his face so that he would look at her but he pulled away from the clasp of her hands.

'We got no choice Girlie. It's either that or we starve.'

We had all stopped eating. We were not hungry any more. Our bellies became filled with grief for the dead woman lying in a mortuary - crushed beyond recognition; the grief her family must be going through and the grieving of a soul so suddenly shocked out of its temple. Eventually the low sobbing began as we cried for ourselves, for our own family, for what we were about to go through. Instinctively we knew a heavy price would have to be paid for such a great loss.

The image of the woman's blood-spattered body haunted Dada every day from thereon. In his dreams at night, his mind was plagued with the image of the woman's lifeless body twisted awkwardly underneath the lorry, and him, staring down at her. Warm smarting blood ran past his shoes, escaping into the nearby gutter on the street. Expressions of shock and terror reigned on the faces of those, chosen by fate to be witnesses. Slowly, an unrecognisable, smiling face, all smashed and bloody came forth from the crowd. Then a long bony forefinger belonging to an old hand beckoned from beyond the grave. She called to him whenever he closed his eyes, tormenting him night after night, forcing him to relive that ill-fated day - slowly driving him out of his mind over and over again. With cold sweat washing his body, he screamed out in terror, waking from his nightmares, only to find that they were his reality. Mama was the one who soothed his pained cries; pieced together his broken nights and hushed him back to bed so that his troubled mind would at least have some respite from the onslaught of his conscience.

One morning not too long after the inquest, he arose bright and early, without prompting or anything.

'Where you going Pa Daidee? enquired Mama, curiously.

'Funeral.'

'Funeral! You crazy? Her family just lost a mother, a sister, a grandmother; they will kill you.'

'You don't have to remind me. Girlie I know you don't understand but it's something I have to do.'

And he did it. He showed up at the dead woman's funeral, making sure to stand well back, as an onlooker. From afar, he watched the sombre picture of grieving family and friends, gathered at the graveside in the pouring rain. Then suddenly a figure in black beckoned to him; and then made its way over to him. One of the mourners, a woman, had coaxed him over to join the others. Holding his head low in shame and despair, his shoulders heaved as he cried. After the burial, the woman who had led him over to the graveside introduced herself to him.

'I know who you are,' she said looking him square in the eyes, but he could not bring himself to look at her.

'I'm Doreen - the daughter of the woman you killed. She was my mother.'

'I'm sorry, I'm so sorry,' he cried, uncaring of the fact that the other mourners were now looking in his direction.

'These,' she continued, 'are my two sisters and my brother. We're a close family.'

It appears they all knew who he was. Everything about him told them of his guilt and suffering. Deliberately, he had put himself at their mercy, inviting retribution for his crime, yet surprisingly, they did not try to attack or kill him, as he thought they might. In turn, they questioned him extensively for answers that would lay their own minds at rest. They listened intently to his tearful account and then, courageously, they comforted him with kind, forgiving hands and words.

'We don't know exactly what must have been going through mother's head at the time,' said the eldest daughter, 'but what we do know is that she just couldn't live without her husband. Daddy died four months ago. She lost the will to live back then.'

This was truly a humbling experience for Dada but it did not make him feel any better. In fact, it made him feel worse. Nevertheless, what it taught him was an invaluable lesson of bravery, love and understanding. They might have forgiven him for aiding and abetting death, in snatching their mother from them, but Dada could not forgive himself.

The deaths of first his father Pinto and now of this woman, left only emptiness inside him, which he filled with anger, resentment and plenty of liquor. As he drank heavily, to try to drown out his pain, we humoured him whenever he came home. We were eager to please because his mood was so explosive, so volatile it terrified us.

'Shall I run the bath for you Dada' or 'Are you ready to eat yet Dada?'

'You see your grandfather Pinto - my father; let me tell you about Pinto,' he'd start saying, before breaking down into a drunken heap, 'he was the greatest man who ever lived on this Earth.'

For the first time we comforted him, putting our arms about his shoulders telling, him that his beloved father was in heaven and that death was not the end. But all those tender moments are so easily tossed aside and forgotten.

Life is one big weather system, susceptible to rapid and instantaneous change.

On a beautiful warm May day, Mama was sitting in the settee in the kitchen, trying to recuperate after washing hoards of clothes and browning chicken for Sunday dinner. The backyard door was wide open. Bright golden sunlight poured in with a cool tantalizing breeze, lifting everyone's mood and spirits to a playful tone. Us kids ran inside to pester Mama with childish questions. To catch our breath, we cuddled up on the settee next to her.

'One day we'll all go to Jamaica. I'll take you all to see Aunt Mary. She going be so glad to see you all.'

'How will we get there?' I asked, joyful that she was still holding on to the threads of that dream.

'We're going to travel in style, by plane; we'll have plenty of money, enough to help Aunt Mary and all her children; enough to build a big beautiful house for ourselves, on a hill overlooking the sea.' Mama's eyes lit up, her face set in a fixed dreamy smile as she relived the vision of her dreams for a moment. We lived it too; imagining ourselves breathing in the sweet air, running around the perimeters of that huge beautiful house, enveloped in the warmth and vibrant colours of Jamaica; that far away land we all dreamt about seeing. The only thing more beautiful was a dream that was born into reality. Aspirations of our most cherished hopes were some way off from that point but what happened next would alter the images in our heads forever.

Cousin Enid breezed in like a hurricane with news of the third death, the last in this sequence of three.

'You kids go outside and play, I need to speak to Girlie on a serious matter.'

Slowly we edged outside, looking back forlornly at Mama. If this was bad news then we wanted Enid to keep it to herself. Failing that, we wanted to share the weight of any heartbreak or misfortune intended for Mama. She was not strong enough to carry it on her own.

'Go out in the backyard and play!' shouted Cousin Enid, shooing us outside.

Outside I crouched down beside the open kitchen window and listened.

'Is what Enid?' asked Mama.

Cousin Enid stood there shaking her head. 'Girlie, I get a telegram from Jamaica.'

'From who? What does it say?' asked Mama sitting up in her seat.

'I've had it for a week now,' said Enid. 'I was too scared to bring to you any sooner.'

'Read it to me Enid,' said Mama despondently. However, Cousin Enid did not read from the telegram. She came over to Mama and clasped her hands.

'Girlie, it's bad news, and I know you going to take it badly. Aunt Mary ...'

'No! No! No! Oh God no, not Aunt Mary, not Aunt Mary,' screamed Mama, jumping up from her seat, to make irrational ubiquitous movements around the kitchen. On hearing the commotion Dada came out from the sitting room and he and Cousin Enid were both holding Mama up, trying to put her onto the settee, as she was now hysterical.

'I was going back to Jamaica for her. I never forgot her; I was always going to go back for her. We were all supposed to be together.' She cried for a while, allowing Cousin Enid to hold her, and Dada to pat her back feebly. Then she wiped her face with the end of her apron, and shrugged her shoulders to focus directly at the messenger of such disastrous news.

'Tell me Enid,' said Mama struggling to control her emotions, 'how did she die?'

An eerie silence descended on Cousin Enid. Dada scratched his head, at a loss for what to do or say. That question went unanswered and so it was repeated again.

'I said, how did she die? I need to know.' suddenly, Mama looked ready to rip Cousin Enid to shreds if she did not divulge this vital piece of information.

Cousin Enid cleared her throat. 'They said, - they said the duppies came to take her away.'

'Enid tell me the truth, tell me right now or I'm going to go mad and I won't be responsible for what I do.'

'I got the telegram last week, but yesterday I get a letter from your brother James. He said Massah Ronnie come home drunk and started beating Aunt Mary and..., well, to what he is telling me, Ronnie give her a blow to the head causing her to fall and hit her head on the table. She died instantly Girlie. Same night he buried her right there on the land, in the corner of the backyard - you know the corner I mean.'

I could not believe my ears. Aunt Mary, my grandmother, had been murdered in her house, by her common-law husband. There had been no investigation, no trial; in fact, Massah Ronnie would get away scot-free. We heard that he had laid her out on an old white sheet in the back room that night and under the cover of darkness, Massah Ronnie had worked the remaining liquor out of his system by digging her grave and burying her. The next morning, he told people she died because the duppies had taken her spirit away. Mama was now sick with grief.

The courts found Dada Guilty of driving without due care and attention and banned him from driving for ten years. His driver's licence was taken away and to top it all he lost his job. He did not feel bad about the driving restrictions for he decided after the accident that he could never get behind the wheel of any vehicle ever again. Being the breadwinner had been in vain for now his life was in ruins. He concluded at the end of the court case, that as long as he lived, he would never again work for someone else. He could not see the point of building himself back up again so he just gave up. He took to the streets for acceptance - at least he still had his life and he intended to enjoy it at whatever cost.

The benefit from the Assistance Board started to arrive. It was posted directly to Dada and only he was allowed to open the letters. He called me to read what he was unable to decode and as I got to the juicy bits of information, he snatched it from my hands. Mama got fifteen pounds a week, to pay the bills and to feed a family of eight, after which Dada hit the streets to seek out friends and acquaintances. Drinking heavily, he tried to drown out his pain by downing copious amounts of neat spirits. We humoured him when he came home. We were eager to please because his mood was so volatile, teetering on explosive and that terrified us - he could go off at any time, so we became peacekeepers when he was around. Anything to keep him calm and happy but he was a stranger to us. We couldn't figure him out.

During that, time there were many tears and many visits from Cousin Enid. When she came for an update on how the court case had gone, she had only one word to say for Dada.

'Reaction!' to her it was divine justice for all the sins he had committed.

'Enid that's not fair, he's going through a really bad time, in fact we all are,' said Mama.

'Like I said to you, reaction take him. Him too wicked sah, him bring it on himself.'

'Look around you; we're all suffering in here. We have to pay the mortgage on the house or they will throw us all onto the streets and what little is left I can barely feed the children with, much less clothe them. In all my years Enid, I never think I'd sink so low as to take handouts from the Assistance Board. I still can't believe this is all happening.' she burst into tears.

Mama cried as she signed the papers for us to receive free school meals. The shame of it alone nearly killed her. She cried for days, just like she was crying now.

'Girlie you know what you need to do, you have to leave him,' Cousin Enid told her. Only you can make it all stop.'

'To tell the truth, I don't know if I got the strength to run no more Enid. You seen it for yourself. I run, he finds me and brings me back to this hellhole. What's the point? Anyway I couldn't run out on him now. He's my husband, he needs me.'

'Well seeing as you not going anywhere, in the meantime, I've got a proposition for you. It will earn you money so I hope you not too tired for that. I need you to look after my children during the six weeks holiday and my tenant Mrs Bailey, she needs someone to look after her two boys. Do you think you can do it?'

Mama took on Cousin Enid's four children and Mrs Bailey's two boys, on top of her own six children. She convinced them that she could handle all the children. She needed the money and they needed someone to take care of the kids during the summer holidays. Altogether there were twelve children in that house. Poor Mama, was rushed off her feet from six o'clock in the morning to six o'clock at night. As you can imagine twelve kids can cause a lot of damage to one house.

Someone found an old broken cup deep in the soil of the backyard. Inspired by films on telly about pirates and buried treasure, we dug holes, deep enough to twist the ankles of the younger toddlers.

'When I catch hold of you, I'm going to wop your tail,' Mama shouted after us, with the belt doubled in two. We didn't mean any harm. Thought if we found some buried treasure then we would be rich and all our troubles would be over.

There was never any rest for Mama. Childminding was never going to be straightforward with twelve children. Some kids are harder work than others. Everybody was in the kitchen getting ready to eat. I went upstairs to call my cousin Janice down for dinner, but she just lay there on the bed, eyes wide open, not saying a word.

'Mama I called Janice down for dinner but she won't even talk, she's just staring at me.

'Quick! Cousin Girlie,' said Yvette, the oldest of Cousin Enid's children, 'Janice is having a fit.'

First Yvette then Mama rushed upstairs, with all us kids following behind. Janice lay there, shaking violently and groaning. We had never seen anything like this before and that made it all the more alarming. Janice had epilepsy and Mama was at a loss for what to do.

'What does Enid do to bring her out of it?' Mama asked, panicking at the sight of Janice's eyes rolling back into her head.

'She puts a stick in her mouth to hold her tongue down, and then she sprinkles water on her face.'

Mama placed the stick Yvette had found in the backyard between Janice's teeth, and sprinkled water on her face from a jug until, eventually, Janice came round, exhausted and dazed. What a relief that was, and quite eye-opening for us as we were not allowed to have any illnesses of any kind. Janice, however, was not by any means the only child with health needs to worry about. Mrs Bailey's oldest boy Malcolm had chronic asthma and her youngest son Daniel was nothing short of a wild animal. Crying and screaming he lunged at anyone who came too close. If his little fingers caught hold of you, he would claw and bite his victim until they bled. We all bore the scars on our faces, legs and arms, so at the end of her tether, Mama marched him home one evening, halfway through the holidays, vexed at his latest attack on the children. She could not manage him any more and she was going to tell Mrs Bailey. She and Cousin Enid had complained to Mrs Bailey on numerous occasions, but all she did was cry and apologise, as she was doing now because she did not know what else to do. Bringing up her two children on her own was tough and anyone could see that she was struggling.

'I want you to use this,' she said after a while, handing Mama a long piece of material. 'Tie him to the foot of the bed; then he won't be able to hurt no one.'

'I'm sorry, I can't do that to a child,' exclaimed Mama, quite aghast.

'I'm his mother and I'm telling you to do that, because if you don't, then I will lose my job; I will lose the room I'm renting from Enid because I won't be able to pay her no more. You got to help me or I'll lose everything,' she sobbed, appealing to Mama's good nature.

Mama didn't have the heart to leave this woman high and dry. She admired something about her, the fact that when her marriage had turned ugly, she had had the guts to pick up her two kids and run.

So Mama took the piece of material from Mrs Bailey and tied Daniel to the bed-foot to stop him attacking the other children, then she briefed everyone not go anywhere within the circumference of the piece of material that bound him, for their own safety. But Daniel was like Samson and at times he broke free which caused all kinds of mayhem.

The following evening Massah Stanley came home the same time as usual. Half past five on the dot, in time to catch the tail end of the children before they were taken home. Trying to get to his room, he held his arms in the air scornfully, as children ran about him laughing and squealing. Cussing bad words all the way to his room, he emerged with silver tray and fine china to make his usual cup of tea. On his way back upstairs, waiting children jumped out of dark corners to frighten the life out of him.

'Pow! Pow! Pow! Pow! You're dead!' they shouted, pointing their makeshift guns at him; two sticks bound together with string.

'Damn kids! All you women know how to do is to breed like fucking flies.'

He said it in Mama's earshot as it was intended for her ears.

'I told you before, this is my house and I want you out. We need the space, me and my six kids.'

'And I told you I'm not going anywhere. I'm a tenant and tenants have rights.'

He talked to Mama as though she was nothing at all and gloated because he could get away with it. He always complained to Dada before Mama could get to him and being a man, Dada was more inclined to take Massah Stanley's view.

Six weeks was an awful long time with nothing to do. Things got broken by accident and Mama always covered up for us when Dada came home.

'No it wasn't the kids; it just slipped out of my hand.'

'I hope you're not lying to me,' he'd say to Mama, eying us up and down suspiciously.

Boredom leads to antics, most of which Mama dealt with herself but one day towards the end of the holidays, boredom came calling again.

'The last one on the bed stinks!' I called and there was a rush to get upstairs into the back bedroom. Seven of us jumped on the bed and at once there came a loud crashing sound. A corner of the bed protruded down into the kitchen ceiling. This was deadly serious. There would definitely be a beating in store for us now. We ran down to the kitchen crying, trying to explain.

'I can't hide this one from your father. He's going to go mad when he sees it.'

We waited solemnly quiet for the inevitable and like a promise, we got it when he drew his belt to beat everyone, even though Mama told him the floorboards were rotting.

For days that big hole in the kitchen ceiling looked down on everyone like a big black eye. Sick of the sight of it, Mama nagged and pleaded with Dada to allow her to get someone in to do the job.

'I need the money to pay someone to fix it,' she says.

But Dada, determined not to part with any cash, did the most extraordinary thing ever. In all our years, we had never seen him so much as lift a hammer or even a screwdriver for that matter, but now he got the ladder out and opened it into standing position, directly underneath the hole in the kitchen ceiling. We stood there in disbelief, while silence fell upon us, holding the ladder as we had been instructed. Wondering what had come over him, we watched in amazement as he mounted the steps of the ladder for the first time. History was being made before our eyes.

'You're almost there Dada,' we said, giving him encouragement as he awkwardly mounted each step. 'Almost there. Just one more step to go.'

But right up there on the top tread of the ladder, his foot slipped. Quickly, we let go of the ladder and stood aside, to give his large frame room for a speedy descent - well there was no use everyone getting hurt now was there? He ended up at the bottom in a disgraceful, crumpled heap.

'Oh Girlie! Girlie my back! my back!'

To stop ourselves from laughing we tried not to look at each other, or at Dada. We breathed deeply through our mouths, knowing that if any of us dared to laugh out loud, we'd be laid up in a hospital bed somewhere, legs and arms in traction, probably sucking food through a straw.

'Are you alright Dada? I dared to ask, trying to sound concerned, which made everyone's breathing quicken to a cough or the clearing of a throat.

'I hope you're not laughing at me,' he warned, inspecting our faces - including Mama's. 'Anybody laugh, I beat them, you hear me?'

'Yes Dada,' we said, helping him to his feet and settling him onto the settee in the sitting room. That was the first and last time Dada ever attempted to do anything around the house. However he recovered enough to keep an appointment with the streets that night.

The next evening was in complete contrast to the previous one. We sat in the kitchen watching television and laughing together. We were totally relaxed and free although exhaustion and depression had driven Mama to seek solace in the sanctuary of her bedroom quite early on in the evening.

It was around seven when Dada came home drunk with his friend Donavon, whom he had been drinking with, and who in comparison to Dada appeared quite sober. The seemingly calm atmosphere changed the instant Dada stepped into the house. He was whispering to Donavon now, something about money. Disappearing into the sitting room, he emerged shortly with eyes blazing.

'I want to know who's taken my ring out of the sitting room. Which one of you was it?'

'We haven't touched your ring Dada. We don't know what ring you're talking about.'

'My ring! The one I left on the table! Find it! If I don't get my ring right now, I'm going to burn down this bomba claa't house with everybody in it. Look for my ring!'

Shaking with fear, we dropped to our knees, like soldiers on a battlefield who had taken a slug in the guts. Wounded with fear, we searched every nook, every crevice the ring could have possibly fallen into. We knew that Dada sometimes misplaced things, but still we searched with tears blurring our vision because there was little hope of finding his precious ring. Shocked by what he had seen, Donavon tried to make excuses to get away.

'Winston, it's all right, you don't have to give it to me now...'

'Shut up! You wait right there Donavon. They'll find it - you'll see.'

But we couldn't. Together we had searched the whole of the downstairs of the house, sobbing as we did so.

'We've looked everywhere Dada. We can't find it,' we cried hysterically.

But those words: 'we can't find it,' were fuel to a fire and as the flames of Dada's temper blazed out of control, we were struck with terror. My legs felt like jelly. Soon, they would not be able to support the weight of my body.

'I want my fucking ring,' he yelled, lifting an armchair above his head and throwing it across the room.

'Winston Leave it! Leave it man!' pleaded Donavon, holding him back, 'I can get it another time.'

But Dada flashed him off. He was madder than we've ever seen him. 'Get me the paraffin.'

'No!' we cried, now stricken with something worse than terror. 'Please Dada, Please don't do it, don't do it!'

But it was too late. Cussing and swearing Dada got the paraffin and began to sprinkle it over the kitchen floor. Seeing this, Donavon ran from the house. Pauline and me, we made for the door, but we were stopped in our tracks.

'Where you think you're going? Get back in here.'

This is it then, I thought. This is where we die. 'Please Dada, please don't do it.' we pleaded, 'we'll keep looking for the ring.' But he dipped a hand into the pocket of his jacket to produce a box of matches. The whole house was screaming, a loud, combined chord of fear; everyone that is, except Mama. It was not her turn to be terrorised tonight. She lay in her bed locked away in a darkened room, her mental health spiralling out of control.

Clovis and Glen, now, sixteen and seventeen - almost men, but not quite - heard the commotion. They were both standing in the doorway of the kitchen now, unable to take the screams anymore. Slowly but surely Dada was losing control of them. The sneering, hateful looks on their faces must have done something to Dada for he caught himself and what he had reduced us all to. Panting to compose himself, he left, slamming the door, muttering something about wanting his precious ring. Trembling, we sank back into the chairs for support. The relief of his departure made us cry and shake uncontrollably. Clovis and Glen comforted everybody.

'Don't worry, you lot. Stop your crying and remember this: we're all growing up, and one day, God willing, we'll all have the guts to stand up to him.' The truth in those words were a comfort. It seemed that our coming of age was the only weapon we would attain to fight Dada with.

The social support system was oblivious to our existence, so we supported each other, as best we could.

In the middle of the night when the house was quiet and still, Dada came home with a dog. He said this dog had followed him all the way home, so he claimed it, and we kept it; a welcome distraction from the turmoil of life.

In the morning we tried to decide what we were going to do with Rover. We were all there pondering on his purpose when Massah Stanley came whistling down the stairs and into the kitchen. We looked at each other, sideways. Something clicked in all our heads at exactly the same time. It had a way of doing that with us. I leaned across to whisper in Pauline's ear.

'What you all whispering about? Didn't your Mama ever tell you it's rude to whisper?

'Rude? Oh what, like when you cuss Mama down in front of us?' I said.

'Shut your mouth you, and don't talk to me like that before I speak to your father,' he sneered, pointing a finger at me in an aggressive manner. He didn't scare me at all, but Rover didn't like his tone and showed him by growling.

'If you set that dog on me,' he said nervously, staring Rover in the eye, 'I'm - I'm - going to tell your father.'

It appeared that Massah Stanley not only had an aversion to children but also to dogs.

'Dada won't believe you because we haven't had time to train him. We only got him last night, remember. If I was you,' I advised boldly, in the tone of bad boys from the Wild West, 'I'd pick up that tray and get going. Go on! Get out of here!'

'I'm going to make your father beat the lot of you for this, you watch and see,' said Massah Stanley, edging away, tray in hand, still annoying Rover with his sustained glare. With cups rattling on the tray he retreated out of the kitchen and up the stairs backwards. Out of curiosity, I slapped Rover's behind to see what would happen.

'Fetch! Rover, fetch!' and surprisingly, Rover charged up the stairs after Massah Stanley. The words 'Rass claa't!' followed by the sound of breaking china made us curl up with laughter. We loved Rover. He was a great dog, destined for great things.

Chapter Seven

Raggle Taggle Gypsy

It was in the early 1970s that we suddenly stopped being coloured girls, and coloured boys, and coloured people. Overnight, we miraculously become black people, and with the word 'black' came a new concept for us; a concept of pride, beauty and love of self. No longer did we look outwardly onto the world, hoping for positive messages of image and self-worth. We found them within, and we accepted and embraced them with open arms. Yep, black is beautiful. Mohammed Ali told us that before each of his boxing matches. His positive rhetoric was a tonic; an injection of love; and we tumbled down the stairs for a fix whenever he was on TV

'Quick! Run! Black people on the telly!' That's what we shouted whenever we saw a black face staring back at us from the screen, so rare was it that everybody in the house instantly dropped whatever it was they are doing, to gather round the TV for the momentous event. Once in a blue moon we saw people like Harry Belafonte or Sammy Davis Junior or Shirley Bassey, but we waited for news of Ali, and his next match, with bated breath. To us, he was everything - genuine, black and proud; he shouted it everywhere he went, and then backed it up with a successful win.

Yep, black is beautiful. At school, we used that statement like a protective shield to guard against those children who called us wogs, niggers, jungle bunnies, darkies and coons on a daily basis. Now we wore our hair in Afros, our halo of crowning glory. We dressed in tank tops and bell bottom trousers, and read literature on our heroes, Martin Luther king, Malcolm X, Angela Davis and Marcus Garvey; food for the soul and we plastered our bedroom walls with pictures of the Jackson Five. Despite all this positive rhetoric though, there was no sustenance for Mama's ailing spirit.

But like rows of corn, standing at different heights in the sun, we grew. Glen and Clovis had left school, Julia was at Woodberry Down Comprehensive, Douglas was in his final year at primary school and Pauline and I went to Clissold Park School. Mama was trying harder than ever to keep it together and had managed to secure a job at an old people's home, next door to our school.

It was a cold grey frosty morning; the kind of morning where you can see your breath in front of you. Pauline, Mama and me walked to school together, linking arms like school chums, with Mama in the middle. We stopped at the newsagent's to buy Polos, Cola cubes and cough candy before continuing on our journey, laughing and talking on the way. Instinctively we knew deep down inside that Mama was desperately unhappy, and beneath our laughter, so were we because it felt like she was with us but some unknown force was trying to pull her away. Before we parted, we hugged and kissed, making arrangements for later that day.

After school we walked the few yards or so to the old people's home on Clissold Road, and as always, Pauline and I braced ourselves for the entrance. As soon as we hit the door, we took in a huge gulp of air and held it before entering. It was pointless really because we knew that eventually, once inside, we would have to breathe out; and when we did so, the pungent smell of stale ever-lingering urine, mixed with cleaning fluids and air freshener, would stick right at the back of our throats. From the huge windows that faced the front of the building, wrinkled faces stared out with blank expressions, from comfy armchairs, which they had been placed in. Their eyes were wide open yet one could easily presume that the lights were on but no one was home. I wondered what was going through their minds. Were they living in the past and was the present an intrusion, a hindrance, or did they register the people who walked by every day? I concluded that this was not a happy home. It was too quiet and sombre a place, almost as though this home was all they had left of the world, the last stop at the end of a journey. It was like watching still life. Day after day, they were propped up by the window, waiting for that great big hand in the sky to reach down and pluck them, like ripe fruit at harvest time. After school we went there to wait for Mama and every day I couldn't wait for her shift to be over. We walked home together through the park; back to our own miserable home, our every step, collecting up the woes we had walked away from that morning.

'Whatever is done in the dark must come to light,' that's what Mama used to say, and boy was she right! Secrets, like a ship's compass, have a tendency to alter the course of lives when they get out.

On Friday morning Cousin Enid sent word requesting to see Mama as a matter of urgency. Mama spent the next few hours worrying what dreadful truth Enid had to reveal. She was under no misconception that it had something to do with her husband so when the time came, she took Glen with her for support.

'I think you had better sit down Girlie,' said Enid, morbidly serious, as soon as they had arrived.

'Well I am here now,' said Mama, putting on a brave face. 'Say what you got to say and get it out in the open.'

'I wanted to tell you a long time ago, but I couldn't bring myself to do it.'

'Tell me what? What is it that you've known about for so long?'

'You've had so much to cope with Girlie, I couldn't bear to overburden you with any more. You not going to take this very well but maybe it's what you need to make a fresh start.'

'Oh for heaven's sake Enid, stop beating about the bush and just tell me noh, you frightening me now.'

'You have to leave Winston,' she said after an eerie pause. Girlie, if you don't, he's going to drive you completely insane, I know it.'

'Tell me something I don't already know,' said Mama

Enid wrung her hands in her lap, hesitating to get the words out.

'He's got kids with other women. '

'Kids! How many children Enid?'

'Five that I know of.'

Mama shook her head. She was speechless. It was a good thing she was sitting down for she would surely have fainted had she been standing. She covered her mouth with her hand to hide the trembling of her lip, tears welling up in her eyes like springs. Her husband had been leading more than a double life.

'I hear that two of them are black, two are half caste and the other one is half Chinese,' continued Enid, 'It's common knowledge. A lot of people know about it and you know what people are like, they're chatting you behind your back. I couldn't hold it no more. I had to tell you for your own good Girlie.'

'You knew! All these years you knew, and you said nothing,' said Mama, angry because in her eyes, she had been betrayed. 'You sat with me, laughed with me, ate with me and you even comforted me when my spirit was low, and all that time you knew and you didn't tell me.' Mama got up to leave. She could hardly contain her rage.

'Girlie, the time wasn't right, you were…'

'What do you mean the time wasn't right? Right for who? Enid, I thought you loved me, but I was so obviously wrong.'

'It's because I love you, why I didn't tell you back then.'

'That's a damn blasted lie because if you love someone, you don't deceive them, you don't keep them in the dark.'

'And that's exactly what your husband is doing to you, when are you going to open your eyes?'

'You know what, I'm not listening to this. You and him are the same - cowardly and deceitful. You were the only person I could trust, more fool me for expecting any better from you. I will never forgive you for being disloyal to me. Never!' And with that, Mama headed out of the house; tears rolling down her cheeks and Glen, running behind, trying to keep up.

Mama had deleted Cousin Enid from her world. She decided then never to talk to her again from that day forth. An act of kindness or betrayal, this revelation had instantly transformed Enid into a scapegoat, who was left to carry all of Dada's sins. Mama blamed her solely, for not enlightening her with the power of truth. What if she had been armed with the truth? Would her life have turned out any different or would the truth have set her free to follow her dreams and map out her own destiny?

It was truly harrowing to watch as Mama's health continued to decline. Us kids were all she had left in the world. We could see what was happening, but being bound by fear, we were helpless to do anything to rescue Mama's mind from her pain and from herself. That guilt would eat away at our hearts forever.

Noticeably ill, Mama had to stop work. Her employers at the old people's home refused to allow her to continue in her present post as a domestic. In light of her fraying sanity, all the friends she made at work, women whom she could have a friendly chat with in the street and the few whom she had invited into her home - it was as though they had all mysteriously disappeared off the face of the earth. Because of Mama's erratic mind, and the fixed look of anger on her face, no one came calling to visit her any more, afraid of what she might do or say next; afraid of what they didn't know or understand, afraid because they too did not know how to help. Loneliness became Mama's best friend. Seeking solace, she journeyed deep within herself to a place where she was excused from the rigorous trials and responsibilities of life. She had no one to tell her troubles to, so at first she started talking quietly to her inner self. But as time went by, her thoughts were invaded by ghosts from her past and she would have blazing rows with them. She had no qualms about giving them a good piece of her mind, at the top of her voice. In that secret place of hers, she found the strength to turn the tables on her husband, to laugh in his face at his attempts to terrorise her, and to give him a spoonful or two of his own bitter medicine. However, she continued to torture herself by going through Dada's pockets at every opportunity, still looking for confirmation that would corroborate his total disregard of her. I watched as her hands fumbled deep in his pockets and this time she pulled out a folded Valentine's card to reveal a message of undying love. Mama left it out deliberately to show Dada that she may be mad, but she knew exactly what was going on.

'Did you take this out of my pocket?'

'What that piece of rubbish. I was just about to dump it.'

'How many times do I need to tell you, don't go through my pockets? How many times? You have no right.'

'I'm your wife, I have every right,' said Mama standing up to him.

'Call yourself a wife; look at you,' he said looking down at her with contempt. 'You don't even cook for me no more. I've had to do that myself. In fact I cook for you but you won't eat it.'

'That's because you trying to kill me! I know how you're thinking. You want me out of the way,' accused Mama.

'That's right, so don't touch anything that belongs to me, you hear me, and keep out of my pockets.'

'We're back to that stupid piece of rubbish I found in your pocket. Why don't you frame it, or better still put it up on the mantelpiece so everyone can get a good look at it and see you for the nasty, no-shame dog that you are.'

'You're sick you know. You're not well. That's the only reason you talking to me like that. If you took your tablets you'd know better,' said Dada, pacing up and down, in between putting on a fresh change of clothes. 'I don't know how much more of this I can take,' he said, playing the victim, as he so often did, 'but I think you trying to drive *me* mad,' he declared.

'Well why don't *you* take the tablets then?' said Mama, bold as can be.

'You keep pushing me like this and I'm going to send you right back to that mad house.'

'You're too late,' laughed Mama wildly, 'I'm already there. This is the mad house. Didn't nobody tell you?'

He walked away as he always did and home life continued to deteriorate, dragging everyone living in Number 27 into that downward spiral of discontent.

The marital bed was no longer sacred, so night after night, Mama locked her husband out of the room they had once shared, forcing him to sleep on the settee in the sitting room. She could no longer bear to have him lying beside her; knowing what lay beneath the innocence his face took on as he slept, for that picture was a lie.

Suspicion and mistrust of all those around ruled supreme. It intensified the arguments between her and Massah Stanley, which became more frequent. Mama couldn't bear the sight of him. She was sure he, like her husband, was in on the conspiracy to poison her - to get her out of the way. If she bought meat from the butcher's, hours later, when she was ready to cook it, she'd say that it had been switched and that someone had replaced it with human flesh. As a result her weight plummeted to dangerous levels. She could hear Massah Stanley now, on his way to the kitchen, so she raced in there after him, refusing to vacate her own kitchen to allow him to cook in peace.

'So what? You going to stand there and watch me make a pot of tea?'

'You think I don't know what's going on.'

'Oh here it comes. Why, what is it now?'

'You've been poisoning my food. I see you, and I want you out of my house.'

'I don't know why Winston puts up with you,' said Massah Stanley, pouring boiling water from the kettle into the teapot, 'You're breaking your family apart.'

'You're a fine one to talk about breaking families apart.'

'What do you mean by that?'

'I mean wasn't it you who breed your wife and her best friend and then walked out on the both of them?'

'Shut your mouth, you mad bitch. You don't know what you talking about.'

'Your wife told me years ago, so save your breath for someone who's going to believe you.'

Clovis walked into the kitchen just then, catching Massah Stanley unaware.

'I thought I told you not to talk to my Mama like that. I will not have you disrespecting her in her own house.'

'You're just a bwoy to me. Move out of my way,' said Massah Stanley, tray in hand.'

'I might be a boy to you but I'll bust your head open same way, try me if you feel you is a bad man.'

'I'm going to speak to your father when he come home.'

'You're pathetic you are, paying next to nothing for the best room in the house. Why don't you do us all a favour; pack up your things and leave. Get out man!'

'I'm not going anywhere and none of you are going to drive me out of my home,'

'Yeh! Well I'm going to make your life hell in here until you do, you watch.'

The twins (Mrs Green and Mrs Andrews) were like the Paparazzi, never tiring of accosting us kids whenever we left the house. They caught Pauline and me again now, just outside. We walked on, away from the house because we expected that they would toddle after us for a while, and just in case Mama was listening by the window. She didn't need to hear the nasty things people were saying about our family.

'I see your father last week,' Mrs Green declared, while hastily trying to keep up with our quick pace.

'Did you?' I asked, showing no interest at all in what they had to say. I knew they were itching to reveal another slice of what they considered to be juicy gossip.

'Yes. You're not going to believe it, he was chatting up a young nineteen year old girl,' said Mrs Andrews.

'Old enough to be his daughter,' piped up Mrs Green.

'He should be ashamed of himself, bringing shame on your family like that, and another thing...'

'I'm sorry we've got to go,' I interrupted, quickening my pace to get away from them, 'we'll be late for school.

'I'll tell you next time then: as a matter of fact, why don't you come by later and we'll talk then.'

'Can't,' I called back, 'we got homework and chores to do.'

They would stop at nothing to try and find out what was happening inside our home; to hear it straight from the horse's mouth, so to speak, but we gave them nothing. Things were bad enough, people whispering and laughing at us. We just wanted it all to stop.

School though, was a safe haven. A delightful place of normality and routine; a place where the mind and body was nourished to grow. However, our minds were too full of troubles to soak up the education given to us; concentrating was hard work. Free school dinners was the only assured meal we had to look forward to each day. Without them, we would have starved for sure. There we grew up into young teenagers, old enough to have a crush on a good-looking boy - too poor and lacking in experience or confidence to do anything about it. It took me two years to realise that I could trust Miss Davis, my English teacher. She supported me, talked with me after class, but did not intrude on my family nor did she send the authorities round because she knew that separation would have killed us all for sure. She was the only somebody I could trust outside of my family. One day, she gave me a handful of leaflets about benefits and welfare funds she said Mama was entitled to.

When I got home from school there was usually a fire raging in the backyard or the remnants of one, still smouldering. It was so commonplace that sometimes, we even warmed our hands by it on cold days. Over a period of time, Mama had burnt most of the furniture, photographs, including those of her children and most of what few clothes we had left. Not wanting to go naked, we had even, on occasions attempted to pull clothing from the fire to stamp out the flames, while Mama stood there having a hysterical belly laugh at us. She threw the leaflets my teacher gave me on top of the flames. She burnt things belonging to everyone except Dada. The much treasured clothes in his elaborate wardrobe remained untouched due to fear. But then, one day he pushed Mama too far over that edge. He produced a padded card some woman had given him for his birthday, with a big red heart on the front. It said: 'To the one I love,' in big gold lettering, and he put it neatly in the centre of the mantelpiece for everyone to see.

'I don't want no one to touch it, right?' he warned

Mama walked past and kissed her teeth, pretending that she was not hurt, although inside, a silent turmoil raged. I couldn't believe he could be so cold and callous as to do that. I sneaked a look inside to see who it was from when he left the room.

"To my darling sweetheart, Winston. Happy birthday to the one I love. Penny." A nauseas feeling worked its way into the pit my stomach then. How could he? How could she? I wondered what kind of woman Penny was, to be giving my daddy, a married man, that kind of card.

'Hey Girlie,' he said admiring himself in the long mirror in the passage, 'your husband's a pretty man, aint he? How do I look?' He made a playful grab for her, trying to cuddle her in a teasing way.

'Take your hands off me. Don't touch me. Whatever love I had for you is dead, dead, dead,' spat Mama, untangling herself from him.

He laughed. 'I know you still want me. I can tell.' He was so sure of himself.

Mama watched for a while as he bounced up the road on that air of confidence, before finally slamming the door after him. After she had locked herself away in her room I sat outside it on the top stair. She cried for a long time that night and there was nothing I or anyone could do to ease her miserable suffering.

The next day she emerged to tackle the housework, trying to keep herself busy. She looked a sorry sight on her knees, putting her back into scrubbing the kitchen floor, although it did not need scrubbing.

'Wicked, dog-hearted, cheating, bastard! You're going to get your comeuppance, you're going to suffer,' she cursed angrily with each movement of the scrubbing brush. She personally wanted to bring about Dada's suffering. She needed to feel some satisfaction from humiliating him, so she racked her brains for ways of making her husband a laughing stock in front of those who knew him well, to expose *him* as a fool, but the plan eluded her as she scrubbed away at the floor.

Not long after, there came a low, distinct yet persistent knocking at the door. Mama dried her hands to answer it. Standing on the doorstep was the 'Ragga- Ragga' woman. That's what we knew them as - the people who went around collecting old rags.

'Hello love, hope you're not too busy.'

'Well I am,' said Mama, ready to slam the door but this woman was persistent, moving forward all the time.

'You got any old rags you want to get rid of?' the old woman, craning her neck to peep around the thin slice of open door.

'No! No rags today,' barked Mama, practically slamming the door in the woman's face now, to walk back to the kitchen. However, when, halfway there, she stopped in her tracks. Quickly she did a U-turn, opened the front door and said, 'Wait a minute, maybe the both of us can help each other today.'

Unseen by us in the next room, Mama swung open Dada's large mahogany wardrobe and emptied it of clothes, leaving only the few items that he had not worn for ages because either they had gone out of fashion or he had grown out of them.

'Here you go, these are nothing but rags, you're welcome to them,' said Mama, handing the Ragga-Ragga woman a huge pile of clothes containing several suits belonging to Dada.

'Oh my, that's very generous of you, very generous,' she said piling everything onto the wooden cart she pushed down the middle of the street. 'God bless you love.'

'I've got plenty more where that came from so make sure you call again,' Mama shouted after her. 'I'll even collect the rest from the dry cleaners for you.'

'Who was that Mama?' we asked after hearing the front door close.

'Just the Ragga-Ragga woman.' But Mama had a spring in her step and a cunning smile on her face. Something was wrong. Drastically wrong.

'Did you give her anything?' I asked growing increasingly worried by her outlandish behaviour. 'Are you listening to me Mama, I said did you give her anything?'

'Just some old rags in your father's wardrobe.'

'Oh my God! You gave her Dada's clothes! Why? Why?' screamed Pauline.

'I told you, it was rubbish,' said Mama more serious than before.

'But he's going to kill you, he's going to kill us all,' declared Pauline panicking.

'Don't tell me what to do in my own house!' shouted Mama.

She was getting angry again, so not wanting the situation to escalate further, we left her alone. There would most certainly be an eruption and all we could do was to wait it out.

First the gate rattled, then came frightened whispers of; 'Dada's home! Dada's home!'

Mama pottered about, still high on her audacious act, as though nothing had happened. Hardly daring to breathe, we watched as Dada took off his jacket and walked into the bedroom to hang it up - then all hell broke loose.

'No! No! No! Oh Christ Almighty God! Not my clothes - not my lovely beautiful clothes. I'm going to kill her,' he said bounding out of the room into the passageway to where Mama was.

'What have you done with all my clothes? If you burnt them...'

'I haven't burnt your clothes,' said Mama fearlessly. She was amazingly calm and confident. Pushed too far over the edge, it was strange now how her madness had evaporated to nothing, all the fear, intimidation and bullying tactics Dada had used to brainwash her into a quiet obedient wife. Madness, I concluded, wasn't all-bad.

'Well, where is it then?' demanded Dada, momentarily fooled into thinking that his clothes had been given a reprieve; that they were safely tucked away somewhere close to hand. A wicked smile spread across Mama's face.

'I gave them to the Ragga Ragga woman.'

'You did what?' screamed Dada, in fit of fury.

'I said,' laughed Mama, now hardly able to control her hysteria because his distress had tickled her so, 'I gave it to the Ragga Ragga woman.'

In surprised silence, I looked first from Mama and then to Dada, as though watching a game of tennis, waiting for what was to happen next.

'You're not laughing now are you? she said boldly.

His eyes glazed over. Repeatedly he clenched and unclenched his fists.

'You know what? He said after a long pause, 'you're too sick to beat.'

'Beat who?' said Mama. 'You ever put your hands on me again and I'll run a knife up under you while you sleeping.'

The effect of those words reaching Dada's ears caused him to swallow hard and to touch his stomach simultaneously.

Mama wasn't laughing any more. She was deadly serious, and that scared him to the core. The painful memory of being stabbed once before was enough for him to back off, but not without the final word.

'I'm going to get Dr Glassman to come take a look at you next week. You're dangerous.'

It's not good to be gluttonous, because once greed has set in, one loses the ability to know when to stop, to know that one spell of good fortune may just be random luck; a one off, never to be drawn on again experience.

Only three days had passed since Dada lost all his best suits to the Ragga-Ragga woman and nothing hurt him more deeply than the thought that somewhere, someone, was sporting his suits, without the necessary style or debonair personality needed to carry it off. That anger had not subsided in the least during the three days that had elapsed. Like an ever-burning lake of negative emotion, it continued to bubble up inside him.

Wondering around the house in his underpants and vest, he first laid out the mish-mash of clothes he intended to wear that day, before going into the bathroom for a shave. He had only managed to shave half his face when there came a low persistent tapping at the front door. Dada came out of the bathroom, razor-sack in hand, and was now standing at the top of the stairs trying to see who it could be. When I opened the door I thought my eyes were deceiving me.

'Hello love. Got any old rags you don't want?'

My God, it was the old Ragga-Ragga woman again. I was terrified, not of her, but for her. She must leave this instant for her own safety. Shaking my head, I mouthed the words 'Go! You got to go.' I even tried to close the door on her, but she just kept pushing forward.

'What was that you said love?'

Again I mouth the word 'go,' with my eyes on stalks, aware of footsteps edging closer.

'Melanie open the door a little wider, let me see who it is,' said Dada, taking slow predatory steps down the stairs towards the door.

'I was here on Friday,' continued the old woman, 'and this lovely woman gave me a load of suits. Wonderful they were. I got rid of the lot the same day.'

At that revelation Dada was shaking with rage. 'It's you ain't it?' he said. 'It's you who Girlie give all my suits to, and … and, you have the nerve to come back for more! You're madder than my wife! I'm going to fucking kill you!'

I don't know what tonic that old lady was on, but judging by her swift, agile movements, she must have been taking a daily dose of some kind of potent pick-me-up for she darted out into the street to where she had left her cart. She picked it up and took off up the middle of the road at the speed of light, with Dada in hot pursuit behind - still wearing only his vest, underpants, with half of his face covered in shaving foam. We were so shocked; we did not know whether to laugh or cry. He chased the old lady halfway down the road, past Mrs Andrews and Mrs Green and past Mr Jones at number 58, who was trimming his hedge. Halfway up the road, Dada finally gave up the chase. The old Ragga-Ragga woman was just too quick for him.

'Knock on any door you want,' he shouts after her, 'but don't fucking knock on mine! You come back round here again and I'm going to murder you! You hear me? Murder you!'

Heading back towards home, Dada realised then that he hardly had any clothes on. Mr Jones had stopped trimming his hedge and stood there staring with mouth and shears wide open.

'What you looking at eh? I said what you looking at? Trim that hedge! Trim it!' threatened Dada. Mr Jones did as he was told and soon the shears moved at manic speed, damaging the hedge, because fear had fixed his eyes firmly on Dada and not on the task at hand.

Then Dada walked towards Mrs Andrews and Mrs Green who were now at the front of their house.

'Lord have mercy!' said Mrs Andrews. 'I feel faint.'

'Sister shut your eyes,' said Mrs Green, covering her sister's eyes with her hands, whilst her eyes were firmly fixed on Dada.

'Good morning ladies,' said Dada, able to style out the most embarrassing of moments.

Chapter Eight

Love Without Compassion

....

It was obvious that Dada had found a new love interest, for he disappeared for days, leaving no money or food in the dilapidated house, which was slowly crumbling around us. Mama was too ill and Dada, well, he just didn't have the time to care. When it rained, the roof leaked in various places. There is no furniture in the sitting room to sit on, because Mama had by now burnt our lucky settee in an attempt to drive her husband away, so we sat on the bare floorboards to watch television; because Mama had also pulled up and burnt the carpets. Around the house, wallpaper still bearing the signature of young children, peeled from the walls. The faulty gas cooker in the kitchen slowly released gas into the air; not enough to kill, but just enough to threaten our senses with its presence. We had no choice but to light the rings to keep warm or occasionally to cook on. We could not afford to call out the gas board because we knew they would immediately switch off the gas supply and stick a health warning across the appliance. We would have to pay out money we did not have, to put things right before the gas could even be turned back on again. We had already been there once or twice before and so we risked our lives because we did not have the money not to and because no one cared. Taking a bath in our house was therefore a tactical exercise. You could easily lose your eyebrows or indeed your life, if you did not know how to run the bath in our house. The old geezer on the bathroom wall had, over the years, worked its way loose. A huge, hideous, monstrosity, it sat there, grinning down at us, terrorizing anyone who entered the bathroom with ambitions of using the hot water. We had no choice but to find a way around the problem and in time, we discovered the process. First, you had to turn on the hot water tap, and then run for your life, remembering to close the bathroom door behind you so as not to get caught up in a mini explosion. Once I made the mistake of standing in the doorway to observe, yards from the geezer, to wait until it was safe to go in - what a mistake. Yellow flames shot out from the boiler, followed by a loud bang, and no word of a lie; that huge flame, that ball of fire, came right over to greet me. It kissed me softly on the forehead before disappearing back into the geezer as if something or someone had dragged it back in. It took me a while, I can tell you, before I could move my legs again and longer still, for my eyebrows to grow back. Just about everything and everyone was falling apart in Number 27, including our physical and emotional health.

With nothing in the house to eat, Mama sent us out to look for Dada. We searched all his old haunts to no avail on that day, and the next day, and the day after that. Mama sent us up to Mr Adebayo's shop to trust some food on credit and to tell him that she would pay him back on Friday. Mr. Adebayo frowned at first, but then he allowed us to fill two big bags with groceries. Of course, his kind generosity had trapped us in a vicious circle of trusting food from him, sometimes up to three times a week and struggling to pay for it at the end of the week out of the thirty-five pounds Dada now gave to keep a family of eight for a fortnight. Nowadays we expected to see him roughly every two to three days, as he chose not to come home to his family every night. He always turned up whenever he was ready to collect and cash the giro cheque, but always, he took his time to return with the housekeeping. We saw him sometimes on our way home from school just on his way to the post office, talking and laughing with people as though everything at home was fine. He chose also to disregard the fact that his wife was ill; and that his children might be cold and hungry. I wanted to take hold of him by the lapels of his jacket and give him an almighty good shaking so that he could see what he was doing to us.

In my heart, I let out a big thunderous bawling for Mama when his fancy woman started dropping him off outside the house at the end of the night. I remember the first night the car drew up and parked across the road. Whoever it was, she drove a plush navy blue jaguar car with soft cream leather upholstery throughout, with a private reg. That car was like a stately home on wheels. We all looked out of the window through the curtains as shut away in her darkened room while downstairs, her husband spoke of love, marriage, money and stars. My heart broke into many pieces for Mama. What was going through her mind now that she had given up?

On Friday evening we made ourselves scarce. Meeting that woman was like betraying Mama, something we would not even lie down at night and dream about. Then around seven o'clock Penny's car pulled up opposite the house and Dada came in and bellowed at us to put on our shoes and come out to meet the new woman in his life. Although I had not even blessed eyes on Penny, already I hated her with a vengeance.

'This is Penny everyone. Say hello,' he instructed, his tone of voice auspicious, as though we were all dying to meet her. Outside it was dark, but the car was all lit up and I took a good look at her now. I wanted to see if there was anything else apart from her money, that had so captivated Dada. I swear I saw Dolly Parton staring right back at me from the driver's seat - big hair, plenty of blood-red lippy and blue eye shadow worn under huge movie style glasses, which she removed to greet us. Again a sweet sickly smell of what must have been literally gallons of perfume, evoked a nauseas sensation in the pit of my stomach and for a moment I felt faint. I loathed her so much I wanted to smash her glasses in; I wanted to black both her blue eyes but instead I said: 'hello Penny,' as we all did with Dada standing over us. Back inside we couldn't speak to each other. We were too choked up with shame and disgust.

After he left, we sat with Mama in her darkened room, which was her sanctuary from the hurtful world outside. She would not allow anyone to turn the lights on. Said she felt safe there in the darkness. Bitterly unhappy, Mama accepted the fact that she had lost her husband, but for a while was determined not to lose her children also. We were all she had left.

One day, completely out of the blue, Mama did something that made Pauline and me cringe with embarrassment and guilt. It was the last lesson of the day at school - history - not long to go before the bell went. The history teacher Mr Bolan was so passionate about his subject and I was so bored by it, I stared straight ahead out of the window; not looking at anything in particular, just daydreaming about Rickie James; the only boy in the world - the one I had the biggest crush on. I imagined him declaring his love to me at thirteen, because in my heart we were destined to be together forever. Lost in a far off dream, my mind travelled a million miles away from reality whilst my body occupied a seat in a classroom during a history lesson. Slowly, the union of my body and mind were awkwardly reunited when suddenly my eyes begin to focus on a colourful image that had come into view. My heart pounded wildly; every beat was deafening. My body was ambushed by waves of intense heat, rising repeatedly from my feet upwards as I stared out of the classroom window in shock. Mama had come up to school to collect Pauline and me, even though we were too old for collecting. She paced back and forth at the gates, her obvious agitation attracting attention. On her head she wore a pink headscarf over her wig, a pair of Dada's black socks which came halfway up her shins; her grey coat was done up way too tight and the worse thing that scared me the most was Dada's thick leather belt dangling around her neck. The sound of the bell had me running around the school, frantically searching for Pauline. I wondered if, like me, she had been staring out of the window and had seen what I had seen. From every class I searched, I peered quickly through a window, watching Mama as she paced up and down getting angrier and more agitated the longer she had to wait. Finding Pauline was a relief but her teacher had decided to give the whole class ten minutes detention. I peered into the classroom through the long rectangular glass panel, made eye contact with Pauline and signed to her that Mama was at the gates. But my frightened antics served to amuse some of the other children in the class.

Ten minutes were up and Pauline bolted out of the class. Both of us nervous wrecks, we rushed down the stairs and out to the gates where Mama waited. Drawn to Mama's colourful attire, Rickie James and a few friends gleefully gathered to observe. We tried not to make eye contact with them, although we knew they were looking. We could hear their cruel sniggering behind us.

'Come on Mama, let's go home,' said Pauline holding onto Mama's coat sleeve, trying to coax her home gently.

'Take your hands off of me, I'm a big woman,' she seethed, drawing the belt from around her neck. 'Why you keep me waiting for so long?'

'I'm sorry Mama but the teacher kept everyone back for ten minutes detention,' said Pauline.

'Don't you dare keep me waiting again,' screamed Mama, lashing after us with the belt. Embarrassment alone nearly killed us and we ran on ahead of Mama, trying to get away.

'Wait for me or I'm going to beat you when I catch up with you,' she called to us, but she was too erratic and people were looking, so we ran all the way home, crying as we went.

We got a shock when we entered the sitting room. Dada was in there, and the whole room has been kitted out by Penny. A beautiful cream shag-pile carpet had been fitted - so luxurious it was like walking on a bed of air. There was a new three piece suite, new twenty-eight inch colour TV, new coffee table, ornaments and pictures. The people who had put it all together were leaving as we arrived, then Mama came in through the front door and now we understood why her mood was so explosive.

'Beautiful isn't it?' said Dada, marvelling at his new surroundings. 'Penny is so good to me. She says she's going to leave me money in her will. I will be a rich man one day. She's such a kind-hearted woman.'

On entering the house and hearing Dada praise Penny so highly, Mama kissed her teeth loudly. 'Enjoy it while you can because I'm going to throw fire on everything in this room.'

'You touch anything in here and I'm going to have you locked up for a long time, you hear me?'

'You expect me to sit back and watch, while you play "dolly house" with your whore? If I was you, I'd sleep with one eye open tonight cause I'm going to wait until you're drawing snore, then I'm going pour some hot oil down in your ears, fry your raas in here tonight.'

Those words terrified Dada. Visibly gripped with fear, he swallowed hard and touched his ears. I imagined him in deep slumber and Mama using a funnel to pour the oil in. Never before had we seen him so scared. Foolishly, we took leave of our senses and laughed out loud in applause of Mama's new-found spark.

'Shut up! shouted Dada. 'It's no a laughing matter. You heard! She's trying to kill me. Tomorrow morning bright and early, I'm going to get someone to put a lock on this door, to keep you out.'

Just then, Penny's Jaguar pulled up opposite the house and she tooted the horn for Dada. We all noticed, including Mama. She turned to Dada now.

'With every breath I take from this day forth, I will spend the rest of my life hating you, you wicked son of a bitch.'

Startled by those words, Dada left the house. Outside, he put on his jacket, took a quick look back, and then sped off into the sunset with Penny. There was no comforting Mama. She wouldn't let anyone near her.

Bright and early the next morning, a new lock was fitted on the sitting room door so that Dada could feel safe at night if he came home to sleep, and, to protect his material interests.

'Get yourself ready,' he commanded me later that day, 'you coming with me to the shops.' His conscience must have pricked hard for he bought belly of pork at the butcher's to cook for everyone. It was when we came out of the butcher's that we bumped into someone he knew. A tall beautiful brown skinned woman with high cheekbones whom he introduced to me as Shirley. I could tell by their tone of voice and the way she fluttered her eyelids that something more than friendship was going on. So, Penny was not the only other woman then, I concluded.

'Bye Melanie,' she said in a sweet voice, interrupting my thoughts. I smiled at her. For some reason, I could not feel hate for her. All I felt was pity. I could have told her then that it wouldn't last, that it would all end in tears. Oh, it made my blood boil and multiplied my abhorrence towards my father.

Back at home, he instructed all his daughters to help with the cooking and delegated a range of tasks. Soon the kitchen was filled with the steamy aroma of delicious smells; he really was a great cook, there was no denying that fact, but the pots were not the only thing to bubble.

When dinner was cooked, I took a tray of food up to Mama's room. She emerged from her room minutes later, heading down to the kitchen. Her countenance was explosive. She was like a hand grenade ready to go off. It was best not to converse with her when she was in this frame of mind, for if someone said a trigger word - that would be like releasing the pin. Erratically she threw her dinner straight into the dustbin, plate included.

'I'm not eating that,' she announced, her mood raging dangerously high. 'It's poison! Why are you all trying to kill me?'

Her wild, riotous temper was subject to deterioration at any time. I kept very quiet.

'Don't be silly Mama, it's not poison or human flesh,' said Julia mockingly. 'We've all eaten it.'

Without warning Mama sprung at Julia, wrestling her to the floor. With our combined efforts, we eventually managed to drag her off but not before she took a bite out of Julia's arm.

'Right that's it. I'm going to get the doctor,' said Dada leaving the house in great haste.

There was blood pouring from Julia's arm and both she and Mama were crying hysterically. Glen briefed us all about what was to come, and we were all whimpering now. Poor, poor Mama. They were going to take her away again. They'd keep her drugged up and locked up. I couldn't even hold her in the short space of time we had left together. She was too distraught.

After a while, Dada arrived back with Dr Glassman; a gaunt looking man, bald on top with curly hair at the sides. We knew him well. He was a sympathetic man; a good doctor but he too was absolutely petrified of Dada. Mama had stopped crying. In readiness to meet Dr Glassman, Mama composed herself as though nothing had happened. She had a way of doing that sometimes and it was hard to believe that this was the same person who had behaved so wildly only a short while ago. It made Dada look foolish in front of the doctor.

'I've had a talk with her and she looks alright to me,' said Dr Glassman trembling as he spoke.

'I want her in the hospital today, so you better look lively and call for the ambulance, right now.'

This time, when they led Mama to the waiting ambulance, she did not go kicking and screaming. Instead, she walked calmly to the waiting vehicle, assisted by the ambulance crew. We cried a different kind of cry this time.

'We'll come and see you later Mama. We love you Mama.'

'Leave her, let her go,' said Dada. 'The hospital is the best place for her.'

I watched enraged as the ambulance sped off into the direction of Hackney Hospital. I shut the door when I saw Mrs Andrews and her sister loitering for news.

I couldn't concentrate at school the next day. Education was like water and my mind was a sieve. All I could think about was Mama having things done to her against her will and it had me scared witless.

After school, two days later, Dada took us kids up to the hospital to visit Mama, still wearing our school uniforms. As long as I live, I will never forget that bleak, decrepit place, Hackney Hospital - dubbed the worst mental institution in the country by the press. Entering the mixed ward was like going through the gates of hell. Deranged men ran screaming wildly through the ward, while staff gave chase. Piercing cries of men and women begging and pleading to be released terrified my already frightened spirit. In the sea of faces, I tried not to perceive the madness happening around because it was too disturbing.

There sitting up calmly on the bed in the middle of the ward was Mama. She hadn't seen us, for she was staring into space. All around her was chaos yet Mama just sat there, not making a sound. In fact she looked like the only sane person on the ward and that included the staff. I rushed over to her and gave her a big hug.

'Hello Mama. It's me Melanie, how you feeling?' She acknowledged our presence but she was shocked into silence so I did most of the talking, telling her how good things would be when she came home. I had to be positive; had to be strong. We brought fruits and drinks for her and Dada brought a dressing gown and bed slippers; then he noticed that she was already wearing a new dressing gown.

'Who gave you that dressing gown?' he asked, curious and slightly annoyed that someone else had beaten him to it.

'Glen and Clovis are looking after me now,' she said, breaking her silence. 'I don't want nothing from you. Nothing.'

Anger etched itself onto his face. His jaw line twitched in annoyance. He would not confront them with it because they were young men now. If they took him on together, there was a growing chance they could probably overpower him.

A bell signalled the end of visiting time, and suddenly I felt as though I had a lump in my throat the size of a Bramley cooking apple. I couldn't help it, I started to cry and the more the tears gushed down, the more disappointed I felt with myself for I had been determined to show strength of character, to keep my visit positive so that Mama wouldn't fret, but I had failed miserably. On that basis, Dada decided that I couldn't visit Mama any more because of how distressed I became.

At home, we tried to carry on as normal, but there was the most intense hatred towards Dada looming in the atmosphere. Despite this, there appeared in our darkness the faintest; most distant, speck of light. And although it seemed a million miles away, because undoubtedly, more tribulation paved that rocky road ahead; we knew that that speck of light represented the beginning of the end.

Chapter Nine

Drunk and Disorderly

....

All the life we knew was a long drawn out storm of turbulent seas. The salty waters that rushed ashore, seeping through every nook and crevice were the tears of our dejection. Our struggles were the cruel, brutal waves that crashed into our lives, knocking us back each time. It required mastery and skill for survival, but sometimes even that is not enough to keep all hands on deck. Like a boat adrift in savage waters, Number 27 rocked with such ferocity it allowed two members of our family to be washed overboard into the icy-cold depths of despair. There was no time to stop and save them then. We had to try and save ourselves; had to go on, if only to prolong our own miserable lives, in the hope that one day, through some miracle, we'd be able to go back to rescue them and that they would still be there afloat - waiting to be plucked from troubled waters.

It's hard to believe when you're a child that nothing is permanent; that nothing lasts forever. One day Dada told us that Penny was ill too, that she had cancer; and that his name had been added to her will. Told us he stood to inherit ten thousand pounds. I wondered why all his women suddenly became ill and it was easy to understand when I saw her drop him off outside the house. These days he didn't come in, unless forced to do so by Penny. He gave her the impression that he was going home to his family when he waved her off and blew kisses after her outside the house, and us kids, we hoped he'd come in because there was nothing in the house to eat. But as soon as the Jag turned the corner, he was out of the gate, and bouncing up the road, towards Shirley's house. It isn't long before Penny began to sample a fraction of Mama's torment. Her suspicious mind got the better of her so she began to circle the block around the house three or four times after dropping Dada off. He watched her from the sitting room window, eyes bulging, waiting for when the coast was clear before Jim Screeching away to Shirley's house, leaving his wife upstairs in her darkened room, his children without food, and Penny driving home with doubts plaguing her mind. She knew he was up to something. She had caught him unawares a few times, when her mind had told her to go round the block again. Not for one second did she believe the lame excuses he gave her. She had enough money to buy herself another top of the range gigolo if she so wished, but like Mama, she did not want no other; just him. I pondered on how two people like that came to be together in the first place. Where did he meet her and how long had this peculiar arrangement been going on?

After three long weeks away, Mama had came home, quiet and sullen with her broken spirit in tow. Slowly, she marched up the stairs, ignoring the welcome from us children, and Dada who was putting a cufflink into place before bolting through the door. At the top of the stairs, Massah Stanley waited to descend with tray in hand. His surprised expression on seeing Mama, turned into a smug smile of satisfaction.

'So they let you out, eh? I Hope they fixed you properly this time. Maybe now I'll get some peace in this house.'

He might as well have been invisible, for Mama said nothing to him. She retreated into the dimly lit room of hers; blocked out every piece of light that filtered in, before locking herself away in the pitch blackness. Massah Stanley continued on his way down to the kitchen and I felt an intense need to smash that tray of his over his head. He was nothing but a blood-sucking leech. I soothed myself with Mama's words, 'every dog has its day.'

Mama stayed in her room for days at a time, sometime weeks, then occasionally without warning, she would surface to go to the shops or perhaps to collect Pauline and me from school.

One day I heard voices coming from her room so I knocked on her bedroom door to make sure she was alright, to find out if there was anything I could get her.

'Why don't you draw the curtains and let some light into this room Mama? I said heading over to the window.

'No, leave the curtains alone! Don't draw them. I don't want no light in here; I want to stay in the dark. It's better for me.'

'I thought I heard you talking to someone. Who were you talking to Mama?'

'Spirits.'

'What spirits you talking about?'

'Can't you see them? They're all around you. So many people coming and going. This house is full of them,' she laughed.

'Mama there are no ghosts in this house, it's just your imagination,' I said, somewhat spooked.

'Girl I know what I'm talking about. They're everywhere.'

Poor Mama. - she worried me so - scared me even.

On the way back in from the shop, I was jumped on by Mrs Green and her sister Mrs Andrews.

'I hear your father's carrying on with another woman who lives on Beatty Road. Did you know about that?' enquired Mrs Andrews.

'And that woman Penny; the one that drives the Jag, she don't have no shame parking outside your Mama's house like that,' said Mrs Green. 'I blame her.'

'Now sister how can you blame her when you know it's all his fault?'

'How can it be all his fault? It's her car. She's the one parking her big ole arse outside. Remember he was banned from driving.'

'You forget sister, he drove his wife mad. You saw what he did to her.'

I stood there for a while looking from one to the other as they threw words about in a game of catch. I was just about to walk away and leave them to it but Mrs Green caught hold of my arm now.

'And another thing, have you seen the way your Mama's been walking the streets with her clothes all torn up like rags? I can't bear to see her like that no more. Why can't you do something about it?'

'Do something about it?' I gasped. Her words had wounded me badly, and I felt hurt and ashamed. 'Don't you think I've tried. I'm fourteen years old Mrs Green, What exactly would you want me to do?'

'There's no need to be so abrupt, I was just saying…'

'That's your trouble. You always say too much; always blabbing your mouths off without thinking. You make me sick the pair of you, I bet you even gossip in your sleep - well give it a rest,' I shouted, 'because it's not helping.' I walked away from them then. It was always advisable to put as much distance as possible in between them and myself.

'We're sorry, we didn't mean nothing,' they echoed together. 'We'll talk again tomorrow eh?'

Time is an incredible thing. We were all growing up so fast, it wouldn't be long before the trail of us children leaving home begun. Indeed, it had already commenced for both Clovis and Glen had girlfriends and occasionally slept out. Julia on the other hand had discovered her own womanly beauty, the opposite sex, clubs and parties and that had the same affect on her as the streets had for Dada. She knew the risks were great, for if Dada ever caught her sneaking out, he would kill her for sure. I told her that often enough, trying to dissuade her from taking unnecessary risks. Mostly there was only one, maybe two nights of the week when Dada slept at home. We never knew exactly which nights they would be, but Julia must have had luck on her side for she always managed to avoid being caught even on those rare nights when Dada had decided to come home unexpectedly. Sometimes we stuffed the bed to make it look as though she was asleep. It was good for her that he was a heavy sleeper. She did not have a key, so depended on me to let her in at around four o'clock in the morning when she returned. I had to listen out for her tapping on the sitting room window; that was the signal. Only trouble was that if Dada decided to come home, the sitting room was where he would sleep, but unbeknown to him, his own snoring acted as a smokescreen, drowning out any background noise. I hated it when Julia went out. It was impossible to sleep so I sat up all night, like a zombie, waiting for her. Only when she had returned safely could I attempt to drift off into careless sleep, while Julia, still excited from the thrill of the night, babbled on about what it was like at All Nations or Phoebes club; demonstrating new dance steps; quietly humming or singing the latest songs she had heard. Yep, we were all growing up, and one by one, the three eldest were positioning themselves to fly the nest. They were practically all independent people now, able to sustain themselves if need be. Julia was working for an import company as an office worker. Inheriting his father's style and love of fine clothes, Clovis went into the rag trade, working for Greeks who would not allow anyone else but him to cut their cloth. They sent a black taxi to pick him up every morning because he lacked the discipline and the motivation needed to get up on time. Glen was an apprentice mechanic. He had a car of his own; a white Ford Capri, with the words 'Mean machine,' plastered across the front windscreen. Every so often he would pull his car to bits, stripping it down

Rive Gauche, Charlie, L'air du Temps and Le Jardin D'amour, every birthday and Christmas without fail; she bought shares in a clothes factory for Dada, who every so often came home with new garments for us to wear. As well as that, she tried her best to get to know us individually. On one occasion, she even defended us against Dada when we got caught wearing lipstick on the street. Silently the Jag had pulled up alongside Pauline and me as we walked to school.

'Where you going looking like that?' asked Dada jumping out of the car. Wipe that muck off your mouth now before I do it for you.'

'For goodness sake Wins,' cried Penny's voice from the open window of her car - that's what she called him; my dad; 'Wins'. 'What's the matter with you? Can't you see they're young women? Get back in the car and leave them alone. Now!'

I did not think there was anyone in the world could speak to him in that way and get away with it; but Penny did, and he obeyed, still growling under his breath.

The day of Glen's presentation had arrived. As we approached the car now, the electric window glided down ever so gracefully. The gold-tip rims of her huge sunglasses sparkled as she flashed a powdery smile in our direction.

'Hello Julia, hello Glen, hello Melanie, hello Pauline.' she greeted us as though she knew us well. 'Come on, get in. Make yourselves comfortable. Where are the others?'

'Oh, Douglas has got a cold and Clovis is still at work,' I told her.

Feeling like a fraud, I reluctantly climbed into the car. She talked to us while we waited for Dada, asking all sorts of questions, trying to get to know us better. She was talking away but there was no concentrating on what she was saying. All I could think about was Mama alone in the darkness of her room. If she could see me now, she would think that even her children had betrayed her but that was not so. I told her the night before, that Dada had planned the whole thing; that we had been coerced into it and that we had no choice but to go along with it; if only for Glen's sake. And I told her how I hated Penny with a passion, just to make her feel better. As the car pulled away from the house, I looked back at the windows. I could have sworn I saw the curtains twitch. My stomach tied itself in complicated knots and inside I was crying again because I couldn't bear to think of my Mama alone and hurting.

The ride in that car was unbelievable. It did not feel like the wheels of the car were in contact with the ground. I could see the appeal all of this had for Dada, for quietly and shamefully, I felt like a millionaire. Just before we got to the presentation, Penny drove us up a high hill and parked the car for a while. It was dark but we all got out to take in a breath-taking view of Essex, all lit up like a massive flat Christmas landscape that stretched for miles in front of us. It was a sight to behold.

When it was Glen's turn to go up on stage to collect his certificate we were so proud, we clapped and cheered the loudest. If Massah Stanley could see us now, he'd probably suck his teeth and say, 'Uncivilized.' Glen however beamed with joy and we wrote the experience upon the tables of our hearts as a day to remember.

When we got home Dada was itching to go out. He had intentions of heading over to Shirley's house but he bided his time; hanging around for a full thirty minutes, taking credit for a successful night out; killing time just in case Penny was watching the house or waiting for him round the corner.

'I've just seen her car go past again,' Dada said, looking back at us excitedly from behind the curtains. 'Did you see her, did you see her? She's like a one woman secret service, but she's not smarter than me.'It was all a game of cat and mouse to him, and he obviously enjoyed the chase. No doubt he would be sharing Penny's torment with his friends over a drink of rum. He left a while later, taking his chances with him.

Fed up with Massah Stanley treating her home like a hotel, Mama, without warning, emerged from her room to bolt shut her front door after around eleven o'clock at night. Anyone who wanted to enter after that time would have to knock. Dada grumbled about it but was far too occupied with other things to mind. However, it caused a world of friction between Mama and her tenant. She didn't like the idea of her home being an open house. Night-time was meant for sleeping so at a certain hour she locked up the house, much to the annoyance of Massah Stanley who would bang and rattle the door so loud it would wake the whole household. Night after week after month this continued and sometimes I made sure that I got to the door first so that Mama would not have to take the abuse. My response to his tempered frustration was always the same: 'This is not your home. This is my mother's house, and you are a tenant. Abide by her rules or move out - you have a choice.'

I could see that he hated me. But that was alright because I hated him back so whenever we had a full house I allowed Mama to get the door so that I could prove to the others the necessity of having a clearout. On hearing the front door bang and rattle, Mama alighted from her room to answer it.

'You fucking lunatic,' blazed Massah Stanley. 'Didn't I tell you not to bolt this door!'

'All you have to do is knock and I will open it,' Mama said.

'Why should I have to knock when I got a key, tell me that?'

Just then, Clovis tore out of his room and down the stairs.

'You talking to my mother like that again?' he said heading for Massah Stanley. But Mama held him back.

'It's alright Clovis, don't start no trouble.'

'Lock that fucking door another night and I'm going to kick it in,' said Massah Stanley, heading for his room.

'Kick it in then,' shouted Clovis, temper bubbling over. Kick it in if you're bad.

But two days later that's exactly what Massah Stanley did. Clovis and Glen were not at home. Everyone who was in for the night had gone to bed. The house was silent and still but for the humming of the noisy old refrigerator in the kitchen. First an audible rattling sound woke the family, then there was shouting and banging, by which time Mama and I were on the stairs, racing to release the bolt. But before we could do so, there came an almighty crash. Massah Stanley had broken the full-length pane of glass. He stepped in through the frame, crunching the shattered glass beneath his shoes, sneered at Mama and I, then marched straight to his room and locked the door without a word.

The next day, when Clovis and Glen saw what he had done to the front door, they decided it was time to take action. I watched in excited horror that day as first they broke into his room, then, unscrewed the hinges to his bedroom door. Once loose, they lifted it off and leaned it up against a wall inside the room. His room, the biggest in the house, was an Aladdin's cave of beautiful things. Silverware and fine china sat elegantly on top of a brass trolley, beautiful pictures hung on the walls and the ornaments added a finishing touch of luxury. Anger made the boys turn the room upside down. But our anger was not only directed at Massah Stanley but more so towards Dada for doing nothing about ousting this unbearable man from our overcrowded home. The boys waited in all day, spoiling for a fight. In fact all six of us were geared up and ready; ready to jump on Massah Stanley's back if need be, to pummel him with fists as painful as the insults he had spat at Mama over the years.

'When Massah Stanley comes home,' explained Glen to Mama, 'you stay in your room. We'll take care of everything.'

'You mustn't throw him out like that,' Mama said, panicking at the speed at which this trouble had escalated. 'Give him at least another day to find somewhere else.'

'Another day?' shouted Clovis in disbelief. 'He needs to go TODAY Mama.'

'You know he's a proud man, at least let him go with some dignity,'

'If he had any pride he would have been gone long ago, but just for you Mama, I'm going to give him *one* day.'

Now that it was crunch time, here she was worrying about giving this despicable man more time. He didn't deserve another second let alone another day.

The tension in the house increased further when Dada put in a brief appearance. He was like a kid, playing out in the vicinity of his home; running back and forth, whenever it suited him, in an effort to maintain control over the household. However, he was shocked at the sight of the front door.

'Who broke the glass in the door?' he demanded.

'Massah Stanley did,' I declared with an air of confidence, wondering what he intended to do about it.

'I bet you any money Girlie start the whole thing.'

'Actually she didn't,' I say, 'it's my fault if anybody's. I thought everyone was in for the night so I bolted the front door before going to bed.'

He looked at me annoyed more than anything, and then mounted the stairs to the bathroom. We all six followed behind as bold as ever. He saw it then - the gaping hole where Massah Stanley's bedroom door should have been.

'Oh Christ Almighty, Where's the door for Stanley's room?'

'He smashed the front door glass, so I smashed his door in – let him see how it feels to be invaded,' said Clovis standing up to Dada.

A death-defying pause followed.

Catching a whiff of conspiracy in the air, Dada's eyes swung from side to side as he examined the faces of each of his children. 'Do you know how long he's been a tenant here with us?' Dada asked.

'Too long,' answered Clovis venomously. 'And here's another question, 'Do you know how long he's been insulting my mother under her own roof, and in front of all her children? Too long. Well I'm not going to stand for it no more. He has to go.'

For a while Dada said nothing, his eyes taking in the sight of his children standing together in unity.

'Well I'm not going to be here,' Dada said hurriedly. 'I don't want nothing to do with any of this.'

After he left we tried to get some normality back into the house by sitting down together to pretend to watch TV, waiting for the volcano - our house - to erupt.

Around seven o'clock, much later than usual, we heard Massah Stanley's key in the lock of the front door, which was now boarded up. We were behind him now, following him up the stairs, in the same way we had followed Dada, earlier that day. He said nothing at all, until he saw the state of his bedroom door and instantly he was filled with rage.

'Who took my door off?'

'Me and him,' said Clovis, pointing to Glen. 'You're taking the piss man. 'You got one day to get your things together and get out. Count yourself lucky that Mama gave you a whole day. If it was up to us, we'd put you out right now, like the dog you are.'

'Where's your father? I want to speak to your father.'

'No use complaining to him, he already knows, said Glen. 'You're on your way out man – deal with it.'

Defeated yet still shaking with anger, Massah Stanley went into his room and leaned the door up against the frame to block out prying eyes. He came rushing out later that night to confront Dada when unexpectedly he heard him on the stairs. He wanted to find out how Dada intended to handle the situation.

'You seen what your kids done to my door. They're trying to throw me out. You have to do something about it. Exercise some control man.'

'What do you want me to do Stanley? They even want me out, so what exactly do you want me to do?'

Those words stunned Massah Stanley. He watched as Dada walked past, indifferent to his plight. With retribution running through his veins, Massah Stanley felt the need to humiliate the family one last time and did so by leaving the house soon after Dada, to return in the early hours of the morning with two prostitutes. Clovis and Glen had gone clubbing together so there was nothing we could do.

At around six o'clock in the morning Clovis and Glen returned home to throw Massah Stanley out as planned but when they heard what he had done, they marched up to his room without hesitation, kicked down the unhinged door and picked him up off the ground from where he had fallen. After giving him a few punches along the way to prevent him from struggling too much, they threw him out onto the pavement where he landed with a thud. God forgive me, I clapped and squealed with delight and then my sisters and I threw his bags on top of him, while from the open window of his bedroom, Mama joined in. She threw out the last remaining plates left in his room, trying to rid the house of all evidence of his existence. Like Frisbees, they sailed through the air, some missing him by inches, smashing around his feet, and some, making direct impact.

'About time too,' said Mrs Andrews, looking down on Massah Stanley with disdain as he lay sprawled out in the street.

'You ought to be ashamed of yourself,' said Mrs Green. 'Call yourself a gentleman. You don't look very gentlemanly now do you?'

'How could you bring prostitutes into Girlie's family home? Don't think we didn't see you. We see *everything.*'

'Nasty!' exclaimed Mrs Green, her physiognomy an expression of someone with a sickened stomach. 'That's what you is - a nasty little man.'

I strolled outside the gateway to stand in agreement with them and to get a close up image of Massah Stanley still writhing around on the ground.

'Mrs Green, Mrs Andrews, for the first time I have to say I totally agree with you. He *is* a nasty little man.' I looked down on him with scorn now.

'Don't you worry yourself Melanie, it's all finished with now,' said Mrs Andrews, patting my hand. 'You tell your mama that too. It's only a matter of time before the same thing happens to your father, treating your mama like that. By the way, how is she? Is she getting any better? We hardly see her any more.'

Mrs Green and her sister both cocked their ears, ready for news.

'She's fine,' I said in a tone that warned them against prying any further.

'We're always here if you need to talk,' said Mrs Andrews persuasively.

Why don't you come over now? We got coconut drops and Gizarda indoors.'

'Actually, I'm a bit busy at the moment clearing up,' I said, edging away from them to quickly head back to the doorway of my house. Massah Stanley was beginning to stir from his momentary lapse of unconsciousness. 'Maybe some other time,' I called.'

Slightly dazed, Massah Stanley managed to scramble slowly to his feet. Madder than ever, he wanted to lash out at an easy target. Face contorted with anger, he fixed his gaze on the twin sisters now.

'Oh, Lord have mercy! Run sister! Run!' cried Mrs Green when she saw him coming towards them on unsteady legs. Managing to let themselves into the nearest of their homes, they slammed the door in his face, just in time. Massah Stanley walked off up the road in a zig-zag line, leaving his belongings where they lay; strewn across our gateway, and out onto the pavement.

'And if you're not back in an hour to pick up all this rubbish then I'm going to get Mama to throw fire on it, so you better be quick,' Clovis called after him.

With Massah Stanley gone, Dada began to come home more frequently, not necessarily to stay, but to assert his authority on anyone he could. Trying to control Clovis and Glen, now that they were young men, was not going to be easy. So instead, he tightened his control on the four youngest members of his family.

He put in place a new curfew of eleven o'clock for Julia to be in by, simply because he knew she couldn't keep to it. Constantly, he questioned her about what time she got in at night, tripping her up a few times because he had been in the sitting room sleeping at the time she said she arrived. Being a heavy sleeper let him down though. It meant Julia was able to slip back into the house undetected and be all tucked up in her bed by the time he awoke.

First thing he'd say when he came home at odd times at nights; was 'Where's Julia?' checking that she was where she should be. I could tell he was setting for her and it was only a matter of time before she got caught out.

Now he was taking on more of the responsibilities of running the house, with Mama too sick to do anything. I handed him a whole handful of bills that had piled up. He made me open each one and read it to him. What a shock it was to find out that a large group of people were queuing up for money we didn't have. The mortgage had fallen behind and they were threatening to repossess the house. We received numerous letters from T Stephenson threatening bailiff action if we did not pay up; the gas board was threatening to cut off our supply as was the London Electricity Board and numerous others had joined the queue. It was a shock for Dada too. He had always left that pressure to rest heavily on Mama's head in the past, but now the tables had turned and on his head be it. He took me to the town hall. Showed me how to pay the rates, and then did the same with the other bills so that I could pay them for him when he was too busy. He did the cooking too, when he felt like it; buying enough for only one meal at a time.

More trouble came calling about three weeks after Massah Stanley's disgraceful departure, to again shatter the fragile normality we had settled back into. It was a Thursday night; Dada had left earlier on that evening and Clovis and Glen were out for the night also. I walked past my bedroom door on the way to the bathroom to get myself ready for bed but had to do a double take when through the crack of the door, the sight of Julia getting ready to go out left me standing motionless. She was wearing a red pencil skirt with matching top, moccasin shoes; and her mass of curly hair was shaped elegantly into a hairnet. I watched as she put on lipstick, puckering up her lips, to a group of admiring men who lived in the mirror. I watched her for a long time, with that sick feeling of fear accumulating in my stomach, making me nauseous enough to want to vomit. Suddenly aware that she was not alone, Julia spun around to find the owner of the watchful eyes that had so rudely invaded her privacy.

'Are you spying on me again you little shit, get in here,' she said, pulling me into the room.

'What you doing Julia?'

'What does it look like? I'm going out,' she announced turning to the mirror again.

'Don't do it Julia. If Dada catches you he'll kill you.'

'For God's sake, I'm eighteen years old. I'm a woman now. He's got no right to stop me,' she said plonking herself down on the bed. 'It's so unfair, I don't tell him how to run his life. Well he's not going to ruin mine; I'm going to do some living before I get old.'

'But why does it have to be tonight? What's so special about tonight?'

'If I tell you something, you promise you won't tell anyone?'

'Cross my heart,' I said.

'I got a boyfriend. I met him a few months ago and I'm meeting him again tonight.'

I realised then that there was no way of talking her out of going. It was obvious by the way her eyes lit up when she spoke about this man that love had thrown her a line and was pulling her in.

'How will you get in without a key? Last time I had to creep past Dada to let you in and I told you then that I would not do it again. I'm too scared.'

'Please Melanie,' said Julia taking my hand. 'Just do it for me one last time and I'll never ask you ever again.'

'Don't say it like that; you bring crosses on yourself by tempting fate.'

'Please Melanie. Dada's gone out. He won't be coming back for tonight. Look, I've got to go otherwise I'll be late. Listen out for my tapping on the sitting room window and then let me in when the coast is clear.'

'Julia!' I cried as she headed out into the darkness.

'What!' She called back in a whisper.

'Don't be long. Please don't be long.'

I sat up all night waiting for her to come back, as I usually did. The only noise breaking the silence was the sound of the old house as it creaked and breathed. Mama in her madness or depression, call it what you will, had moved all the bedrooms around, feeling the need for a change. She did that a lot. As I lay on my bed in the room adjacent to the sitting room, my tattered nerves tricked me into believing that there was a tapping sound coming from the sitting room window. I was terrified of the dark yet I could not risk turning the lights on for fear of attracting unnecessary attention to myself which could possibly foil Julia's plan to get back into the house safely.

Quickly, I raced into the sitting room, my heart in my mouth. Dispelling my fear of ghost and ghouls, I stared out of the window to see if Julia was waiting to be let in, but there was no one there. My over-active imagination, coupled with the strong wind that blew outside, had got the better of me.

Suddenly, a huge black shadow glided pass the window. If it had been an apparition, I don't think I would have minded much - they cannot hurt you. Dada was making his way through the gates. Hastily I tore back into the bedroom to feign sleep, knowing that within seconds his formidable presence would enter this room and that he would wake Pauline from her sound and peaceful sleep in the usual abrupt manner.

The bedroom door swung open. Both Pauline and I sat up when he switched on the bright light. I wiped non-existent sleep from my eyes to match Pauline's motions.

'Where's Julia?' he shouted.

'She's - er -she's sleeping,' said Pauline, in a voice that was both sleep-induced and fretful.

'I'm not stupid; I can see she's not here. What time did she go out?'

'We can't remember, we were both sleeping.'

Suspiciously, he eyed us both, his whole body engulfed in anger. I prayed for this monster to quickly fall into a deep slumber, so the effects of the liquor would wear away the danger that Julia was now in.

'I'm going to give her the hiding of her life when she comes home; think she can take me for a fool. This is one night I'm not going to sleep. I'm going to wait up for that bitch. I'll show her to take liberties with me.'

It was the middle of the night, and there was going to be trouble. A sickly feeling invaded my being. I had long since decided that in a year and a half, as soon as my sixteenth birthday came, I would be off - anywhere far away from this God forsaken house. The tension was unbearable; it kept me awake. I lay there in the dark, ears tuned to the slightest sound, waiting for that dreadful moment to arrive. The hands of the bedside clock went round and round. Hours had ticked past and I was just beginning to drift into sleep, when around four o'clock in the morning a low but distinct tapping could be heard on the sitting room window. Thinking Dada was out cold in a deep slumber, I tiptoed through the dark passageway to the front door.

'Get back in your room,' a sudden voice in the dark sneered menacingly.

'Don't beat her Dada. Please don't beat her,' I begged. Then followed another short series of tapping on the door.

'I said, get back in your room,' he threatened again and I knew that Julia was in grave danger.

'Julia, Dada's at the door,' I warned, trying to prepare her for a beating.

Slowly he opened the door, throwing me a furious glance for calling out.

'Get inside the house now,' he said, allowing her to take two slow steps towards him before forcefully dragging her in and banging the door shut.

Slapped and punched with so much force, Julia screamed out in pain. Her half finished pleas for him to stop were interrupted in the most brutal way and once again, I was too frightened of what he would do to me if

I tried to help. I screamed and begged for him to stop; my eyes witnessing what I thought to be murder. Pauline and I cried out for God, and He sent Mama.

As sick as she was, Mama unlocked her door. She raced downstairs in an effort to save Julia from being battered to death. It was the first time she had come to Julia's defence, for Dada had made the mother-daughter relationship they should have had difficult, from years back.

But before Mama could get to her, another blow to the stomach sent Julia reeling onto the floor, then, when she was down; Dada followed it up with two hefty kicks to the stomach. Julia screamed out in pain.

'Take your hands off her,' screamed Mama tearing at Dada's face and clothes, pummelling him with blows to make him stop. 'You not going to kill my daughter. I won't let you kill her;' she screamed placing herself between him and Julia. In the next brief pause, Mama pushed her husband against the wall and he panted with rage as he stared down at Julia's crumpled body. It was his duty to exercise control over his family, to show us that we were mere possessions and the seriousness of what would happen if we ever dared to disrespect his authority again.

'Julia you all right?' Mama cried.

'Let him kill me! Mama, let him kill me! I want to die; I can't take no more.'

Time stood still then. With everyone frozen to the spot, only the sound of heavy breathing could be heard. Eventually, Dada stormed into the sitting room without a word, leaving Julia lying there on the floor in the passageway. Mama, Pauline and I helped her to her feet but she was in a bad way. We managed to get her onto the bed and covered up. Without warning, Julia took hold of Mama's hand and held it.

'Thank you Mama,'

'For what?' Mama asked, a little taken aback.

'For being my Mother; for being here. You go back to bed and get some rest. I'll be alright now,' Julia said; trying to convince Mama that she was fine. That night, Pauline and I fetched water for Julia to drink and did everything we could to make her comfortable. Awoken by the sound of groaning some two hours later, I saw Julia, holding her abdomen, her body tightly curled into a ball. She looked up at me with watery eyes, and then started vomiting heaps of yellow bile onto the bedroom carpet. I got a pail and placed it beside her and throughout the rest of what was night and into early day, she practically filled it.

'Julia you got to go to the doctor. Something's wrong.'

'I'll be all right. I just need to sleep for a bit, then the pain will go.'

Nevertheless, she continued to wince in pain.

'I think it's your appendix Julia. You need a doctor.'

'My what?'

'Your appendix - I saw a programme on television about it once. They said if you don't get to a doctor on time and it bursts, then it can kill you because it releases poison into your body.' I was sure my diagnosis was right I; had a special interest in health and biology, and Mama always said I'd be a doctor or a teacher so now I put my skills into practice.

'I'll come with you, but let me sleep for a while.' She grimaced in pain again.

'No! You got to come now. I'll help you get dressed,' I said throwing the covers off; giving her no choice.

Supporting some of her weight, we made our way to the doctor's surgery. Julia limped all the way there, through Clissold Park and along Church Street, to where it met Green Lanes.

Doctor Glassman, who was evidently shocked by Julia's appearance, examined her stomach after warming his long bony hands and she screamed out in pain again when he touched the spot.

'It's an appendicitis. You need to go to hospital for an operation straight away. How did this happen,' he said looking from one to the other for an answer. We had agreed beforehand that no matter what, we would not to say anything about what had happened.

'It started hurting when I got up this morning,' Julia said avoiding his gaze, as did I.

'And what about those cuts on your face, when did that happen?

'I, I also fell down the stairs this morning.'

Doctor Glassman eyed us both with suspicion.

After the ambulance arrived at the surgery to take Julia off to the hospital, I raced home to let everyone know what had happened. I telephoned Glen and Clovis from a call box and went home to stuff a few of Julia's belongings into a bag.

'We're going to have to have to do something about that man and soon,' said Glen. We'll talk about it later. Right now we have to get to the hospital and make sure Julia is all right.

When I told Dada about Julia needing a life-saving operation, he sat there on the settee stunned into silence.

'I got to go now,' I said. 'We're all going up to the hospital.'

Not a word was uttered from Dada's mouth.

After she came out of theatre, we gathered around Julia's bed and waited for her to come round.

'She's awake. How are you feeling Julia?' Pauline asked.

'I'm OK, just a bit sore that's all,' she whispered back quite despondently.

We put flowers in a vase; fruit in a bowl and made small talk to keep Julia's mind from what she had been through. She looked so pitiful rigged up to a drip; catheter hanging seriously beside the bed. Her left eye was completely closed and the size of a golf ball. It was hard to believe that we damn near lost our sister. Some of us were sitting on the bed or on chairs, telling jokes to cheer Julia back to health. She laughed so hard she had to call for the nurse who made her hold a pillow against her stitches, and we got a stiff warning from matron. It was so good to see Julia laughing, and not dead. But the smile was wiped from our faces and we all started to attention beside Julia's bed when we saw Dada entering the ward.

His bleary eyes scanned the large room and affixed themselves to where we were. He began walking over towards us and that's when I noticed he had been drinking a beverage much stronger than water or tea. 'Please God,' I asked, 'don't make him cause a scene.'

'All right everybody?' he said with a false smile that didn't fool me for a second.

'We're going now,' said Glen. 'Got to make sure Mama's OK,' and both he and Clovis left hastily without a word to Dada.

'I bought you some fruit, a dressing gown and some slippers,' Dada said, not looking directly at Julia. I think they'll fit you.' Then when his eyes finally came to rest on her, he burst into tears. I looked up into my father's face. Shame and guilt were killing him. I could tell he must have wanted so desperately to see his daughter but had needed courage to do it; so he had had a drink. And that one drink had probably turned into a few drinks until he felt he was ready to face her.

'You hate me don't you? All of you hate me,' he sobbed loudly.

'I don't hate you Dada, you're my dad,' said Julia from her hospital bed. 'I will always love you.' She said it so lovingly, I will never forget.

'I never meant to hurt you, I was just so angry with you.'

Crying uncontrollably, he attracted the attention of the matron who was watching and listening intently from behind her station.

'Come on; it's time you all left Julia to get some rest now. You can come back later if you want,' she said, ushering us out of the ward.

Humouring Dada on the way, to cope with our embarrassment at him being drunk and to contain his mood, we jumped on a 243 bus from St Leonard's Hospital to Stoke Newington. He did not follow us home though. Instead, he waved us off at the top of

Church Street, to our relief, and went straight into The Three Crowns pub to drown his sorrows, all over again.

'You have a boyfriend don't you?' he asked Julia three days after she had come home from hospital.

Julia responded by nodding her head, nervously.

'Well, bring him round to meet me. I want to talk to him.'

That sounded ominous in itself, but at least he was making an effort to do the right thing. Over the next few weeks, Dada cooked with a passion, like never before. He cooked a range of foods intended to build up Julia's strength. He made beef soup, oxtail and butterbean soup, chicken soup, mackerel and banana with cornmeal dumplings; each as delicious and mouth-watering as the one before.

Strong enough to now lead her love interest into the lions' den, Julia invited her boyfriend Dennis round to meet her father. From what he had heard about Dada, Dennis knew that he would eventually come face to face with the man who had so much control over the woman he loved.

'Dada this is Dennis,' Julia said, swallowing hard.

Dada said nothing at first. He took his time to eye up this slightly built young man, from where he sat on the settee. Then, satisfied that he was too lean to be considered a threat to anyone, he stood up to overshadow him with his size.

'Pleased to meet you sir,' said Dennis offering a trembling hand.

'You can call me Dada.' Dada shook Dennis' hand so hard, his shoulder looked as though it might pop out of its socket. 'Come sit down right here, so we can talk. So where are your people from?'

'My parents, oh they're from Barbados.'

'Oh,' said Dada, patronisingly, as though enlightened, 'small island people. That's nice, that's nice. Where you live?'

'I live in Hackney, in Clapton in fact,' said Dennis, taking care not to give him the exact address in case this man should ever come looking for him one day.

'Tell me now, how long have you been seeing my daughter?' He looked at Julia while Dennis struggled to answer.

'About a few months I think,' said Dennis. Beads of sweat that had been sitting on his forehead like tiny pools, swelled and overflowed; which Dennis wiped swiftly away with the back of his hand. Dada moved closer to him, staring him square in the eyes now. 'So what is your intention with my daughter?'

Pauline, Douglas and I were in the sitting room with our hands over our mouths to stifle our desire to laugh, whilst waiting for Dennis to conjure a suitable answer.

'Well,' said Dennis, clearing his throat after much consideration, 'I love Julia very much. I'm going to take good care of her and treat her like the diamond she is.'

'That's the right answer,' said Dada jumping to his feet. 'Shake my hand.' He shook Dennis' hand more vigorously than the first time, and then patted him so hard on the back, it made him cough.

'Welcome to the family, Stick. I have to call you Stick because if breeze blow, you'll break in half.' That image must have sweet him so much for he broke into a loud raucous, bellowing laughter that shook the house.

We laughed too; laughed at how terrified Dennis was of Dada.

'You want a drink Stick?'

'No sir. I'm all right thank you sir.'

'I said call me Dada.'

'Yes Dada, I mean, I mean no thank you Dada.'

Dada left the room laughing all the way to the bathroom in which time Dennis managed to down two double shots of rum to steady his jangled nerves. On Dada's return he noticed the decreased amount of rum in the bottle and laughed out loud again.

It seems that dark episode in Julia's life had brought to an end the physical violence that we had endured in the past. It did not however bring to an end our fear surrounding Dada, for we knew his potential, his capabilities.

A few months later when Julia started vomiting into the pail every morning, I knew it was definitely not her appendix. She was pregnant and it was just a matter of time before she too, like Clovis and Glen, left home.

'Please don't tell anyone Melanie,' she begged.

I was going to be an auntie, an Auntie. This new title made me feel so grown up.

'Of course I won't tell,' I said; joyous on one hand and deeply saddened that my siblings were one by one flying the nest. Everyone was tripping over themselves to get away; all trying to escape the house that held so many bad memories for us; all confident that they could make a better success of their lives. I wondered what was to become of Mama when everyone had gone. What kind of existence would she have? For that's all she was doing now; existing; totally withdrawn from the world.

With her pregnancy beginning to show, Julia left for the Mother and Baby home opposite the Mothers' Hospital, in Clapton where she would eventually give birth. Unable to stay with Dennis in his one room rented accommodation, Julia was lucky enough to be given a room in the home, along with lots of other young girls her age, who had found themselves in the same predicament.

In the month of July, Julia gave birth to a little girl weighing in at six pounds. When she brought her baby round all wrapped up in a papoose to introduce her to her family; miraculously, Mama actually drew her curtains for a while before holding the child to take a close and intent look at her.

'Lord have mercy,' smiled Mama.

We all peered into the baby's face to see who she looked like.

'She looks just like…' I began.

'Cousin Enid,' Mama finished. And it was true. It was as though Cousin Enid was staring right back at us.

I was in my final year at school when Dada called me to him one day.

'I want you to go round to Shirley's house tomorrow, after school. She wants to see you about something.' he told me the address and how to get there. It was a demand I dared not disobey. I spent all day wondering why on earth this woman whom I hardly knew would want to see me of all people - why not one of the others?

After school the next day, I walked the distance to Shirley's house. When I got there I pushed the wooden gate, walked up the path and knocked on the door. I could hear someone coming so I took a step back; it being a strange house and that. Slowly the door was opened wide to reveal a shocking secret. Shirley stood there, her stomach as big as a beach ball. I couldn't move or speak. It was such a shock. The moment I saw her, tears welled up in my heart. Suddenly I felt sick to my stomach.

'Hello Melanie. Come in. As you can see I'm seven months pregnant.'

I went into the living room and sat down without saying a word.

'Would you like something to drink?'

I was too dumbfounded to answer her.

'I know it must be a shock to you Melanie but I needed to see you. The only reason me and your father got together was because he told me that him and your mother were finished; that they did not have a relationship together any more. My baby's coming in two months,' she said rubbing her huge stomach.

I kept my eyes on the floor for most of the time; it was too hard to look at her without feeling anger.

'It's not been easy living with Winston. He tells too much lies I can't believe anything he says anymore. I was pregnant before you know. Five months pregnant but I lost it because of your father. He's not an easy man to live with you know.'

Who was she telling? Me or herself? Instinctively, I knew the unborn child she spoke of had been beaten out of her. At fifteen years old, I had already experienced living with that man for longer than she had known him.

'I feel so sorry for your mother and what he's done to her,' continued Shirley. I feel like I'm going mad myself, that's why I needed to talk to you. I looked up at her with tears in my eyes. Her voice seemed so kind, honest and genuine it was difficult not to feel anything but pity for her, seeing as she already had three small children to take care of, two of whom were still in nappies.

'I need to ask you something. How long has he been seeing Penny?'

'My God, you know about Penny?'

'Of course I know about that bitch.'

'She's been around for years now,' I said, without worrying that Dada would find out.

'He's only with her for her money,' she spat like an embittered woman. 'You know how he met her? She was the wife of the boss who owned the lorry driving company he used to work for. He knew the man well. They were good friends and then they fell out when she started having an affair with your father, around the time of the accident. She don't have no right flaunting hers nasty self outside your mother's house; knowing the woman is not well. And you know something else I've heard about this Penny, is that she's in the hospital every minute having abortions for him.'

'She's got cancer,' I said, 'that's why she's in hospital so often.'

'Well I know for a fact, she's had more than one abortion,' said Shirley, seemingly unaffected by what I had just revealed.

'I'm sorry I had to tell you this, I know he's your father but he's driving me mad. You don't have to worry though, I won't say a word about what we talked about. He won't know a thing. And don't you tell him anything I said either.'

When I got outside into the fresh air I walked the few yards to the bottom of the road on trembling legs. Too weak to carry on, I stopped for a while to lean against a wall for support. The tears would not allow me the privacy of my home. Distressed for Mama, I cried my heart out. There was no way I could tell her about this, it would just finish her off for sure. Why had Dada involved me in the first place by sending me round there? Did he even consider how I would feel? Fifteen years old and I had to keep this secret from everyone, just in case someone leaked it to Mama. I did not want her to hurt any more - to feel pain on top of more pain.

A few months later, Dada ordered me to the hospital with him following the birth of his child. Then, when the time came, he made me sit with Shirley's children while they went out to register the birth. I held their little boy in my arms. He was beautiful, I thought, as I looked down at him. He hadn't asked to be born and I did not have it in me to resent him. I put him in the cot, hushed him to sleep, then set about entertaining Shirley's three other children.

Two weeks later, it came to my attention that the cat had been let out of the bag when I saw Mrs Green and her sister hurrying towards me.

'Is it true what we heard?'

'What have you heard this time Mrs Green,' I said trying to sound disinterested.

'Well,' said Mrs Green, looking over each shoulder in turn, 'I hear your father had a baby boy with that woman who lives on Beatty Road. It's true ain't it?'

My outer countenance was that of total indifference. Now that Mrs Green and Mrs Andrews had perceived the latest episode of my father's shenanigans, the whole neighbourhood, no doubt, would have an update on our suffering, and renewed glares of ridicule, pity and interest would inevitably follow.

My father's cruel and insensitive attitude meant that he was a vehicle out of control, still unrelenting in his attempts to run Mama and us kids off the road. Mama of course, had been hit a number of times, by this runaway vehicle and survived, yet instinctively; I knew that it was only a matter of time before another member of the family would be permanently maimed by Dada's reckless determination to be a free, commanding spirit.

'That man is unbelievable,' continued Mrs Green.

'Unbelievable!' echoed Mrs Andrews.

'Can't you kids do something about him? I tell you it breaks my heart watching what he has done to your family.'

'Breaks my heart,' repeated Mrs Andrews; her small hand patting her flat chest at the same time as shaking her head sorrowfully.

I turned, walked away solemnly, into the bleakness of my dreary home, quietly shutting the front door behind me. Apart from the knowledge that Mama was upstairs in the stillness of that dark room, the house felt deserted. I glanced up at the grey ceiling from where I stood in the hallway and at the layout of what was before me. I hated this house - detested the resonance of its dank, mournful atmosphere. This cold, innate place was an entity unto itself; a living breathing thing that had drawn strength from the most potent emotions of residents past and present. We were unwelcome guests. As long as we remained here under its roof with my father, Mama was never going to get better - I knew that. Things could only get worse. And once more, in a dark moment of reality, where unforeseen dangers lingered out of view, fear had tightened its grasp on my already imprisoned spirit.

Those two meddling women, Mrs Green and Mrs Andrews were right. We had to do something about Dada, but what?

Chapter Ten

Uprising

....

Sweet sixteen was like honey on my tongue for the first time, and the transparent doors of a confectionary store, full of life's pleasures were thrown wide open for me to enter into. My birthday would come and go, like any other ordinary day so I drew strength from the fact that I had reached the age of consent. Legally, I now had a say - a voice. Presents don't always come in tangible boxes tied up with brightly coloured ribbon, for the greatest gift for me on that day, was the gift of my young adult life, the choice to put in motion my own decisions; my chance to orchestrate what **I** wanted from life. I was a free spirit, breathing in a new lease of life and it felt like I had just opened Mama's grip, to see the three little birds that I had accidentally suffocated come to life again. The choice to walk away from my desperately unhappy life was placed firmly into my lap. But as I sat with Mama that night, in her darkened room, with the peaceful moonlight seeping through the crack of the curtain, I listened with tears in my eyes as she talked about moonlight in Jamaica, childhood games and tales of jumbies. Recollecting favourable memories, made Mama laugh out loud with glee. But in the next instant, her girlish chuckle, full of all its bitter-sweet nostalgia, slowly descended into a soft, hearty cry, and although overwhelming was my need to escape this hell where I was forced to watch the suffering of those I loved, I knew I could not leave her, not now, and all of a sudden, the flame of my earlier excitement was snuffed out. Instead, my fears were ignited, forcing me onto a deeper level of reality to reveal what I must face. The only way to help Mama, long-term, was to get her away from Dada and away from this godforsaken house. Yet what was also apparent was that it indicated that one day, I would eventually have to leave Mama behind in order to set the wheels in motion. The precise juncture at which to make such a move was never going to be easy, nor ideal - not with the volatile presence of my father still looming. The one consolation was that I would escape the choke of this house for the last time. How many lives are there in one lifetime I asked myself? My heart was torn in two pieces - a piece for Mama and a piece for me. Mama's piece was for keeps: therefore to rescue her from a life of degradation was to save my own heart.

I wanted to help, so I got a job; my first job as an office junior, working for a company called S J Hartley in Old Street, in the city. There I make countless cups of tea and coffee for the staff and in particular for my boss, Mr Taylor, a short bespectacled bald headed man, who grimaced and gave me a peculiar glance when swallowing the first mouthful of beverage. Both they and I longed for a new worker to relieve me of my current duties. I put to use the copy-typing skills I had learnt at school to type countless letters and my speed and efficiency met with praise and smiles of approval, which raised my esteem. But I was at war with the duplicating machine and quite often, got covered in ink. At this, my colleagues, old enough to be my parents or even grandparents, expressed impatience, bemusement or utterances of 'Oh dear.'

Contributing to my keep liberated me into a social circle of friends: a circle, which re-introduced me to my first boyfriend, Charles, whom I had known from school, since the age of eleven. And do you want to know what it was about him that caught my eye? It was his attire; his 'air of the world' countenance and his good looks. Here he was, all grown up, suited and slick. He had that magic of persona; that zing, that pazzazz - call it what you like - he had it, and all of a sudden my world was coloured with a cherry-blossom tint. Unbeknown to me, there was no mistaking the fact that I was my mother's daughter. I started dating Charles secretly, making sure to get in by eleven o'clock lest it should be a night when Dada decided to put in an appearance. I detested the hold he still had over me.

In a matter of weeks, Charles, who was an only child, had introduced me to his family - his mother, father and tenant, Hubert who when he drank too much, sang at the top of his voice and strummed his guitar with conviction about a girl who had broken his heart - leaving Charles' mother to shout: 'Hubert! Hubert! Stop that damn noise at my head!'

Apart from that, and the two killer guard dogs in the backyard, here was a normal functioning family who communicated with each other.

His parents, who lived in large end of terrace house on Rendlesham Road, had given their son everything within their power to give; everything a young man of Charles' age, could possibly want. For some reason unbeknown to me, they liked me - treated me like the daughter they had never had.

'Melanie you thirsty? Would you like a drink?

'No Mr Clarke.'

'Clarkey,' Charles reminded. 'You must call him Clarkey.'

'It's hot in here. Melanie are you too hot? Charles go get Melanie some ice-cream from the freezer.'

'Thank you ... Clarkey, but I'm OK.'

'Dinner will be ready soon. You are staying to dinner ain't you?' that was more of a command which Charles answered for me, and I gratefully accepted.

'Kick you shoes off, relax,' said Clarkey, I'll call you when dinner is ready.'

I was blessed to have good people around me; friends who waited patiently outside number 27, as I ran in to check on Mama; friends who raised my weary spirits once I had withdrawn from that house, sullen and deflated. Going into that house was like entering another world.

Almost four seasons came and went, and still my reluctance to leave Mama kept me firmly anchored to number 27, but nothing lasts forever, which I concluded, isn't always a bad thing.

In the beginning, I stuck by Dada's rules: I did nothing to upset the fragile equilibrium of the household, but hope as I did, for a better tomorrow, staying close to Mama had not brought about any improvements in her emotional or physical well-being. I was being unrealistic, hoping for a miracle, but still I hoped, because I kept the faith - and I don't know what else to do except pray, and it seemed as though I'd been praying all my life. Yet I persevered to continue hoping because perseverance was the key, and at the end of every day, I still believed in the magic of the world; the silver lining of every cloud, the light at the end of a tunnel, the promise behind every rainbow and the comfort of a peaceful calm at the end of a storm. Despite my efforts, and the efforts of my siblings, Mama's mental state was in a continual spiral of deterioration. There was no longer from time to time, the odd flicker of any improvement in her health. She dumped food, bought for the house, especially meat because she was always suspicious of it being human flesh and because for years now, she had been convinced of a conspiracy to kill her off by poisoning. As you can imagine, she was perilously thin and what little clothes she possessed hung miserably from her bony, bedraggled frame whenever she left the seclusion of her room to start yet another raging fire in the backyard to burn things she said had been swapped by intruders; items of clothing, a piece of furniture and more frequently, her own bed, which we children had to replace hastily. She took up smoking too and proceeded to smoke cigarettes in quite an unconventional way, by putting the lit end into her mouth.

'Mama what are you doing? You got the cigarette the wrong way round.' I moved towards her to take the cigarette carefully out of her mouth, but she pulled away.

'No. It's good this way,' she said. 'I want to burn out my insides. It's cleansing.

'Mama don't talk rubbish, you going to do yourself an injury.'

'You too young to understand, too young,' she trailed off, then popped the cigarette back into her mouth and turned away from me.

'Mama please listen to me,' I protested, but my words fell on deaf ears. She could not hear me. To my annoyance, she responded to the interjection of voices in her head - the lost souls of restless entities tuned into her frequency of despair. Again they set upon her, all clambering to occupy the temple of her body and mind, if only for a short time.

Life carried on as normal for Dada: he came and went, only to look upon Mama with scornful disgust whenever their paths crossed. I looked upon him in the same way, irritating his discomfort. Over time, the penalty for my silent disgust made me the focus of his attention and for some reason, void of words or actions on my part, my presence was increasingly a threat to him.

I met Maureen at the office in which I worked. Thankfully, she joined a team of mostly, middle-aged workers a few months after I had started and almost instantly, she and I became great friends. I introduced her to Basil - Charles' best friend. Both men were always together. They were as thick as thieves. Often, they would meet us for lunch and together we dined out on Luncheon Vouchers in near-by cafes or bistros.

Neither Charles nor Basil worked, yet they were always slick - sharp as the razor my father used to mark his cards. They certainly had an eye for style: Cecil Gee, Burberry, Fred Perrier, Gabicci; the names were endless.

At noon, one week day, Maureen and I came down the long metal steps of the side entrance which led out into a courtyard round the back of the office, to see Charles and Basil attending to something with fevered interest. We followed their eyes. The Securicor van, which delivered the wages - our wages, was parked in the courtyard. Alarmed, Maureen and I looked at each other. Charles and Basil were almost salivating when a guard alighted the vehicle with a black case in either hand. From where Maureen and I stood, it looked like an easy target.

'Hi there, come on, let's have something to eat,' I said, breaking their concentration.

As we walked away, they both kept craning their necks backwards, making sure they had not missed anything.

Basil looked at Maureen intently then asked: 'Is that Securicor van here at the same time, every week?' he looked across at me also.

'I… I think so, I'm not sure,' stuttered Maureen.

'I've never noticed it before,' I added.

After work that same day, I went back to Maureen's house to get ready for a night out. We sat on the carpet in her bedroom, listening to records, as teenagers do. Strewn around us on the floor were vinyls - 45s and LPs. We shared a four-pack of Cherry Bs we had bought on the way in, so we were in high spirits, giggling about anything and everything.

'Seriously though,' said Maureen with convicted sobriety, 'I'm really worried they're going to do something stupid, like rob that Securicor van.'

'You know what that would mean don't you?'

'What?'

'We won't have any money. We'll both be skint.'

Maureen runs her hand through her hair and says: 'Could you imagine that!' She took another swig from the Cherry B bottle. 'When I'm broke, I'll have to go to Basil and say, Basil, I need some money for bus fare: could I please have my wages?'

We both rolled around on the vinyls, giggling and laughing at the prospect.

When we stepped out with Charles and Basil on that same warm, summer evening, the merriment of Cherry Bs stepped out with us. And later that night, although they complained about how young the night was, they all walked me home.

'You know you can come back with me,' Charles said, 'you don't have to stay here.'

'Or, you can always come home with me,' said Maureen.'

'No, honestly you guys, I haven't been home for two days. I need to make sure Mama's all right. You all go and enjoy yourselves, I'll see you tomorrow,' I called. The fading remnants of cheer began to drain from my veins as I waved them off. I walked up to the front door and primed my key for the lock.

As though by some dark and sinister force, the door flew open without my even touching it, and quick as I flash, I was hauled in by a hand and thrown against the wall in the passageway.

'Where you been?' he demanded, his eyes a blazing red furnace, his fists, like his teeth, clenched.

'Dada!' I exclaimed in shocked surprise.

'I said, where have you been?'

'Dada, it's... it's only ...' I glanced down at my watch.

'Shut up!' he interjected, not wanting to hear the utterance of another word from my mouth. But I chanced to defy that control, for as a young woman, I had a voice and a right for it to be heard.

'... quarter past eleven. I didn't realise -'

My defiance served only to enrage him further and he lashed out. First the shocking sting of a large open palm, followed by the back of a hand caused me to stagger. Momentarily stunned, I slowly steadied myself against the wall. As soon as I had gathered my faculties, the pain he had inflicted upon my being, transformed itself into the most intense hatred. I stood up to my full height, side on, (just two centimetres below his chin) my panting chest heaving with rage. That was the very last time he was going to hit me. Right there and then, I wished to be a man of equal stature and height. Oh how I wanted knock him out cold, to beat him senseless, then step over him, but instead I stood there staring deep into his eyes. All I could see were his eyes - not him, just his eyes, and all the wickedness that lay beyond.

'Don't look at me like that!' he shouted, suddenly perturbed. 'I said stop looking at me like that!'

But I didn't stop. With my chest still heaving with fury, my persistent glare smashed to pieces the narcissistic pride he hid behind, exposing him for the misogynistic, power-thirsty charlatan that he was.

'Get up to your room! Go on! Get out of my sight before I kill you!

Slowly I withdrew; dropping my gaze to his feet in utter disgust as I turned to leave.

'This is my house you hear me, my house and as long as you're under MY roof, you will do as I say,' he asserted. 'I'm going to come home at the same time, every night, just to make sure you're in the house. I'll show you to make a fool of me.'

The sound of the front door slamming, before I had even reached the top of the stairs told me that I was free of his presence. So this was it. The time to leave this house was upon me for I could not remain here under these circumstances for another day.

Mama opened her bedroom door to me, her eyes anxiously searching my physiognomy as I entered into the solace of her peaceful abode.

'Why is he doing this to me?' she cried, 'Why? What have I ever done to him? He's running all my children out of their home: first Glen, then Clovis, then Julia and now you. That's what you've come to tell me haven't you? You're leaving too.'

We shared a deafening, most truthful pause because Mama was right, we both knew it.

'Not straight away Mama; but when the daylight comes, I'll have to go.' My words wounded her like a knife and she began to sob bitterly. 'Mama stop crying, it will be for the best, you'll see. I have to leave you to make myself stronger, then I can come back and get you away from Dada and away from this house for good.'

'If you leave Pauline will be at your heels. Please don't leave me alone with that man, I tell you he wants me dead.'

As fearful as I was, I tried to be her strength to dispel her fears but my voice wavered and tears pricked at my eyes. I knew what she was thinking; that I was going to walk out of this house and out of her life. I sat beside her on the bed and put my arm around her shoulders.

'Mama it will only be for a while, I'll come back and visit you regularly during that time, as often as I can. You must believe that I will never stop thinking about you. There will be times when you think that everyone has forgotten you, but remember this - Mama: as there is a God, I vow to you now, that I will come back to get you out of here.'

Those words made Mama cry even harder.

'Tell me about Jamaica,' I coaxed. And so I led her; guided her; into the sweetest memories of a faraway place and time; a place she most probably would never bless her eyes on again. Outside, the sudden windswept rain of a passing storm sung a haunting lullaby against the panes of the window.

In the early hours of the morning, Mama fell asleep, and when the daylight had finally poked its head over the folding darkness of what was night, I threw a few things into a bag, kissed Mama goodbye and left my solemn oath in the form of a note beside her on the pillow. It me grieved badly to leave behind three of the people I loved most, in the world - Mama, Pauline, who was visibly depressed and Douglas, who was too quiet for words. I bid that house a triumphant goodbye as I departed, glad that I would not fall victim to its warped charms.

Choked up, with an ambivalence of elation and intense guilt, I did the hardest thing ever. I walked away.

When Charles opened the door to me, I fell into his arms, a tearful mess. His parents came out to see what the commotion was about and I fell into their arms also. Immediately, they sat me down. I was given cups of tea, and through much sobbing, I told them the whole episode of what had happened and parts of the past I was willing to divulge to enable their understanding of my distress. They consoled and advised me with a tenderness I had scarcely known. They knew of my family but still they accepted me, made me feel welcome, as though I was part of their family, and so I took up residence with them. Thank God, they saved me; until the time when I could save myself.

Freedom however, did not come without its sacrifice. I had to be very vigilant when visiting Mama, and these visits were more like a game of cat and mouse in my pursuit to avoid clashing with Dada. Living on the outside made the house appear a more desolate and lonely place. None of my siblings had dwellings of their own which could serve as a temporary sanctuary for Mama. With the exception of Pauline and Douglas who were still at home: and Julia who was still at the mother and baby home, awaiting re-housing; we all lived with partners in their family homes and even though, at night, we lay our heads under a different roof, Dada's hold over us was just as strong as it had ever been. I was never going to allow myself to be ruled by a man - ever. An equal partnership, though rare, was my only compromise.

It was not all a bed of roses living with Charles. Everything happened so fast. Following the initial honeymoon period of about three months, I discovered two things which changed my outlook on life forever.

Trudging back through the snow, towards the home I shared with Charles and his family, on a cold January morning, I was struck by a sense of awe and wonder, which was marred by the guilt of Mama's long suffering, not yet brought to an end. The family doctor had just confirmed that I was about to become a mother - me! A mother! It was at that precise moment I felt a mere child myself, frightened, helpless and dazed. Amidst my fear for Mama's safety, and my confusion about life, a higher being had seen fit to bestow blessings upon me. A most precious gift had been handed to me and with every bone in my body I was determined that my child would not be exposed to the horrors I had endured throughout my childhood. I would have to be even more vigilant when visiting Mama if I did not want to end up in hospital, like Julia had.

Charles was over the moon when he learnt that he was to become a father. It was a bow, a brass button, a stripe on his newly decorated male countenance, which inflated his chest to almost twice its size. His parents, Miss Ida and Clarkey were overjoyed when Charles and I broke the news to them. They were sure that responsibility was what Charles needed to help keep him on that straight and narrow road he had traversed for quite some time.

Quite unexpectedly, the second discovery came the morning after Charles had disappeared under the guise of purchasing of a newspaper. Once before he had done this, saying that he had slept over at Basil's place even though I had my doubts then. But now I was beside myself with worry: something was amiss.

Downstairs in the kitchen, Clarkey washed pots and pans, wiped units and cooked breakfast at the same time.

'Here,' he said, placing a cup of tea and some toast on the table, on my entrance. 'You must try to eat something.'

But I could not eat a bite, not a morsel. Instead I fretted and wrung my hands together.

'Anything could have happened to him.'

Mr Clarke walked over to where I sat, around the kitchen table. 'Melanie, the good news is, Charles don't have another woman and he is alive and well and I am positive there is nothing wrong with him. I don't know how to tell you this,' said Clarkey, worry lines etched across his forehead, 'He's been arrested. He's in jail.'

'Jail! Why, have you heard something?'

'We don't need to hear, we've seen it before, many times.'

Just then, Miss Ida entered the kitchen to share with me her secret shame. Apparently, Charles had been incarcerated by Her Majesty's Service, on more than the one occasion he cared to mention in the early days of our relationship, even though he assured me then that it was all in the past and that he had moved on.

'Since he's been with you, that's been the longest time he has stayed on the outside - and look at this,' said Miss Ida, raising her arms in dismay. 'I thought he put this behind him. The shame I've had to go through when people come and tell me that he is in the Hackney Gazette again; and me sitting in the courthouse like a fool. I'm not doing it anymore, so you got to talk to him,' pleaded Miss Ida, her voice now streaked with desperation. 'Tell him you and the baby need him, or your child's going to end up with a jailbird for a father.'

Again my heart sank, and it sank deeper still when later that afternoon, after being remanded on bail, Charles put in a appearance to confess to an earlier crime for which a court hearing had been set, and to feebly attempt to convince me of his innocence of the crime committed the previous day.

Naturally, he made every effort to find work, so that it would set him in good stead for his pending court appearance. However, getting a job was not the problem; Charles could talk his way into anything and in the effort of acquiring work, he was successful time and again. The difficulty for Charles lay with holding down a job, because he was not accustomed to taking orders. Sometimes a job would last a whole week and sometimes only half a day. To tell the truth it was wearing me out.

'Charles you're home early, what's going on?'

He sucked in his breath, puffed and panted, then made the kind of hissing sound a builder makes exactly prior to delivering a verbal quote. This was not a good sign. Someone had upset him.

'I've had to jack the job in, ain't I,' he announced, in his sticks-man, cockney accent, as though it were through no fault of his own.

'And you were doing so well,' I sympathized, disappointed yet again but more ashamed of how pathetic I sounded. 'What happened?'

'Well,' said Charles, adjusting his neck and stance as though getting ready for a fight. 'I've gone into work this morning, and the foreman, he's nagging me - "do this, do that, pick that up, you're not working fast enough," and by tea-break, I'm brewing, I mean, really brewing. I swear to God, I feel to knock him out and done, but I held it down cause I need the job.'

At that precise moment, I breathed an inward sigh of relief. At least his job was still saveable.

'Then after tea-break,' continued Charles, 'he starts giving it the big-un again.'

'I don't understand. Why did you have to quit the job? Why did you walk off site?'

'Because I told him; I says to him: "listen mate, I didn't leave my nice warm gaff to sweep floors." Then, would you believe it,' gasped Charles, expressing his earlier astonishment, 'he starts giving me a bit a lip.' He demonstrated at the same time with one hand in the shape of a talking mouth.

'So what did you do?'

'I decked him! The sap!'

These bouts of aggression however, did not stop at his place of work. As you've probably gathered, Charles had a temper - a very volatile one.

About a fortnight after he had 'decked' his boss and two weeks before his court appearance, his parents, Miss Ida and Clarkey invited both of us along to a birthday party a friend was throwing for her thirty-year old son.

'Charles, make sure you don't drink too much, I don't want you embarrassing me and your father. Melanie, watch what he's drinking, I got to try and hold my head up in front of these people.'

In the latter hours of that evening, the four of us, Charles, myself and his parents walked the short distance to the party. Music and a chorus of, chatter and giggles greeted the ears before the eyes. Guests standing outside the house looked up as we approached; to acknowledge, to smile, to say a polite hello. We entered the house and drinks were quickly placed into our hands.

'Remember what I said,' Miss Ida whispered in a warning tone, 'conduct yourself like a gentleman.'

'Settle down Mum,' laughed Charles, mockingly playful, 'you're too stressed.'

Judging by the look on Miss Ida's face, she was not in a playful mood; nevertheless, she proceeded to introduce Charles and me to friends she had known for many years, before we followed the sound of music, into a large room at the front of the house.

The living room had been emptied of all furniture, except two bamboo chairs and a glass coffee table, perched precariously in a pile in the corner. All that remained in the middle of that big space, apart from guests who lined the perimeter of the room, was Mark. It was *his* birthday, so naturally he was centre of attention. There in the middle of the room on his own, he danced to the applause and delight of everyone, wearing around his neck the biggest gold belcher chain I had ever seen, to which was attached his drink. Confident of his appeal, he spun around. Everyone's attention was on this one being. He was the star of the show. However, at that precise moment, something told me to transfer my eyes away from Mark's gyrating to view the expression Charles wore on his face.

'Who the fuck does he think he is? He's taking the fucking piss ain't he? Look at him.'

And look at him, is exactly what Charles did for most of the night, studying his every movement, growling under his breath every time Mark walked past, muttering juice-filled insults like: 'The sap! The plum! The lemon!'

Again I was humouring a man. Trying to make him see that he'd got all hett up about nothing. Anyhow, everything would be fine as long as he remained standing right beside me as he now was. That way, I could keep an eye on him.

'So you're Melanie,' came a female voice from behind.

I turned towards the voice; smiled, opened my mouth to speak but then came an almighty crashing sound; and screams thrown up to the ceiling fell like torrential rain. Rolling around on the floor were Charles and Mark: it appeared the latter had been caught off-guard. All I saw was Charles on top of Mark; his arms, bent at the elbow, working like pistons on an engine as he repeatedly pounded his victim. When eventually Charles had been prised from Mark, and carried outside, I heard his parents in the background apologise profusely before making a quick exit. We stepped out into the cold night air of the street, to face Charles and the front door of the house was shut behind us.

'How could you do that? And in front of all our friends.' Miss Ida bursts into tears and Clarkey puts his arm around her shoulder.

'Come on Ida, let's go home.'

I was not a worldly woman, however there was the ever-present resonance of disquiet within me, an alarming feeling of déjà vu, which my senses repelled. I was gripped with the fear of making the same mistakes as my mother; of retracing her steps on that same road to hell. It could only be a matter of time before that level of aggression was turned against me and I shivered at the thought.

When the court case came up, I did what Miss Ida suggested: I wrote a letter to the judge pleading with him to be lenient, given my present condition.

The judge looked directly at me as though to apologise for his intended action.

'Due to the serious nature of this crime and previous convictions, I have no alternative but to impose a custodial sentence.'

What a blow this was to me and my unborn child.

'However,' continued the judge, 'in light of the fact that the defendant has pleaded guilty to this, and a number of other charges, and that he is soon to be a father, I impose a sentence of six months for each crime to run concurrent.'

Charles was lucky. He had got off lightly. With good behaviour he could be out in four months. He was taken down to the cells and I waited anxiously to see him before he was transferred to a destination as yet unknown to me.

Everything was a mess. So much for leaving home to seek my fortune, to save Mama. Good fortune I discovered, was in short supply.

I started receiving letters from Charles, who made a request for me to write every day and when I did not meet that request, he accused me of having affairs.

'Damn cheek!' Exclaimed Clarkey, when I shared one such letter with him. 'Write back and tell him you have better things to do with your time. Tell him, he put himself in there, not you! Tell him to stop writing them stupid letters, and that if he's going mad, to keep it to himself.'

In my response to my most recent correspondence with Charles, I passed on Clarkey's message and I also delivered an ultimatum. I conveyed that much as I loved him, I could not allow that love to destroy me or my child.

There was so much time to think; to look into the future to see what awaited me if I did not diverge from this path to make my own way in life. Although I did not want to be the creator of a new broken home, I decided to give Charles one last chance to make good. Everyone is entitled to one mistake. Still, even I knew it was not wise to place all of one's eggs into one basket, so, without breathing a word to anyone, I made enquiries about alternative housing.

Out of this world was the sensation that washed over me when for the first time, I felt life moving within my womb and consequently, my whole being was aglow in celebration of womanly pride and the untold mysteries of the miracles of life. I needed the comfort of my mother now more than ever, to be once again cradled and rocked by her arms alone. The guilt and shame of failing my mother gnawed away at me with every passing moment she remained trapped in that confounded situation.

Visiting Mama was always risky. I took care, first making sure, as best I could, that the coast was clear. The sight of me in my present condition would infuriate Dada - leaving me wide open to danger. Nevertheless, I had to see my mother, but for obvious reasons, it just could not be as often as I wished. Therefore, I decided that should Dada show up during one such visit, my feeble plan of action would be to hide out in Mama's room. I would be relatively safe behind her locked door, if, I remained silent until Dada had left the house.

Time is the tumbling, fast moving clouds, carried along by a strong wind that rolls into weeks and months. I wrote many letters during that time; kept many appointments and tried my utmost to look forward to what I hoped would be a better future.

With only days to go before Charles was released and the birth of my child, I prepared once again to see Mama because when the baby came, I wasn't sure when next I would see her. I wanted to assure her also that I was in the process of getting myself together and that a few months after the baby was born, I intended to get a nanny, in order to go to university and train for a career in teaching. I had to lift her spirits because things were at an all time low and simply could not get any worse, or so I believed.

'Do you want me to come with you?' asked a concerned Clarkey. 'Give me two minutes, I'll get my coat and shoes on.'

'No Clarkey, I'll be fine, honestly. I'll be back in under an hour.'

Pauline's repressive countenance let me into the house. Although she greeted me warmly, the dark rings under her eyes told a sorry of her own desperate longing to escape.

Slowly, I climbed the stairs; knocked at Mama's bedroom door and waited patiently for it to be opened. The idea of her being cooped up behind lock and key in this gloomy place frustrated me whilst I waited, even though I understood why Mama did it, and how safe it made her feel. After a long while, I entered into the moroseness of her room.

'Melanie, thank God you're here. I'm worried about Douglas, so worried,' she said, wringing her hands together.

'Why, what's wrong with Douglas?' I asked, suddenly alarmed.

'He's not well. He's sick. Look after him.'

Something in her voice caused a cold shrill to run through my body. The full realisation of why Douglas had become so quiet, hit me with terrifying consequences. The madness we were all so terrified of had claimed my brother. I looked in every room for Douglas then made my way downstairs to find him making tea in the kitchen. For a few brief moments, I hovered in the doorway - Douglas oblivious to my presence. He reached up for the teabags and I noticed then that the cupboards were practically bare.

'How are things Douglas?' I said after stepping into the kitchen to make my presence known.

'All right Melanie,' he said in a cheerful voice, not making much eye contact.'You know I'm a Jehovah's Witness now, don't you?' he announced with pride.

'A what?'

'A Jehovah's Witness. A soldier of God, prepared to fight His battles and defend Him on a higher plane as well as here on earth. You should come and worship with us. My church,' he says, throwing a dreamy upward glance in the air, 'is called The Kingdom Hall. 'I have many brothers and sisters in the Kingdom Hall.'

I was speechless. I could not recall him speaking in this way before, nor had I seen him look so happy, as though the surety of his hopes and dreams were at last guaranteed. I knew he had developed an interest in theology for I had seen him avidly reading the Bible on a multitude of occasions during this quiet period he had been going through. He stirred the tea, going round and round the cup in anti-clockwise fashion. *Watchtower* magazines covered the table and I flicked through them searchingly whilst Douglas talked with passion about the only thing that offered him true hope; the only thing that had stretched its hand to reach out to him. As he rambled on about the Kingdom Hall, I looked up at him and my eyes filled with tears. Once again, panic rose high within my stature, renewing its attack on my despair. If he didn't get help, and fast, the nightmare we went through, (were still going through with Mama) would begin all over again.

'Melanie, have you ever thought what heaven is like?'

'Douglas why are you thinking about heaven?' I asked, rocked to the core with fear. 'You're alive; you got to think about living; here and now.'

'But Melanie, there's a better place; a beautiful place, and you know what? I can't wait to get there.'

Dear God, when would there be an end to our suffering? How much more could one family endure before it crumbled, disintegrated to nothing? The fevered urgency for Mama and Douglas to leave this house was stronger than ever before. I knew that if they spent another year here; it would most certainly be their last on this earth. I left holding my stomach, barely able to support my own frame.

Charles was released from prison in time for the birth of our beautiful baby boy, who we named James, by now Mama's fourth grandchild. Glen and his girlfriend had had a boy after Julia's baby, and then Clovis and his partner had also given birth to a boy. Now that I was a mother, I knew Dada would not be so aggressive towards me. Believe it or not, he had some morals, in that he could not kill the mother of a helpless, nursing child. I did not have to hide any more as Dada showed little interest in James and I whenever we visited Mama.

Up until two weeks ago, Pauline had been living at home. But quite unexpectedly, the opportunity to escape had suddenly opened itself to her when she met Joseph, a Nigerian student, studying law. For her, it was ever-lasting love - everything she had been waiting for. Seduced by what lay beyond the open door in her darkness, Pauline entered in, but unbeknown to her, she represented Joseph's passport to citizenship and freedom.

Pauline left word that she had an announcement to make and that she wanted to see everyone back at the house; so we all met up, together, at Number 27, for what was to be the last time.

'Look everybody,' Pauline announced after arriving by herself. 'I'm a married woman.' She flashed a ring at everyone and we were all gob-smacked, speechless. We couldn't believe that she had got married and not invited us to the wedding. From courtship to marriage, it had taken two weeks in total for Joseph to get that ring on her finger. At first glance, it appeared to be a whirlwind romance. Dada was vexed to high heaven because Pauline was his property and it was an insult, a slap in the face, that he had not even been asked to give her away. Not a single word escaped his lips and where there should have been cause for celebration there was an atmosphere of rising tension and animosity. The only decent thing left for us to do was to congratulate Pauline, and so with the exception of Dada, we shifted our disappointment to one side and did just that. Dada on the other hand, tried to hide his simmering fury by pouring himself another glass of rum and opening the newspaper to the betting pages.

Then, one by one, we drifted upstairs to see Mama in that same room - the room in which Pauline had broken the sink after swinging on it that very first day we moved in. The room where we had once sat happily, eating mashed potatoes and drinking Treetop orange squash; that same room which over the years had become Mama's prison of conscience. A long eerie silence descended us as we stood there in the dark around Mama's bed. It was a message; a distant calling that only we could hear in the stillness of that room; a telepathic communication that arrived on the back of a thin slice of light that pushed its way in through the slightly ajar door. It revealed to us that the time was now right to do whatever was necessary to take Dada's wife away from him. He had no interest in her whatsoever. It suited him very much to have a down-trodden wife as an asset to his notoriety, and even though it had always been within his power to set her free through some amicable arrangement, his ambitions for her could not stretch that far.

Downstairs in the comfort of the plush living room, Dada padded around on the shag-pile carpet, in complete contrast to how Mama was living upstairs. They were a married couple who presided in two separate worlds, under the one roof.

'Dada we're worried about Mama, she's sick bad and she's not eating. She can't weigh more than seven stones,' I told him.

'Well I cook food and she won't eat it. What you want me to do?'

'It's just that she's in such a bad way, and Douglas - he's not well either.'

'Do you think I don't know that? I know he's sick. Yesterday I sent him to the shop to buy cigarettes for me and you know what he turned round and told me? He told me to get off my fat lazy arse and go buy it myself. He said that if I wanted to kill myself, I should use the sharpest knife in the kitchen. So I know he's sick because he wouldn't talk to me like that if he wasn't now would he?'

For a moment we conceived that Madness had also given Douglas the bottle to say things we were still not been brave enough to say ourselves. Apparently, according to Dada, I would need to be mad first, to tell him what I really thought of him.

'So, what you going to do about it Dada?' Clovis asked.

'What do you expect me to do? I've had enough. I washed my hands of Girlie a long time ago. A man should be proud of his wife but how can I be proud of *that*?'

How dare he speak of my mother in that way. The desire to speak up in Mama's defence was so strong but we held our tongues, everyone except Pauline.

'Well why don't you sell the house and let us find somewhere else for Mama and Douglas to live? Pauline asked. 'This house isn't doing them any good. In fact it's killing them.'

'Sell which house?' He shot Pauline and the rest of us, a threatening look and abruptly stood up to his full height. 'Over my dead body!' he bellowed with such conviction.

The appeal of that idea, though very agreeable to us, had triggered something quite ugly in Dada and a new-found determination in us, his children. We could feel the heat of his temper rising as he glared down at us and not wanting to be on the receiving end of his anger, we quickly departed. He had left us little choice but to resort to drastic measures. If he wanted a fight to the death, then so be it. Somehow, we would have to sell the house from under him; a daring mission that would raise hell itself.

Soon, Clovis, Glen, Julia, Pauline and I, began to hold regular meetings at each other's homes and we are buzzing with the optimism of seeing Mama and Douglas free. We put into place, a firm plan of action; however, our plans were hindered somewhat, because in the mean time, Douglas' health was deteriorating fast and he was extremely adept at eluding the doctor's appointments set for him.

He had stopped attending the Kingdom Hall but that did not stop all the brothers and sisters he had in the church from coming round, trying to coerce him back. They knocked on the door all hours of the day and night, while Douglas cowered inside, confused. Like vultures, they waited outside, ready to pounce on his vulnerability should he emerge. They pushed prayer books and notes through the letterbox and told him that God loved him.

The only way to get any respite was to insult them, which I did on a few occasions, but they were persistent people. Desperate to escape the pressures and torments within and around him, Douglas was one day driven through a pane of glass. He jumped through a window, cutting himself badly in the process, to run screaming down the road, lashing out at anyone who came too close. He was arrested that day and taken to hospital where they held him down and heavily sedated. We visited him in hospital for over two months; saw how agitated he had become and cried when big burly men wrestled him: held him down, strapped him onto the bed or worse still, into a straight jacket to inject him, while we stood around helpless. And then, like a baby, he would drift into a peaceful sleep. His deterioration set our plans back for a while. Nevertheless, we realised that we could not wait any longer for him to improve. It wasn't going to happen just yet and although that realisation was as bitter as the cud, we had no choice but to swallow, and accept it.

Time was not on our side. We had to move fast, using the fact that Dada was illiterate to our advantage. It was a pity his reading skills did not stretch further than the horses for here was a gamble he was sure to lose. Therefore, without the aid of estate agents (who would struggle to highlight the best features amongst all the dilapidation) Glen and Clovis started the process of a private sale, and within four weeks, we get a date for completion, via solicitors.

It was only right someone broke the news to Dada, to give him time to make alternative arrangements but that prospect terrified us to the core. Two weeks had gone by and still he was none the wiser. We sat in Pauline's one bedroom apartment in Wood Green, sick to our stomachs with a combination of hysteria and fear.

'Who's going to tell him?' asked Julia. I would, but last time I made a stand, he put me in hospital. I had to go under a knife.' she laughs and Glen laughs with her shaking his head.

'He's knocked you out cold before, ain't he?' Clovis says, looking at Glen. So I suppose you don't want to tell him either.'

'Don't look at me,' said Pauline, placing a tray of drinks on the table beside the window. 'A coward man keeps safe bones: you ever heard that saying? Well I'm a woman and I'm also keeping my bones very safe: I'm stopping in tomorrow. I'll take care of the children. Let me know when it's all over - if you still alive.'

'Why don't you tell him Melanie, you're braver than us,' said Julia, trying to humour me into fronting this dangerous deed.

'Hey look, I value my life just as much as you do,' I retorted, 'although - I will tell him, because someone has to.' They breathed a sigh of relief. 'But not on my own. I'll do it if Clovis and Glen comes with me.'

The night before the final conflict, I sat up in my bed turning over a multitude of thoughts whilst Charles slept peacefully beside me. I looked at him with a mixture of love and pity. He had become more domineering, quick to lash out. Our relationship was on a dead end road, so yet again I played the waiting game; waiting for an opening to make yet another escape.

I wondered whether Mama had eaten or if she was warm. With the end of our nightmare in sight, I allowed my mind to drift back over all the years of cruelty and turmoil I had seen in that house during my childhood; over all the things that Dada had done to Mama and I cried for the way he had let her and the family down. Rage took over from fear. No longer would I hold my tongue. I had to say something. I had to let him know what I really thought of him. I pulled the cord on the bedside light switch. My body was weary but my mind, wide awake, raced like the horses backed by my father.

The next day, there was such an urgency within me to see Mama. Fuelled up with the anger I had accumulated from the previous night, I felt ready to take on the world. I set off with determination in my step, stopping only to pick up a few things from the shops and then I paused for a while outside the fish and chip shop before going in to buy a piece of fish for Mama. I know how much she loves a piece of rock. I turned the corner from Church Street into Yoakley Road and walked down a few metres, till the house came into view. In the distance I saw the flashing lights of a police van and car parked outside the house. In the brief moment that followed, I was frozen to the spot. I fathomed to think what crime had been committed. I gathered my senses together, to race down the road towards home with all kinds of horrors racing through my mind. I was across the road from the house when I saw Clovis being led out by two policemen; his hands cuffed behind his back, blood dripping from his face.

'Clovis what's happened? I cried. What's going on? Is Mama and Douglas OK?'

'Melanie I can't bear to see Mama like that no more. I turned over the sitting room,' he declared before being bundled into the back of the waiting police van.

I rushed into the house. Three more policemen were in the sitting room talking to Dada. He shot me a venomous look when I paused briefly in the doorway. I took the stairs leading to Mama's room by two, to see if she was safe. Her door was slightly ajar.

'Mama you OK?'

She did not say anything, just lay there in her bed.

'I bought you something to eat Mama. I know you like rock don't you?'

'Thank you Melanie,' she said in a voice, weak and low. 'I was so hungry.'

Tears poured down my face.

'Don't you worry Mama. We're going to get you and Douglas away from here very soon. Just you prepare yourself. Pack what little you have and be ready: it could be a matter of days - two weeks at the most. We've sold the house. It's over Mama, it's over.' I kissed her face. 'Now I'm going to give that bastard downstairs a piece of my mind.' I marched into the sitting room, pushing past police officers to confront my father for the first time. He stood up as I approached.

'What are the police doing here?' I demanded, madder than I had ever known myself.

'They're here because your no-good brother came in and destroyed my property.'

'So who called them?'

'I did,' he said, coming towards me with shoulders hunched over in aggressive fashion. 'I told him I was going to get him arrested for this.'

'How could you call the police on your own son? Your own son.'

'Look what he's done to my things! Look at it! Everything is damaged.'

'That's all you've ever worshipped isn't it - your things; your suits, your gold, your money, you make me sick to my stomach. While you're down here, living your high life, my mama is upstairs starving; your youngest son is screaming out for help and all you could do is worry about material value. You're a pitiful excuse for a father, do you know that? All you do is to walk street and breed women. Why do you keep breeding them? If that's what you think being a father is, then you haven't got a clue.'

'That's right!' he shouted, with tears in his eyes, ready to put on a show for the officers. 'My father left me when I was seven years old, so I don't know no better.'

'Don't you dare try to twist and manipulate this situation,' I interrupted. You are not the victim here. You have destroyed lives and caused so much misery to so many people because of your selfishness. You knew what you were doing. You just didn't care, but you know what, time catches up with everyone,' I warned. 'Wickedness will not prevail. Your time is up.'

I saw the anger, the hurt my words had caused. Unable to speak for a moment, his eyes blazed with rage, and in the next senseless moment he lunged forward and made a grab for me. Well acquainted with what his hands could do, I managed to jump out of the way in time for the police to make a grab for him. One of them radioed for more help.

'You little bitch, talking to ME like that, ME!' He was almost foaming at the mouth now, and there was no doubt that eventually, he would overpower the three officers who restrained him but I had to tell him to find alternative housing before I left.

'I just want to hold you,' he said to me with such passion, 'so I can wring your fucking neck. Let go of me!' Again he struggled to break free.

'If you wasn't such an illiterate bastard,' I announced with glee, 'you would realise that we've sold the house from under you! Your days here are numbered.'

'The only way you're leaving this house is in a coffin. I going to fucking kill you,' he shouted, putting up a more ferocious struggle to break free from the grasp of the three officers.

'You'd better go now,' an officer managed to blurt out as Dada knocked his helmet to the ground in the scuffle. 'Quick!'

My body, awash with adrenaline, vibrated as I walked up the street. The dirty deed had been done. Its release was ecstatic, and at sweet last, we were able to bathe in the glorious light at the end of a tunnel.

Chapter Eleven

Blast from the Past

....

The day Mama finally left that house had always been envisaged by all to be a great day, a perfect day - in fact it was grey, overcast and spitting rain; a day filled with nervous uncertainty, for who knew what lay on the road ahead, or round the corner for that matter.

When she emerged from the house, wearing the new navy overcoat we had purchased for her, Mama looked frail, frightened and confused. She couldn't have been more than six and a half stones in weight. It was then, if ever, we realised just how close she had come to death, how reverently she had willed it on to release the gnawing of her agonising pain.

The house was emptied of all our belongings, what little we had. Now instead of the uninhibited noises of yesteryear, there was profound silence, broken only by the sound of our every movement, which ricocheted around an empty shell.

Back in '66 although Number 27 Grayling Road had been a mere stepping stone on our journey, it represented the core of a plan that would take us back across thousands of miles of ocean. This house had been a symbol of hope and prosperity: a sign of better things to come and so within its walls, we cemented all our hopes and dreams, and with the passionate yearning of immigrants, we had believed whole-heartedly, that one day, it would yield up Jamaica as its bounteous reward. The last thing we had expected was to be delivered into the midst of a harsh and bloody battle for survival; to look on, helplessly, as our most cherished hopes and dreams slipped from our grasp, like smoke that faded into nothing. Wearing the cloak of that bitter knowledge, we were silently aggrieved, for we would leave the house with considerably less than what we had come with. Walking away from this nightmare of heartbreak and disappointment should have been easy for everyone, but for Mama it would prove to be an emotional minefield; the aftermath of a bitter war in which not only she, but her youngest son also, had been seriously wounded.

Outside, although rain spattered in our faces, we looked up to the grey sombre heavens above our heads and gave thanks for the long-awaited arrival of this day, bleak as it was. Mama sat in the front of a Dolomite Sprint and through the rain-spattered windscreen, she peered up at the house for one last time - a quick glance, then without much ado, she turned her head forward, and we were, all of us, including those in the van behind, as ready as could be, to enter onto a new road; to start a new life, free of Dada's menacing control, and to see what we could make of it.

Number 27 Grayling Road was sold at a great loss; not only because of what had happened there, but because it was in the most decrepit condition - all of it, apart from the sitting room. With Mama and Douglas free, we were able to breathe again. However, we were not, by any means, out of the woods yet. We still had to find them somewhere permanent to live and we needed help in managing Douglas' illness better, to stop him from being arrested and sectioned, which had become a frequent occurrence.

For about six weeks or so, they lived in a high-rise block on the Haberdasher Estate in Hoxton. It was the only place we could find at short notice, without involving the authorities. We wanted Mama and Douglas to stay together. We did not want one or the other to become lost in a deplorable mental health system for we had been exposed to its practices; saw what horrors really went on beyond the security of its secret doors, and therefore were reluctant to willingly entrust to it our precious Mama and Douglas, without first making enquiries to understand the type and level of care that would be given. It was an uneasy time because both their mental states were highly charged so as a precaution, we had the windows in the flat nailed down.

In approximately eight weeks, we purchased the first of two three-bedroom properties, one in Wanstead, and then a year later, another in Walthamstow, with the intention to continue expanding as soon as the equity had risen. After a shaky initial start, the long process of settling Mama and Douglas into a stable environment had begun.

A most remarkable thing occurred during this period of re-establishing ourselves as a family and as individuals. Equipped with the tools of self-empowerment we surged ahead with our personal lives and in our careers.

With Charles still gracing Her Majesty with his presence, I decided to call his bluff. I put an end to our relationship on a Saturday afternoon and took control of my life. I rented a two-bedroom conversion with garden, got my child into a local day nursery and enrolled at university, with the hope that one day I would attain qualified teacher status. Education was a wonderful vocation. I soaked up literature on Vygotsky, Bruner and Piaget and I was empowered with words, confidence and the new-found freedom of knowledge that was open to me. My brothers and sisters were also guided towards their chosen careers. Glen, as you know, was a mechanical engineer; Clovis who had inherited his father's love of fine clothes went into designing; Julia worked for the Royal Courts of Justice and was also studying to become a barrister. Pauline found her niche in marketing and worked her way to the top within a very short time. We were all as happy as can be, given our current situation, all except Pauline whose personal life was in a mess.

From the first time I had met her elusive husband, in that one bedroom apartment he shared with my sister in Wood Green, I had taken an instant dislike to him. Pauline supported him: a student who already had a string of letters after his name. Irritating was the repugnance of his plastic smile; the way he moved and paced quietly in the background, translucently obscured by his lack of interest or support for his wife. I could see right through him, down to all his dishonourable intentions and I unleashed onto him the discomforting pierce of my glare, which always had the desired effect - to drive him out of the one bedroom apartment. Then, after a while they moved into a two bedroom flat just off the Old Kent Road.

For a long time Pauline had suspected him of being unfaithful. A mother herself now, she chose to suffer in silence like Mama had done before her, hoping for things to improve to keep her family intact. But when she broke down and cried about the emotional stress she was under, one Saturday afternoon, it was a problem no more. Clovis and Glen, were only too keen and fired up; after they heard what had been going on, they were set to put Pauline's husband out, in the same way they had put Massah Stanley out, years earlier. They arranged to meet at her flat at eleven o'clock on Tuesday and purposely chose a weekday to see what the element of surprise would throw up. The whole saga was relayed to us not long afterwards.

Pauline had gone in to work at Dickens and Jones as normal on that Tuesday but had left early, feigning illness. Turning the key in the lock, she entered her home, leaving the door slightly ajar for Clovis and Glen. In a quick sweeping movement, she entered her bedroom, ready to pack her husband's belongings but the shock, which greeted her, caused her to retreat backwards, out of the room. Standing over the kitchen sink, her blood boiled rapturously. She was going to give them a wake up call like none they had had before.

On her bed lay two entwined sleeping bodies; the sheets weaving, in, out and around them like a wicker basket.

'Wake up you slumbering low-life,' she said, splashing the bucket of cold water over them and then followed it up by also throwing the bucket at them, which caught Joseph just above the eye.

'Pauline! gasped Joseph in a rich Nigerian accent, after seemingly swimming for breath. 'I promise you, it's not what it looks like. We were just studying.'

'Tell me something, what do you take me for? You know why I came home early from work today? I thought I'd have a clear out.'

'Do something Joseph! Don't just sit there!' pleaded his female companion, trying desperately to pull the sheets about her.

'Oh baby, he's not going to do anything - but I am.'

Pauline rolled her sleeves up as she usually did when about to take part in a fight. She was a woman born with muscles; like Cousin Enid. She always had them, hence the reason why she'd fight all my battles when we were at school together. Sometimes I'd have the whole school in hot pursuit behind me because my mouth had got me in trouble again. I couldn't fight my own battles, but one thing I was able to do, with long skinny legs, was to run like hell. I knew that if I saw Pauline in the distance, everything would be all right. She'd stop them in their tracks. Pauline would catch hold of me and put me behind her, from where I'd give the assailants two fingered gestures. Then she'd roll her sleeves up, crack her knuckles real loud, and say: 'right, who wants to go first?'

In two swift steps she rushed to the naked woman on her bed and was upon her in no time at all, dragging her kicking and screaming to the front door.

'What are you doing? shouted Joseph, trying to pull Pauline off. 'Let go of her. For God's sake, she naked. You can't let her go out like...'

In the struggle, Pauline's elbow met Joseph's chin and his head and body jutted backwards.

'Trust me, my husband, she'll learn a valuable lesson from this. She'll learn never to open her legs in another woman's bed again. Now get out, you whorite!' screamed Pauline, giving the woman an almighty shove.

Just then, Clovis and Glen showed up; their serious faces, in time for a shock.

'What the ...!'

Without another word they dragged Joseph off, back into the bedroom as Pauline slammed the front door. In the background she could hear her husband taking a beating, and the unknown woman she had put out, was also beating down the door for her clothes, but Pauline was in no hurry to save either of them. Calmly, she walked into the kitchen and pressed the switch on the kettle to make a cup of tea.

Annoyed by this woman's persistent hammering though, Pauline eventually opened the door and dangled her dress. 'Is this what you want?'

Relief lit the eyes of this nameless woman, like fairy lights on a tree.

'You can have it, but first I'm going to redesign it slightly, for you,' and with all her might, Pauline ripped the dress into two neat halves across her knee. 'Here you go. It's going to be all the rage. Let's see how you wear that, and count yourself lucky you got off so light. Now get away from my door before I rip you to shreds.'

Back in the bedroom Joseph, who was just coming round, sat up to gather himself.

'Get your things together: you're leaving,' said Glen.

'Not tonight. I've got nowhere to go. I'll go tomorrow!'

'No you won't leave tomorrow or tonight - you're leaving right now.'

And so with the help of Clovis and Glen, Pauline spring cleaned her husband right out of her life and filed for a divorce.

The house was always full on Saturdays; the day when Mama got to see all her family in one go. Having grown up with strict gender roles, the boys mended, repaired and fit fixtures, whilst the girls shopped, cooked and took care of the kids. After dinner, we all sat in Mama's garden, where she had started a little vegetable plot of carrots, beans, tomatoes, onions and garlic. We laughed and loved whilst the children played; three generations of the same family united under one roof.

Life over the coming years was a juggling act, not without pressures of its own, although nowhere near the hell, we had all been through. It was a time to heal; a time to replenish our ailing spirits; a time to rekindle and reacquaint ourselves with some of the lost hopes of bygone years; and most importantly, a time to give thanks for the mercy of lives spared, to understand, to accept and to grow in strength despite what fate had handed us.

At the age of twenty-seven, I graduated from university, a fully fledged teacher, to everyone's surprise and delight. Overjoyed, Mama's eyes glistened with pride. It was because of her that I had achieved so much. She was the one who encouraged regular visits to the local library and who, when we got back, would say, 'now let's play school.' She made learning a game, a joy, and a pleasure and although it was hard to soak up the knowledge at school, her principles on education remained with me always - her gift to me.

More than anything, I wanted to see Mama and Douglas restored to their former selves but I learnt fast to face the reality of things because the kind of traumas they had been through would not heal overnight. Time is the master who healed deep wounds to the silky-smooth touch of a scar that would always abide as a reminder, in mind and body.

In 1989, just a little over ten years since Grayling Road my brother Douglas was now stable on the medication he was taking. The downside however was that he spoke only when spoken to; never smiled and never made eye contact, but at least he was no longer agitated and did not pace up and down arduously any more. He was calm and relaxed. When I think back to our childhood, I imagine we are playing football in the backyard, or the sun, pouring through the branches of trees we climbed, the expression on his face as we fought with swords made of sticks; then I remember how cruelly Dada treated him and I am saddened all over again. Sometimes I grieve for him because in a way, it feels as though I have lost a brother. It took both Mama and Douglas seven years to realise that they were never going back to that dark place and time from which they had come, but forwards, hopefully on to better things.

Freedom was, once again, hers for the taking, but Mama could not bring herself to reach out to it, let alone take it. That would be like rewarding her errors of judgement and for that, she judged herself unworthy of happiness. She had failed as a mother and wife and therefore deserved to be punished for her sins. Moving on was not an option. She possessed neither the desire nor the energy to reach out and take what was rightfully hers. Aunt Hilda and Dada had in turn left their mark on her. Their curses convinced her that beauty had indeed eluded her, and that she was a raving lunatic whose existence was worthless and so now she lived out the self fulfilling prophecies that had become her life because it was all she knew.

Mama had not mentioned Dada's name in all the years she had been apart from him. We did not want her upset in any way and so we all signed an invisible treaty to that effect. The man who had boarded the SS Ascania, back in 1958; the one whom she had waved off at Kingston Harbour - my father - was nothing more than a distant smudge on our troubled past. Undoubtedly, Mama still despised him, yet what had always remained crystal clear was the fact that a confounded part of her, of which it seemed she had no control, still loved him deeply - with the same ageless passion that had long since taken up permanent residency in her heart. Mama could not move on. To move on is to love yourself enough to forgive yourself but all her woes had been of her own making and Mama simply could not forgive herself for that; not ever.

'Why don't we go for a drive in the country or even a walk,' I asked yet again, one afternoon.

Mama kissed her teeth: 'I got so much work here to do and you want me to drive around the countryside like a fool. Why would I want to do that?'

'Don't you think you've had enough time to grieve - you need to start living again. All that was done to you in the past is behind you. And if I was you,' I said on hearing the others arriving downstairs in the hallway, 'I'd draw the curtains before Clovis gets up here. You know how much it upsets him to see you sitting in the dark.'

'Look at you,' said Mama changing the subject as she often did when confronted.

'You should be married now. You too young to be walking life alone.'

'You can talk, I'm just following your lead.'

What I did not tell her was that Nathan, whom I had introduced her to as a friend only a few days previously, was going to be the love of my life; that he had restored my faith in the opposite sex and that I had possibly made a very important decision.

'Don't follow me, I'm old, my life is over.'

'That's a load of rubbish and you know it.'

'What's going on?' Clovis asked Mama after first entering and scanning the room, which met his instant disapproval.

'Nothing's going on, Mama said defiantly. 'What's the matter with *you*? And why are your eyes all sunken into a hole? They look like two shipwrecks, side by side.'

I couldn't help but laugh as I looked at Clovis. Mama certainly had a way of exaggerating things for her own amusement but Clovis was not amused; he was more frustrated with Mama's lack of effort to move on with her life than with her antics to throw him off course. Glen, Pauline and Julia entered the room also.

'What have I told you about drawing the curtains in the daytime?' Clovis breezed over to the window and pulled the curtains apart with much force, to permit the sunlight to flow into the room. Mama kissed her teeth again and gave Clovis a look, which said that he was over-reacting.

'If I come here again and see these curtains drawn in the daytime, I will personally tear them off the window and throw fire on them myself, do you hear me? When it is daylight out there, your curtains must be open in here, and at night, when it gets dark, then you can draw them, got it! I won't tell you again, so don't say you haven't been warned.'

'Look at him,' says Mama, now in her element. 'He's stiff, staring, mad, and you've lost weight.'

'Talking about losing weight,' I interjected, 'guess who I saw in Walthamstow Market yesterday.'

'Who did you see Melanie?' Pauline asked, and Mama cocked her ear, to receive the information.

'Cousin Enid!'

'Cousin Enid! You never did,' gasped Julia, 'It must be nearly fifteen years since we saw her last.'

'What she doing so far from home?' asked Mama, trying hard to show disinterest, yet, unable to hide her curiosity.

'Shopping, what do you think. Unlike, some people, she gets out and about. You need to take a leaf out of her book and start living.'

Mama pretended to avert her interest, but I could see she was intrigued to know what had become of her cousin.

'How did she look? What did she have to say for herself?' asked Glen.

'Remember how big and hefty she used to be, well, she's really lost a lot of weight. Said she saw you Mama; called to you and how you just walked right past her.' Mama kissed her teeth again, but I ignored her to continue. 'She wants to see you again Mama.'

Then Julia asked the question that was on everyone's lips: 'Did you give her Mama's address?'

'No I did not, but she'll find out soon enough. I've made arrangements for her and Mama to meet in just over two weeks time.'

'That's fantastic! blurted Pauline. 'That's just what you need Mama, it'll do you good, you'll see.'

'Whether you like it or not,' said Clovis looking directly at Mama, 'Cousin Enid is coming here to see you in a couple of weeks, so you better just shape up and don't embarrass yourself.'

'I'll take you shopping. I'll get you some new clothes so you can look your best when you meet Cousin Enid.'

'I don't want new clothes, I don't want to see anyone, I just want to be left alone. Why can't everyone just leave me alone?'

'Mama now you're behaving like a spoilt child, behave or you'll get the back of your legs slapped, joked Julia. 'This is your new lease of life. Now you got something to look forward to.'

'I'll do your hair. I know a really nice style that will suit you.' I touched her hair but she pulled away from me.

Whenever she felt anxious, Mama did what she knew annoyed us most, sometimes enough to make us want to scatter - she started cussing aloud. However, we were not unperturbed by Mama's antics, so we stood our ground, ignoring her and talking amongst ourselves.

Then Clovis broke a code of silence and blurted out: 'well guess who I saw bouncing down the road towards *me*, on Thursday?'

The question, 'Who?' trailed off from our mouths into a knowing whisper, and a gust, a sudden chill, came over us.

'Dada!'

Just the sound of that name: 'Dada,' killed Mama's cussing dead in its tracks and opened the floodgates for a torrent of bad memories to come flooding back. A dark momentary silence befell the room and all its occupants.

'He can't hurt us any more,' I reminded everyone, attempting to douse any sudden flicker of anxiety, but despite my efforts, after many years of not seeing Dada, there still emanated from each of us, including myself, the essence of fear. 'What did he want?' I enquired stiffly, after a brief pause.

Mama held her head down, looking into her lap. I wondered what was going through her mind.

'He wants to see you all again,' revealed Clovis after a pause. 'I told him the best I could do was try; said I'd talk to you all.'

And all of a sudden, the terrifying nightmares that I had put to rest, now resurrected themselves. I dismissed the idea of being at his beck and call; I wasn't going to bow down to him, as I had been forced to, as a child, when he commanded I remove his shoes each evening. To foolishly, hand back control would be futile, possibly dangerous. 'If I don't see that man ever again, I'll be glad,' I declared with vehemence.

'You should be so lucky,' jeered Clovis. 'Guess where he's just moved to? Fernbank Road - two streets away from you. You're going to be seeing him all the time.'

I was absolutely flabbergasted - why around the corner from me? Avoiding him was going to be difficult to say the least.

'You can tell him from me,' I hissed, 'that I don't ever want to see him, or speak to him again as long as I live and that if I see him on the street, I intend to keep walking: I hope he does the same.'

'I'm not interested either,' dismissed Pauline, coolly, putting her arm around Mama's shoulder.

'Count me out too,' said Glen.

Surprisingly, to us all, Julia spoke up on Dada's behalf.

'Maybe he's sorry. I think we should give him a chance; life after all is short and at least now, he's making an effort. It's better late than never.'

'How could you say that?' I asked, 'surely you haven't forgotten what he put us through, especially Mama and Douglas.'

'Melanie, all I'm saying, is that people change. Maybe he's changed for the better and if he has, then maybe we should give him a chance.'

'Give him a chance! I'm not even going to give him the time of day. It's as much as he has given us. Don't get me wrong, I don't have a problem with any of you wanting to see him, but I don't want him anywhere near me or my mother and I'm sorry but I think we should change the subject.'

We spoke no more of him then, and Mama I vacated the room, followed shortly by the others.

It was inevitable that at some stage, I would come face to face with Dada; so outside, I kept my eyes peeled waiting for the inevitable to happen and you know what they say? If you expect something to happen, it usually does.

Maureen had recently moved into a new two bedroom conversion within walking distance of my place of residence, and at the time, I was so glad for her, I promised to return a favour by helping her decorate her new home. I had visions of having a pyjama day, as I called it - watching slushy movies, in the luxury of having nothing pressing at hand. I was in the midst of that at one o'clock on a Sunday afternoon when the phone rang.

'Melanie, it's me Maureen, what you doing?'

'What, right now?'

'Yes, right now.'

'Well I'm in my pyjamas, on the settee, watching *Imitations of Life*, and eating popcorn. Why?'

'Well I'm sorry to spoil your fun but you said you'd help me to decorate, and I'm decorating today.'

'Today! Oh no, come on Maureen,' I gasped. 'I'm having a ME day. Can't we do this tomorrow, or in the week?'

'I helped you to decorate when you moved in, and besides Mel, you promised,' she said confidently, trying to tempt me out of my house. 'I've cooked a big pot of soup, and I've got plenty of liquor.'

'I'm in! I'll see you soon,' I said, and we both laughed, and I hung up.

About a third of the way to Maureen's house, my mind was occupied with a multitude of things. It was a warm May day; a day that assured a glorious summer of memorable sun-kissed experiences, synonymous with that year. A warm breeze caressed my face, and I inhaled a deep breath, ready to delight in the awesome magic of nature, but just then, in the distance, something caught my attention and for a moment, it took my breath away. I will not lie to you; a feeling of intense panic came over me, followed by the compulsion to hide, yet despite this, I kept the rhythm of my walk. The figure of a well-built man with a renowned bounce in his step approached. I recognised my father immediately. As he marched imperiously towards me, with the same arrogant pride he had always worn, I noted nothing about his countenance to suggest that he had suffered the slightest pang of anguish or sorrow for his part in the miseries of Mama and Douglas. Inside, I seethed with anger. My head held high, I refused to be intimidated by his stance. Nearer and nearer he came and it was like Showdown at the OK Corral. Who was going to break first? It was not going to be me. He looked at me then - a pleading look which tried in vain to break his rocklike austerity and I averted my eyes; ignoring his presence, my step unfaltering. We walked right past each other and after a while, when he was a good way in the distance, I glanced back briefly, in time to see him adjust his head forwards again. With my heart pounding its way to a normal rhythm, I exhaled a huge sigh of relief. A sudden cloud of sadness tries to consume me

'And about time too,' were the words Maureen greeted me with before she realised that I was not quite myself. 'Melanie, has something happened? You look as though you've seen a ghost.'

'I've just seen Dada, on the way here.'

'I was right then. I'll pour you a double brandy. What did he have to say for himself?

'Nothing. We walked right past each other.'

'What are you saying to me? He must have wanted to speak to you. I bet it was you who didn't make the effort: I know how stubborn you can be.'

'Tell you the truth Maureen, I just couldn't bring myself to talk to that man.'

'But Mel, at the end of the day, he's still your father: blood is thicker than water and family are not supposed to behave like strangers.

'Maureen, I know what you're saying but it's just the way things are and I'm happy with that.'

In the two weeks preceding Mama's said reunion with her cousin, I had seen Dada, either from a distance or in close proximity, on a few more occasions. Thankfully, he knew not to speak to me, and wanting to hold onto his pride, for he was a very proud man, had marched straight ahead. Although Julia and Clovis thought that Dada was deserving of another chance, I felt quietly smug because I knew that under no circumstance would they coordinate a reunion with him without me. I stood in the way of what he craved most but I wanted him to suffer; I wanted to smash his arrogant pride; to reduce him to nothing, so that he would disappear from our lives once and for all.

On the Saturday of Cousin Enid's visit, Mama scrubbed the house from top to bottom, as usual; bathed and washed her hair, then came to join us all in the garden.

'Quick! Get me the comb Julia,' I said. 'I'm going to do Mama's hair for her.' This time, surprisingly, she did not object.

'Just plait it,' she said. I don't want nothing too fancy.'

A few die-hard black hairs presided amongst a sea of greys but I proceeded to plait them into neat cane-rows.

'Mama have you decided which of the two dresses you're going to wear when Cousin Enid visits tomorrow?'

'Neither of them. I don't understand why she wants to come here. I just wish people would leave me alone.' Stressed, she started cussing under her breath and Clovis gave her a sideways glance.

'You better not start any of that shit when Cousin Enid gets here - make yourself look stupid.'

Mama gave him a filthy look and I changed the tone a little.

'Do you remember how we all used to dream about going to Jamaica? Let me take you on holiday Mama.'

'What, so everyone can laugh after me. No sir. They all know what happened to me - that I was in the madhouse.'

'That was all in the past, and besides, people change and move on.' Julia gave me a curious look then.

'I'll never set foot back on that island as long as I live,' Mama said with conviction.

'What about the dream you had of a house overlooking the sea. With five houses in England, you've got enough money now.'

Mama kissed her teeth and said despondently, 'Why can't you hear when I say that dream is dead.'

'For you maybe. I've always kept that dream alive. I'm booked on a flight next month,' I said, knowing the surprise my revelation would cause. They fired questions of concern in my direction.

'You can't go by yourself,' Clovis declared.

'Where are you going to stay?'

'Are you serious? How long you going for?' asked Mama.

'But I've heard it's dangerous out there,' Pauline said trying to get me to reconsider. 'What if you wander into the wrong part?'

'Give me a chance to speak,' I interjected at last. Firstly, I'm not going by myself - Nathan booked it, so I'll be going with him. We're going to stay with friends of his in Montego Bay, for two weeks. Julia, will you look after James for me while I'm gone?'

'I might, if you bring me something nice back,' she agreed, to my delight.

We talked about Jamaica through the changing shades of the afternoon as it descended into the evening twilight.

Cousin Enid was ready and waiting when I called to pick her up the following day; overcoat buttoned sensibly to the top and handbag draped across her arm.

'Aren't you a little hot in that coat, Cousin Enid,' I asked as she got into the car. 'The sun's shining.'

'Don't let that sun fool you, I've been to church this morning. It's nippy out there,' she said, in her Jamaican cockney accent, shrugging her once broad shoulders. 'How's Girlie?'

'Better than she has been in a long time, although occasionally she still has her dark moods when she feels scared or threatened in some way.'

'I see your father in Dalston last week. I just give him one look. I can't stand him. He is a wicked, wicked, man. When last you see him?'

'A couple of days ago as a matter of fact,' I said indifferently, 'but we don't talk. Try not to mention him to Mama. It still upsets her sometimes.'

On our journey, I attempted to fill her in on the fifteen years, which had lapsed since she had seen Mama.

'Well, here we are,' I said, pulling up outside Mama's house. 'Remember, try your hardest not to mention Dada, and take no notice if Mama starts cussing or rambling: it's her way of hijacking the conversation, or trying to scare you off. I'm afraid she doesn't like herself very much.'

I led Cousin Enid through the hallway and upstairs to Mama's room, where she was seated on her bed, watching TV.

'Look who I've brought to see you Mama.' I leant over and kissed her, then moved out of the way to reveal Cousin Enid. Mama eyed her briefly from head to toe and Cousin Enid stood there, eyes brimming with tears.

'Girlie let me hug you. I been wanting to see you for so long. How you be?'

'I'm all right,' Mama said, watching closely as her cousin dried her eyes with a tissue she had pulled from her pocket.

'You looking well Girlie. You have on put weight,' said Enid, placing herself in an easy chair beside the bed.

Telling someone they were weighty is considered an insult by most, but for people of Mama and Enid's generation it was a compliment; a sign of good health.

'What happened to you? asked Mama. 'You used to be so much bigger. And what's happened to all that hair you had? You don't look like the Enid I used to know. You've changed.'

'I got sugar on the blood and high blood pressure. The tablets I've been taking cut my hair, plus the doctor said I had to lose weight so I've been going to exercise classes.'

'And how's brother Rodney? You still together?'

'Rodney?' Cousin Enid scorned. 'That man getting on my damn nerves. I can't stand him.'

Mama laughed. 'You don't still beat him do you?'

'Of course I beat him, if he step out of line. A woman needs to be in control of her own destiny. I'm not going let no man trample over me like...' she stopped herself then, realising that she had stumbled too close to what was still a sensitive matter.'How have you been since I seen you last? It's been a long time,' Enid said, trying to steer backwards. But it was too late. She had triggered bitter resentment. It was unavoidable really.

Mama held her head down low, lost in the darkness of the past. 'He was so cruel,' she blurted tearfully. 'Put me in the hospital so many times. Treated me like a dog, after all I had done for him. I had nobody to turn to.'

'You had me Girlie,' cried Enid, assuring Mama of her commitment to their kinship.

'I had no one. Aunt Hilda always said I'd amount to nothing. She was right.'

'Miss Hilda? She died must be three years now. I can't remember what she died of.'

Mama ignored this revelation; swept right over it to someone else who had come into her mind.

'I wonder whatever happened to Vi Tugman, you remember her?'

'She died about - let me see - about seven years now. I think they said it was a heart attack.'

'Have you heard anything about Millie Smith?'

'Last I heard she was living in Canada.'

The word 'Canada,' trailed off Mama's lips.

Curious to find out what had become of all the people she had left behind, Mama reeled off a long list of names, most of whom it seemed had died or were living abroad.

'You remember Bobsy, don't you?' blurted Enid after a pause in the conversation.

'Bobsy? Which Bobsy?'

'Your Bobsy. Miss Beulah's Bobsy.'

'What's happened to him? I suppose he's dead too.'

'No sah. He's alive and well.'

'Who is this Bobsy? I asked curiously, having heard his name mentioned so many times.

'He proposed to Girlie in Jamaica but she turned him down for that fool - your father. Bobsy really loved your mother. It took him years to get over her. Eventually, he married a woman called Dorothy. They came to England in '72 and had three children - two daughters and a son.'

'I'm glad he's happy - he deserves to be.'

'Which happy! Him and his wife argued from morning till night. It was anything but a happy marriage. Anyway, she died about three years ago now and he's been living in that big ole house in Croydon all by himself ever since. He's in Jamaica at the moment. His mother passed away two weeks ago so he went home to bury her.'

'Miss Beulah dead?'

Enid shook her head in answer. 'When he phoned last week, I told him I was coming to see you and he gave me a message to give you. He said when he gets back from Jamaica, he'd like to come and visit you. He's hoping to take you out for a drink or something, I believe.'

The prospect of facing the man whom she had rejected years ago alarmed Mama greatly. 'I'm not ready to see anyone, I'm still recovering, I need more time. Enid, don't make him come here, I'm begging you. Tell him I can't see him.'

Enid kissed her teeth. 'You need to start getting out and about - cooped up in this house like some kind of frightened chicken, well I'm taking you to church next Sunday whether you like it or not, so make sure you're ready by nine-thirty sharp.'

I left them alone together, to make tea and refreshments and checked on them occasionally. I relaxed more when I heard raucous laughter coming from Mama's room.

The following Sunday, Enid showed, and with much fussing and cussing to dissuade Enid from taking a mad woman to church, Mama took the biggest step she had taken in years, and left the house with her cousin.

Every Sunday after that, Mama gave a repeat performance, sometimes even putting up even more of a resistance. Mama was not a sociable person. Being amongst people unnerved Mama somewhat, but had it not been for Enid's bullish determination, Mama would have opted for the safety of a hermit's life. .

'You know Bobsy's back from Jamaica,' announced Enid one day. 'He's been back two weeks now and he wants to see you next week Saturday. I want to be here with you all, but I got the grandkids that day, so I gave him your address.'

'You gave him my address? Why would you do that? You know I don't want to see him. Tell I can't see him, please Enid, for me.'

'Girlie there is no reason why you can't see Bobsy.'

'I can't, I just can't see him,' Mama cried, her voice streaked with dread and shame. I'm not the person he thinks I am.'

'You name Girlie ain't it? Well it's Girlie he wants to see.'

Everything was happening just a little too fast for Mama. There was the distinct possibility that she might buckle under the strain of social overload and retreat further back into her shell. She was not a people kind of person. The sniggers, the whispering and the laughter that had wounded her so much in the past suddenly surfaced to a full-scale panic. She was certain that Bobsy too wanted to ridicule her downfall as a way of avenging her for rejection.

Riddled with anxiety, Mama started cussing: 'Trying to control people's lives, damn liberty-taking, cruel and heartless. They don't have no mercy; who can't hear must feel - one day the wicked must fall,' and along those lines her rambling flowed.

'Anyway,' said Enid, paying no mind to Mama's inadvertent attempts to throw her off course, 'remember we're going to church tomorrow so make sure you ready when I come for you.'

Mama cussed her way through the following week, especially when anyone was around to hear; hoping that we would deem her too unstable to meet with Bobsy.

But being cruel to be kind, and ever hopeful, we took a risky chance, knowing that it would most likely fail. We ignored her pleas and instead, reassured her that Bobsy's intentions were honourable.

Peering discreetly through Mama's bedroom window a week later, I sighted a bespectacled gentleman, standing on the doorstep; flowers in hand. I was both nervous and excited for Mama, but someone should have told this respectable man that Mama didn't care much for flowers.

'Now remember Mama,' I pleaded, fussing around her appearance, 'your best behaviour,' As usual, Mama kissed her teeth, which could indicate trouble.

In no time at all, Bobsy was upstairs, knocking politely at Mama's door, before entering.

'But wait! Is you dat Girlie?' he said excitedly. 'You do remember me don't you? My God, I thought I would never see you again. So how is you?'

'You brought flowers?' Mama said in a stiff monotone voice.

'Yeh, beautiful aren't they,' he said, taking in their fragrant allure. 'You like them?'

'People bring flowers for the dead,' announced Mama, looking at the floral tribute with distaste, which took Bobsy a little unaware.

I shot Mama a warning glance.

'Not just for the dead, but for the living also, and you alive ain't you?' said Bobsy.

'I hate flowers,' Mama declared directly. 'You shouldn't have - you shouldn't have brought them.'

'I'm sorry,' Bobsy said apologetically. I won't make that mistake twice.'

Mama gave him a look, which said: 'you won't get the chance.'

'I suppose you don't like flowers either? Bobsy said, turning to me.'

'Me? I love flowers.'

'Then these are for you.'

'That's very kind of you Bobsy,' I said, hoping to ease his nervous tension.

'Let me take your coat.' I glanced over at Mama, and instantly I received her vexation, loud and clear because she wore it on her face: her discomfort and irritability now bordered on downright rude.'

'Don't be put off by that look Bobsy,' I said, drawing attention to Mama's physiognomy, 'and don't let her frighten you off with her cussing.'

Bobsy laughed, more to Mama's annoyance. 'I heard all about that from Enid. You not going to get rid of me that easy, not this time.' His gaze became more serious and intense now.

'Would you like a cup of tea, Bobsy?' I interrupted.

'You know, I have never drank a cup of tea in all my life.'

'Really?' I say in surprise.

'I wouldn't mind a cup of coffee if you have it, that's all I drink.'

'Sure,' I said, and as I headed towards the door, Bobsy turned to focus his attention on Mama.

'How long has it been Girlie?' Mama didn't answer. She stared straight ahead, as though at a loss for words. 'Must be nearly thirty years.' Still there was no answer from Mama. He pulled an object from his inside jacket pocket. 'Have a look at this. These are my children,'

Mama took the photographs from his hands and I watched them both as Bobsy proceeded to put a name to each face, musing about the characteristics of his children. Mama studied the photos for a good while, then handed them back without comment of any kind. Bobsy it seemed was unperturbed by Mama's silence and so he did all the talking, in the hope that something he said would provoke a response from Mama.

After serving them with beverages, and giving Mama a few warning glances, I left them alone together. They had a lot of catching up to do.

Downstairs in the living room, my siblings and I discussed excitedly our hopes for Bobsy to remain a strong feature in Mama's life, knowing that at any minute, it could all go horribly wrong. Ever since I was a little girl, I had dreamed that one day, Mama would find a man who would love and respect her for who she was.

We waved at Bobsy as he drove off down the road and watched until his car had disappeared out of sight.

'We probably scared him off,' Julia laughs.

'I'm not so sure' I pondered. They call luck a lady, but there was something loyal, just and promising, about Bobsy but who knows what else the tides will bring in.

Chapter Twelve

Jamaica Calling

....

I love all things with wings: birds, planes and my angel of mercy, who had forgiven my earlier sins and shown me clemency. Aboard flight ML630 to Jamaica, an indescribable excitement arrested my soul. My spirit ascended to heights I had only ever dreamed about, and I was flying higher than a kite. Lighter than a feather, surging above, below and through clouds of brilliant white, towards a mystical island in the sun - my island, by the blood of my ancestors, and so I claimed it as my own before I had even blessed eyes on it. Suspended in mid air, I got a little taste of the sweet joy behind the solemn promise I had made, years ago, to the most high one. He said: 'ask and thou shalt receive,' and so I asked. I said: 'Dear Lord, if I can just get Mama on a plane; and if at the very moment she sets down her two feet on Jamaican soil, you come to call for me, then I will gladly depart this world with you. I will not be afraid, because my soul will be elated in the joyous knowledge that Mama, after many years of being lost in a forest of confusion, had at last, found her way back to her homeland.

Here I was, wrapped up; cradled, on a pilgrimage, an odyssey to set in motion a chain of desirable events, or so I hoped. Nearing the end of that flight, I looked out onto the world, waiting to capture and store forever my first glimpse of a great and dear place - and there it was. The island of Jamaica burst forth into view and my eyes beheld a beautiful vision, a chimera that had previously lived in my mind for many years as a childhood fantasy. Surging towards my love, with wings outstretched, I came into land, swooping low over palm trees, which danced freely in energetic salutation, throwing their long palms this way and that, in the most radiant sunlight. And when my feet were placed on the tarmac of Donald Sangster Airport, in Montego Bay, a solitary, unruly tear escaped my dignified composure, and I knew I'd been blessed.

After collecting our cases, Nathan and I were met by Devon, our host and his friend Lloyd who greeted us warmly. We walked over to a red jeep, threw all our luggage in the back and took off on the open road, towards the parish of St James, a short distance away. I was like an uninhibited child; I stared at everything, trying to take it all in - the people, the structure of buildings, vegetation, the sky, everything. For the first time in my life, I saw all colours, in their most vibrant form. I felt like I had died and gone to heaven.

'You OK?' Nathan asked, his arm around my shoulder.

I affirmed by nodding my head in quiet awe of my surroundings.

'Welcome to Jamaica,' he whispered and kissed my forehead before re-entering an ongoing conversation with Devon and Lloyd.

The large house which Devon inherited after his mother had passed, was situated on a two acre plot of lush, green land. Outside, two other inhabitants whose names unnerved me slightly for different reasons, were there to greet us: Money was a young man of about twenty-two years, and Killer was brandishing a bloodstained machete and turned out to be the house chef.

Nathan and I sat down to a hearty meal, and as the evening aged gracefully, the night began its slow ascent. When it arrived, it was what it was, as black as night; the blackest of nights and the sounds of the day were drowned out by the creatures of the night who sang their preamble in perfect harmony. Exhausted I took myself off to bed. Serenaded by the lullaby outside. I eventually drifted into a deep, rejuvenating sleep which was interrupted it seemed, all too soon.

'Melanie, Melanie wake up!'

'What is it, Nathan?' I gasped in a sleep induced stupor. For a moment, I feared that Killer had lived up to his name and had gone berserk with his machete.

'I want you to come with me. I want to show you something. Hurry up!' he said with great urgency. Anticipating some horrible blood-stained scene, I allowed him to lead me out onto the verandah. Evidently still jetlagged, I attempted to ask why he had brought me out here in what seemed the dead of night.

'Shh!' he said, 'Listen!' And the tuneful synchronicity of the night's anthem touched me again. 'Beautiful isn't it?' he said. 'I woke you up so that we could be together at the birth of a new Jamaican day.'

A steaming cup of fever-grass tea revived me greatly whilst Nathan and I observed with glee, the subtle change of shades before us, until at last, a new dawn broke through the darkness and the song of the day began all over again. A symphony orchestra was at work. Down at the bottom of the yard, in the first light of the day, I discovered a hammock and a swing hidden by the stretching branches of a large rubber tree. Something magical happened to me that day, as I swayed gently to and fro in the hammock under that huge rubber tree, drinking rum and milk. I was totally entranced by this strange yet enchanting new world. Deep down inside, I felt that I had always known this place; I could almost swear I'd been here before. Suddenly, a doctor bird graced me with its presence, fluttering around as though it had come to deliver an important message and I must have been mad or something: maybe I really needed a doctor, because I started talking to it.

'Hey there little fellow, beautiful spirit; look at you. Thank you for coming to greet me like this.' I marvelled as it continued to dart around, thorough in its inspection. Eventually it flew away, leaving me with a feeling of complete and utter contentment. I lay back and closed my eyes. At that precise moment, I had tasted paradise and fallen hopelessly in love. I had been bitten, quite badly, by the bug, and I was sure I would never recover. I saw Mama's dreams so clearly and it became clearer still with each passing day. For the first time, I truly understood how displaced Mama must have been feeling all those years ago.

My holiday with Nathan was like the wings of the doctor bird - it moved at great speed. Two days before our departure back to England, we went on a shopping excursion to Kingston. Not long after we arrived, Devon had started drinking and so Killer took the wheel on the drive back to St James. At speed, we headed towards home along the mountain range and through the blackest of nights. In the next surreal moment, the car was suddenly spinning out of control, up there on the cliff-face. All speech and laughter ceased. The male passengers who had braced themselves for the impact of the crash, were entranced by an eerie stillness. My piercing screams were the only sound to break the monotony of that deadly silence. I was not ready to die; I would not go quietly. In slow motion, Killer fought with the wheel but the car continued to spin in a sequence of deadly moves - towards the edge of the cliff, towards the cliff-face, then towards oncoming cars, and so it went on for what seemed an eternity. Miraculously, the car came to a jolting halt, facing the direction in which we were originally heading. In disbelief, I breathed a sigh of relief.

A Rastafarian man drove up alongside us, wound down his window, looked at the occupants of the car, then said: 'You're lucky you know dread! You're lucky.' And as his car cruised slowly away, he repeated those words, 'You're lucky!'

We drove the rest of the way in complete silence and those who had been drinking were stone cold sober and sat bolt upright.

Back on British soil I headed straight towards Mama's house and when eventually I saw her I was choked up with emotions.

'Thank God you're back!' she said. 'I missed you. Why did you stay so long? Don't go away for so long again, you hear me.'

I embraced her with all the love and understanding of what her soul yearned for; all that was missing from her life, then stood back to take in her melancholy countenance.

'Mama I told you I would be away for two weeks. It seems longer doesn't it? I missed you so much. You know whenever I looked out over the sea, I felt as though I was a million miles away from you and England.'

'I'm just glad you back safe and sound. Now I can stop worrying.'

It was Saturday, so I waited for all the family to gather before I revealed all the things I had brought back from Jamaica.

I do somewhat shamefully declare that between Nathan and I, we had brought back sixteen bottles of white rum, about three bottles of John Crow batty, three bottles of Red Label wine, two bottles of rum cream, mangoes and guinep, amongst a host of other things, including wood carvings and rolls of pictures.

'I can't believe they let you on the plane with all this,' laughed Mama.

Great minds think alike for Clovis appeared before us, holding a tray of glasses.

'I'll pour the drinks; you tell us all about Jamaica,' he said.

'I don't know where to start,' I gasped. 'We had such a wonderful time out there, Nathan and I are going back in a few months.'

'When?' gasped Julia. 'I'm coming with you this time.'

'I'm so glad you said it first, Julia. It would be a dream come true if we all went back together - all of us. How about it Mama?' I said, turning towards her. 'It's what you've always wanted.'

But Mama's composure of indifference said it all.

Nevertheless, nothing could dim the illuminating glare of the visions imprinted on my mind. 'Well I beg to differ, because I saw that same dream with my own two eyes. It's alive and well. It's so beautiful Mama, you got to see it again.'

'For them to say how I went all the way to England to seek my fortune and ended up in a mad house? No sir, not me.'

'Well you can put me and Glen down for a start,' said Clovis. 'I'm not missing out any more. Life's too short, man. Hey Mama, you can bring Bobsy with you,' he teased.

The look of disgust on Mama's face told Clovis that he was treading on shaky ground.

'How is Bobsy by the way?' I asked.

Mama kissed her teeth. 'That man won't stop from blighting my days. Why did you have to make him find me? Now he's like a sticking plaster. He's round here all the time. I just feel like he's stalking me.'

'How can he be stalking you?' I ridiculed. 'You don't go nowhere to be stalked.'

'Well he's stalking me in my own home; that must be worse.'

Mama seemed genuinely put out by Bobsy's visits, even the mention of his name in fact, but at the same time, when she spoke of him, there was a strange glow about her person, which did not deceive my attention. All the same, I was not too hopeful for the viability of their relationship because Mama, as you know, was her own worst enemy. In a few more weeks, maybe months, Bobsy would most probably eventually tire of her ways and she'd be right back where she started, still punishing her unforgiving self, in denial of her heart's desires - a martyr to the sparse limitations of her own joy and happiness. For now, though we were together, thank God, which we celebrated by talking way into the night, and with the utterance of each word, the magic began. The distant calling of a land far, far away, which I had already answered, was audible, no longer to my ears alone, but to all those around me and like a phoenix rising from the flames, the dreams of yester-year resurrected themselves.

Back only a few days from my so-called pilgrimage, I still had a Jamaican spring in my step; its enduring warmth in the tone of my voice; the shade of my skin; beneath which, the spectre of Jamaica was regenerated through veins that carried it to a hopeful heart. Feeling incredibly blessed, I was still on that high, imagining myself in busy Kingston as I made my way through the streets of Dalston, after booking the next holiday. I turned into a side street to leave behind the bustle of the high road, but there ahead, in the distance, I saw an all too familiar figure coming towards me. Again my step was unfaltering as I marched forward, determined not to make eye contact with Dada. I did not incline to stop, neither it appeared, did he, and so we walked right past each other, yet again. I had come within close proximity of him or seen the back of him disappear down a side street on many occasions now. Unperturbed by these chance encounters, I had learned to take them in my stride for there were many more occasions to come, when our paths would cross.

Soon after my journey to the Caribbean, I answered the calling again and embarked on a holiday of a lifetime. This time, the Ambiance Hotel in Runaway Bay, Jamaica was where we were all taken to spend two weeks in a haze of glory; still unbelieving that at last my siblings and I were in existence on Jamaican soil. It was a homecoming for Clovis, Glen and Julia, for they had not seen where they had spent their formative years for almost a quarter of a century.

Two days after arriving, we loaded ourselves into the large minibus hired for the duration of our holiday, and took off towards Vere, in Portland Cottage to visit one of Mama's youngest sisters, Aunty Dattyu. The scenery outstretched before us was very rural: evidence of poverty or people struggling to make a living was all around. We asked locals for the only directions we had - the name Dattyu, and they pointed us towards her house. This was not an area frequented by tourists, that was obvious. Minutes later, we pulled up outside Dattyu's house and alighted from the vehicle. An old wooden shack, home to Dattyu and her family of six, stood precariously at an angle. It did not, however, look out of place surrounded by neighbouring houses of similar build. That was the house my Mama had been born into back in the 1930s and my heart swelled with an ambivalence of joy and grief to know that she had survived and come through such a difficult start to life. A few meagre goats wandered around to graze on the sparse grasses that sprouted here and there on the dry dusty land. We called out to Dattyu, and at first a little boy of about six years old emerged, followed by two older males and then a woman whom I presumed to be Dattyu. Instantly, I saw my mama in her face, her complexion and her build. She was overjoyed to see us and after hugging everyone, shooed the goats and dogs into different parts of the yard before disappearing into the house. I looked about me and took in the rugged landscape. On this land lay the body of my grandmother, Aunt Mary, whom I had heard so much about and who had met a premature death at the hands of a drunken man. Then under the cover of darkness, those same hands had buried her out in the yard. Wandering around, we come across her grave - the mould of an open Bible at its head. With Aunt Mary being an elder, we should have looked up to her, but now in a state of grace, we stared down at all that remained of her - a concrete memorial. From the moment we called her name aloud and started speaking to her, we felt her presence, and that of our ancestors all around, encompassed in the warm sunshine that enveloped us.

Carrying smiles of excitement, a few receptacles for drinking and a big bottle of rum you knew was kept only for special occasions; Dattyu emerged from the house with quick legs.

'Aunt Mary is so glad to see you all,' she panted, 'so happy. Mek we all drink and celebrate together.'

She opened the bottle, poured a good measure around Aunt Mary's head, then into cups which we raised in honour of our grandmother; the spirit of her blood, alive and racing through all our veins. What little Dattyu had, she shared with everyone and we sat and talked until the setting sun beckoned us back to Runaway Bay.

At sunrise, the following morning, Pauline, Julia and I took an early morning swim in the hotel pool, waking everyone on campus with our childish antics, our laughter and squeals of delight. After breakfast, we set out to Treasure Beach in St Elizabeth to visits the graves of our grandfather Pinto and great grandmother Mammee Jule, who had paved the way for Mama's journey to England all those years ago. Leaving the serenity of the air-conditioned vehicle in the middle of a hot Jamaican summer, I could not believe the sweltering heat that hit me. Everything was still in what must have been nearly forty degrees of heat, even the goats that grazed motionless on the hills were like still-life, and one's immediate instinct was to seek out the shade of a tree or house - anything.

We travelled the island for the duration of our holiday, sometimes staying in different hotels. But wherever we were, by nightfall we would find ourselves beside the waters of the Caribbean Sea. Drinking Wray and Nephew, under skies that occasionally offered a spectacular lightshow of a distant storm, we marvelled at the multitude of diamonds that filled the vast night sky above our heads. However, in all of that sweet reverence, the absence of Mama and Douglas to share in our paradise left a bitter after-taste and a lump in the throat. It was the only one thing that blighted the feeling of immense bliss and it was made all the more difficult by the fact that on paper, Mama was still married. The promise she had made before God to let only death part her and Dada reigned supreme. Neither one had sought to get a divorce and I supposed that in some strange way that meant something to Mama, but that thread of hope meant that her life was on hold - a prisoner to the fulfilment of that promise that was their marriage. He had humiliated her; scandalised her name yet still from wherever he was in the world, he was very much in control of her life. I took in a gulp of what was my last night on the island.

A chaotic affair ensued, prior to boarding the flight back to England, simply because my siblings and I behaved like dry-land tourists in our effort to take Jamaica back with us. Maria, (Glen's partner) decided to go one better than me, and had packed a smaller suitcase inside another, at the start of our holiday, to show she meant business. With neck strings bulging, we struggled to lift our cases onto scales, which when read induced shocked surprise and disbelief. Two bemused airport attendants rushed to our aid, unsurprisingly.

'My God! What you have in these cases?' one enquired. 'It's only a plane you know - only a plane.'

'A plane crash is a easy, easy thing to happen,' exclaimed the other attendant, implying that if the pilot met with any difficulty during the flight, it would be because of the cargo we carried. 'You can't take Jamaica with you, you just have to keep coming back.'

'Keep coming back,' he said. I mused on those words as the plane lifted up into the air and Jamaica became a series of bright lights - fireflies, in the night sky.

On our return to England, we told Mama of the beauty of her homeland and with eyes that glistened with tears; she re-lived each moment of our experiences. We told her how we had seen the resting place of Pinto and Mammee Jule in St Elizabeth; the stifling heat and then we give her news of Portland Cottage, Dattyu and Aunt Mary's grave at the bottom of the yard. Her heart-felt sadness at being too late to fulfil her promise to take care of them in their old age caused her tears to flow freely as she sobbed openly. I put my arm around her.

'Come now Mama, you mustn't cry. Aunt Mary, Mammee Jule and Pinto, they all doing fine, resting in the sunshine. There's no more pain for them, no more struggling.' It was all I could think of saying, but still Mama wept, and my heart wept bitterly with her; for no matter what she did, she would never see those people she loved in the flesh again - not in this life-time. I couldn't bear to see her shed tears so I changed the course of conversation by telling her about the one-legged man at the mall in Kingston, who when he had set eyes on a plump Maria from a distance, had decided that she must be the queen bee of the family. Maria, who was always careful with her money, if not a little mean, tried to make a run for it, her hands restraining her unruly bosoms, but the one-legged man was like a top sprinter on crutches: he gave chase, and would you believe it, he caught her. Maria parted with a few hundred dollars then, for sheer effort on his part. Mama's tears of sadness, turned into tears of laughter. There and then, if I had said 'Mama get your things together, we're going to Jamaica,' I think she would have gone. However, I knew that once the days and weeks had passed the ghosts of her past; her denying of self would still hold her back. There had to be a way to get Mama to return to her island, if only for a holiday. We had, up until now, exhausted every avenue where that was concerned, but we refused to let that deter our future efforts. Forgiveness, I concluded, was the key. To move on as a family, we needed to talk about the past; to forgive each other for our shortcomings in the early days; to rid ourselves of the guilt, the fear and the helplessness which, to some extent, still haunted who we were. Since leaving Grayling Road, we had become a chrysalis, a cocoon, waiting, hoping for the day to come when we would all emerge *together*, in a new light. Until then, even poor Bobsy, who had months earlier bought a new house closer to Mama, could only ever be part of the scenery but not a significant feature in Mama's picture. Yet that must have been enough for him because he was reliable, punctual and loyal. Forgiveness I concluded again, could change not only our lives but the lives of others around us.

A lot happened during the following eighteen months. Request followed request from Dada to see his family again and I, no longer angry, just stubborn, ignored the messages from friends and family, by still passing Dada on the street whenever we saw each other. He expected me to make the first move; to be the one to approach him and that, I determined, was his role, as the parent, the father. I decided to put him on the back burner until he came to his senses on the matter.

My siblings and I took it in turns to travel back and forth to Jamaica on a building mission and in between time, Nathan and I had another addition to the family, a little boy we named Matthew. Yes, I was blessed to have Nathan as the father of my children. I watched them together, in the knowledge that my children would always have the sweet memories of a significant male to call upon. I thought about my brothers and sisters, mostly Douglas, and how having a good father would have shaped him differently. It might have been enough to have saved him from himself. Striding outdoors alone in the middle of winter, I heard Clovis and Julia's argument in support of giving Dada another chance. I supposed there was the possibility that he was a changed man, as Julia had so eloquently put it. Time has a way of doing that to some people, but where my father was concerned I found it hard to believe, nonetheless.

I was walking through busy Wridley Market on a fresh and chilly October day when I caught sight of some mangoes on a stall. I picked one up in a gloved hand, and was in the middle of sniffing the sweetness of its aroma when suddenly, something else caught my eye. Dada was standing right beside me, as large as life, glaring down at me.

'I need to talk to you,' he said, in a low voice.

With the mango still glued to my nose, I could not ever recall seeing him with such a forlorn look in his eyes; eyes I had not looked into for many years. And now, humbly, he had plucked up the courage to approach me. Strange thing was I did not feel an ounce of fear, standing there in the middle of the market, just shock at his sudden appearance, because it seemed as though he had stepped out from behind curtains.

'Hey you!' shouted the Jamaican stallholder, jolting me out of my initial shock. 'Yes you! Don't sniff my mangoes. Put it down! PUT- IT-DOWN!'

I looked at Dada. I could tell that his temper was rising by the way he bit his bottom lip repeatedly, as though he was getting ready to punch someone or something. Maybe he had not changed after all or maybe those changes were too subtle to reveal themselves in a situation such as this. I studied his reaction carefully.

'Don't you dare talk to my daughter like that, you hear me?' he shouted, prising the mango from my hand and promptly throwing it full force into the stomach of the stallholder. 'You say one more bad word to her and you're going to see what I do to you and this stall.' Deep down, I was touched by this display of solidarity.

'What did he say?' enquired a passing female shopper.

'Said she mustn't sniff the mangoes,' enlightened my father.

The woman gave the stallholder a backward glance. 'Feisty!' she exclaimed. 'That's why I don't shop with you. You too renk.'

If looks could kill, that stallholder would have dropped down dead, sprawled across the top of his mangoes, because we all three gave him the deadliest cut eye, at the same time.

'I must talk to you, today,' Dada said more seriously. 'Can you come round later?'

I nodded to confirm. How could I refuse?

'You know where I live don't you? It's number 23.'

'I'll be there,' I said, and we parted company then.

It was a strange encounter to say the least, and as you can imagine, I could not wait to tell the others.

'He's going to want to see us all isn't he? Oh I'm pooing my pants, just thinking about it,' Julia said nervously. I'm so glad it's you and not me. Phone me later and tell me how it went.'

After replacing the receiver, I sat there in nervous contemplation, tapping my fingers on the telephone table, the coiled wire still entwined around the fingers of my other hand.

'Hey, what's wrong? You look a little tense. Has something happened?' asked Nathan.

'I bumped into Dada in Wridley Market,' I said in a matter of fact kind of way. He said he wants to see me later.'

'Oh well, it's about time the two of you started talking. Did he give you a time to come round?'

'No he just said later.'

'That means he's waiting for you. You should go soon and get it out of the way. Do you want me to come with you?'

'I'm not afraid of him any more. I'm more frightened of myself and what I might say.'

'Well that's a good thing in my books. Get it all off your chest and clear the air once and for all. This is probably the best opportunity you'll get to speak your mind. He can't hide from the truth.'

Chapter Thirteen

Any Day Now

....

As if by magic, in the next crazy moment, I was standing outside a four-storey block of flats. My bold upright countenance a show of strength, I walked the paths that led to Dada's two-bedroom apartment, rang the buzzer and waited. Then the heavy, audible footsteps of a giant pounded towards me and all my childhood fears - the guilt, the helplessness and the most intense anger - came flooding back on the heights of a great wave, which instantly drowned my courage. All over again, in a split second, I relived the terrifying memories that I had locked away in the darkest, dustiest, most distant corners of my mind. I felt the pain of a child, beaten, time and again for telling the truth, a child powerless to stop her mother from being committed to a mental asylum. I hated him for all the times that Mama was dragged from our arms by the ambulance crew, and him, watching our chaos silently in the background; the times he terrorised us by threatening to burn the house down with us still inside; for almost killing Julia and for his confounded attempts to kill the spirit of our family. With my heart racing its own marathon, I moistened my dry throat and asked God for courage: to guide my mouth and to instil me with wisdom for the trial ahead. All of a sudden, the door was prised open and I tilted my chin upwards in a brazen manner and said, 'Hello Dada.' At last, it seemed that I was finally ready to confront my father.

I intended to get this over and done with, quickly. My intention was not to remain in his presence for longer than I could bear so after entering his abode, I stood in the centre of the living room facing my father. He looked me up and down.

'Have a seat,' he commanded before he caught himself and adjusted his tone.

'I mean, sit anywhere you like. I'll pour you a drink.'

I scanned the room, saw what was obviously *his* throne, and decided that that was where I would sit. When he turned, his step faltered at the sight of me in his chair and as he handed me a drink with unsteady hands, I was aware of his efforts to read my physiognomy.

'I'm glad you came Melanie,' he said before throwing the full contents of the glass into the back of his throat. 'I've been wanting to talk to you for a long time, but first I've got to do something.'

And to my annoyance, he disappeared into the kitchen from where issued a delicious smell, to emerge minutes later, with two plates of hot steaming food, which he placed on the table. Here he was, trying to manipulate the situation to his own gain, when all I hungered for was understanding as to why he had hurt my family so badly.

'Taste that and tell me what you think it is,' he said, his eyes, hoping, waiting to be praised for his culinary delights by way of diverting my focus.

Observing him suspiciously, I sampled a mouthful of food. As expected, it was divine, although I couldn't quite tell what it was. Nevertheless, it was not my intention to inflate his ego. I thought back to when I was a child and how he would use food then to break the ice.

'It tastes like chicken, no, prawns. What is it?'

'It's lobster. Isn't it beautiful? What do you think?'

He waited now for the kind of verdict that would indicate a smooth path ahead.

'It's good. You've outdone yourself,' I said half-heartedly. I heard his inward sigh of relief.

'I know we have a lot to talk about, but first, let's eat, then we'll talk.'

I didn't force the issue. Food is a blessing, a pleasure. Emotions were high though and I was sure there would be tears - whose, I did not know.

We ate, not in silence I might add, for Dada nervously churned out information on the recipe; the secret ingredients he had used, and what he had done to the lobster to get it to taste this way. He talked of fishing ventures in the Caribbean Sea, how to set and retrieve lobster pots. I knew everything there was to know about fishing and lobsters. An expert now, I could write a book on the darn things.

Whilst he cleared the plates away, I poured myself another drink and one for him and that's when the talking really started.

'So, I hear you're a teacher now.'

'That's correct. I graduated six weeks ago.

For a moment, his eyes glazed over, his countenance a mixture of deep shame and immense pride, both at the same time. 'I'm so proud of you,' he began, and I shifted impatiently in my seat, ready to get up and leave at any second. 'If only you knew …' there was a pause and then, 'how's Girlie?'

I looked at him, hardly believing that he actually cared at all.

'Mama? She's fine. We take great care of her, and now that Bobsy is in her life again, she's so much happier. She is a new person.' I just had to let him know that Mama was no longer the wreck he had left behind; that he had not succeeded in destroying her completely. However, I gave no indication of the fact that Mama still loved him so desperately that she was unable to move on with Bobsy.

'And Douglas, how's he doing?' he enquired.

'He's OK. He could be better though.'

'I've bought some clothes for him. Let me show you,' he said half raising himself to do so.

'Why did you want to see me Dada? I demanded, fed up with his beating about the bush. 'Surely it wasn't to cook me dinner or to show me clothes you've bought for Douglas.'

He wiped a stray tear from his face.

'I had to see you Melanie. I couldn't take it no more, watching you, my own daughter, ignore me on the street. Do you know how bad that hurt me?'

Surprisingly, I was incredibly calm in the presence of a man whom I had plotted to kill on many occasions.

'First and foremost, you are the parent, you are supposed to take the lead: and if I remember rightly, the last time we spoke, you said you were going to kill me; that you'd put me in a box.'

'Come on Melanie, you know I didn't mean those things. You made me so angry.'

'Oh and I didn't have anything to be angry about, I suppose,' I said cynically. 'The way you drove Mama and Douglas into the ground and out of their minds was despicable; it was a crime against humanity itself - how could you? You treated us worse than dogs. We had a terrible life back then. Terrible. We didn't deserve that, none of us; to have people looking, laughing, and gossiping about us. You have no idea of the shame and the guilt we carried. Do you know that as a child, I used to lie down night after night and pray to God to come and take me out of the hell that you created.'

I was just getting warmed up, so I did not expect what came next. I never thought that I would live to see the day when this giant of a man would crumble, but now he broke down and cried, in front of me. Nevertheless, I observed his blabbering distress with suspicion. I had always known him to be a scheming man: a shrewd man. Maybe this was just an act on his part, to gain my sympathy. If it was, he had missed out on a lifetime's opportunity to be a great actor for his performance was worthy of nothing less than a Grammy award.

'I know I've been a terrible husband to Girlie and I failed you kids as a father. Believe me, I wish I could go back and change all of that but I can't, and that will always grieve me. May God forgive me for what I have done to my family because I can't forgive myself. I have to just live with it.' He shook his head and cried even harder. 'Melanie, I love all my children: I just want the chance to be the father I should have been a long time ago.'

Well what do you know - Dada was also seeking forgiveness.

'I'm so sorry,' he sobbed repeatedly.

And there it was; that blessed word I thought I'd never hear him say; the word that restored hope for humanity.

'I'm willing to forgive, but I can never forget - you made sure of that - and where Mama's concerned, only she can forgive you for what you have done to her, the same for Douglas.'

He kept his head bowed low and again I watched him intently. If I could count every teardrop that had fallen - all the tears that still fell during a solemn, private moment of remembrance, it would amount to a lifetime of antipathy, yet I was weary of hating, for it was not within my nature. Negative, wasted energy consumed too much precious time.

'Do you know what, Dada, it's time we stopped mourning for the past; time we all started looking forward to greet whatever the future has in store for us. It's bound to be better than before.'

'I know Girlie don't want to see me again and I can't blame her, but tell her - tell her I'm sorry; tell her if there's anything I can do for her, to let me know.'

I put my arm around his whimpering shoulders with some reservation. Maybe he was saveable after all - only time would tell.

After that, I really began to get to know my father for the first time; began to understand him as a person.

Slowly us kids started coming round, with the grandkids, to gather at Dada's place once a month. Oh, how he loved the attention. How he took pleasure in feeding his family with the generosity and lavishness of a serving king. He did anything to make memorable the time spent with his children and grandchildren. Every effort; all his energy, he put into convincing the world that he had changed for the better. The way he doted on his grandchildren was unbelievable. They got away with things us kids never could.

When the weather was fine he threw open the patio door and took them outside to play football, in between browning the chicken. We watched with an ambivalence of tender covetous longing, as he pushed the children high on their swings, talking with them about their young lives, something he had never done with us. Even though he had put on weight and sported a beer belly, (a rum belly we called it) he charged around the turf playing football with his grandchildren until he was out of breath. Indoors, he turned his baseball cap back to front and entertained them with moonwalks, claiming to be the choreographer who had taught Michael Jackson such moves. After dinner, he sat them down and told them boyhood stories about Jamaica; stories we were hearing for the first time, with all the actions that went with them. Everything about him made them laugh, as it did us when we were kids, except we were not permitted to laugh aloud. By the time we are ready to leave, he was asleep in his chair, snoring in deep, contented slumber.

To begin with, we were amazed at the new improved Dada, although I was not totally convinced that he had altered his characteristics that drastically. Dada had always battled with his thirst to be in charge and it was not long before cracks began to show in his display of fatherhood renewed. He became increasingly demanding; occasionally raised his loud voice and Julia and Pauline reverted to the timid children they once were, although safe in the comforting knowledge that they did not have to live with him. I, on the other hand was not at all fazed by his half-baked attempts to get attention, and that pissed him off in a quiet, niggling sort of way. If we missed a gathering due to other commitments that had arisen, (e.g. Mama or if the children had chicken pox) his mood would suddenly turn quietly thunderous, the effects of which could be sensed from afar. He would sulk and lay on the guilt real thick when we next met up.

'I take sick last week, you know,' he said in a tone determined to shame us for not being there.

'Did you? With what?' I asked.

Sinking into his chair, he puffed and blew and shook his head for a while, to express the seriousness of it all. 'I nearly dead!' he announced dramatically.

And Pauline, Julia and I tried not to laugh. We dared not look at each other in case we made the situation worse by inflating his already tumultuous mood. We were used to his antics. We had heard it all before, and the words, 'I nearly dead' evoked laughter in us, not concern, because it had become his catchphrase, synonymous with him alone. It was his way of making us feel sorry for him, so that he could assess whether he was loved and who loved him the most. But he needn't have worried himself about love.

The women on the block flirted shamelessly with Dada, to the annoyance of his new belle, Little Black;

an Antiguan woman he had hooked up with. She lived in the block facing his. As I said, some things never change. I kind of liked her, though. She baked birthday and Christmas cakes for the grandchildren and was more than happy to assist with setting up family banquets and the entertainment. As it turned out he and 'Little Black' as he called her, (because she was short and dark) were evenly matched.

'I got an old man you know,' she said as we walked to the shops to buy more bottles of beer. 'Your dad knows about him.'

'Does he?' I said hardly surprised.

'Yes. I'm not prepared to give him up though, he's got too much money; he's loaded.'

'How old is old? I asked, aware that I was prying.

'Nearly eighty,' she said and I gasped inwardly so she did not hear my shock.

'He bought me these rings and this chain,' she said showing off the jewellery around her neck and outstretched arm. 'He buys me clothes whenever I want; pays my bills and pays for all my holidays; in fact he knew how much I wanted to go home to see my mama, cause she's not very well you know, so he booked my fare; gave me a thousand pounds spending money. Good aint it? Girl, you see when he did that for me, I fling some pussy up underneath him there and then. Wouldn't you do the same?'

I almost choked on my own spittle when I heard that. Call me a mother of two, a prude if you like but I saw her in a quite a different light as she danced back into Dada's front room; bottles of beer under her arm. As Dada's sidekick and his love interest, Little Black supported whole-heartedly Dada's efforts to amend his wrongs with vested interest.

Somehow, I had to tell Dada about the forthcoming event of baby Matthew's christening but this was an extremely sensitive matter, simply because in Dada's eagerness to please, I was fearful that he would try to take control of the event. Despite this worry, I would have no choice but to invite him and at the same time, break the news that Nathan's mother had beaten him to the post by offering to do the catering. It was not going to be easy so, for the time being, I put off telling him.

In all the years over which her grandchildren had been born, Mama had never once left the house to attend a christening or family function. I knew how nervous she felt about being amongst a large group of people. Given her feelings about socializing, I recruited Bobsy - good, old, faithful Bobsy - to be there to administer a bit of gentle persuasion, and it worked. I was relieved when she agreed to come to the ceremony in the church, even though she chose to give the party afterwards a miss. Turning up for the service would be a major achievement for Mama - if it came to pass. Ever faithful to Dada, and a martyr to her past suffering, she had never stepped out with Bobsy by her side before. In her eyes, it wasn't right - she still being a married woman and all that. But Bobsy had the patience of a saint. He would not desert her, for in the last few years, he had become a loyal, doting, most trustworthy friend. With him, there was no turmoil, no pressure: just calm and peace. Bobsy was the best thing that had happened to Mama in years and we thanked God for the day he came back into her life. Although their relationship was platonic, there was a closeness between them that I had not witnessed with either of my parents. Embedded within their affiliation, was the existence of love and mutual respect so it was only natural and quite obvious that Bobsy wanted more. I had a feeling that any day now, he would pop the question. But how could Mama commit when she was still a married woman?

Cooking together in Mama's steamy south-facing kitchen on a Saturday afternoon was a joyous affair; a bonding time for all female members of the family. At the same time as chopping and stirring, we danced, sang, and laughed at anything that took our fancy; totally detached from all our previous troubles, which seemed a million miles away.

'You haven't changed at all, Melanie,' said Mama. You still skinny and you still love to wine up yourself.' Mama laughed. 'I remember how I used to laugh until I cried, watching you dance as a child because you were like a stick insect.'

'Do you remember,' laughed Pauline.

'What about the time you did a striptease, Melanie?' says Julia

'She ran right under the blankets to hide and I wanted to beat her, Lord knows I tried' laughed Mama, 'but how can you beat a skeleton.'

I didn't mind that I was the butt of their jokes.

'Where did all that time go?' I mused, sobering our laughter. 'I mean look at us; we're all mothers now. How did it happen?

'You really want me to explain, Melanie?' says Julia.

'You know what I mean. It's as though we're all on a conveyer belt or a fast train, moving through life at a speed we have no control over.' I turned to Mama. 'I have achieved almost everything I want in life. I've got a good man, two lovely children, a good job, a nice car and last week Nathan and I put an offer in on a house in Walthamstow, but the one thing I want, more than anything else in the world, is to see you in Jamaica Mama. When I'm nearing the end of my journey, I want to have that memory to fall back on, to keep me going. Let me book us all a holiday Mama, please.'

'You know what my answer is,' Mama, said, dismissing my pleas.

To illustrate a point, I deliberately steered the conversation onto the subject of her estranged husband.

'I don't know why you've blown this thing way out of proportion. Going to Jamaica is not such a big deal. Dada phoned me last week to tell me he's going back to Jamaica straight after the christening, him and Little Black.

A smile lifted one corner of Mama's mouth. I think it was the name 'Little Black', but she remained silent, battling to keep her face expressionless as she did whenever we spoke of Dada.

'Do you know he came round with a pot of soup balanced on the handlebars of his bike when I had the flu,' interrupted Pauline. 'Do you think he's up to something?'

'Ahh,' sighed Julia. 'That's so kind of him. I know he's a pain in the arse, but maybe we should tell him to stop trying so hard to please everyone.

'Leave him,' I said, 'he's just going through a spiritual cleansing. Let him get on with it, if it makes him happy. It will make him a better person. Do you know, I actually got round to telling him about Matthew's christening and he begged me to let him do the catering, I mean begged me.'

'I thought Nathan's mum was doing the catering,' said Pauline.

'She is.'

'So what did you tell Dada?'

I scratched my head. 'I said yes, only because he looked like he was going to cry. Anyway, it's all sorted. Nathan's mum has agreed to do the buffet and Dada will do the meat dishes. But I'm so worried. He's gearing up like a contender about to take part in big competition. I just hope a fight doesn't break out between him and Nathan's mother. '

The forthcoming event of Matthew's christening had gathered speed. It would be a catalyst for change, however small, for Mama - breaking new ground with Bobsy, for Dada - publicly proving to the world that he was a good father, and for Bobsy, who was thrilled about accompanying Mama to an event after years of pursuit.

I strolled round to Dada's place to finalize the drinks list and the menu with him. Waiting patiently at his front door after ringing the buzzer a few times, I noted two middle aged women, clothed in sensible attire, going from door to door. They saw me and smiled but I do not return the gesture. Eventually Dada let me in and disappeared into the bathroom.

'I'm having a bath,' he shouted. 'Put the kettle on and make me a cup of coffee.'

I made two cups of creamy coffee and was sipping mine leisurely in front of the television when suddenly the buzzer went off. Someone was at the door.

'I'll get it,' I said, opening the door.

'Who is it?' Dada shouted, splashing about frantically, but I didn't answer him.

Standing there on his doorstep were the two smiley happy women I had seen knocking on doors on my way in. Looking them up and down, I knew exactly who they were and what they were. Jehovah's Witnesses. You could spot them a mile off, wearing their drab 'Christian' clothes, those sensible shoes, briefcase in one hand; copies of the *Watchtower* in the other. I disliked them immensely, although not half as much as Dada did. To some extent still in denial, he more or less blamed them entirely for Douglas's predicament.

'Hello there. Sorry to trouble you. We'd like to talk to you about God.

'Who is it,' shouted Dada again, more insistent than before, but still I didn't answer.

'I'm sorry, but I'm not interested. You'd better go,' I said, trying to get them to leave right away.

'I beg your pardon. What did you say?'

'I said, I'm not interested.' I retorted more clearly.

'What, do you mean you're not interested in God!' said the one wearing spectacles, appearing somewhat astonished.

'I said I'm not interested in you, or what you're peddling, now please leave.'

'Not before we tell you about the kingdom of God; it will only take a while.'

'Melanie who is it? Is it someone for me?' called Dada again, refusing to give up.

'It's Jehovah's Witnesses Dada. They're just going.'

'No! No! Tell them to wait there for me, I got something for them,' he said, as if he had been waiting for them to call round and pay him a visit. Maybe they had patched up their differences.

'Is that your father in there?' asks the bespectacled woman.

'Yes it is. This is my father's place.'

'Oh we'd like to see him too,' beamed the other woman, presuming to kill two birds with one stone.

As I turned to go back into the front room, Dada emerged quickly from the bathroom; rushing past me towards the front door whilst tying the belt of his thick towelling dressing gown around his waist. He looked them up and down.

'Didn't I tell you people to stop fucking knocking on my door?'

'We - we just wanted to talk to you about God, that's all,' said a now nervous voice. It won't take long.'

'Yes. We wanted to ask you,' interjected the bespectacled woman, pushing her glasses further up the ridge of her nose, 'what do you think heaven is like?'

'What do *I* think heaven is like? Dada repeated. 'I think it looks something like this,' came Dada's voice.

My God, the screams; they were so loud, so piercing; I thought somebody must have died and gone to heaven. I rushed into the hallway to see *Watchtower* magazines strewn all over the doorstep.

'What's happened, Dada? What's happened?' I asked, thinking he had hurt them in some way but he just walked right past me, laughing as he went. With my mouth wide open, I puzzled about what had taken place. I followed him into the living room. It was then I saw that wicked glint in his eye. The same one I had seen that day when the Ragga Ragga woman called round the second time. He was sitting in his chair now, slapping his legs, shoulders heaving; laughing his head off. Then it dawned on me why they had screamed and why he was laughing so.

'Oh God no. Tell me you didn't Dada,' I said. But he was still laughing, harder than ever now. Something was really sweeting him, too much.

'Tell me you didn't flash those two Christian women, Dada.' Dear God, I was in shock and all he could do was to chuckle hysterically.

'They get more than they bargained for today,' he laughed. 'They won't come knocking here again, that's for sure. I give them enough sweet dreams to last a lifetime.'

'You mean nightmares don't you?' I retorted in annoyed fashion, giving him the kind of look a disappointed mother would give a naughty child. He laughed, until his eyes were running with water.

Holier than thou was the Reverend Pryce who would be taking the service. You would think, with him being a man of the cloth, that he would be sweet natured, loving and giving with all his brothers and sisters. However, it was with utter disgust, and scorn that he looked down his nose at the failures of society, those who in his eyes, lived their lives on the sidelines of his Christian values. There was no rejoicing in his church or heart for the lost sheep who had lost their way, just contempt.

In order to finalize the ceremony, I had arranged to meet with the Reverend Pryce and now entered the church grounds, closing the squeaky wrought iron gates behind me. A down and out tramp, who had sought refuge in the doorway of the house of the Lord, lay slumped across the steps. That old tramp probably thought this was a place where Good Samaritans hung out - how mistaken he was.

Coming from the side entrance of the building, Reverend Pryce made his way over to greet me. A beaming smile revealed two shiny gold teeth, but that smile dropped from his face like a lead weight the moment he clapped eyes on the tramp.

'Hey look here. What you take this thing for? I tell you people already, don't come back in my church. Come on! Get up! Get out of here before you get me mad.'

'Oh poor thing,' I said, looking into the glassy, weathered eyes of the tramp, wondering what had happened to him in between being born, supposedly a beautiful baby boy and becoming what he was now; a smelly mess; his grey matted hair probably infested with lice. What paths had he taken in life to end up a down and out tramp?

'Here's some change,' I said. 'Get yourself a cup of tea and something to eat.'

'No! shouted Reverend Pryce. 'Don't give him nothing. He bring this on himself. Keep your money. Remember you have to pay me for the certificate of baptism.'

Our party of excited guests gathered inside the church: Mama, looking incredibly nervous with Bobsy, who was in high-spirits, by her side, followed by Cousin Enid and the rest of the family. We were determined to be on our best behaviour because we knew that Reverend Pryce was feisty enough to haul you out if you so much as coughed when he was in the middle of one of his moralistic speeches. With the church full, we all sat facing him, waiting for that precise moment when the Lord said it was time for him to begin. We could see that time was nigh because droplets of sweat, which had appeared on the Reverend's forehead, now began to roll down the sides of his face and both his arms were outstretched in front of him - a sign that something was about to happen. Around his neck dangled two gold belcher chains, on which hung a medallion and a cross. On the fingers of his outstretched hands, he wore four rings. As he opened his mouth to speak, his gold teeth glinted in the sunlight, which seeped through the stained glass windows. He was a replica of Dada. The only difference between the two was that Reverend Pryce wore a white collar.

A hush descended on the congregation and we all waited with bated breath for the service to begin.

Cousin Enid turned to Mama and said, 'Watch him no, going on like the spirit of the Lord is within him. From what I've heard about him, he better mind God don't strike him dead up there in that pulpit.'

'And the Lord said: "Thou shalt not worship vanities." Those were his opening words.

'What a cheek, just look at him,' gasped Maureen, my godmother. As my best friend, she had solemnly sworn to behave; to refrain from cussing or using any kind of hardcore Jamaican expletive for one day, but her outburst produced sniggers from the sighted, and tuts of disapproval from the blind - his supporters. My group of family and friends, tried hard to stifle our laughter, but Mama let it pour out, which attracted the Reverend's attention.

'Shh!' hushed the women in the pew behind.

We all turned around, shushed them back, and cut our eyes at them, all at the same time. They didn't say a word to us after that.

Agitated, Reverend Pryce's temple began to pulsate. Knowing him, he wouldn't let this slip. Surely we would be punished for Mama's outburst.

After a short introductory speech, we sang the first song. With an air of importance, the choirgirls held their bosoms with one hand and sung their hearts out for Reverend Pryce, smiling a sweet, seductive, secret smile, but everyone had heard the whispers. We knew that more than just praying took place when Reverend Pryce visited them individually in their homes. Everyone knew, except his stuck up wife, who thought her high colour made her better than anyone else. As long as the money kept rolling in that's all she cared about and conveniently for the Reverend Pryce, it made her blind to what was going on right under her nose and deaf to the whisperings that trailed behind her.

As expected, when the hymn had concluded, Reverend Pryce set about his revenge by preaching about unmarried mothers, looking directly at me and occasionally at the eight other women sat before him holding babies. His damning words had us all cringing with shame, causing our eyes to genuflect as we hushed our babies, whether they needed hushing or not. Silently, I prayed to be saved from the onslaught of his attack and out of the blue, my prayers were answered. Like a blessing, a beam of sunlight shone through the stained glass windows, then came a whisper that floated high up into the eaves of the roof and echoed around the church.

'The peas! The peas!'

People shifted in their seats, turning their heads to trace the origin of those words.

'The peas! The peas!'

Mama, Cousin Enid and Bobsy were unable to hold in their laughter any longer.

Apparently, Nathan's mother had left her peas on the fire back at home and was now checking with the rest of the family, who were also checking with each other to see whether anyone had remembered to turn off the fire from under the pot. The problem was, they were not all seated together. Mama adjusted her hat and covered her face with her hands to hide her laughter but her shoulders were still convulsing.

'The peas! The peas!' Those words were said with urgent eyes tearing out of their sockets whilst the rest of the congregation now began to giggle at the thought of someone's Sunday rice and peas ruined after so much effort had been put into cooking them.

'The peas! The peas!

In the next moment a large group of people got up and tore down the aisle, not only to save the peas, but possibly the house as well.

Apart from the further fiasco of two women getting in the spirit during the hymns, which left Mama, in hysterics again, and the Reverend Pryce trying to catch and christen a screaming seven-year-old dreadlocked child whom he said had the devil in him, everything went fine.

'You know something?' announced Mama breathlessly, outside the church, 'I had a really lovely time. It was a wonderful service. I'm so glad I didn't miss out on this.

But this is too much excitement for one day. Take me home please, Bobsy.'

The blessing of the table back at the house was a swift affair even though the Reverend Pryce had been persuaded to do it for a fee of ten pounds after backing out from his initial promise to do it free of charge. Despite all the dramas, the christening was a great success, for Dada at least. To those who knew him, he had triumphed in his battle to win back his family.

Mama, on the other hand, was not in search of anything for herself and following that event of the christening, I noted that something was amiss.

'How's Bobsy, Mama? I asked one afternoon. I haven't seen him for nearly two weeks now.'

Mama kissed her teeth. 'Feisty! She exclaimed, 'I told him not to come back round here.'

'You did what!'

'You heard me. I told him I don't want him round here anymore.'

'Why would you do that? Bobsy's been a loyal, caring, trustworthy friend to you,' said Pauline.

'That man is damn well out of order.'

'What could he have done that was so awful?' I asked.

There was an awkward pause and then, 'He put question to me,' Mama said with annoyance.

'Do you mean he made a pass at you Mama?' Julia asked.

Mama ignored her completely.

'I bet Bobsy asked you to marry him. Am I right Mama?'

'Out of order and bright!' said Mama, confirming my suspicions by slamming the cups on the counter, almost breaking them in her vexation. 'I'm still a married woman.' and subsequently started to weep. I put my arm around her and gently hushed her.

'In name only Mama,' I reminded softly.

To our quiet dismay, Mama had rejected Bobsy for a second time. She was lucky, blessed enough to have gotten a second chance with Bobsy, but there was no way he would allow her to humiliate him a third time, and who could blame him? The happy-ever-after marriage to Bobsy everyone had hoped for was just not meant to be. Thus, he disappeared from Mama's life and left her with the only things she had to look forward to - growing old in loneliness.

Chapter Fourteen

By The Grace of God

It came as a complete and utter shock to us all - a bolt out of the blue, something I had not expected to happen, ever. Call it childish ignorance if you wish, but with all the progress we had made as a family, I believed that my parents were invincible; that they would always be here with me, on earth, in body, because they had come through many trials and tribulations and survived. I cry for them both now, for the thousands of miles they had journeyed away from all they knew and loved, so that their offspring could have a positive start to life in Britain, whose prefix 'Great' was said with pride. Mournfully, I wept for all the sacrifices that were made - the love that was lost, the dreams unfulfilled - especially the dreams. Finally, I had come to terms with the fact that Mama was never going to return to Jamaica. Never going to fulfil hers and our most treasured dreams, and truly that was a bitter, most sorrowful pill to swallow, because no matter what I do or where I turn, I am still chained to that dream; and I suspect that's how it will always be.

It happened in the autumn of 1995, the season of harvesting, when, without warning, all our lives were turned upside down once again. I thought I knew all therewas to know about the joys and the pains of life. How mistaken I was. With the nights drawing in I went round to check on Mama and Douglas, and found my mother in a peculiar state. She was not herself. Quite unexpectedly, it seemed that her health had deteriorated. She was behaving erratically about something; pacing up and down and I was in shock, for all of a sudden, my worst fears for Mama's health and well-being had surfaced.

'Melanie, you got to go and check on that man,' she said tearing her eyes out at me. 'Something's wrong. I know it. I can feel it in my bones.'

'What man? Who you talking about Mama? Do you mean Bobsy?'

"No! Not Bobsy,' she said, wringing her hands impatiently. 'What's the matter with you? I'm trying to talk to you but you're not listening to me.'

Her distress was my confusion; my fears, and for a moment, I was frightened for her. So frightened.

'Something's wrong with that man - something bad. You got to go and find out for me.'

Then it dawned on me. "That man," as she called him, was Dada. That was how she had referred to him even when we were back at Grayling Road, after he had obliterated every speck of hope for their marriage. He had changed from the kind, considerate man she had fallen in love with, years ago, into an impostor; therefore, she refused to use his name ever again and he became

"That man." In over twenty years, she had mentioned "That man" about three times.

'What man you talking about, Mama?' I was almost daring her to say his name.

'You know who I'm talking about. He lives beside the market. Something's happened to him, something bad. Please, I'm begging you: go and find out for me Melanie. Phone Julia and the two of you go find out.'

'I'm sure he's all right Mama. I saw him only three days ago. I'll call him as soon as I get in, then I'll call you. Try not to upset yourself.'

I drove home in the pouring rain, whizzing past yellow lamplights, people running for shelter and the windscreen wipers, swishing this way and that in fast motion.

As soon as I got in, I called Julia and told her about Mama's state of mind and what she had said.

'Dada's fine,' she says. I saw him on Friday. What's Mama on about? That man is as strong as an ox. Nothing's wrong with him. I wonder what's got into Mama. This is so unusual for her. I'll ring Dada later and you give him a call as well and I'll talk to you afterwards.'

But much later, after unsuccessfully trying to contact Dada a few times, I heard from Julia again.

'Melanie I can't seem to get hold of him but I'm sure he's fine. Dada's a street man. He's always out and about, unless he knows we're coming round.'

We agreed not to worry, and I promised to pay Dada a visit after work the following day.

At the end of a hectic day at work, I went home to get changed but before I could leave for Dada's place, my temperate peace of mind came crashing to an end.

Quite unexpectedly, Clovis called with what unfolded to be alarming news. Dada was seriously ill in hospital.

'Who Dada? He's as strong as an ox,' I said.

'Melanie I'm serious. The old man is critical. He's in a lot of pain. They're talking about sedating him so you better get over here soon. Phone the others and let them know.'

I dropped the phone then. Something in his voice told me to be terrified and I was.

Mama was right. She had known, but how?

I grabbed my keys from the dresser, jumped into the car and sped off towards Julia's house. I called her on the way to tell her the news and there are no words to describe our shock. I cursed and swore every time the traffic lights jumped to red, or if the person in front was driving at too leisurely a pace. Julia called again, demanding to know where I was.

'I'll be with you in ten minutes. Be ready. Phone the others and let them know.'

'He's not going to die is he, Melanie?' asked Julia, seeking the comfort I could not give.

'I don't know, Julia. Oh God I'm so scared for Mama because if anything happened to him I'm sure it would kill her.'

We drove to the hospital in silence, Julia and I, anxiously trying to dodge the heavy evening traffic. With no parking space in the grounds of the hospital, we left the car about three streets away. Frantically, we ran all the way there without stopping; silent, quiet confused tears of past and present moistening the fear etched on our faces. We didn't care who was looking at us. Everything in the world was a blur, a pending catastrophe, for there was no doubt of the effect it would have on Mama, and we could not lose Mama for she was the heart of the family.

As we approached the entrance, sitting there on a bench in the grounds of the hospital was Mary. People round here called her mad Mary to describe which Mary they were referring to; a highly educated black woman, who had gone off the rails. Her eyes lit up when she clocked us running towards her. So predictable was she, I knew exactly what words were going to come out of her mouth.

'Have you got a cigarette please, darling?'

I tried to answer her as I raced pass, to show acknowledgement, but nothing came out, not a word, just my panting breath. After racing up the stairs, we were eventually let in to the waiting room of the ITU. We knew it was gravely serious when we saw Bibi, his sister, standing there acting all sisterly.

'Brother Winston's in a bad way, a bad way,' she said, shaking her head and crying into her tissue. 'I don't know if he's going to make it through this one.'

'I'm going in to see him,' I said marching towards the door but Bibi stopped me.

'They won't let you in. They won't let anyone see him yet. They say they're fixing him up.'

'Fixing him up? What do they mean, and when and how did you get here?' I asked, for I had not blessed eyes on her for over fifteen years.

'He called me. Told me he was sick bad, and that he needed to talk to me.'

'Well? What did he say?'

She stammered for a moment, her voice, trembling with fear.

'He said - he said he wanted me to bury him,' then began to cry into her tissue again, only harder.

'I'll go and see if there's any word on how he's doing.' said Julia.

A sudden chill went through me then. It was over three hours before they would let us in to see Dada, three at a time. Julia and Clovis went in first with Bibi.

They emerged minutes later, crying, weak, and hardly able to support their own weight.

'He's real bad Melanie. I've never seen him this way before,' cried Julia.

'Come in with me, Julia. I don't think I can do it on my own,' I said, fearful of the sight that would greet me.

When I saw Dada amongst the wires and tubes that were plugged into him, I gasped in solemn disbelief. Rows of cold sweat dripped off him. I touched him to try to shake him awake, but alarmingly his skin was ice-cold. It was as though I had touched a dead man. 'He's cold. Why is he so cold? And why is that machine bleeping all the time? What's going on? Is he going to be all right?' A thousand questions pummelled my mind.

'His blood pressure has dropped. That's why he feels cold but we're working on that. He is very ill. We should know in the next twelve hours or so if he's going to pull through. Hopefully he'll respond to the drugs we're giving him.'

I spoke to my father then.

'Hi Dada. It's me, Melanie. What you playing at? 'bout you laid up in a hospital bed. Get up and sort yourself out, man.'

'Yeah! A big arse-staring man like you. Get up,' said Julia trying to laugh him out of his unconsciousness. We talked to Dada for a while. We had a strange and eerie conversation where we asked questions and answered them for him as well. Fretful for what this could possibly mean for Mama, we returned to the waiting room, to wait for Dada to pull through. Throughout the night the monitor attached to my father went off frequently.

But we don't say a word. In silence we sat, all lost in our own thoughts; the bleeping of the monitor the only thing to startle us back into reality; to stare into each others' eyes with panic, for a brief while. In the grey visitors' room we waited as the autumn wind and rain outside lashed the windows, until much later - hours later in fact - daylight forced its way through the dark night and the sun began to rise. Slowly, movement around the hospital gathered speed as staff clocked on and off their shifts.

Eager to find out whether Dada had made any progress during the night, I marched in demanding to speak to a doctor. We were told one would be with us shortly and when eventually he arrived at around nine o'clock in the morning, we all stood up.

'Your father is alive but he has not responded to any of the drugs we gave him. I'm going to speak with you all privately in my office. Get the family together and I'll see you shortly.'

It sounded like bad news but miracles happen, don't they? Moments later, after we had rung around, family and friends started to show up, crowding the corridor outside the ITU. The doctor taking care of Dada called four of us into his office: Bibi, Clovis, Julia and I, and through the square panelled glass of the door, we were told that Dada was dying; that one by one his organs were shutting down. He had minutes, maybe a couple of hours at most to live.

Despite all that he had done to us, all the cruelty he had dealt us, we slowly gathered around Dada's bed to be with him in his final moments on Earth, to say one last goodbye. I held his hand and wept not just for him, but mostly for Mama and the fear that this news would totally destroy her. His nails were pink then. But like the autumn leaves outside, how quickly life withers away and die. As predicted, his blood pressure began to freefall. I begged him not to go for Mama's sake, but then came that dreadful noise. The continuous, uninterrupted bleep of the monitor. I broke down and sobbed heartily then for Mama; for lost love, hopes and dreams, for the fragility of life and the finality of it all. And my big sister Julia stepped out of her normally submissive role to take charge.

'Stop it now and get a grip on yourselves,' she commands, sobering Pauline and me almost instantly. 'Don't let him go like that. Let him go in peace.' Then she took hold of Dada's other hand, and started patting it gently.

'It's all right Dada. We're going to be fine. You go in peace. Look, Pinto and Mammee Jule, Aunt Mary and all your friends; they're all waiting for you; all waiting to receive you. You go in peace Dada.'

I glanced down at the hand I held, and noticed his once pink nails had started to turn brown at the base; where the blood was leaving his body. The doctor present pronounced his time of death and checked his details for the registrar.

'Before we sedated him, he gave his date of birth and age as; sixty-one. Is that correct?'

'Sixty-one! Is that what he told you?' I said, drying my eyes with the back of my hand. 'He's sixty-eight years old: would have been sixty-nine next month.'

I looked at him, shook my head and cried some more. He even lied about his age on his deathbed.

I had to leave the room for a while to allow others who had gathered to say their farewells. On shaky legs I walked out into the bright corridor and into what seemed a different world.

Clovis, Glen, Julia, Pauline and I sat on the benches outside at the front of the hospital, silently stunned. I hoped this was all a bad dream we would awaken from, but with faces we recognised from back in the sixties forever arriving to pay their last respects, I realised this nightmare was really happening. Apparently, news travels fast in Hackney. Right there and then I wanted to hold my mother, to shield and protect her from any harm, but mostly, I was filled with the compelling need to treasure her, because death had driven home to me the fact that we are just mere mortals. After a while I spoke.

'How are we going to tell Mama? You know she loved him so - still loves him.'

'We can't tell Mama, said Glen. 'This will kill her.'

'She don't have to know. She won't be none the wiser. She hasn't seen him for years,' said Pauline.

'For God's sake, she has a right to know that her husband has just died,' I said.

'I don't want to lose Mama too,' Pauline cried. 'I don't know what I'd do if that happened.'

I comforted her and we all cried again with the bewildered feeling of emptiness, synonymous with death.

'I'll tell Mama,' I said, 'and I'll make sure that Bobsy is there when I tell her.'

First I called Cousin Enid to break the news.

'That damn bastard. Serve him what is right, he isn't good you know. That man was no good. He tried to kill off Girlie. He thought that she would be dead before him and look at that, now him dead. You tell Girlie yet?'

'Not yet, we're on our way round there now.'

'Oh my God, you know this is going to kill her don't you.'

'I know but I have no choice, I've got to tell her.'

'Of course you must, I'm just saying that she's not going to take it well.'

I had made arrangements with Bobsy to meet round at Mama's house, but I arrived ahead of him. Douglas opened the door and greeted me warmly, which was a shock to me because he was always so distant. He never made eye contact, but now that was different.

'Hi Melanie. It's good to see you. Come in, come in. Mama's in the bathroom.'

He pointed in the direction.

'Are you feeling all right Douglas? You look kind of different today.'

'Melanie, I've never felt better, thank you. Mama's just through there,' and again he pointed.

I found Mama in the bathroom, singing as she washed clothes by hand; her mood, in complete contrast to that of the previous day.

'I'll be two minutes, I'm just rinsing out these two blouses, then we can sit and talk.'

Again she sang and I studied her, whilst trying hard to stop my eyes from welling up in case she turned around and saw. Her soothing melody took me back to my childhood for a brief while, but not for long. I had to prepare her for what was to come. I opened my mouth to convey that she should expect visitors at any minute, but she interrupted my intention.

'You know the strangest thing happened today,' she reveals. 'For the first time in years, I hear Douglas singing and laughing. I couldn't believe it. I tell you it was such a joy to me. Such a joy. I think he's getting better.' She wrung out the last blouse and dried her hands on a towel. 'Come, let's go upstairs.'

At the top of the stairs, I heard the others approaching so hurried back down to greet them. Clovis entered, followed by Bobsy, Glen, Julia and Pauline. We entered Mama's room and instantly she was surprised to see everyone, especially Bobsy.

'I didn't expect to see you, Bobsy,' Mama said. 'How you been keeping?'

'I'm fine thank you Girlie. I know you told me not to come back round,' he said sheepishly, 'but I couldn't keep away.' Then she looked at us, her children, taking note of our sombre faces.

'Why you all here today? It's the middle of the week. Is something wrong? What's happened?'

I moistened my throat and lips to allow the disastrous news to ease out.

'Mama you'd better sit down,' I said after a pause. 'It's bad news.' but Mama chose to remain standing, looking from face to face.

'Will someone tell me what's going on?'

'It's about Dada. Dada's dead Mama..'

'Dead?' she exclaimed with disbelief. 'What do you mean dead?'

'He died earlier today in hospital. That's where we all coming from.'

All of a sudden, the weight of her body grew too heavy. She sank down onto the bed, and the room fell deadly silent. In that quiet interlude, we waited for a response - tears, laughter, rage, anything, but there was nothing but the blank expression of her physiognomy.

'How did he die?' she asked quietly.

'Heart attack they said. It will be on the death certificate when we pick it up tomorrow.'

'I'm so sorry Girlie,' exclaimed Bobsy. 'If you need me to do anything, just say.'

'I need you to go,' Mama announced, 'all of you. I want to be on my own, I got a lot of work to do. Come on, up you get.'

Would you believe it, Mama was throwing us out in great haste.

'I'm staying the night with you Mama,' I said.

'I'll take the couch in the living room then,' said Clovis.

'No you can't. You all going home to your families. I've got a lot of work to do. Go on. I'll be fine,' she insisted.

'Don't you even want to talk about it, Mama?'

'I want to be on my own. Stop worrying yourself. I'll be fine.'

We left promising to phone later and to return first thing in the morning.

That same night, I lay awake, anticipating the arrival of the storm that was brewing on the horizon, because I could feel Mama's pain, her sadness: I knew she was agonising about the one man to whom she had given her heart. A crescent moon graced the peaceful night sky with its presence and knowing that death had come close enough to touch my life, I drifted into a strange, unsettled sleep.

For the next nine consecutive nights, we held a 'Nine Nights,' the equivalent of a wake. We took turns to cook and provide liquor for family and friends of Dada. I had never been to a Nine Nights before so in between respites, I watched the motion of people going to and fro, sucking the meat from chicken bones, sitting in Dada's favourite chair or lying on his bed. It was all too surreal. During this period, I even sometimes forgot that Dada was no longer with us. Once or twice, I marched into the kitchen to ask him a question, only to find him not there.

We held family meetings in his bedroom to plan the funeral. It had to be done but at the same time it felt so invasive, sitting there on his bed talking about him as if he wasn't there; while music played in the next room. Dada's children, we took charge of the funeral, choosing a style he would have appreciated. In the days following Dada's passing, we registered his death: we visited the undertaker to choose a casket for him; and went to the cemetery to search the permitted areas for his place of rest. We found it in the conservation area, where an oak tree marked the spot. We visited St Mark's church to plan the ceremony, we purchased garments for Dada to wear, and also booked a steel band to add that flavour of the Caribbean on the day.

We did this all for Mama; for the name of the family, so we could show that we had come through the most disastrous of times and survived, that we had forgiveness in our hearts and so that we could hold our heads high at this low time, amongst people who had witnessed the earlier torments of our former lives.

Unsurprisingly, Mama refused to go to the funeral. No amount of persuading could sway her decision. We eventually accepted that so it would be, therefore we did not continue to force the issue - it was her prerogative after all. But Mama's unshakeable determination not to attend Dada's funeral did not rest well with Bobsy. Her reluctance to take his advice agitated him greatly, but did not deter his efforts.

'You know something Girlie,' he announced, 'I believe you should go. You need some sort of closure between you and Winston: put it all behind you.'

Mama gave him a look, which said he was being insensitive. 'I am not going to that funeral and I will not discuss it any further.'

She killed the conversation dead but I knew that would not be the end of it.

The sting of death has a way of tugging at the heart strings, unearthing buried memories to the surface of our emotions for us to battle with all over again. It forced us all to take a good hard look at ourselves; and to try to conceive the legacy that we would leave behind when the time came for us to depart this earth. Since Dada's passing, Mama had not openly shed a solitary teardrop for him. But there was no doubt that in the privacy of her solitude, she was grieving. Her eyes looked tired and drawn and her countenance took on a mournful stance.

The day before the funeral, Julia, Pauline and I made an appointment to see Dada in the Chapel of Rest for one last time before his exit. I needed to be sure that he was looking his best. Pauline decided to remember Dada as he was but gave me a gold cross to place in his right hand. We entered the small room where he lay in his casket. We felt the presence of his spirit all around us. I went to the foot of the casket and spoke to him and in my heart I heard him say not to worry; that he was fine; that he was sorry, that he would always be there watching over us. I placed the cross Pauline had given me into the palm of his right-gloved hand. By his side, we neatly placed his white baseball cap and sunglasses.

'Dada you're looking sharp as usual,' I told him, and we stood there, Julia and I, just looking at him, still in disbelief at his present state.

Then something, which can only be described as miraculous, happened. In the silence of the room we were suddenly amazed. We looked at each other, Julia and I, then, back at Dada's face.

'Did you see that Julia. Did you see that?'

'My God Melanie, he's smiling. Look at him, he's smiling away. You old ginal you.'

We did not make that happen. Neither of us possessed the power.

The day of the funeral seemed a long time coming after Dada's passing and now that it was here, a dark feeling had enveloped my very being. Early in the morning, I went round to see Mama, hoping that maybe she had changed her mind because, as Bobsy had put it, she needed closure. Burying her husband would put to rest all the ghosts of the past, which still haunted her, once and for all. But she was adamant about not attending and though I respected her wishes, I could not allow this last opportunity to elude me without trying to sway her judgement. Sometimes what we need is not what we want. And sometimes we make decisions we later live to regret. I did not want this to be one such occasion for Mama because she had lived with enough regret and it was high time she cast off that cloak of being a victim, to walk through life, a new woman, free from compunction.

'Mama are you sure you don't want to come? It will be like medicine to you. It'll do you good.'

'I can't! I just can't! she cried, and suddenly, I saw just how hard she was struggling to conceal her distress.

'It's all right Mama. Please don't upset yourself. You don't have to do anything you don't want. Remember, you are your own woman now. You're entitled to change your mind at any time. I'll keep an eye out for you just the same.'

With an ambivalence of the most intense love and sorrow, I hugged Mama, I kissed her soft face; told her that everything was going to be all right. But how could I know that?

Two black horses wearing feathered headdress took Dada to St Mark's Rise church. Clad in black, the mourners waited outside; their voices, their movements, hushed by the sight of the horse-drawn casket approaching. A steel band played 'Amazing Grace' in the background as the men in his family who were the pallbearers for the day, carried Dada into the church. During the sombre service, my siblings and I l frequently turned around, to see whether Mama and Bobsy had arrived, but I could not see them in the sea of people sitting behind: some crying openly. How could a man who had shown so much cruelty have been so popular?

At the end of the service, when hundreds of people queued for the viewing, I concluded that Mama was most probably saying her goodbyes in her own way, from where she was. Suddenly amongst the sea of mourners, I sighted a pair of familiar faces. Cousin Enid and Brother Rodney made their way over to us.

'Where's Girlie? Did she come?' panted Enid, peering around searchingly.

'We tried everything Cousin Enid, but she point-blank refused.'

'Good! Serve him what is right. I don't know what I'm doing here,' she said. 'I only came to support Girlie in case she changed her mind. Your father was a wicked man. I will never forgive him for the way he treat my cousin; wicked I tell you. And look at the kind of funeral you give him.'

She peered around in vexation at the queue of people curling around the large church.

'He didn't deserve this. It's too good for him.'

'Enid shut up your mouth in the church,' said Brother Rodney, eager for her not to say what she might later regret.

'Who you talking to? I'm not a hypocrite!' she said, 'I'm only saying what I feel. And stop telling me to shut up!'

'So are you going to say one last goodbye then?' I interrupted, so that their bickering would not escalate.

'I can't even bear to look at him,' she said, casting her eyes over in the direction of the casket, only a metre or so away. 'Then again, maybe I will take just one last look. I am not going to the graveside though. You'll see Rodney and the kids there.'

After peering into the opened casket at Dada, she walked off, shaking her head, and Sam Cookes' 'A Change is Gonna Come,' filled the open church.

In a break in the crowd, I spotted Eric, Glen's long time friend. I was shocked to see him standing there at the back of the church grinning away; and eyeing up the women; wearing what looked to be his best suit. What was he doing here? He had an important job to do.

'But wait, isn't that Eric over there, Julia?' I said, pointing him out. She looked over and spotted him in the distance.

'Shouldn't he be delivering the food to the hall?'

We sent someone over to find out if he had carried out those tasks, but before anyone could reach him, he disappeared into the crowd outside. Like my father, he was a womaniser and we should have known better than to trust him where there would be a gathering of women.

There were two empty seats in the first car, where Mama and Bobsy should have been, so we hovered for a while. However, it was futile of us to pin all our hopes on the chance that Mama would change her mind.

Vigilantly, we tried through sheer desperation, to see if we could catch sight of them in the crowd. But instead, as the car pulled away to Dada's final destination, we got another glimpse of Eric chatting to yet another women, this time on the steps of the church. 'Oh When the Saints,' rings out from the steel band, as the mile long procession leaves for the cemetery along a planned route. The clip-clop of horses' hooves was deafening as it carried us nearer and nearer to The City of London cemetery. When eventually we arrived, friends of Dada's were already there partying from the opened boots of cars laden with food and drink.

'Peace and love Winston,' they shout after the horse drawn carriage. Women who had been more than just a friend to him in the past, showed up in their droves, shamelessly seeking attention. Maybe it was just as well that Mama was not here to see this shameful parade. One woman even has the cheek to show up in a red halter-back dress, which plunged so far down her back it almost showed her arse. As she sauntered across the field, in full view of everyone, I heard two middle-aged women say: 'Eh, eh! Where she going like that? She better mind she don't catch up cold in her back.'

I smiled for the first time in days when I heard that, but then I heard something else that wiped the smile from my face and instead, put one on John's face. John was Clovis's friend. Everybody knew him and of him, for he showed up at every 'dead house' and funeral; regardless of whether he knew the person or not; an opportunistic free-loader but he was pleasant enough, all the same.

John was standing right beside me, when someone whispered in my ear that, in true Jamaican style, the van carrying the first load of food and drinks for the reception had been clamped outside the church.

'What!' laughed John, already tipsy with drink. 'Food get clamp to rhaatid,' was his annoyed expression.

I just looked him up and down. How dare he make a joke out of such a serious situation? As for Eric, I wanted to cuss him, for skinning his teeth on the steps of the church, probably at the precise moment the van was being clamped down the road. But I held it down; there was a time and a place for everything and here at the graveside, was not it.

With the sun straining to break through unyielding clouds, we gathered now for the final act, staring down at Dada's casket, now his embodiment, for the last time.

Suddenly, from behind, there came s a slight rustling sound. The crowd began to shift and it was as though I had had been tapped on the shoulder. I turned around, and then to my delight, saw Mama coming towards us like an uplifting breath of fresh air, accompanied by Bobsy. As she stood beside me, I saw the pain in her eyes but also I saw her courage; the strength she must have summoned to take such a brave step.

'Mama I'm so proud of you, so proud.' I whispered.

We hugged, rubbed her shoulders and back in warm greeting: kissed her cheek; then held onto each other for strength, and the service continued. Throughout, Mama showed no outward sign of tears or distress, even when they lowered the casket into the ground. She did not weep like me; like Little Black and the others who were unable to contain our grief.

The finality of Father Simon's words drew a poignant line underneath our past lives; punctuating the ending of an era with a profound full stop. Life changes indeed. Bitter-sweet is the knowledge that nothing stays the same forever.

The men folk - Dada's sons, grandsons, cousins and friends - covered him from the world by shovelling blankets of soil onto the silver casket as the graveside hymns were sung like a lullaby to a baby. The older women were strongest. They drowned out the sound of weeping by singing louder with enforced surety and passion until Dada was but a mound of dust and soil.

Mama looked on as they decorated him with flowers and I could not stop the tears from rolling down my cheeks, no matter how hard I tried; so desperately sad was I for her. Some cry for the dead, but I cried for the living. We wanted to give my mama the world; to protect her from all harm, yet now, the only man she had ever truly loved was lying dead, underground, beneath her feet. Death had indeed touched us all and in so doing had fuelled my disquieting fear of one day losing Mama.

'I'm so sorry, Mama. I know this must be so hard for you.'

'I'm fine. Look at me. And you dry up your tears now because I'm right here with you.' She glanced around at the autumnal effects of the season and inhaled a deep breath. 'It's very strange. We are all like leaves on the branches of trees, and you know that every leaf has a time to fall, whatever the season or weather. Those of us who are still standing - well, that must mean, it's not our time to fall yet. Our work is not done. So until then, the best we can do is to live good with everyone in our time on the earth.'

Remarkably, Mama was a pillar of strength to me and my siblings that day, when it should have been the other way round. I hugged her again, and then we did the hardest thing ever. We turned our backs and walked away.

After the clamps had been removed from the van that carried the food and drinks, the planned reception went smoothly, amongst a barrage of speeches, drinking and dancing, for Dada so loved to party. Later, when the reception was coming to an end, people came up to us to shake hands; to offer condolences and to say that Dada's funeral was the wickedest rave they had ever been to. I muse on that to this day.

And still, time runs away with us, through the autumn, the bleak winter and out into the glorious spring. Eased by the mystery of new life, we held our grief with dignity. They say that in this world, we have only one life to live, and it passes very quickly. And I say that in that one life, we live many other lives, where we evolve into yet another person of our being, through a series of awakenings; like a flower coming into bloom. It seems an awful thing to say, but Dada's sudden death, strangely, brought about a rebirth for Mama and Douglas. By dying, Dada released all that he had forcefully taken from them in life. It was on the eve of Dada's death that Douglas found his joy and what a blessing it was, to be able to talk, laugh and joke with my beloved brother once again.

Free from the chains of a destructive love which had kept her bound, Mama found forgiveness; not only for Dada I might add, but more importantly, for herself; for it is only when we are able to forgive ourselves that we can even begin to contemplate the forgiveness of others.

After wandering lost and confused for so long, theirs was a new beginning along a path that would lead them back to themselves and their hearts' desires.

And now, thousands of miles away from Mama's house in England, we kids are sunning ourselves on the beach in Jamaica, sipping our favourite drinks - rum and milk, rum-cream, strawberry Dakari, and Pina Colarda. Douglas and I swim in the sea every day and it is just like old times when we used to go swimming; running through the park with our sausage roll towels under our arms. In the distance, in between the branches of palm trees, we see the back of a house; the seven bed roomed house we had built for Mama. On the way up, we see her and Bobsy on the veranda; we wave, they wave back at us. I remember the promise I made to God, but He is gracious in his wisdom; I also get to live the dream and I am so thankful.

Long, long ago when we were kids, Mama planted the seeds of a dream in each of our hearts. Yet, although we endured many storms thereafter, those seeds took root and sprouted strong and new within her offspring. The undying love we have for Mama is the warm rays of the sun, which nourished those dreams. And now, in the sunrise of a new dawn, the end of our story is just the beginning and we give thanks that we are all here together in Jamaica, the land we love.

About the Author

Born in the early '60s, Jacqueline Parchment grew.up in Hackney - London where she lived for over thirty-five years. She now resides in Waltham Forest. She is the mother of three grown up children and has been in the profession of education for almost twenty years.

www.jacquelineparchment.com

Lightning Source UK Ltd.
Milton Keynes UK
UKOW02f0147011014

239411UK00001B/2/P